The Portal at the End of the Storm

The Portal at the End of the Storm

Quantum Touch Book 6

Michael R. Stern

For Linda
With my gratitude and all my love

Acknowledgements

An author often thanks those who have helped create the final product. Rightly so. No story can be complete without the assistance of others. I want to thank my wife, Linda, for tolerating the ups and downs of creating in obscurity. I want to thank those who have read parts of my books and offered constructive suggestions to make the story clearer, and hopefully better. But at this point, I want to thank the fictitious persons who are my characters. We have lived with each other for half a dozen years now. I have enjoyed our time together.

I want to once more thank Amy Davis of Riverfog Writing Group, who has patiently tolerated my extended learning curve. I am a better writer because of her teaching.

Thanks to my publishing team at Next Chapter Publishing.

Special thanks as always to the teachers who have inspired this book, Gilbert Ashley and Russell Fritz. My memories of them have made this creation fun, no funner.

And as always, thank you so much, those of you who have read my work. I hope you feel your time was well spent. For those of you who have read the entire Quantum Touch series, I am deeply grateful.

Chapter 1

Fritz

EIGHT YEARS. All that time, I've waited. When would that day come, the day they find me? A couple of times the cops must have seen the heels of my shoes on the way out. I've been lucky, so far. Working off the books, working hard and keeping my head down has kept me out of trouble, or the electric chair. The two men in the corner are paying too much attention.

Not many students leave college with a back-up marketable skill, or a need to work to get through the four years. I did. The demand for short order cooks has kept me in a position to rabbit when the walls closed in. Still, I wonder what's happening in the real world, my real world.

"Hey, Kraut, you got that order yet?"

"Scotch-Irish on my mother's side, and hybrid English on my father's. And who are you calling a Kraut, Ms. Frankfurt."

"Hey, asshole. Does that work better?"

"If it works for you." Cindy Frankfurt has been a pain for the past year. But she pays me on time and other than regular insults, she knows, or rather suspects that I'm not on the up and up with her. Need to know, Cindy, and you don't.

Eight years is a long time to be gone, from family and friends, from a comfortable life, a job teaching history that I looked forward to after

I found the portal. In that life, I had a son. And in that life, the last thing my wife, Linda, said to me was "I don't love you anymore." In that life, I even had a different name. I had a friend. Ashley. I'm sure Ash and Jane are married by now. Eight years is a long time for a time traveler to be stuck in one place, but I never thought I'd be stranded in an alternate dimension. Believe me when I say that time travel can be unpredictable.

When my shift here ends, all I can look forward to is my dumpy efficiency apartment, and maybe a trip to the library. I don't buy books anymore. I don't buy much of anything. Thank God for car leases. At least, I'm not stuck with constant repairs anymore. Hiding and running has been a nuisance, but it's easier to hide in plain sight. Here, now, it's just me. I have no family, no roots to tap to give my life a sense of continuity. I have accepted my anonymity, both sadly and gratefully. I've even heard that the Feds are looking for me. Will I ever find a way back?

I tapped the bell at the window to get Cindy's attention. "Number seventeen, up. Eggs over easy, home fries, bacon and toast. Times two." The two suits in the corner look suspiciously like law men. I've had too many brushes with the type not to know. The back door is only a few feet away. I'll be keeping an eye open in more than one direction until they're gone. I haven't seen those two before. No extra pepper on the potatoes. No reason to make them mad.

Cindy did her usual ballet of serving and bussing. I had to admit, she was good. A lot of banter, anything for a tip. She stopped for a moment at the window and told me they had complimented me on the perfect over-easy eggs. I glanced at the table. The guy on the far side kept his eye on me. I nodded to him and told her to tell him I said thanks and come again.

"Tell them I make nice waffles, too."

She cleared the other empty tables and started the routine lunch prep. We had about an hour until the crowd would begin to trickle in. I unlocked the back door, but stayed near the service window to see what they would do. When they had finally exited, Cindy waltzed into the kitchen, and told me I had a new fan.

"When he left, he said again, 'My compliments to the chef.' Then he asked your name." I must have blanched because she reacted swiftly. "What's wrong?"

"Nothing. My stomach just grumbled." I remember a phrase from my youth that has proven true—if you can't think big, think fast. Ashley had hit the proverbial nail on the head. I lied well, and I had had many situations where lying had come in handy. But it didn't always work out.

"Uh-huh. And I have a bridge to sell. Those guys upset you. I saw. You hardly took your eyes off them. Who are they?"

"Never saw them before. And I hope I don't again. No one even notices a chef in a place like this unless something's wrong. They're suspicious."

"You're paranoid." I disagreed. Cautious, not paranoid, but I let it pass. They were cops, no doubt. In my old life, having a cop behind me at a red light gave me butterflies. Having them invade this world shifted my strategy for escape into high gear.

She watched me go through the motions for lunch, but I could ignore her more easily than forget why I worried about two guys who just had breakfast. I worked faster than I needed to, and then told her I'd be out back having a smoke.

I poked my head out into the alley and checked for unwanted guests. No one, nothing. I took a deep drag, then sat in the chair I'd salvaged from a dumpster ages ago. As alleys go, this one was pretty usual, except cleaner. The trash guys around here are careful. Never have seen that before. And I make a point of picking up the occasional flotsam and jetsam that drifts back here. Linda would appreciate how neat I've become.

For eight years, I've avoided any contact with the people from my old life. On the bad days, I hold myself back because I've already messed up their lives, not just mine. And the damage to them is nothing compared to what I had set loose on the rest of the world. That's why I've expected that eventually I would be found. President McCain wants me strung up to the nearest tree. At least that's what he'd allowed his vice-president to say. She meant it, even if he didn't.

After an uneventful lunch crowd, I finished up and went home, stopping at the ATM to grab the cash I'd need until the end of the week. I stashed the bills in my pants pocket, not in my wallet, ever. Over the years, I've learned some of the tricks of the street. Check to see if anyone's watching. Never have a lot of cash, but always have some.

That's when I spotted them. As I walked to my car, the guy who watched me in the shop sat in the passenger's seat as they went past. His quick glance gave away his pretending not to notice. My chest tightened and my pulse raced. I watched until the car turned out of sight a few blocks down. By the time I reached home, my nerves had calmed, and I had my plan ready.

Over the years, I have collected backpacks. In the car trunk, ready for escape, I had a few changes of clothes, extra toiletries, only the necessities. My small apartment didn't have room for me to be a hoarder, so packing the rest would require little time or effort. I hadn't planned to leave yet, but when I went to work in the morning, I could choose to vanish or not. Some of my old life had remained, like this lesson from Tom Andrews—always be prepared and always do the unexpected. Wow, Tom Andrews. I haven't thought of him in years. The head of the president's secret service detail, killed during a failed assassination attempt. That was a sad day.

Caution has served me well, just not soon enough to have kept me from being here. I had originally planned to fix things and just go home. The portal had been my friend. Not this time. I've found it easier to blend in, chameleon-like, where I wouldn't be a curiosity. After a few years out west, I'd come back to where I pretended to be just another East Coast guy going to work, going home. Some days, I hoped to be caught just to end the monotony.

We restocked on Saturdays since most customers worked nearby and spent the weekend at home. My job included ordering supplies for the next week, which allowed time to analyze my predicament. This world wasn't real, at least not for me. I had no relationships, no friends, not even an occasional one-nighter. "Solitary Man" ran through my head, a tune that would remain until a new one could replace it. Elections were over, Christmas just around the corner.

After orders had been placed and my late breakfast crowd had departed for Saturdays unknown, Cindy dragged out her holiday decorations. I had been a minimalist when putting up lights meant extra unnecessary work. Linda and I had agreed that just the two of us didn't need it. I wonder if she'd decorate for TJ. This year, in that life, he had just had his first birthday. Or does he even exist, if I've been here all this time? I never have figured out the various permutations of time travel possibilities.

"Are you gonna help?" Cindy called, as she pulled a big box from the storage room.

"I hadn't planned on it."

"Change your plans." I abandoned my to-do list and carried the box to the dining area and at her direction began untangling the multi-colored twinkle lights.

"You know I have things to do, Cindy."

"Yeah, and one of them is helping me with the decorating."

"It's almost lunch time and I'm not set up."

"No one's here. You have time."

"This crowd won't care."

"I do. I love Christmas." A smile, seldom seen by me from this hard-bitten, tough-talking woman, changed her face.

"You should do that more often."

"What?"

"Smile. It takes ten years off."

"Just do the lights." But her smile returned.

In the year plus I'd worked here, we hadn't talked much about anything personal. I certainly didn't want to share, that California concept I'd run away from years ago. I'd guessed her to be in her 50s, and probably not bad looking at a younger age. A little wrinkling, a little gray mixed into the brown. And being on her feet all day, a pretty nice figure held up by shapely legs. I guessed she'd had a rough time of it. But I'd never asked. That would have meant letting down my guard. *Thanks, Tom. Caution. I know.*

She caught me staring as I unwound the tangles. "What are you looking at?"

"Knots," I lied. "You know, you can get new lights for three bucks per hundred at the market. This is stupid. Why don't I go get some new ones. And when you put them away, wind them and wrap them. You won't have this mess next year."

"Will you get them after lunch, then? We can decorate this afternoon."

I don't know what possessed me, but I told her I would. Maybe eight years was softening my resolve, or just my need for human contact. "Just no music."

Chapter 2

Ashley
NOVEMBER 27, 2016

Jane said that I'd been hard on Linda. I was, and on her mother, Emily, for not telling us everything before this mess got completely out of hand. I told Jane that both her life and mine had been upside down for the past six months because of them.

"You know that's not fair, Ash," Jane said.

"Maybe not entirely. But a lot. Jane, I love you. And I love Fritz and Linda like family. More. I can't believe I can't find him. Yesterday, I randomly followed each of the nine books to where he'd paperclipped. Today, only the ones I think he would have chosen. Tomorrow night, I want to go in the exact order he left the books on the desk." Now that I can open the portal, the real weirdness of paperclips in a book on a desktop keeps running through my head. Although I knew it, it was one of those things that you don't really think about. Until you have to do it yourself.

"Do you think you know where he went?"

"My brain says he went to find Robert E. Lee. But inside the portal, that doesn't feel right. Like the portal is trying to tell me to look somewhere else. Classes are going to be relaxing compared to this."

That's how I felt. At first, I sensed Fritz's pain. I know what damage the months without Linda and TJ have done. He'd begun smoking

7

again, up to a pack a day, and he had bought a whole case of Jack to just get through the long nights. I tried to reason with him, then bully him. He's one stubborn cuss when he makes up his mind to be. Kind of like me.

But right now, with Jane watching me, I'm angry, really angry, at Fritz. He took off into the portal. He had to know that I'd come after him, but if he wanted me to find him, he wouldn't have made it so hard. I'm angry because he took the easy way. And left me to sort out the chaos.

"I'm going to try to talk to General Lee tomorrow. Maybe he can give me some advice like he gave Fritz way back when. Or maybe he's seen him. Jane, I hope I can find him soon. I want to marry you. I've waited for years and I'm tired of waiting."

She grinned at me. "Ash, we've only known each other a little more than a year." Her dark eyes sparkled, like in a fairytale movie.

"I've wanted to marry you for my whole life," I said. "I just had to find you first." I took her hand and squeezed. She did what came so naturally. She reached to the leather satchel hanging on the chair, and took out a yellow pad and pen. "So you're going to record all my romantic sayings?"

"No." She scowled, intending to make me laugh. "Those are recorded. You know I have the house bugged." Then I did laugh. "Ash, I think we should have a record of as much detail as possible in case this takes longer than you think."

"Let *me* write it. As I go through, you can ask questions to get to the least important, most miniscule factoid you can conjure. You know, government at its best."

She jerked toward me and I sat back, dodging what I expected to be a right cross that never came. Shaking her head, she said, "While you're writing, I'll make dinner. But before you start, would you do my back? It's itching like the devil, enough that scratching it would feel good even if I opened the cuts. I could get bloody." More than a month after her abduction and rescue from the barn, the wounds hadn't healed completely. A recurring image, finding her in the barn with those knife slices down her back, remained as palpable to me as I'm sure they were to her.

"Sure," I said, and followed her to the bedroom.

By the time I started writing, I desperately needed a shower and food. But the shower could wait. While Jane reheated whatever we had in the fridge, I took the stack of books and made a list of titles in the order I visited Fritz's clipped selections.

The first stop had been Kitty Hawk. McCullough's book. It had been a fun read, but stepping inside its pages enlightened me about how to proceed.

"Here's another one, Wilbur." The younger dark-haired man pointed at me as I walked into their work shed.

"What do you want?" I answered him as abruptly as he had asked.

"I'm looking for someone. And he's been here. Have you seen him?"

"Would I be correct if I said the name Russell?" Wilbur asked, nodding to his brother.

"I think you already know the answer is yes." I asked when he'd been there.

"Who are you?" Orville asked.

"My name is Ashley Gilbert. Fritz is my friend and he's lost."

"He acted fairly certain of his location when he came here," Wilbur said. "He had a lot to say this time."

"This time?"

"I met him a few years ago in Dayton. When he left, he walked into a glowing rectangle. When he showed up here, we three spent a few hours talking about what he said would be accomplished here."

Orville said, "It's out there, Will."

Orville had tried to look busy, but he stood in the shed opening looking at the fluorescent rectangle, the portal. I told them that Fritz and I had found a way to travel through time and space. They both laughed, not at my statement but at the idea that they were about to change the world through flight. I understood the irony.

"How could he be lost, Mr. Gilbert? He came here, just as you have. And he left through your portal. As I presume will you."

I asked again when Fritz had visited.

"What's it been now, Will? Nine, no ten days?" Wilbur nodded. "Why is finding him so important to you?"

I'd never put it into words before. Fritz and I had just meshed right from the start, my first day teaching English at Riverboro High. We'd just talked between classes, like we'd known each other forever.

"I'm the butter to his bread. He's the salt to my pepper." I looked at the workshop. "I'm his propeller, and he's my wings. Alone we work fine. Together we soar." I glanced at the brothers. "I'm his Wilbur, and he's my Orville." I hesitated at their grins, and asked, "Which of you has the best sense of humor?"

Wilbur stiffened, his lips forming a thin, taut line. Orville shrugged. I waited. They answered at the same time.

"Orville," said Wilbur.

"I do," said his brother, and they both laughed.

"In that case, I'm his Orville and he's my Wilbur."

"Mr. Gilbert?" Wilbur asked. "The moon. Does man reach the moon? Mr. Russell said we did."

I asked him if he'd read Jules Verne. He shook his head.

"Not too far in the future from now," I told him. "On July 20th in the year 1969, a man named Neil Armstrong was the first, will be the first, to set foot on the moon's surface. But, what's as exciting is that we had the communication technology to be able to watch it right here on earth. The future, gentlemen, is astounding," I said, "and you are an important part of the foundation we will build on. Now, I have to go. Having met you is a great honor. I have given you a gift, a glimpse of the future. Use the knowledge judiciously."

When I finished the first story, I checked the time. Already nine o'clock. Tomorrow school would begin again, with the final push to Christmas vacation. Jane asked me where I'd been.

"Chatting with Orville and Wilbur. No wonder Fritz wants to use the portal." I pushed the pad across the table. "Here." She pushed it back.

"Ash, you have to find him. The portal may be fun, but it's destroying our friends' lives. So keep writing. Where did you go next?"

"Germany. Of all the places Fritz could go, he went to see Hitler in prison in 1924. That's when he wrote *Mein Kampf.* Fritz paperclipped the one picture of Hitler in his cell."

Jane asked me why Fritz would pick Hitler. Curiosity more than anything, I told her. For a brief moment, I could visualize Fritz with a gun, one step inside the portal, a quick shot. Hitler would be dead, and he would be gone. A shiver ran down my back.

"What's wrong?" Jane asked.

"I wonder if Fritz considered shooting him?"

"He would know he'd create cataclysmic changes. He wouldn't take that chance."

"I'm not so sure. I honestly don't know what he would do. His state of mind is nothing like anything I've ever seen. Just leaving, giving up. It's not like him at all."

"Did Hitler see you?"

"No. I looked and left in less than five seconds."

"You should write that as part of your description. In case things change, it'll be a place to look and see if he's the reason."

When she asked me to describe Hitler, I said I only saw his back, but from the photos, his anger lived on the surface. Dead eyes. No joy beneath. I expected his cell would be like we see in American prison documentaries. Instead, I had seen a fairly large room with a large window, which swung open to the inside.

"Why was he in prison?" she asked.

"In 1923, the Nazis tried to overthrow the government. History books call the attack the Beer Hall Putsch. I need to read more about it, but Fritz said that besides writing the book, Hitler learned a strategic lesson, which he used effectively. From that point, he used the political system to bring the Nazis to power. They became a force the government couldn't ignore. So the German president appointed Hitler as chancellor. He rose to power preying on the fears of the people."

"Write that all down. If nothing else, it's a good start on a book. Then get a shower. You're pretty ripe." Her eyes beamed at me and I finished recording my notes quickly.

Monday morning came too soon. Jane had a meeting with Colonel Mitchell about closing down the secret airport now that the elections were over. I suggested that they might want to delay closing it until the president left office. "He may still be a target. Richter, I mean Koppler, hasn't been put away."

"I agree, Ash, but the president is beginning to wind down everything, so he's ready to hand over the keys on January 20."

"If you talk to him, tell him I still have a bet I expect to win." She chuckled and kissed my cheek on her way out the door. I had only a few minutes to gather my thoughts and my lessons. The stack of books called to me, so I took the remaining seven to the car, along with my game plan for the day.

After homeroom ended, the day should have been busy, but I pulled the plug. For each class, I assigned different writing projects, long enough that they couldn't finish it in class, so it would carry over as their homework. While each class wrote, so did I.

I paid close attention to the next book, General Longstreet's memoir, the one Lee had told Fritz he had asked Longstreet to write. I had stepped through no more than three feet from the general. I had barely enough time to look around. His binoculars were aimed at a wide field covered in smoke, and he didn't hear me come through. Loud, repetitious cannon fire didn't distract the two soldiers running toward me. As I took a step toward the portal, General Lee stepped through the door onto the porch. I didn't wait to make contact. With all the smoke, and so little wind, I don't know how anyone could see anything, but the woods teemed with men preparing. Pickett's Charge would soon follow.

By the end of the first period, I had completed my description of five seconds at Gettysburg, and had started making notes on the next book, Professor Guelzo's history of the battle. Fritz pursuing Lee made sense to me because Fritz said that book read like a novel, one of the best he had ever read. I found out right away I wasn't prepared for my next visit to the past.

Fritz had clipped the pages where the Confederates had retreated from Gettysburg, and camped at the banks of the Potomac in a downpour. If Fritz had been here, I think he would have left quickly. On the heights, the Union army formed up, with the chance to put an end to the Army of Northern Virginia, with its back to the swollen river. Lee's army had escaped, so I had no reason to get any wetter.

"Mr. Gilbert." Yanked back to the present, I wiped the imagined and remembered rain from my forehead. Jay Bennett had his hand up.

"Are you done, Jay?"

"Not yet, but do you know when Mr. Russell will be back? We want to get started on the tournament. We're already falling behind."

Susan added, "And we were supposed to help Delport High set up their own tournament."

I told them I didn't know, but they might be smart to talk to Ms. Chambers. Liz had helped Fritz with last year's history baseball tournament and unless I could find him, she would be their best bet. History baseball and smiling students. Maybe Fritz's best idea ever. I made a note to talk with her, but how would I explain Fritz's situation? Once again, a burst of anger sizzled in me that he'd chosen to leave when so many people were counting on him. I hadn't ever considered how much we all impact each other's lives.

I told the class to get back to work, anxious to return to my own. I opened the fifth book, Koppler's self-absorbed memoir of his service in government. I would never read it. Why Fritz had bought it surprised me on so many levels. I turned to the pictures and returned to my trip into the Koppler family history.

I had gone twice to this scene. I walked into the middle of a party and left immediately. I reset the paperclip to re-enter to a more remote spot. Before I returned, I looked at the pictures of an estate with a large Georgian brick house, surrounded by gardens and a huge lawn in the rear. The house looked as large as a three-story football field. Wanting to avoid being spotted, I set the clip at a shrub-hidden spot on the side of the house, and poked my head into the portal. Three fully grown rhododendrons that had only a few flower petals remaining concealed my entrance. I estimated a late spring event. About thirty feet away, three men stood talking. All three wore tuxedos and held champagne glasses, as their guests, I assumed they were guests, milled around and some stopped to say a word. In the background, a large open tent enclosed a dozen or more tables corralled by folding chairs. Long serving tables down one side provided a choice of food to the line of people holding plates out to the servers.

If Fritz had come here, he probably didn't stay long, but two former presidents, waiting to greet their hosts, held me in place. After my close scrutiny, the three men standing and holding court for the plebeians were related, one somewhat younger than the other two. No doubt remained that, even in younger form, these were the men we had been chasing. I stepped back to the present, but as I crossed the portal, I could sense Fritz's essence, almost as if he'd sent off a foreboding, ghostly message. I noted then that I would search that book again.

Class ended and the next began, pretty much without me. I needed to get through the remaining books, and plan my next steps. Maybe for the first time in my teaching career, the kids just didn't matter. I finally understood what Fritz meant by "the portal at work."

The next book I opened with mixed feelings. Churchill. But Fritz had selected a photo of him as Prime Minister during World War II. As one of the best-protected people in the world, he hadn't met us yet. Spending the Second World War in a British prison didn't appeal to me, so only a peek and gone. Too bad, because I've always been curious what 10 Downing Street looks like on the inside. I stepped in, saw him yelling at someone, waving his cigar, and caught his eye. I left before he could say a word. Likely, he said nothing about a sparkly rectangle appearing and disappearing. But he would remember it, and maybe even me.

As if I were living in a time-lapsed day, classes came in, sat, looked at the assignment, and wrote. If they were noisy or misbehaved, I didn't notice. As if I were in a sound-proof bubble, I kept working my way through. Jane said to put down as much detail as I could remember, so before the day ended, I reread my notes and added the little things. When the final bell rang, I had made it to the last book. I'd visited Dallas, stood in Dealey Plaza, looking up at the Texas Schoolbook Depository and listening for those supposed additional gunshots, but too many people nearby sent me scurrying back through the portal before President Kennedy's motorcade reached me. Then I went in search of Ben Franklin, who we'd met before, and who I hoped would remember me. As I stepped in, I saw Franklin walking in quick-step toward me.

"Mr. Gilbert, nice to see you again. Is Mr. Russell on his way?"

"Afraid not, Dr. Franklin. He's lost somewhere in time. I'm looking for him. You haven't seen him by chance?"

"Sorry, m'boy, but I haven't. If I do, I'll let him know you're searching."

I thanked him, shook his hand and left him to explain whatever any of the others might have seen. I checked the caption on the page to see again where I'd been. The Constitutional Convention. Franklin had only recently returned from years in France and his jovial welcome indicated his happiness to be home.

As my last class departed, I began to pack up. The last book could wait. The picture's caption read, "Good news or bad, he was there." Lincoln leaned over the telegraph operator's shoulder, reading an incoming message. I wanted to speak to George, but before I could get out my door, I had visitors, the Dough Twins.

"Hi, Mr. Gilbert," Rachel and Nicole said in unison. In their three years of collecting for charities, now seniors, they had perfected their presentations, their cadence, and their matching clothing and haircuts. They knew about the portal, and had conversed with the president, intimidated the Speaker of the House, and shaken hands with Benjamin Franklin. I anticipated an enjoyable year with them.

"Hi girls. I'm going to the office and then I'm leaving."

"That's okay," Nicole said. "We'll walk with you."

"What can I do for you?" I asked.

They crossed the room to my desk, looking around to be sure we were alone. Rachel asked in a conspiratorial whisper, "Is Mr. R off spying again?" I think my hesitation alerted them, something I regretted right away.

"What's wrong? Can we help?" Nicole asked.

Rachel said, "We won't say anything, Mr. Gilbert. You know we can keep a secret."

Their offers, as genuine as any I've ever had, tempted me to tell them, but when my classroom door opened again, my instinct to keep them ignorant took over. "No girls, I haven't spoken with him. Maybe he ate too many turkey sandwiches." They left, but neither of them took their eyes off me on the way past Liz Chambers and out the door.

"Hi, Liz. What can I do for you?"

"I just spoke with Susan and Jay. They said you told them to talk to me about the tournament."

"I did. They're getting antsy because Fritz hasn't been around."

"Ashley, I have no idea how Fritz set this up. You know more than I do."

"You know Fritz gave the kids the credit for 'their' tournament." She nodded. "Well, he meant it. Once the teams were chosen and the teachers assigned, he kept George mollified and gave them advice when they asked."

"What about all the questions?"

"You still have the list, don't you?"

"Yes."

"And Susan probably has marked off every used question, so that's a start."

"Isn't he coming back? Did something happen?"

"Between us, okay? Your oath to the president, okay?"

"The portal?"

"Yup. He went in and the power shut off. He could be anywhere."

I didn't elaborate. Her stunned look froze on her face until she asked, "Can anyone find him?" I told her to take a seat and I watched her eyes grow wider as her eyebrows inched higher. Her hand reached up slowly and remained covering her mouth as I related the events of the past few days.

"Ashley, I'm so sorry. You have a tremendous burden to carry. Poor Linda. How awful for all of you. Look, I know I can't be much help, but if you need me, please don't hesitate."

"Thanks, Liz, but for now, if you can handle the tournament, I'd be grateful. I'm sure Fritz wants to see it work out. Let the kids tell you what needs to be done. I know you can handle George." At that point, in spite of the seriousness of the situation, we had a short laugh.

As she left, she turned and said, "Good luck. And you have some visitors." Nicole and Rachel were standing at the door.

"Girls, I need to speak to Mr. McAllister and then I need to leave. Walk with me to the office, but make it quick."

Rachel said, "Mr. Gilbert, we just wanted you to know that whatever you need from us, like taking over your classes or something, we'll do it. You know—if you need to help Mr. R."

I stopped and turned to them. "Rachel, Nicole, I really appreciate your offer. And you can help me. It'll mean you can't be in the tournament, but I want you to help Ms. Chambers and the tenth graders set things up."

"Does that mean Mr. R isn't coming back?" Nicole asked.

"Girls, you took an oath to the president. It's possible he may be gone for a while. You said you know how to keep a secret. So no one can know. I trust you, okay?"

To end what had been one of the strangest days I'd ever had teaching, I spoke to George about what had transpired only three days earlier. His usual annoyance with a crimson touch never materialized. When I told him that I would be using the portal as long as necessary to track Fritz down, he asked if he could help. My first thought matched the one Fritz would have had. *The portal at work?* Until now, I had never appreciated what must have weighed on Fritz nonstop.

"Thanks, George. I think you need to be prepared in case I can't find him."

"Ashley, I know you will. I have complete confidence in you. Lois does too." What a way to end the day. After ten years, he had paid me the greatest compliment ever.

* * *

I FINISHED MY notes about my glimpse of Lincoln, and spread the sheets from the pad on the dining room table. I stacked the books so I could review the places Fritz had paperclipped, and Jane could look over each stop.

When she came in, I had been searching for a clue as to where Fritz would have met Lee as he escaped across the Potomac. I remained convinced that Lee was the most likely destination. But, safer spots, and certainly drier ones, made more sense as a meeting place. Fritz's mighty disdain for thunderstorms had a good reason. After all, lightning hitting the school, almost killing him, began our portal adventures.

"I ordered dinner," I told her. "My notes are on the table. If you want to look them over while I pick up the food, we can talk about it while we eat."

"Should we invite Linda?"

"No. Not yet. I want to do this with as little emotion as I can. You and I can do that. Do me a favor though. As you go through each scenario, think about if you get a feeling." Jane's feelings have impressed me as to their accuracy in reality.

"Ash, you were in the portal all weekend. *Your* feeling is the one that counts."

After dinner, she finished reading and making her own notes, and we started from the beginning, this time filling in details as she asked her questions. We'd covered all but Franklin and Lincoln, so we bagged it until morning.

Before wrapping up for the night, I gave a moment's thought to Linda. On Sunday, after my whole day in the portal, I asked her if the possibility that she might never see Fritz again had crossed her mind. When she grew angry, first at me, then at Fritz, I yelled at her, something I had never done before. When I told her that in my opinion she had behaved like a spoiled brat instead of a wife and mother, she launched into me about Fritz caring more about the portal than her or TJ. I retorted something unkind about her father and money, and our chat would have escalated if her mother hadn't stopped us.

"Ashley, stop now," Emily said barely above a whisper. "Enough destructive words have been said in the past six months to last a lifetime. I won't allow either of you to wreck your friendship. You'll both need each other to get Fritz home."

As I gazed at the ceiling, Jane kissed my neck. I told her I wanted to write Linda a letter to apologize. But I wondered if I could depend on Linda to help.

"Come to bed. It's getting late. You can do it tomorrow."

"No, I want to do it now while it's on my mind. I won't be long."

"Oh, I forgot to tell you," she said. "I went to the doctor today."

Chapter 3

Paris, France

THE MANY-NAMED man sat alone in a corner reading the Tuesday edition of the International New York Times, a cup of coffee in his hand. Unconcerned with the information his lawyer had provided, namely of the government's knowledge that he had skipped the country, he had agreed to meet the lawyer for breakfast. Arthur Salzmann approached the table and waited. Koppler, known to his waiter as Richemartel, gestured for the man to sit.

Before Salzmann had pulled his chair in, the waiter arrived with a freshly-brewed pot and a cup and saucer. "Merci, Armand. Two house specials, s'il vous plait."

"Oui, Monsieur Richemartel."

"Arthur, lose the frown. I haven't skipped. When they want me back, you'll let me know and I'll come back. All this publicity is arduous and upsetting. I needed to get away."

"Thomas, you're not talking to the reporters or the lawyers. This is me. The only thing that you're upset about is not controlling the new Cabinet. Your Caballeros have turned on you. The case is filling in with eyewitnesses. You may be my brother-in-law, but I doubt any lawyer anywhere can get you out of this mess."

"You'll be leaving tonight, Arthur. By the time your plane departs, I will have shown you how you will get me out of this mess. It's going to be quite simple. They have nothing but circumstantial evidence of crimes I couldn't have committed."

"What about the teacher? The president himself saw you attack with that blade in your boot."

"The president. No one believes him. He's old news. He's packing up to leave. Russell attacked me. What boot?"

"Come on. I've known about that blade for years. Joseph bragged about how he built it for you."

"You've never seen it, have you?"

"No, but Joe…"

"Joe is dead. Shot by the intruders. You, of all people, know how his imagination got the best of him. Arthur, how many times did you have to get him out of trouble, even as a kid?"

Koppler watched as the arguments slipped away from his brother-in-law, the final fact sucking the air out of them. "Now you know how you're going to get me out of this mess. Let's eat."

When Armand returned carrying their breakfasts of croissants, cheese, fruit and imported Danish ham, his customers had vanished.

Chapter 4

Ashley
TUESDAY, NOVEMBER 29

I stuffed five books into my briefcase, carried the other four, and dumped everything on the front seat. On the way, Jane's tease had me shaking my head. When she said she went to the doctor, I'd almost fallen out of the chair. She laughed. "He said I need glasses." I wonder how long she'd waited to use that line. Her laugh still lingered when I'd climbed into bed.

The traffic crept steadily on the road to school. I listened to the news, always a source for possible future class assignments. About halfway, the radio shut off, and my car stalled at what was normally the nicest spot on the drive. Through the windshield, a full panorama of earth and sky decorated an overcast with a pink sky background quivering, as if time-lapsed shock waves had pulsed across the entire view. I rolled down the window expecting to hear explosions. Tapping on the dashboard, I hoped to hear a report of what had just happened. The sky went out of focus. I rubbed my eyes to clear it up, and as quickly as the radio blinked off, sound returned, the distortion vanished, and my car started on its own.

On the days when Jane left early, I did too, so an almost full parking lot bewildered me. I must have taken more time watching the sky than I had paid attention to because homeroom was about to begin.

I ran past more cars than usual, and when I gripped the door handle to enter the school, a strong surge of energy ran up my arm. I jerked my hand to free myself of the shock but pulled the door open instead. When I walked in, the door released my hand, the buzz still running through me.

I strode through my open classroom door, but a woman I'd never seen before sat at my desk.

"Good morning, Mr. Gilbert. May I help you?"

"This is my classroom." The kids began to laugh.

"Not today. Your classroom is two doors down on the other side of the hall."

That's Fritz's room. "Oh, yeah. Thanks. Sorry." Laughter followed me into the hall, which bothered me much less than knowing something had changed and not knowing what. As I walked the short distance, the ugly tan color in the halls yelled to warn me. When the door across the hall opened, I figured I was in trouble.

"Morning, Ash." Sandy Horton's smile might brighten up anyone's day at some other time. Today, she just turned me on my head. "Are you okay?" she asked. "You look like you've seen the proverbial ghost."

"Hi." *Not proverbial.* "Late start. See you later."

I scanned the room. Had I caused these changes? The painful greenish-tan walls had returned. No homeroom to attend. The shelves contained a library of history and biography. It was Fritz's room. And now my room. Sandy had left Riverboro a year ago. My morning paper waited, folded on the desk. I set the books down, put my briefcase on the floor, and sat at Fritz's, my, desk and gasped at the headlines.

I did a double-take at the large black letters, and then checked the date. The same one as when I'd left the house, Tuesday, next to the last day of November, 2016. The headline, "First Black President Outlines His Agenda," used up most of the front page columns with stories about his plans for the Cabinet, the economy, and his views on foreign policy priorities. In a small box, outlined in a heavy black border, a memorial to James Koppler, former advisor to presidents, smacked me in the face. The last line said the story continued on page eighteen. I flipped the pages. A picture, the same one I had paperclipped, headed the story, along with a prominent photo of Koppler. The story told of the assassination attempt which took the lives of his brothers, Thomas and William in 2008, but had left him in a coma the past eight years. The story noted that the killings took place just before the election that had propelled the first woman into the presidency.

What the hell did he do? And where is he now? I continued reading until the bell for first period rang. I folded the paper open to the story, folded it in half again and set it to the side. *Now what?* A sullen group of ninth graders began to stroll in, and I received more than one stink-eye as they sat down. I opened my desk drawers to see if they might contain any idea for me. From where Fritz always kept his lessons, top right, I removed the folders and opened the first period notes. Written in my hand.

"Good morning, class." I waited, serenaded by dead silence. "Did you all complete your assignment?" Nothing again. I didn't know any of these kids. I checked the seating chart. "Let's try a different approach. Jamie Brompton, tell us one thing that you found most important." I hadn't looked to see if I could find their homework assignment.

"Mr. Gilbert, the most important thing is I can't believe you made us read that stuff. Stuff isn't the word I want to say, but we're in school." The class snickered.

"I'm glad it made an impression. Now, tell us why you feel that way."

"I can't imagine killing one billion people all at once. Your questions were nuts, too. 'What would be the most efficient ways to kill that many people without harming others? How would that benefit the rest of the world?' Even Hitler and Stalin together only killed twenty-four or twenty-five million."

"Only? That's a pretty large number, don't you think?"

"Not compared to a billion. And the writer made the President of the United States the one who ordered it. So you asked us to write what would happen if that story were real. Do you think this is funny?"

"Did you come up with answers? How about the rest of you?"

Jamie continued, his anger bubbling just below the surface. "Nuclear weapons wouldn't work. Biological weapons have the chance to escape to the rest of the world. I figured drones, chemical weapons, and poisons worked best. If we kill all the animals, the people would starve. We could poison the water supplies. No food, no water. That would eventually turn one on the other and they'd end up killing each other, or eating each other just to have food. But I couldn't figure out how to get rid of all the bodies."

"Mr. Gilbert, Mr. Gilbert, I know."

I glanced at the seating chart. "Go ahead, Walt."

"I keep asking you not to call me that, Mr. Gilbert."

"Sorry … Walter."

"Or that either." The class responded in full-blown laughter.

"So, what should I call you? Remind me."

"Jack."

"So answer the question … Jack."

"All the people who don't get killed should pile the bodies and then we send drones with napalm."

"That's a lot of napalm. And a lot of drones. Did you think how you get the live ones to collect the bodies?"

"Tell them the only way for them not to get some dreaded disease is to get the bodies isolated."

"If they don't want to, then what?"

"What Jamie said. Chemicals and poison."

"Wow. You guys are pretty bloodthirsty. Anyone have anything to add?"

"Mr. Gilbert, I have a question. Why would you want us to think like killers?"

"I don't. But I want you to understand how easy it could be for a government, elected by its people, to get out of control." *Well, that came out of nowhere. And pretty easily.* My flipping through notes located the assignment, a book I'd read a few years ago about a president elected because no one believed him when he said all sorts of outrageous things and most people didn't vote. "If you read the entire book, you'll see that the president turns on American citizens later. The author tried to draw a parallel to the rise of the Nazis. He created a situation where Americans became so disgusted with government that they gave away the freedoms they said they valued. Not so far-fetched if you listened to all the campaigning we just finished. See you tomorrow."

While they were leaving, I pulled out the folders and read the next class quickly. Tenth graders. Familiar names at least. I looked at the assignment. Then I checked the next period. I looked at my fourth period class folder as the bell rang. I, well not me, had given all of them the same homework. Why choose such a bleak subject? I had to come up with a quick answer, but I would never have assigned it.

By the time the second period ended, my first task was clear—to figure out what had gone wrong, and I had to work fast. As I headed to the cafeteria after my fourth class, Sandy caught up to me and asked where I was going. When I told her, she frowned. She asked if I felt okay. I said I was fine and why did she ask.

"Because you have a class now. You have lunch next period." I stopped in mid-step.

"Thanks. See you later." As I turned back to Fritz's classroom, my classroom, I asked myself what other weird things would surprise me. I found out just around the corner. On the floor, surrounded by a group of students, two girls were wrestling, punching and yelling. Classrooms were emptying and teachers stood by, blocked out by the three-deep circle of students.

I started to force my way through when Liz Chambers grabbed my arm. "You don't want to get in the middle of that, Ashley. This fight has been brewing for weeks."

"I'll stop it." I elbowed my way past the outer layer of kids, but the closer I stepped the tighter the circle became. The students were hold-ing me back. Still on the floor, Rachel and Nicole continued to damage each other. They both were bleeding from facial cuts and I could see sharp-edged rings decorating each hand. I shoved past the inner circle and went to grab each girl.

Someone grabbed my collar and pulled me back. I planted my foot, balled my fists and swiveled, only to be facing Tom Jaffrey.

"Are you nuts?" he asked. "The police will stop this. Chief Shaw handles this without our help."

"They'll hurt each other."

"And be gone from here forever. Don't worry about it. And Rachel and Nicole likely will spend their college years in jail. The cops are here now."

Behind us, coming from the trophy case, a row of officers in riot gear walked toward the crowd. A second row entered from the parking lot. The squeeze worked because no new students joined the gathering. All the classroom doors were being guarded from the inside by teachers except for the three teachers in the hall. Another group of ten police officers came around the corner from the main lobby, all carrying handfuls of manacles.

Police broke through the circle using their clubs to poke the kids or smack arms or legs. Thirty-seven kids had been slammed against lockers, cuffed and hauled to the vans waiting in the parking lot.

A man I'd considered mild-mannered grabbed my arm and pulled me down the hall. Tom Jaffrey, at least four inches shorter, looked up at me and shouted. "What's the matter with you? It's not our responsibility to stop this behavior. We can get hurt."

"So can the kids," I said. "What's going on here?"

His anger, not at the kids, but at me, added to my confusion. "If you start breaking up these fights, teachers will be expected to step in. We need to get these bad apples out of here."

"But Rachel and Nicole ... they're friends."

"What world do you live in? They hate each other. They've been looking for trouble since they were freshman. Extorting money, starting fights, bullying younger kids. Now we can be rid of them. They can take exams in jail."

"But they're both smart kids. We shouldn't let..."

"Let them ruin their lives? Have you forgotten the kids they've stolen from, had assaulted, and Johnny Clayton, knifed just before the last football game he could have played in. He only talked to Rachel, and Nicole stabbed him in the leg. Just talking. About a physics exam."

I told Tom I'd forgotten about that. In fact, Johnny had played, had been All-State, and had received a sizeable chunk of money to attend Princeton, playing football as a freshman.

"Sorry, Tom."

"Damn, Ashley, us stopping these little bastards would be as likely as stopping the wars in the Middle East."

Once the ruckus ended, I went into my classroom, to a class sitting quietly.

"So who won, Mr. Gilbert?"

"No one. Were any of you involved?" I looked to see all the seats were full. "Good. No one."

"What's going to happen to them?"

"I don't know. I don't understand it. I've never understood why anyone wants to hurt others."

Two voices from the back had my answer. "That's easy, Mr. Gilbert. Do unto others," said the first. "Yeah. Before they do unto you," said the other.

I held the door for them on the way out and looked up and down the dingy hallway that just yesterday had been a distant memory. Perhaps more distant than I appreciated.

When the final bell rang, I sat at my new desk. What could have gone wrong? *The portal.* Before I could have a cogent thought, my door opened. The principal's arrival couldn't have made the day any worse. Wrong. Red-faced before he said a word, he started shouting before the door clicked shut.

"Will you control that girl? She's making me crazy."

"What girl?"

"Susan Whatshername"

"Leslie. George, calm down. She's not worth a stroke. You look like a beet."

He pushed the door open. "Don't be a wiseass. I don't know why I put up with you."

"I have a contract?" I offered. "I'm a good teacher? Uh, maybe you think I'm handsome, debonair and humorous. So you're envious?"

George shot daggers and headed out. His final words made me duck a bit. "Control that girl."

Sandy had heard my last comments as George departed and bit down to keep from laughing. I had retreated to my desk and wrote as fast as I could to capture all that had occurred since my drive to school. The words galloped from my pen as though I sprayed them on the yellow pad. When Sandy said hello, I jumped.

"Sorry to startle you. You don't look much better than you did earlier."

As though I hadn't heard, I kept writing. She sat down and waited until I placed the pen on top of the pad. "I didn't mean to be rude, Sandy. I needed to get this down."

"What is it?"

"Just some notes."

"About what?"

"You wouldn't believe me."

"Try me."

"I can time travel."

In spite of her skeptical look and sarcastic comments, I related what had happened over the course of the past year and a half. I'd always been able to talk to her, but my reality had changed. She did teach here. So I began to explain what had happened today. Fritz always talked about what could happen in spacetime if history were altered. The examples he used, I used now. If Kennedy hadn't been shot, would Viet Nam have lasted. If Lincoln hadn't been assassinated, or if slavery had been outlawed in the Constitution. If Hitler had been killed before he could start the war. If Lee had listened to Longstreet and moved away from Gettysburg. What would life be like now? Those were the books he'd picked.

"What books?"

"The ones he left as a trail. You know, once we even took you to see Shakespeare."

"You know I love Shakespeare."

"I know. You did in my other dimension. You told him the names of Romeo and Juliet."

"You're kidding. I named a Shakespearean play? That would really be a dream."

"It's a nightmare for me."

We talked a little longer, but I could tell she'd grown uncomfortable. I'm guessing that in this new dimension, people act pretty much the same. Well, clearly not. But Sandy always fidgeted if a particular topic bothered her when we talked. Her frown however made me wonder if she were an ally, someone I could count on here, or if she had other concerns. I didn't ask.

When she left, saying "see you tomorrow," I finally had a quiet moment to look at the big picture. I had entered some kind of alternate universe. I knew it, but no one else did. Everyone I'd met today went about their business like nothing had changed. No surprises. What happened? When? Retracing my steps, the radio, the sky, the buzz at the door. That had to be where I crossed over. But why? How?

The portal always left a trail, usually on Fritz's desk. He outlined books or pages to compare when he went through. But this desk had some pencil marks and an intact desk lock. On the other hand, when I marked my desk, in my room, not this one, I used an indelible marker. I had to check. I peeked in on my way out, and tried the door to the empty room. Locked. I headed for my car. *Maybe Jane will have an idea.*

Chapter 5

Jane

THE COMPUTER SHUT off. That had never happened before. The lights went out. Our back-up systems and emergency power didn't activate. I'd been checking my computer for messages that required immediate attention. The lights abruptly switched off. As suddenly as it had cut off, power returned, and everyone went back to work. I rebooted and waited, hoping no files had been lost. If we had been cyberattacked, Tom Andrews needed to check my entire system. Important information should not have been in jeopardy. Supposedly, the firewalls were taller and wider than the proposed wall along Mexico. I chuckled at that, but my computer contained files about the portal and my relationship with the president that no one else needed to see.

After a few messages from the server about searching for corrupted files, everything had returned to normal. While I waited for the reboot to complete, my cell buzzed with an unexpected caller.

"Jane, do you know where Ashley is?" asked George.

* * *

Ash's car was gone, so I drove to the school. A bright red anything stands out, so the Mustang was easy to spot. I walked into the school but someone else sat in his chair. At the office, I asked George if he had any information. He said he found a substitute at the last minute, but still no call from Ashley.

I called Linda while I walked back across the parking lot. Something had happened, I told her. He made it to school and vanished. She said I should stop by whenever I could. I said I'd come by after work.

Colonel Mitchell's men were busy packing. The colonel had told me that General Beech said the president didn't want to leave a trail to the portal.

"Yeah. The world's all of a sudden a paradise," I said. "Are you taking everything?"

"Not yet. We'll rotate five to ten guys and a medic, just in case," the colonel said. "I don't think the boss plans to tell the new administration about the portal or this place."

"Do you know his plan for Tony?"

"Tony stays, for a while anyway."

"When are you leaving, Colonel."

"I'm going at the end of this week. I'll be back after New Year's, probably to shut down. I think they want us off the radar before the inauguration." He grinned. "It's been quite a year, hasn't it, Colonel?"

"It sure has. Wait. What?" His grin expanded and the men nearby began to clap.

"The general told me this morning and said I could tell you. Congratulations, Lieutenant Colonel Barclay." Although I hadn't really noticed them, cheering, smiling soldiers surrounded me. Every one of them had been part of one portal mission or another, and most had been in all of them.

The choking sensation prevented the words of gratitude and appreciation from being said. "Thank you. All of you," I sort of croaked. When the colonel reached out his hand, the men lined up behind him to shake mine, sunburst smiles on all our faces.

After the unofficial ceremony, I asked Colonel Mitchell if I could speak to him privately. We found an empty table in the lobby area. I told him that Fritz had disappeared into the portal and that Ashley had spent the weekend trying to figure out how to find him.

"General Beech told me about it yesterday," he said. "I wish I could help. I like Fritz."

"A new twist wriggled in this morning. Ashley's missing. He went to school. His car's parked in its usual spot. But no one saw him or knows where he is. I think he may have gone after Fritz."

"That kind of takes the sugar off your promotion. Sorry. Again, I wish I could help. Does the president know about this? Does the general?"

"Not yet. It's only been a few hours. He may turn up. Still, I'm worried. He wouldn't just take off and for sure he wouldn't skip work. I don't think he ever missed a day until last spring. After Palestine."

I'm sure he'll be fine, Jane. But maybe we're closing this place too soon. We may need it."

"Not if no one can open the portal, Colonel."

I drove past the school. Ash's car sat right where it had been earlier. George would have told Ash to call if he'd shown up, so I continued home. I checked everywhere. Normally, I'd have clicked into 'analyze' mode, but I was just plain worried. Before I called Linda, I phoned the president. Ms. Crispen connected him right away.

"I've been expecting your call all day, Jane."

"Sorry, Mr. President. We have a problem here. Thank you for the promotion. I know you made it happen."

"Actually General Beech made it a point before I leave here. It'll be effective on December 15. But what's the problem?"

"I think Ash went after Fritz." Then I told him what the day had been like.

As the story unfolded, the president said, "If he and Fritz are both stuck inside, we need to make sure the portal's protected, or they won't have a way to get back."

"I was thinking the same thing when you closed the airport."

"Well for now we can't use it to go anywhere. I hope we don't need it. But maybe we should slow the change-over."

"Especially since Koppler's loose."

"Jane, or should I say Colonel Barclay, let me think about this for a bit. I still have six weeks or so. If he's still after me, or Fritz, we should have a plan to respond."

"I'll think about it, too. Thank you again, Mr. President."

My next call did nothing to ease my concern. Linda had no news from Ash. She invited me for one of Emily's creations, and since I had no intention of cooking for myself, I accepted. When we disconnected, my phone buzzed. To add to the strangeness, no name popped up on my caller ID.

Chapter 6

Linda

I SAID, "THAT'S weird." Jane had just told me a strange story.

"What is?" Mom asked.

"Ashley is missing." I told her what Jane had said.

"Do you think he went after Fritz?"

"I don't know. Without thunderstorms, how could he? Maybe Tony will know."

"Well, I wouldn't worry just yet. Let's start getting ready for the holidays. Would you mind if I use Fritz's car while I'm here?"

"Not at all. He won't need it." As if a pipe had sprung a leak, a trickle flowed down my cheeks that just wouldn't stop. "What am I going to do, Mom? I knew coming back would be difficult, but I can't make any sense of this. I'm gone, he's gone. What next?"

"Hopefully, he comes back and you stay put. Ashley and Jane get married and you all live happily ever after."

I dried my eyes and laughed. Mom does have a way to make the difficult seem silly. And easier to fix that way. "But Koppler is still free. That still worries me."

"Linda, that's not your problem right now. He can't undo the election. The government is wise to him, so he won't get away. Take care of the baby, make the house ready for when Fritz comes home. Start working on what you have spent years getting ready to do. Or is that

MBA just for show? You dreamed about your bike shop, and Fritz shared it with you. He supported every step you made. That's your work—the baby, the house, the shop. The rest will be whatever it is."

"Thanks, Mom. But what if he doesn't come back?"

Mom looked squarely in my eyes. "The baby, the house, the shop."

Mom had raised her kids, Joe and me, in the relative normalcy of an affluent community. She had been an active volunteer in many organizations and causes over the years. She matched perfectly with my father. She offset his bluster and argumentativeness with practicality and logic. I even think she cancelled out his votes. I had learned over the past few days she not only knows how to cook, but she can bake, something I have never been good at. So I've helped her. Ash and Jane and the rest of our occasional crew got to sample Mom's skills. She'd said only a few days ago that she believed the old adage—as kids got older, their parents got smarter. Then she just smirked at me, hands on her hips.

"You know, Mom…"

"Yes, I do. About time you figured that out."

"That's not what I mean. I fell into a trap that I made myself. Walking out like I did. I can't believe I didn't make more of a fuss about the portal. It's dangerous. It changes lives. We just went along because it was good for the country."

"It was, wasn't it? Think of all the good things you did."

"Mom, Fritz and now Ashley can time travel. Every time, they set things in motion that brought us to where we are now. Remember how mad you and Dad were when Joe and I played with matches. Well, we've been playing with them again, only this time, the matches are sticks of dynamite. And what did I do. I became a stereotype, the woman upset because her husband didn't listen. I walked out like he cheated on me. I've been so stupid. Look at where we are now."

"Linda, I can see both sides. I tried all summer to get through to Fritz, and he always said that you would come home, but you needed to find out for yourself, on your own. But, he's been miserable. He started smoking again. And drinking. He didn't know that I could hear him at night, calling for you. I couldn't pry you away from Tim, so I just had to wait. And I did my best to minimize the damage of you and your father together."

"Why didn't you say something?"

"I did, but you weren't listening. You and Fritz have been perfect together all these years. Part of that, I think, is that both of you are pig-headed, but you're both so smart that eventually you were able to compromise. Or really see the other's viewpoint. Unlike what your father thinks, Fritz was the best you ever brought home." She took a deep breath, I remember, because that's when she said that Ashley would find him and bring him home. "That's why I don't want you two at odds. It's not helpful."

Chapter 7

Ashley

I GRABBED THE newspaper and headed to my car. I read for the dozenth time the memorial notice for James Koppler. He'd been shot in 2008. How could he have just died if Fritz had killed him a year ago? Could this be another cover-up? From my own experience, that possibility wouldn't come as a surprise. I looked up but the real surprise struck hard—my car was gone.

The lot emptied faster than a keg at a frat party, so only a couple dozen remained, and none were red. I reached in my pocket and my keys jingled. I turned around to report the theft at the office and to call the police. The door opened and Sandy and Tom Jaffrey walked out.

"What's wrong?" Sandy asked.

"What makes you think something's wrong?"

"Your face."

"My car's gone."

"Have you checked at home? Maybe your girlfriend took it."

"She has her own. You know about her?"

"You said you took it for repairs." She looked at me as if my head were on backwards.

"I did?"

Tom had been listening and shaking his head. "Are you okay, Ashley? You're having a bad day, but are you sure you're thinking clearly?"

"I'm fine, Tom. Just getting over too much turkey."

"You don't like turkey," said Sandy.

"That would mean I had too much," I said. I tried wisecracks to get out this corner, but they glanced at each other, frowning. "I need to get to the office, so I'll see you later."

"I'll walk with you," Sandy said. "In case you need a ride."

By the time we reached the office, lights were out, the door locked, not a breathing body around. Rather than say anything, I shrugged. George never left this early and Mrs. Sweeney never left until he had gone.

"Call your girlfriend," Sandy said. The tone in her voice told me that no love was lost between them. I dialed Jane's number.

* * *

A BUZZ IN HER PURSE made her jump. Alone in her office, the quiet allowed her to concentrate on the plans for changing the status of airport security officers. She looked at the caller ID. "Who the hell is Ashley Gilbert?"

* * *

SANDY DROPPED ME off. We barely spoke on the way. As I opened the car door, she said that I should get some rest. "You're not yourself. People noticed. That time-travel story is amusing, but don't let others hear it. Ashley, we've been friends for a long time and I know you better than most. If you want me to get you some help, just let me know. But you need to do something soon."

I stared at her, letting her words find a proper translation. She didn't believe me. No surprise. I thanked her and closed the door. My car wasn't in the driveway, either. When I opened the door, I did a double-take. I had expected a light blue paint job, but stark white greeted me. Grease streaked the light blue carpet. The stripped-down frame of a ten-speed bike stood in the middle of the room. Oily parts surrounded the frame.

A voice I recognized called from the rear of the house. "I didn't hear your car." When she walked into the room, I couldn't take my eyes off her. "What the hell is wrong with you?" She snorted. "This time."

"Someone stole my car. What do you mean, this time?"

"Did you look under your desk? In your briefcase? Put your stuff down and let's go look. Honestly, if your head wasn't attached..." I let my eyes follow her around the room. "What... are you... looking at?"

I had no explanation for Linda being in my house.

She drove me back to the school in the ugliest car I think I've ever seen—a lime-green Corvette.

"You know, I think *you've* lost it." She pulled up next to a beat-up black Toyota Camry.

"Oh, right." No wonder I didn't see it.

"We need to have a long talk when we get home." I thanked her for the ride and got out. My keyring contained an unknown key, but it had to be the one I needed. By the time I opened the door, Linda had merged into traffic.

My problem slapped me. I didn't belong here, but worse I didn't know the person in this world. Whatever had happened, this world was angry and apathetic. I had to find Fritz, but I also needed to figure out how to get us back to our own time. Without artificial access to the portal, only thunderstorms would open the gateway. I needed to find out which classroom to use, which desk, even which paperclips. Had the school been hit by lightning in this world? Who can I talk to? Who can I trust? From all I've seen, I might be on my own. Twisting the key, the motor sputtered and started. Ten minutes later, I pulled in the driveway.

She had left the front door open, so I expected her to be waiting when I closed the door.

"Where are you?" I asked.

"In the bedroom. Packing."

"Packing what?"

A moment later, we stood face to face. "I'm taking a break, going home for a few days." She said that when she returned, she would move out. "Ashley, you're a nice guy, but this isn't going to work. I need more. Frankly, I never expected that a relationship with a teacher would be as bad an idea as my father said. But he nailed it. I'll get my stuff out when I get back."

That might have been the best news I'd had all day.

She left with a suitcase and not a word. I had no idea how long she'd been here. I waited until I couldn't hear her car and with my pad of notes, I began to look around. The bike parked in my living room had a metal shield that read, "Miller Racing Co." In smaller letters, in quotes, "Fast and Easy." A can of some kind of oil, drips running down the sides, sat on the carpet. The lid added a new stain. A small paint brush rested in a grease puddle. I read the label, which told me nothing about how to clean the damaged rug, but the name of its manufacturer grabbed my attention. Badenhof Chemicals, Ltd. Another dead guy reincarnated.

I rubbed my hand on the streaks. Dry and brittle, the fibers crumpled. She'd even managed to drip on the couch. I took notes. In the kitchen, piled dishes filled the sink, with cans and bottles spread on the counters. The mess reminded me of a time, not long ago in my other life, when I lived alone. Her bicycle drawings, advertising and a letter covered the table. The dining room table looked more like a bike repair shop than a place to eat.

In the rear of the first floor were two rooms. One had been my bedroom, the other a guest room. My office and library in the old days, yesterday... this morning, were upstairs. No longer. Spread over every surface were bike magazines, tools, and parts, with markers and their marks everywhere. She'd used the walls to make notes to herself. This woman resembled the Linda Russell who had been my friend for years as much as a dog resembled a bird. In less than a day, I'd seen a world I couldn't wait to leave.

The other first floor spare room had survived unscathed, almost. Again stark white walls begged my question. Who am I and what am I doing here? I climbed the stairs, dreading the scene I might find. So far, her concern for my house and my things was negligible. It could have been worse. The bedroom, now upstairs, had been rifled, almost like a burglary scene from a TV detective movie. I would have to check more closely to see what else she took, but the household cash which I kept in the desk was gone. But was it? Did I keep cash or anything else in the same place in this life?

Before picking up, I stood in the middle of the room and slowly turned. I could pile everything in a corner and then decide, but I wanted to see what I could find out about me.

I checked my desk first. On the right side, the drawers contained evidence that in this world I taught history. Old lesson plans, lists of students. My notes. On the left, the deep bottom drawer held upright folders. Thumbing through, my financial life slid by, folder by folder. As I removed them, one comforting fact emerged. I had more than $10,000 in a savings account. If I were stuck here for a while, I could get by. The rest contained paid bills, which I studied to be sure that new ones got paid. In the middle drawer, stationery supplies and a checkbook were untouched.

I removed a flat gray box from the top left drawer and set it on the desk top. It was locked, so I pulled out the key ring and found one that fit. Inside, two plastic bags, side by side, a pipe and a lump of tin foil joined a packet of cigarette rolling paper. Both bags, sandwich size, were pretty full. I had no doubt what they contained. I opened the foil and three chunks of soft brown clumps wafted a unique aroma. Sandy's voice rang in my head. In this life, I was at the least a recreational drug user.

Already in trouble, I had no intention of adding more. Both bags and the hashish were down the toilet, but I also had to check for more. At that moment, I understood that I couldn't change the person I was, am, in this dimension until I found out more. Until Fritz found the portal, I'd rarely had more than five hundred dollars in savings. Where did my new-found wealth come from?

I began a systematic search, starting with the bedroom. I'd seen enough cop shows on TV to look at everything. I shook each item on the floor, folded it and made a pile. I stripped the bed, and removed the mattress, looking for holes where something might have been hidden. Next, I checked the box spring which gave a clue. The mesh had been replaced with a stronger though similar fabric that had numerous staple holes around it. Rather than tear through, I went to the kitchen for a flashlight. In my old life, this morning, I had a junk drawer. Here, a different drawer had what I needed.

Stapled around the inside of the frame, a series of small bags reflected the beam. *Now what?* My first instinct was to flush it all. But in this world, Ashley, me, wasn't a recreational user. *Better to keep looking for now.* What I did know for certain, I needed to find Fritz fast, and get out of here. *Well, Ollie, a fine mess you've gotten us into this time.*

I worked my way around the bedroom. Dressers, under the rug, the closets. I found a false bottom on the frame of a shelf unit inside the closet and released the latch. Filled with small bags of weed, and a notebook, with some kind of coded names and numbers. Even without the Caballeros, I had another mystery to solve. And how many other hiding places were still left to find?

Room by room, my hunting yielded half a dozen stashes of what I assumed to be cocaine, mostly, and a variety of marijuana. The more I looked, the more worried I became. If I wanted to survive here, I had to quickly learn how he, I, handled the business, something I didn't really want to know. More importantly, if I had traded places, where did he go? Had he entered another dimension? Did he face the same dilemma as I? Could he get back on his own? Could I coexist with other me in this space? Had Fritz ever thought about any of this?

I finished the easy sleuthing, but still had the basement and the attic to check. Head pounding and knees wobbling, I sat for a moment, and glanced at the clock as my stomach played like Mount St. Helens. The clock announced that I better get something to eat. I headed to WaWa for a sandwich.

As I parked, two car doors opened and two young men blocked my way.

"Where have you been? I've been here an hour," said the younger, a tall, skinny kid in a light jacket and jeans. His constant eye flicking side to side and glances over his shoulder revealed his agitation. The other guy, the size of more than one linebacker I'd played against, stood with arms crossed. "Did you get my stuff?" was all he said.

"We can't stand here," I said. "I fell asleep and forgot. What did you guys want? Help me out here." I sincerely hoped that would work.

The big guy said, "Two and one."

"That's not helpful."

"What did you do, turn narc? Two coke and a grass," he whispered as the store door opened. To cover the awkward silence, I laughed. "You got it or not?"

"No."

"I have promises to keep. Go get it."

The young kid said he had people to see tonight, and told me he had expected six bags of weed. "You usually have it in the glove box. Don't mess with me." With a closed fist, he tapped his chest.

"Let me check. I'm still a little groggy." I climbed into the car and leaned to the glove compartment. When I pulled, the door resisted. I didn't want to break the lock, so I worked around the key ring for a match. The correct key yielded two paper bags with initials written in black marker and closed with staples. But who they belonged to, I had no clue. They both saw the bags, so I had no choice but get out. I opened both to check the "orders." I flashed thumbs up and they each reached into a pocket.

"How much?" asked Linebacker.

"What did we agree to?" I had no idea what the right amount would be.

"Four." He handed me four one-hundred dollar bills. I turned to Skinny, who passed me folded paper. I started counting.

"It's all there," he said. As he left, he said "Next week, be on time."

Linebacker looked me over, a scowl on his face. "What's wrong with you, Ash? You act like you never did this before."

Having been around Fritz for so long, I had learned that a convincing lie offered the only tool available to me. Fritz had been good at instant lies, and now I had my chance. "I tripped and hit my head. I'm not sure where I am. And I don't even know who you are."

"So you just showed up with the stuff by accident?"

"I came to get a hoagie."

"I'm outta here. Hope you don't remember my name." He hopped in his car and backed out, as a police car pulled into the parking lot.

Rather than loiter outside, I went in and ordered. The police officer waited at the register, a man from the other dimension. Jim Shaw greeted me and then said, "Wasn't that Bob, Mr. Gilbert?"

"Who?"

"Bob, Bob Easthill. You were just talking to him."

"Oh, I don't know him. I just bumped into him at the door. Big fella."

He leaned in and looked in my eyes. "Don't you remember him? Played football at Riverboro. He was always in trouble. You had him in your classes for a couple of years."

"I knew he looked familiar." I needed to get out, away from the police, and say as little as I could. Things were getting weird, weirder. I paid for my sandwich and headed for the door.

"Mr. Gilbert," Jim Shaw said. "Aren't you forgetting something?"

Did we have some kind of ritual we went through, like asking him a history question, or something else about Riverboro? I started to panic. "No, I don't think so."

He pointed at the back where I had ordered. "Your sandwich."

"Oh yeah. Right. Thanks." I didn't have butterflies. Rather a full flock of something larger flapped at my insides. *How did Fritz do this?*

Waiting for me just outside, Jim Shaw said, "Be careful of Easthill. We know he's selling drugs, but haven't found anything on him, or at his house. I'm not interested in him so much as where he's getting his supply. That's why I'm here now. The manager saw him and called. I got here just a little too late."

"I'll keep my eyes open, Jim. Thanks."

He snorted. "Jim? No one's called me that in years."

"Sorry. That's your name, isn't it?"

"Well, yeah, but even in your class, I used my middle name, Brian."

"I must be getting old. Sorry, Brian." He shook his head and headed back to his car. "See you around," I said, and when I sat, I exhaled until I thought my lungs were coming out.

Chapter 8

Ashley

MY FIRST DAY as the new me could not have been more unlike me, and I had no idea of what more to expect. To keep as unaffected, distant, from this world as possible meant I had two jobs to do. First, I needed to find out as much as I could about this Ashley. I needed to protect myself in this world, and second, if I was to become a bad guy, I needed to shift into my new role quickly.

I stuck my no-longer-interesting sandwich in the refrigerator. A quick look in the open door informed me that food shopping topped my to-do list. The shelves were almost empty, except for a couple of cans of diet cola and an open half gallon of hopefully drinkable milk. At least, no lingering odor of old and mold assaulted me.

My unexpected yawn made me look at the clock. Already after midnight, I had to get some sleep before I could face another day like today. What to wear pushed me back to the bedroom. Years had passed since I needed to think about where my clothes were, so I took my list and checked closets and dressers. Fortunately, new me (I have to find a better name to call myself) had a sizeable, comprehensive and compatible wardrobe from which to select. At least, I didn't need new clothes right away. I decided then that I would rearrange the house so it was mine again.

I've traveled extensively so sleeping in strange beds wasn't new. Except sleeping in my own bed, wearing a different person's clothes, driving a strange car, even though it was me, angered me. For the time being, nothing I could do would change anything. When I finally hit the bed, on top of the bedspread, I closed my eyes hoping this whole day had only been a nightmare. *Only.*

Day two in my new life started earlier than I would have chosen. An old clock-radio began blasting early morning DJ chatter an hour earlier than I usually get up. After a quick shower, coffee would have been welcome. Not today. I grabbed one of the sodas and reviewed my notes. I had acquired a foreign skill-set. I guess all the reading and conversing with Fritz and Linda had rubbed off. Or maybe this life was my real one and I'd been living in the wrong universe until now.

"No, that isn't right. I would feel comfortable here if that were true." Hearing my own voice startled me. "If I can find Fritz, we can get out of here." My mission, my primary objective, my singular goal, suddenly loomed as if the Rockies had sprouted in my kitchen. I needed a careful plan, and a new list. I had the books, but no idea of how to enter the portal from here. To make matters worse, with December only a day away, thunderstorms were unlikely for months. "What if I can't get back?" I know that Fritz talked to himself, but I never had. Another question to find an answer for. *Is there some residual Fritz in me? The same thing that made the portal open for me?*

A soft tap on my back door snatched away my reverie. Not yet six-thirty. Even the sun still slept. Pushing the curtain aside, my stomach flipped. Nicole Ginsburg looked in from the top step. *I don't like this guy.* I opened the door.

"Got any weed, Mr. Gilbert? I have the cash."

"All out, Nicole."

"You said today."

"Sorry. How did you get out of jail so quickly?"

Her smirk added another layer to my discomfort. "My dad knows a lot of people. But I'm suspended, so I figured I should make the best of it. So, when will you have more?"

As dismissively as I could, I said, "Never. Too many people are watching. I'm done. You can pass the word. How many people do you know that get it from me?"

"Everybody knows."

"Then tell everybody the sign says out of business. Now, if you'll excuse me, I have to get ready for classes."

"You're gonna piss off a bunch of people."

Looking at her, an idea began to form. "I may have something special for you and Rachel when you get back. Let me think on it."

"I hate her."

"I know, but maybe I have a way to put that to good use. For both of you. Have a nice day, Nicole." I shut the door.

If I meet other me, I might shoot him. Me.

Knowing my car this morning, I parked in my usual spot. At least the one I'm used to, and headed straight to the office. I asked Ms. Sweeney if George had a minute. She scowled and told me to find out myself. I knocked on the closed door, another new feature. George rarely had his door closed in the morning and I almost never wanted to talk to him, no matter what time of day.

"What?" I opened the door, asking for a minute to chat. "I don't have time to chat. What do you want?"

"Mr. McAllister, I want to try something between now and exams, and wanted to discuss it with you."

"Quickly. You know how we do things here."

"Actually, I don't. I do know that I don't like what I've seen lately, and I want to change things in my classes. Just me. It won't interfere with anyone else."

"So, what is it?"

"Instead of lectures and discussing homework, I want to spend the next couple of weeks on current events and let them do all the reading at home for their exams."

"I don't care what you do, as long as you cover the required material."

"Here's the rub. I want to tell them that if they don't pass the exams, they fail for the semester. No exceptions."

George's usual crimson didn't materialize. He said that if I wanted to fight with parents, he wouldn't stop me, but to leave him out of it. Then I told him that beginning in January, I wanted both Rachel and Nicole transferred to my class.

"They'll be your headache. Better you than me. Nicole's father is influential with the school board. Rachel's mother will be in your class as much as you are. I've kept them separated since ninth grade. It'll cost you your job if you screw up."

"Thanks, George. I have an idea. We'll see how it works. Thanks for your time."

"Your funeral. I'll always have time for that."

I didn't know what he meant, and didn't ask. I thanked Ms. Sweeney on the way out. She didn't look up. I stopped at Sandy's classroom on the way.

"Good morning," I said, as cheerfully and as opposite of everything I'd seen.

"Why are you so happy?"

I plunged in, ignoring her. "What are you doing after school?"

"Going home."

"Do you have time to talk? You said you would help. Did you mean it?"

"I have a few minutes."

"Not here. Let's go somewhere we won't be interrupted."

Returning to my classroom, I opened my desk and took out one of Fritz's yellow pads. They weren't mine. I titled the page Current Event Topics and started a list. I needed around twenty to reach vacation. Today's question would help me get my bearings in this world. "What is the proper role for teachers in our society?" I made some additional notes, but the rest of the questions could wait. If I was stuck here in this world, I intended to create one that I wanted to live in.

My first class would set the stage. With three classes of eleventh graders, I expected that word would spread. I wrote the question on Fritz's blackboard. It had been years since I had used chalk. I girded myself for the change. They would meet a different me. Only a couple of students came in. The rest loitered outside the door. I stood in the hall until the bell rang and when the last boy took his time going in, I put a hand on his shoulder. When he tried to shrug me away, I squeezed.

"Don't push."

"Don't test me," I said. "I know kung fu." He twisted and encountered my smiling face. "Go sit down."

I scanned the faces as I waited for a quiet I didn't expect. For two minutes, they ignored me, as I looked at them, eye to eye. When I had enough quiet to continue, I cleared my throat.

"Welcome to day one of the rest of your lives. We're going to change some things around here. You will all have responsibilities as we approach exams."

"What, like cleaning erasers?"

I set the hook. "Not what I had in mind, but Paul, that's good. I'll expect you here every day until the break for five minutes after school. Each day you don't show up will drop two points off your exam. With about twenty days left, that means if you score a perfect one-hundred, you'll get a sixty. Would anyone like to tell Paul what a sixty means?"

"Fail" was the uniform answer, called out by almost all.

"So I'll see you after school. And thanks for your help, Paul. Now your jobs will be to read and study. You know what you are supposed to read. You might want to study for the exam together, test each other and cover each of the sections we have been through. Here's why. I'm not reviewing. If you have questions, I'll answer here. But your responsibility is to pass the exam. If you don't, your grade will be…" I put my hand to my ear.

"F," they yelled, except for the FU from the back corner.

"FU? Fordham University. Is that one of your choices, Paul? I snickered at his glare. "Okay, here's what we are going to do. We're going to talk about the world you live in and the one you will someday be the leaders of. How many of you think you want to be teachers?" Two hands. "Gail and Ken." I pointed to the board and asked each of them how they would answer the question. Ken said that first of all, teaching was a job and they were hard to find, it was a profession, and he could teach a subject he liked. I just listened. When he finished, I pointed to Gail.

"Mr. Gilbert, I want to be a teacher because the world is changing. We need to learn a lot more than people did fifty or a hundred years ago. Not just for jobs, but for solving complex and serious problems that affect the whole world."

"Does anyone have a comment?"

"I do," said a voice by the window. "School's boring. So are teachers. Same stuff every day. What do I care about something that happened to a bunch of people two hundred years ago? They're dead."

Ken said, "That's ridiculous, Bill. Everything that happened is a foundation for where we are today."

Only once for the rest of the class did I step in to quiet them. I tapped the blackboard to bring their attention back. Just before the bell, the last answer summed up the class period. "The role of teachers should be to teach students to analyze facts, in whatever subject, and find uses for wherever our lives will lead."

When the bell rang, all I said was "See you later, Paul," while the rest were packing up.

"Come on, Mr. Gilbert. You can't be serious."

"Are you willing to take that chance?"

The classes that followed were aware that something had changed, but each tried a different approach to challenge me. I think that my smiling at them and not talking confused them, all of them, but each class eventually joined in the mood. One senior, on his way out the door, said he thought this class had been the best he'd ever had.

Sandy waited until my room had cleared. She asked where we were going. I suggested the coffee store. Paul walked past us and into the classroom, and started banging the erasers. I stuck my head in and told him to take them outside.

She waited until he was out of earshot. "Too crowded and too noisy," she said.

"How about the Mill? It's too early for the dinner crowd, or even happy hour."

"Okay. I'll meet you."

Another item to add to the list, the Mill had survived the time warp. I counted on that same survival of my relationship with Sandy. The Mill had survived, I saw as we entered, but not as the family restaurant I expected. I asked her why she agreed to go to a strip club.

"You want help and we can talk here, maybe better than anywhere. Let's find a corner."

"No. This isn't the place I know. How about a diner nearby? Any one of them will be quiet now. How about the Jersey Queen?"

"Closed. Two years ago. They couldn't clean it up enough after the flood."

"Then you pick. I'm not doing so well."

"We can walk. It's just down the street. Waverly."

"Lead on MacDuff."

"You know that's not a real quote from MacBeth."

"But it has its own meaning now. So, lead on, Ms. Horton."

"Ashley, I haven't been Ms. Horton since my first year here. As you well know, my married name is O'Connor. Like the Supreme Court Justice. You've commented enough times about it."

"Let's just go, shall we?"

"You really are weirder than usual."

We walked in the diner and took a distant seat. Not having eaten since lunch the previous day, I ordered a meal and she ordered a soda. When the waitress left, I started.

"Look, Sandy, I know you don't believe my story, but the past twenty-four hours have been nuts. I'm not sure about anything, especially me. You said you would help. So now I'm asking what did you mean?"

"Everyone knows you have a drug problem, Ash. And some people suspect you're a dealer. Are you?"

"Apparently. But I'm not, not in my other world."

"Oh, stop. That's denial in the worst form."

"What I told you is true. How could I not know about the Mill, or fighting in the school, or even your last name. I ran into a cop last night, who I know as Jim Shaw, who is training now for the secret service. This guy told me his name is Brian. It's the same guy. In my other life, I'm an English teacher. Tom Jaffrey teaches physics. Rachel and Nicole are best friends since they were five. They collect money for charities. How could I make this stuff up?"

"You've always had an over-active imagination."

"You're not being helpful, Sandy. I may be stuck here for a while until I can make things right again. So if you seriously want to help, I need to know everything you can tell me about the other Ashley. Frankly, I don't care if you don't believe me. I'll prove that some other day. For now, I need to know what kind of person I've replaced." I took out my yellow pad and set it on the table. I wasn't hiding my notes and she read them upside down. That might help convince her, though I doubted it. I'm not sure I would believe me either.

"Who's Fritz?"

"Like I told you yesterday, he's a teacher here. In fact, I'm using his classroom. He's the one who first opened the portal. But that doesn't matter now. Tell me about me."

"You've been at Riverboro High for ten years."

"Good. That's the same."

"According to the stories, you started to change, and whatever caused it, happened in 2008. You turned moody, stopped your involvement in student activities, and except for occasional visits to the gym, you came to work, taught, and left. Someone told me you had some kind of argument with Mr. McAllister about a teacher."

"Do you know about what, or who?"

"Something to do with dating, I think. I don't remember her name. But she was a French teacher."

"Good, that happened too."

"You never missed school sports. You went to all the football and basketball games, even the away games, and then…" she snapped her fingers. "You just stopped."

"What about personality?"

"You've been the same as long as I've been here. You used to be the faculty comedian with a joke for everything, even if people didn't always understand."

"And the drugs?"

"I don't know. No one ever talks about it."

"And all these things derive from my colleagues who seem quite interested in my comings and goings."

"You were a good teacher. Then you just began going through the motions. Someone said you had planned to go to law school."

"The bio still matches. Did anything happen in the spring of 2015?"

"Only that the school was hit by lightning. No real damage but we kept getting shocks for a while."

"Where was I when that happened?"

"I don't know. At your desk, I guess. Why?"

"That day, Fritz held the door open for me when the lightning hit. That started his ability to open the portal."

"And he could time travel?"

"Right."

"So how is it that you can time travel since no one named Fritz teaches here?"

"Sandy, the story is complicated and since you don't believe me, it's not important now."

The waitress brought my meal and Sandy's drink, and I considered all she had told me while I ate. She sipped and stared at me. If the school was electrified, Fritz's desk might still be the catalyst.

"Thanks for your help," I said. "At least I have something to work with." I took another bite of my sandwich. If anything could have elicited a sense of joy, her curiosity made me think I had a way through. It wasn't as important that she believe my story as my having a chance to prove it. I explained the desk, the doorknob and the paperclips. I told her that I had to rely on thunderstorms since I no longer had access to the air force.

"And how did you have access to the planes before?"

"I want to tell you the whole truth, Sandy, but this part sounds so far-fetched that I'll undo any belief, small though it may be, that I may have given you."

"Tell me anyway."

Just having her willing to listen drove me on. "So, the day Fritz found the portal, he was showing George that nothing had happened to his classroom. When he opened the door, now this was before we figured out how it worked, when he opened the door, he was looking into the Oval Office."

"That must have surprised her?"

"Well, see, here's the problem." I hesitated because I was about to blow my small amount of credibility. "In my home dimension, the president is Barack Obama, not Hillary. She just lost the 2016 election. Things are reversed. Obama won the primaries in 2008 and she served as his secretary of state."

"You're kidding, right?" I shook my head. "So he's already been president. And what was that like."

"Contentious. All eight years. But in spite of the obstruction, he got a lot done. He could have done much more with some cooperation. Most importantly, he got a formal agreement to bring peace in the Middle East."

"You'd never know from what we've seen the past eight years. She tried but no one paid attention."

"As a woman, she had mountains to scale in that culture. The place of women has a long way to go to reach equality, even equality of opportunity."

"Do you think he'll try to do it now?"

"We used the portal to make it happen. He doesn't even know about it. You and I are the only ones who do, here and now. And I'd like to keep it that way until I can figure this all out."

"Did you really meet Shakespeare?"

"Yes, and so did you. Really. I think he liked you."

"And if you get the portal working, will you take me?"

We had reached a decisive moment if I wanted to earn her trust. "I'll show you how to set it up tomorrow. Keep it ready."

She raised her glass and sat back. "You know that none of this is possible."

"I know. But despite that, everything I've told you is the truth."

She placed the glass on the table, slid out and put her coat on. "You've given me something to think about, Ash. See you tomorrow."

"Thanks for your help."

Chapter 9

Ashley

DAY THREE PROMISED some stability. After my conversation with Sandy, I had scratched off chores on my increasing number of lists, buoyed by the fact that I had an ally. Food resided in a clean refrigerator and freezer. Cabinets were stocked with in-date supplies. My bed now had clean sheets, and I had a new underwear supply for two weeks. I shivered at the thought of wearing someone else's clothes, even if I was that person. And last but not least, the Riverboro sewers ran freely with contraband. Other me might be pissed if ever he returned, but not sleeping on thousands of dollars' worth of drugs made sleep come quickly and last through the night. I even tolerated the clock-radio, especially since the coffee waited, hot and fresh. My priorities had already simplified. In other words, I'd created a livable surrounding, and hoped I wouldn't be here long.

My classes considered a simple question on the third day. "Elections are over. Did voting matter?" I expected a heated discussion from these mostly white, mostly middle class kids. Most of them were not old enough to vote, but they would have opinions.

Before the day started, I went to the office to see if anything would rattle my upbeat start. Ms. Sweeney saw me approach in the hall and came to meet me. "Mr. Gilbert, he wants to see you. I came to warn you. He's mad about something."

In all my years in my old school, Ms. Sweeney had never come out from behind the counter to talk to me, or anyone else that I could remember. I'd seen the old George explode before, but given that everything here leaned to worse, I walked in with trepidation.

"Morning, George. You want to talk to me?"

"Sit down." That didn't bring cheer to my heart.

"What can I do for you?"

"You can stop making my life complicated." The sound he made struck me as a growl. I wasn't sure if he was trying to be funny. The look on his face said no. "After school, I've arranged a meeting for you with the school district's psychologist."

I couldn't mess around. Something bad had happened. "Psychologist? Why?"

"I'm privy to some stories about you. I'm not jeopardizing my reputation or the safety of my students for your eccentric ideas."

"Do I have any input on this?"

"Sure. You can say anything you want. Even 'no.' I wish you would because if you give me any trouble, you'll be looking for a job."

I nodded, my lips pressed together for a moment. "So my input is—I'll see you after eighth period. If I may ask, where did this poison pill come from?"

"I've caught wind of some rumors. So be here."

My search for Fritz hinged on being here, so no cage-rattling. When I returned to my classroom corridor with no information to draw from, I waved to Sandy, and walked to her room.

"Have you been to the office this morning?"

"Yes. Why?"

"George is in a rare mood. He said he's heard rumors about me. Just wondering if he said anything strange to you. He wouldn't tell me what or who told him." I watched her to see if she had been his source. She didn't look at me, but instead rearranged items on the desk top. She didn't have to say a word. "See you later."

With my choices now limited, I proceeded through the day as I had planned. My students rose to the challenge in each period, which surprised me, after what I'd seen. The kids showed their family biases in answering, but their willingness to discuss voting in terms of policy outcomes fascinated me. When the discussion turned to how government should work as opposed to how it did, they found places to compromise. I wondered if Fritz had these kinds of discussions. In spite of my looming meeting, my day was fun, no, funner, than any day in recent memory.

In one American History class, a student asked if I thought term limits were good or bad. I picked up a piece of chalk, and squeaked two columns, yes and no. "All right, what are the pros and cons? What are the reasons on both sides? I waited for answers. Slowly, hands began to rise.

"Mr. Gilbert, we've talked about how the Founding Fathers envisioned government. Citizens, regular people, would return to their real life after serving. Now, their real life is all about getting elected over and over. I read that like ninety percent of Congress always gets re-elected no matter how bad they are or how little they get done. That can't be good for the country."

"So, Dave, are you in favor of term limits?"

"I'm not sure. Wouldn't it matter how long the terms were allowed to be?"

Another hand went up. "From what we studied in ninth grade, I think government is pretty complicated. The House of Representatives has lots of committees, covering everything. I think that learning all the stuff they do, and the rules they have, would take years."

"It shouldn't take years, Mary," said Laura. "Look at all we learn in just an hour a day. If they can't learn what they should fast, then they aren't doing their job. And we pay them." She looked around the class. "We don't get paid and we learn. Why can't they?"

"Well then, how long should they serve?" Mary answered.

"I don't know. What do you think, Mr. Gilbert?"

I told them that what I thought wasn't part of the discussion. They were doing just fine without me. "Tell you later."

Dianne said, "We hear on the news all the time about lobbyists and special interest groups. And the news talks about how those groups control Congress. They write bills for Congressmen to introduce. They pay fees and contribute to campaigns. Once they control a congressman, or enough of them, doesn't that corrupt the system?"

Heads shaking and calls in agreement were interrupted when Bob said, "You have to control a lot of people to get a majority vote."

"But if staying in Congress for a long time is possible, you can get them a little at a time. Then others see how much the lobbyists give to campaigns, and then they want that, too. I read that Congressmen spend half their day asking for money. No wonder they don't get anything done," Dianne said.

Dick jumped in. "Twenty committees and regular subcommittees meet regularly. I looked it up. So much information can't be absorbed when everything changes all the time. If you have term limits, the members who leave will be the most knowledgeable."

"And they'll be the ones most set in their ways. No room for new ideas or changing information," said Jason. "Old guys like things the way they are, the status quo. I think term limits should be no more than two terms, just like the president."

"But the president has two four-year terms. What about changing the Senate to four years, and only two terms, and no more than four two-year terms in the House," Jerry suggested.

While they discussed and sometimes argued, I forgot to write on the board, but I listened in awe. These were sixteen and seventeen year old kids. They weren't the same mean-spirited kids I saw on Tuesday. For a moment, I envied Fritz. I enjoyed teaching this way. *I have to thank George for letting me try this.*

As we neared the bell, Laura asked, "Mr. Gilbert, now what do you think?"

"I think you guys are terrific. This has been great. One thing you didn't mention, however. How do you get Congress to vote for term limits? They would be voting themselves out of a job. Don't answer. We'll talk about that another time. Keep reading."

After the class emptied, I wended my way through the crowded hallway, past the banging lockers, toward the office.

"Ashley, wait for me." I swiveled to see Sandy running to catch up. "Hi."

"I have an appointment with George."

"I want to talk to you first."

"I'm in some kind of trouble and I don't want to make matters worse." I locked eyes with her. "I know it was you, Fredo." Her stunned expression confirmed my earlier suspicion. I continued to the office without her.

George stood in his doorway, his face already a light shade of irritated, and he waved me over.

"We'll meet in here."

"Fine. I want to thank you first. I just had one of the best classes I've ever taught. All I did was ask one question. I hope the kids had as much fun as I did. So thanks again. Now, what's the plan?"

"Don't be so damn glib. This is serious."

"How could I possibly know what you're talking about?"

"Dr. Whitehall will be here in a minute. So will Chief Shaw."

"Chief Shaw?"

"The police chief. I want him to hear this too."

"You're having me arrested?"

"We'll see."

My instinct told me to leave, with a few pointed suggestions of what he could do. But I wasn't in a position to go on the offense yet. In my other world, George's office had been spruced up, thanks to Fritz. This one shared the same ugly color as the rest of the school. George had stacks of papers everywhere, but had made room for three chairs. I took the one closest to the door.

"Sit in that one," George said, pointing to the one farthest from the exit.

"I'm fine right here. I'll stand up so your other guests can get by. George, what's this all about?"

"You'll see soon enough."

We sat staring at one another with not another word said for several minutes. I tried to think of an appropriate analogy for the atmosphere being thick. But I kept returning to the image of a meat slicer cutting bologna, or in this case, baloney. When the others finally arrived, George shut the door.

He said, "Mr. Gilbert, I've invited you here..."

"Invited?" I kept my tone as friendly as I could. "You ordered me at the threat of losing my job. I'm here. Now what's this about?"

"Allow me, Mr. McAllister," said the doctor. "We've received stories about your strange and erratic behavior. I've been asked to determine if your actions are a potential danger to the students."

I had reached the end of my patience. "With all respect, what the hell are you talking about?"

George's complexion reminded me of Fritz's tomatoes in late summer. "Let's start with interfering with the police just a couple of days ago. That action goes against school policy."

"I was trying to break up a fight in the halls. No police were around at the time. They showed up later." The doctor wrote notes.

"Don't be belligerent, Mr. Gilbert. We have received a report that you believe that you can time travel. That you are here from another dimension."

I just looked at him. I had Sandy nailed. I couldn't help myself. I chuckled.

"Well?" George glared.

"Well what? I didn't hear a question."

"Well, is it true?"

"Is it true that I can time travel? I think I'm the wrong person needing his head shrunk."

"You're pushing your luck."

"Yeah, I'm really lucky." I could feel my control slipping, and although I didn't know this man, I couldn't give him a chance to pounce. I sucked in a chest full of air, and let it out, allowing me to regain my composure and a moment to think. "I know where you got the time-travel story. I only told one person."

"So," said George. "I need to hear it. I'm responsible for the safety of the students. I won't have aliens teaching them."

I summoned every ounce of control and tried not to laugh in his face. Or punch him. Even in another dimension, he was a pain in the ass. "I'm writing a book and I wanted to test the plot. Who better than an English teacher to try it out on."

"What do you mean?" George's rising color said that I'd won. He might not like the answer, but he couldn't deny that my knowing his source unraveled his argument.

"Let me continue, please, Mr. McAllister," said Whitehall. "The teacher who told the story indicated concern for your well-being, as well as the students. Tell us about your book."

"Are you going to buy it when it's published. I don't want to give away the story." I smiled at him. Fritz calls it my Cheshire-Cat grin.

"Trust me, Mr. Gilbert, when I tell you that we deem this a serious issue."

"Doctor, trust me when I tell you that there is nothing that I consider to be more serious than accusing me of endangering children. So far, my actions have been exemplary, quite the opposite of what you are implying. My story, if you must know, is about a history teacher who can time-travel. Imagine the value of bringing history to life for readers, especially kids."

"Well, how did you get here from another dimension?" George kept digging a deeper hole. I wanted to get him a backhoe.

"Other than walking through *your* door, and finding myself at the Salem Witch trials, you mean?"

"I don't have a lot of time for this nonsense," said the police chief. "So let's get to the heart of this. I caught up with Bob Easthill with a customer. He said you were his supplier. We asked him if others bought from you. He gave us the names of at least three kids who are students here. All three said the same thing. They bought from you. Why would they say that?"

"Mr. Shaw," I said, "do you intend to arrest me? I think I may need an attorney. It seems the three of you have me guilty of something you've concocted. This story is better fiction than I could ever write."

"I'm not arresting you now. We are investigating the claims, and we will be looking for evidence."

I wanted to say something sarcastic like arrest me so I can't travel to another dimension, but I kept my mouth shut. Fortunately, I had dumped the drugs other me had hidden. I hoped I had found them all. "Okay, so what happens next? I haven't done anything that remotely resembles what you are all claiming, but I can't help but wonder when the other shoe's going to drop. I do my job and I think I do it well. My record shows that, doesn't it, Dr. Whitehall? George? I don't take time off. Have I ever refused anything you asked me to do?" I didn't really know the answers, but from what Sandy had said, other me kept to himself, but didn't really bother anyone. Looking from face to face, I received no response.

"George, whatever the reason you choose not to like me is your business. But I'm not crazy, I'm not a drug dealer, and I'm not a slacker. If you want me to leave, that's fine. When my contract ends, I'll go. Unless you gentlemen have something more, I have a book to write."

As I started to leave, George said, "You're still responsible for disturbing things. That girl, that tournament."

"George, I'll make it simple for you. Do you want the tournament?"

"No, of course not."

"And she needs your permission, right?"

"Of course."

"Just say no." Tempted to slam the door, instead I left it open.

Waiting in the hall across from my classroom, Sandy took a step toward me when I came around the corner. I said nothing, but held up my hand and shook my head. Nothing she could say would overcome her betrayal.

"Ashley…"

"No."

"Let me explain."

"No." Without a missed step, I pulled the door open and went to grab my coat and briefcase. She followed me in. "Sandy, I almost lost my job. So don't bother." I brushed by her, and held the door for her to leave. I've never handled tears well and hers were like twin waterfalls. "Look, I'm not who or what you think. I have a task to accomplish and no one is going to stop me." As I headed down the hall, I stopped and turned. "If you want to help me, find a book about Ernest Hemingway and the Lost Generation. Find a picture of a book store named Shakespeare and Co."

"And then?"

"Paperclip the page, and wait for a thunderstorm."

I had one thought when I got home. Make sure the drugs were gone. So the yellow VW Beetle parked in front of my house wasn't a pleasant surprise. Another character from my other world walked up my sidewalk. After my inquisition, only raised suspicions could accompany her to my door.

"Hi, Ashley. I need to talk to you. Can I come in?"

"Natalie, I really just need to do something. Alone."

"Ash, you're in trouble. Brian Shaw talked to me a few minutes ago. The police are getting a search warrant."

"This is getting weirder by the minute. Why would he tell you?"

"He likes you. He said specifically to warn you. He has to look. His job, you know. He said you're a good teacher. I came right away."

"Look for what?"

"Ashley, we dated for a year. Don't deny what I already know. I'll help you look. You need to be sure everything is gone. He's bringing dogs. I know every inch of this house and a few places you might not even remember. I made a mistake introducing you to our friend, Ms. Miller."

How weird everything had become.

Chapter 10

Ashley

SHE RECEIVED another call from Chief Shaw, saying they were on the way. He'd called earlier and Nat had texted back, telling him to find something to do for a half an hour. Then she told me we had a lot to do and not much time. She had been right when she said she knew the house better than me. Other me had more stashes than Carter had liver pills. When she told me to get the bike out of the house, I asked why.

"You're an idiot. Just do it."

"Why?"

"Put it behind the house. Lay it down. That fits you, not caring."

"What are you talking about?"

"Ashley, are you forgetting why this model is so expensive?" She huffed at what must have been my blank expression. "Get it out. Now. Hurry."

Rather than risk her ire, which I had seen in my world, I did what she asked. How she had held off this raid, this assault on my privacy, with a cell phone, made me curious. Natalie and I had a lot more to discuss. Planted, the seed of that thought began to germinate. I'd have to be more cautious after the Sandy episode. Before she left, I asked her what she was doing later, when the police were gone. She had answers to my expanding list of questions.

"When they leave, call me."

"What's your number?" She cocked her head, then put her hand on my forehead. She said I didn't have a fever, but asked if I'd lost my mind. I told her I was trying to find it. I held out my phone. She held hers out and said now I had it.

"I'll see you later." She pulled away as the red and blue flashing lights invaded my street.

I didn't know if I should stand at the open door, but they were, after all, coming to visit me. It seemed rather silly to close the door and open it again, so I just left it open and sat in the living room. When the doorbell rang, I called "it's open," which should have been obvious to them.

Two officers preceded Chief Shaw through the door. He said he assumed I understood why he was here, and I shrugged.

"I expect you're following up on our conversation with George. Do I need to do anything?"

"No. Just stay where you are. One of my men will be here with you."

"Do you have a search warrant?" That question made me feel like an actor in a crime show. He rolled his eyes, and handed me folded legal-looking papers. "Thanks."

"We're bringing in dogs."

"Sorry, but I didn't buy any treats."

One by one, six policemen and two dogs began to dismantle my house, room by room. I couldn't see what they were doing, but I imagined that they had undone what I'd cleaned up only two days ago. Kind of like Groundhog Day. They were methodical and organized. I could hear drawers opening, but never close. The clomp of wood on wood said they were stacking the drawers, and I would have more work when they left. Whether I'd be leaving with them remained a question.

When I stood to get my briefcase, the officer told me to sit down. I had classes to prepare, I told him, and I wanted my notes. He repeated his request, a command, really. I asked if he would mind checking with his boss, and despite a clench-jawed grimace, he called Shaw. I explained that unless they were taking me away, I had a job and work I still needed to do. With a wave of his hand, I judged he had just given me permission.

Even with surveillance of my own homework, I managed to prepare my question for Friday's discussions: "What one thing would you want to know more about?" I thought about the advances in technology and ease of access to information as the basis for the growing knowledge economy. I became so engrossed, I didn't notice when the Chief stood across from me.

He cleared his throat to garner my attention. "We're done. It seems you've been rousted for a rumor, Mr. Gilbert. We'll be clearing out."

"Sorry I don't have a box of dog treats to offer."

His stark expression lingered until he figured out I was serious. I asked him if he had a minute to chat.

"Let me get my guys out of here first. I'll be back." He ushered the men and dogs out the front door and in a matter of minutes he stepped in.

"So?" I asked, as he took the seat across from me.

"You want it straight?" I nodded. "I know you had drugs here and I'm glad you got them out. But this is the last warning. Next time, no mercy."

"I'm not a drug dealer, so there won't be a next time. But I have a question. Why are you letting me off?"

"You don't know?"

"Wouldn't ask if I did."

"Mr. Gilbert, think back. I was in your class for American History." Of course, I didn't know that. "You caught me with three joints I planned to sell. Don't you remember?" Again I shook my head. "Well, you took me and the joints into your classroom, crumbled the joints into your trashcan, and we went to the boys' room. You flushed your entire can and backed up the toilet. The only thing you said to me, 'stop being stupid.' I haven't forgotten. I don't know what's happened to you since, but like they say, 'What goes around comes around.' So stop being stupid."

"I know Nat told you to wait. Why did you?"

"I owe her. She wrote a piece that changed public opinion about police. You must remember it. When the kid got shot with the stray bullet? Anyway, she wrote that the time had come to stop judging based on news stories, and that the police have a hard and dangerous job. Bad apples make the story, and make the thousands who really are public servants look bad."

"I guess I owe her now too."

"Maybe more than you know. Don't take it for granted. That'll not only piss her off, but you'll be making me your enemy."

"Message received. Thanks again."

Primed for the morning onslaught, I still had no idea how to find Fritz. How long would I have to wait for Thor to send me some luck? Following the chief's admonition, I called Natalie to thank her. Her question caught me off guard.

"What are you doing the rest of the night?"

"Nothing."

"Do you want company?" Her sensual tone enticed, and my answer surprised us both.

"Not tonight, but how about breakfast on Saturday?"

She chuckled in resignation. "Still hard to get. I'll pick you up at eight-thirty and we'll play it by ear." My phone went dead.

December continued to be warmer than usual according to the ten-day forecast on my computer. Unseasonal storms were expected for the Gulf States. All I could imagine on my way to school was Chris Hemsworth laughing at me.

My classes performed admirably. In a world changing so broadly, the list of things they wanted to know more about grew each period. I left the list on the board, adding each class's ideas. My fifth period class had another agenda after I told them they had homework. When I asked them to tell me one thing they wanted to know more about, "Like what?" was the first response.

I said, "For me, I want to know more about mosquitoes." Scrunched faces of disgust and fidgeting as they scratched told me I had struck a nerve.

"Why? With so much to choose from, why pick something so annoying?"

"We've learned to control them, how to prevent bites, and still we can't kill them off. Is there something we can learn about survival from them?"

The day's best answer came from a tenth grade boy. "Girls." I didn't say, but I had to agree. I looked forward to their homework lists. Fifty things they wanted to know more about.

Although I anticipated an enjoyable morning on Saturday, I hoped that Nat would be a trustworthy confidant. The yellow Beetle ground to a halt with her downshift. In her other world, she drove a hybrid Focus.

"Where are we going?"

"Breakfast."

"I know, but where?"

"Best buffet around."

I had no idea until we pulled into what was a garden center in my world. Here a full parking lot and a line out the door warned of an indefinite wait. I suggested we go someplace else. She shook her head and said, "You're an idiot." The owner met us at the front door and after a hug and cheek kisses, we were escorted to a booth in the rear, behind an uncleared table.

"This table won't be available until you're ready to leave, Natalie. So glad to see you again."

"We'll be a while, Niko. But pad the bill. He," she pointed to me, "can afford it."

"Thanks for that," I said. She smiled. "And thanks for your help with the cops. You seem to know me better than I do."

"Now, my old friend, do you want to tell me who you really are?"

I stopped looking at the menu and jerked my head up so that we were eye to eye. No twinkle, all business. "What do you mean?"

She kept her eyes locked on mine, reached out and grabbed my hand, flicking my nail tips. "Brian told me about your meeting with McAllister and the shrink. Writing a book, my ass. Spill it, Ashley."

"What did he tell you?"

"Nothing you can't tell me again. I've interviewed politicians for years, so believe me, I know a lie from any angle you can think of. I want it. I want it now. I want it all."

I recognized this version of Natalie, even if we were from different worlds. Tenacious, a word that had her teeth marks as the definition, unyielding and determined. I had always found her attractive, sexy even. But this one had a thin coating of nice over the hard-as-nails reporter across from me. She still held my hand. The warmth that passed between us contradicted the hard look she gave me.

"I can time travel."

I expected a laugh, some form of dismissal, disbelief. She sat back, reached into the saddle bag she called a purse, removed a pen, a pad and a recorder. She leaned her chin on her right hand, and asked, "When did you stop chewing your nails?"

So, other me bit his nails. I had never been a nail biter. "Is that the giveaway?" She nodded. "Nat, no recorder. My life is too messed up as it is. If you want me to talk, it's off the record." She reached to the OFF button. Then I started.

"So I exist in another dimension." Not a question, just a surprise to her when I had told her most of the story.

"Yup. Maybe more than one. I don't know yet."

"And you can't do anything without a thunderstorm?"

"Right. I think my desk, the current one, will still work, but I don't know until I can try it. And I can't find Fritz until I know everything works. I've got to try to find where he went and soon. Being here may not last. If he's the reason the world is jumbled, then it stands to reason that everything he does forces more changes. I just don't know yet."

"Paperclips, really?" I thought back to Nat's first encounter, not unlike this one. Not skeptical, lots of questions. And she shut up when she first met the president. "And to find Fritz, you have to meet Robert

E. Lee, Winston Churchill, the Wright Brothers and Abraham Lincoln." Her smile tugged at me like a magnet. "I'm not letting you out of my sight." A genuine smile, totally disarming. "And all I have to do is wait for bad weather. You're a lot more interesting than you, I mean, you know, the other you."

Chapter 11

Fritz

CHRISTMAS WENT on hold the minute I returned. Our new customers were what I expected—cops. Seated at the same table as their first time. Cindy sat rigid, across from them. The look on her face flashed a warning, but not of what to fear.

"He's back, so let's go," said the one who had stared at me on his first visit. All three of them stood.

"Russ, take care of things, will you?"

"What's up? Where are you going?"

"I'm being questioned. I asked them to wait until you got back."

"Do you have a lawyer? Do you want me to find one?"

As she stepped to the door, she said no, she'd be back soon. They pushed her into the back seat of the car I had spotted at the ATM, and she looked at me as they pulled away. She mouthed, "Help."

I didn't know where they were taking her, or what I could do, besides keeping the place going. So instead of going home, I decorated. I had been at it for about an hour, not only the lights but the other junk she'd collected had some place to go, when the phone rang. I had never answered it, so the ring made me jump.

"Call Flynn Connolly, you've met him. Tell him I'm at the police at City Hall. He'll know what to do."

"Are you being arrested?"

"Don't know yet. Call him. Now. And keep the place going." She disconnected.

The man she wanted me to call carried a brogue as heavy as a barrel of Guinness, and hung up the phone faster than a Belfast bullet. And I had no idea what "keep the place going" meant. Or when she'd be back to keep it going herself.

I began a list, some things don't change, of what I would need to do. Cleaning up the decorating debris came first. My job was easy. Cook. She did everything else. I thought about what I needed to buy (she did that), how to cook and juggle twelve tables and four booths (she did that). Pick up, wash up, clean up, sweep up, close up. She did all that too. I'd never let that fact reach my conscious thought. *She is quite remarkable, yup.* I continued the list in detail, until I reached my last question. What should I do with the money? I counted it, made a note for the register, and put it in my pocket.

Although I'd locked the front door, I left the back door unbolted. When it slammed open and three rather large men of dour countenance walked in, I stopped wondering about me, and addressed what they were doing.

"Sorry, we're closed, and that's not the entrance."

"We know." The wild red hair exploding from his head identified one Flynn Connolly. He headed for his destination, and he ignored me.

"What do you want? Is Cindy all right? Is she in jail?"

"Not now, bucko. We've got to move fast." They pulled up one of the floor runners, exposing the opening to the cellars. I didn't even know we had a basement. "Turn off the lights in the kitchen," he told me. "Then hold the trap door open for us." A series of wooden cartons were lifted up to the floor, and I moved the tables to make room. I'd seen enough movies to guess what they contained. When a dozen crates had been removed, one of the men backed a truck as close to the back door as possible.

"Give us a hand. We'll be out faster." I lifted and gauged the weight of a case of rifles. In less than ten minutes, the truck pulled down the alley and into the night.

"Where's Cindy?" I asked, as the big man reached the door.

He snickered. "I expect she'll be out soon. I'll tell her you Christmased the place up. Oh, and she said to take the money home. She'll settle up with you later."

"What's this all about?"

"You don't need to know."

"If you want me here on Monday, I need to know."

"She trusts you. I don't. I do know that you're not who or what you say you are. So until I trust you, you don't need to know. You read too much, too many real books to be a know-nothin', say nothin', just doin' my job, kind of guy."

That little tidbit raised warning signals. "What books I read aren't any part of this. How do you know anyway?"

"I make it my business. She hasn't kept help as long as you since she opened this dump. And now you have regulars and you're attracting attention. That wasn't the plan."

"What in hell are you talking about?"

"Make you a deal. Tell me who you really are and if I like the answer, I'll think about what you're entitled to know."

"Let's just say I'm an illegal alien, who knows those boxes didn't hold used car parts."

"Smart-ass answers aren't what I was lookin' for. I know you aren't Russell Furst. I know that you don't exist, anywhere, you have no official records. We've looked. So Mr. Furst, what's your story?"

"You wouldn't believe it if I told you. All *you* need to know is that I'm here and I have no interest in being involved in anything illegal."

"So you're running and hiding. Just what I thought."

"You're guessing."

"Listen to me, and listen carefully. Cindy is a concern for us, for lots of reasons. Believe this red hair when I tell you that nothing happens to her that I can prevent. Now close the place up, go home, and be here all the earlier on Monday. You'll be needin' some help, I imagine. I have your mobile number. You'll hear from me by evening tomorrow." His quick turn revealed the gun holstered beneath his left arm. Seeing his back and hearing the door click shut, I locked it, both the locks, and stared at the closed door. Involvement with gun runners and people who carried them placed below last on my to-do list. But I had nowhere to go, so I closed up and went home.

Monday morning came as early as it did any other day. I opened the back door and waited for the help that Flynn had promised. Loud pounding on the front door took me away from setting up breakfast. Not surprised, two young women and one long, skinny man walked in, accompanied by my new Irish friend.

"This is Seamus, and the girls are Jane and Kathleen. I'll be back at 5 p.m. Finish up and close up, but don't leave. Let the girls go when you're done. Seamus will stay with you. He knows what to do."

"What do you mean, 'what to do?' "

He grabbed my right shoulder and leaned in to my left ear. Squeezing my shoulder, hard, he said, "Do … what I say. And keep your mouth shut. If you need anything, send Seamus." He removed his hand, turned and left through the back door.

"Well," I said, taking a deep breath, "let's get to work. Ladies, would you set the tables. Seamus, I need to start with the batter. If I get it started, will you mix it?"

A new brogue met me. "I've worked for Katie before, Russ. I know me way about the place. And I can cook for ya if ya wish."

"Good. But who's Katie?"

He turned seven shades of red, and reminded me of Ted, my student in my other world. "I mean Cindy. You know."

"Okay." I let that slip of the tongue hang around on a back burner for the time being. "Then I need to get the potatoes started. I cook 'em on high and move them to a low heat to keep 'em warm."

"And you'd be tellin' an Irishman how to cook potatoes?"

That made me laugh. "Well, I guess I am. But I've done this alone for so long that I have a system. Sorry."

"I know. Ka … Cindy's told us. Been here a few times meself. You're good. We like the waffles, too."

By opening time, everything was ready. But the expected, usual trickle became a steady flow and then verged on a mob. The suits were plentiful, including our cop newcomers. I told Seamus to go out back and call Connolly, let him know the cops were in the house. He carried a half-full trash bag out to the dumpster, and came back, whispering local cops were in the alley. I told him to take over the grill, and went out front.

"What do you guys want? You're upsetting my staff. What's this all about?"

The staring guy said, "Let's go outside."

"Fine." He followed me out the door. "Look, I just work here. I'm holding down the fort, but you're making life difficult." I was talking to a rock.

"Your name is Russ, right?"

"You know it is. So why do I have a full house when maybe we get twenty or thirty for breakfast on a Monday. Are they all yours?"

"Not ours, but Cindy's Cozy Kitchen hit the news over the weekend, so people are checking it out. Your crowd is a lot of press. You did a good job on the website." He stopped my next question. "She told us. And I looked."

"So if they aren't yours, why are you here?"

"We want to talk to you."

"Why?"

"Because Russell Furst doesn't exist."

I tried to hide the intimidation and my tensing muscles. "I'm right here."

"Cut the crap. We're not interested in you or your story. Your boss has been storing and shipping small arms, rifles and pistols, to the provos in Northern Ireland. We just haven't caught her at it. So you can tell us and then we can let you be."

"So let me understand. You want me to tell you all I know about an international gun smuggling plan and you'll go away?"

"Yep, that's it. Simple, huh?"

"Yeah. I don't know anything, so I can't tell you anything. I come in early and leave by mid-afternoon. If I had something to say, I'd tell you." I watched his reaction, meeting me eye to eye, and hoped the lie would be undetected.

"I suspect that's not true. But we'll be watching."

"So when's Cindy coming back?"

"When we're done with her. And we'll have eyes on you."

Self-restraint took over. After years of repartee with Ashley, and a wise-crack at the end of a conversation, this guy didn't crack a smile, unlikely to appreciate my humor. As I returned to the kitchen, he called across the room, "Good waffles."

"Secret recipe. Stop in again some time." Relief and anger were fighting for first place.

"Oh, you can count on that."

Just as promised, Flynn Connolly walked in the back door with Cindy close behind. The Christmas lights brought an endearing smile to her otherwise worried face. With their arrival, I put my coat on, but she said not to leave yet. Seamus locked the back door as the three of us sat in a booth.

"Thanks for looking out for the place, Russ."

I took the cash I'd been holding, laid it on the table. "No problem. But I think you better start looking for a new cook."

"Not a good idea," Flynn said. "You're invisible here, and Kate will need to be away to visit her sick mother. Off and on for a few months."

"Let me tell him, Flynn. My name's not Cindy."

"I guessed that one already."

"My father, two brothers, and six cousins have been murdered in the last ten years by agents of the Queen. Flynn's family raised me in the States to keep me safe. But things at home are worse than ever. Northern Ireland is the last gasp of the British Empire, and they won't let it go. We here are their only source of help anymore. The rest of the world doesn't care. A civil war they call it, a religious war. But it's not. It's a war to gain our freedom from their oppression. And it's personal."

In my world, the wars in Northern Ireland, the Troubles, had been resolved more than two decades earlier and peace had slowly found a home. In this one, the world seemed hell-bent on its own destruction. None of the efforts to keep peace were working, as the Middle East boiled, China had become the world's largest naval power, and the oceans had begun to change the US coastline. The US had slid out of the forefront of economic, political and social dominance. Influence in global affairs had all but dissolved with our constant internal in-fighting. Everyone, at least according to one media source or another, was a terrorist, and they all called themselves – "So you're a freedom fighter?"

"I am, and proud of it."

"It sounds to me like you want revenge. That won't solve anything. It never has. I know that for certain."

"Do ya?" Flynn's red hair flamed in every compass direction. "Then now is the time for you to tell us your real story, bucko."

"No, it's not, and not here." Tom Andrews' tall figure and serious face flashed before my eyes. "I can't believe you'd be so careless. Have you checked to see if this place is bugged. A cop or a cop's accomplice has been in every seat in the place."

Flynn reached into his pocket and pulled out a plastic bottle, a knowing grin on his stubbled face. Crushed particles that looked like some kind of ground spice took up half the container.

"This place is checked constantly," Cindy said. I wasn't ready to accept the name change. She held out what I thought to be a rosary. "It sends a message to my computer which links to a cell phone. It buzzes when it detects uninvited transmissions. Bugs. I grind them up. That's why we have two meat grinders. So this place is safer than any." Having included me in one little secret, she asked, "So, Russ, what's your story?"

Chapter 12

Fritz

"**I'M A TIME** traveler." I'd learned over the years that if you said it right, the truth could be told and accepted as a lie. I remember having that thought a while ago and how strange I felt analyzing lying. That had been a good lesson to learn. I'd studied body language, facial expressions, tones of voice. Amazing what you can learn watching the news, especially in an election year.

I continued my story, surprised that they didn't interrupt. Even Seamus had taken a seat at a nearby table. I didn't need to elaborate. A story so far-fetched needed no twinkle lights. I neglected to mention that I was also a murderer.

When I ended, Flynn rubbed his stubble, but before he said that he didn't believe a word, Kate said, "So for eight years you've wandered. No family, no friends, no way back. Sounds a lot like me." Her sad smile contained both genuine sympathy and a touch of sensuality. "No girl friends?" I shook my head.

"Oh, stop." Flynn glared. "Then why's your photo in such a prominent place in the FBI files?" *He knows?* "Yeah, we've had you pegged for quite some time. They don't have a name to attach and it's old news now, so you've been lucky. But you can bet they'll piece it together. Those fellas that took Kate are suspicious. They'll figure it out. So you better stay where I can keep you out of trouble."

"What did you do, Russ?" I filled in the rest. "So, you went back in time and killed the men who tried to kill you, screwed up your life and you ended up turning all of time on its ear."

"That's pretty much it. I just wanted my family to be done with it. At least, they're safe. I didn't expect to turn everything upside down, but I hadn't planned to be going back anyway. I've had plenty of time to think about this. History, the past, doesn't want to be changed, and I'm here now, because history fights back. In ways I'd never considered. I've tried not to mess up here in case that affects the other dimension."

She reached out and placed her hand on mine. "You're a freedom fighter, too."

We closed up and Flynn asked if I would give Seamus a lift. I told Kate I'd see her in the morning.

"You never know." Her smile returned.

Seamus climbed in and told me to head into the Northeast. I've never lost my fascination with Washington, but rarely now would I cross the bridges. I'd burnt mine already. The Monument gleamed between the buildings as we turned down K Street. He directed me to a bar called McNamara's, emblazoned in fluorescent green, and said he lived in an apartment upstairs. He told me to park and come in for a beer. I said I wanted to get home.

"I'm not really askin'. Flynn has some things to discuss." A minute later, a pint of porter bubbled in front of me, delivered by one of the waitresses who'd helped out at the café. Jane placed four menus on the table. I quizzed her with a glance.

"They're on the way, Russ. Can I get you a snack?" I told her I'd wait. All eyes were on me, mostly Irish eyes, I guessed. I would find out later that I had sat in Flynn's seat of power. Moments later, my other helper delivered another pint of porter. "I'm still working on this one, Kathy."

"I think you'll find no shortage tonight, Russ. So I hope you know how to drink."

"I'm a little out of practice, I'm afraid." More than a little out of practice, I'd stopped drinking anything stronger than diet in case I needed to hit the road fast. Another lesson learned in a small town near the Nebraska-Iowa border, when a local constable posed a question as to why an eastern accent found itself so far from home turf.

"Then, these are your spring training. The regular season opens in just a few minutes."

She was right. Flynn and Cindy walked in to opening day ovations without the need of a public address announcer. She waved and sat down next to me while Flynn worked the room. The handshakes and hugs reminded me of a reunion of long-separated friends. I asked Cindy. She said Flynn had a ritual. They all loved him and most had been pulled out of harm's way when Flynn had come to their rescue.

"You know all these guys, too?"

"Every one. Some for most of my life. What are you eating?"

"I didn't look." She pushed a menu in front of me.

"Look. Kelly's one of the best chefs around. She could have her own TV show and make some of them look like fast food drive-in cooks. Do you like corned beef and cabbage? Drink up. It's on the house." For a woman who'd spent a couple of days in jail, she exhibited more animation than I'd ever seen from her. And no tips were involved. For the first time in years, I had a warm, belonging feeling, like I'd come home.

While Flynn continued to make the rounds, the crowd came to say hello, one at a time, with a handshake for me and a kiss for her. I asked her what she'd asked me earlier, and she told me her story.

She'd been shipped to America for the first time at eight years old when the Troubles were at a crisis point. The Connollys were related on her mother's side and had raised her like a daughter. She'd gone to school and returned home for a few weeks each year. She said she had been back and forth for the past thirty years. In that time, cooking for crowds and cleaning guns at safe houses rounded her education. She had opened Cindy's Cozy Corner sixteen years before.

"And running guns since then?"

"All we can get, every few weeks."

"When did the cops find you?"

"A long time ago. And a lot of them are sympathetic. I go through this a couple of days every few months."

"I never noticed."

"I didn't tell you. Just a couple days off, I said. So you were a history teacher?"

"Hold on. You already know my story. So you came here at age eight and you've been doing this for thirty. How old are you?" She laughed and chided me for my impolite question. "I'm a teacher. The history doesn't fit with the math. So?"

"I'm thirty-nine, and I'll never have another birthday."

"We're all having corned beef," said Flynn. I looked at the empty chair. "He'll be here. Have another porter, Russ."

"Still working on this one. So Cindy, what's your real name?" I asked.

Flynn chuckled. "You think your story's strange."

She said, "Kathleen Scarlet O'Hara. My father loved 'Gone with the Wind,' although he rooted for the rebels."

"What did you do before you became an international criminal?" Flynn turned a hard glare on me.

"He's joking, Flynn," she said. "I did like most American girls. I went to college. My bachelor's is in political science, with minors in history and music. Georgetown. I'm a well-educated terrorist."

"That's not a joking matter, Kate. You've done the family proud. And she's learned a useful thing or two, like picking pockets, taking out bullets, and she can make a disguise for anyone. That's been real useful. Oh, here he is, finally."

The last person I expected sat down. Flynn waved to Jane, as I gaped at the staring cop. "Russell Furst, meet Tim McNamara. We named the place for him." A stronger handshake than I expected squeezed my hand.

"So where's my dinner?" he asked.

While I ate, I listened to the chit-chat, and a report of all the police activities surrounding my new friends. Friends—that was a word that had vacated my vocabulary for quite some time. The corned beef melted in my mouth and I'd never had cabbage and boiled potatoes that tasted so good. My fourth pint of dark beer guaranteed a swimming head and a hangover in the morning.

"And what do they have on our friend here?"

They had my attention in spite of the porter. "Nothing yet. But the secret service has been told that with a black president, they needed to tie off loose ends. You're one of those, Mr. Furst. I have a friend who's pretty high up at the Bureau, and she said they were opening any and all cold cases that might pose a danger. That includes shooting campaign donors."

My companions laughed while I gagged on my last bite. When I could finally swallow, I asked how long they'd known. Flynn said they did a better job vetting employees than the voters ever did. McNamara said he'd checked me out my first week at the job. Facial recognition turned a match at about sixty percent, so he dug further. The picture from the Koppler security system wasn't good enough, but nothing else fit. "We kept a close eye on you, and you made the rest easy. Regular routine, you showed up for work, never a problem. Never went anywhere. So we left you alone. When you told me this afternoon that you didn't know anything, we knew we'd made a good choice. You're a pretty good liar. My partner didn't suspect a thing."

"So, what do I do now. If you've figured it out, then someone else is bound to, eventually." Kate excused herself, stepping out of sight in the back. "I don't need any trouble, and neither do you." My head cleared fast. "I think it's time for me to move on."

"I told you before, we can protect you better than anyone. Kate needs someone we trust to keep the shop running while she's gone. If you go, you'd have to start over with no background to verify anything."

"You could vouch for me."

Flynn said, "And why would I do that? I want you here. I'll not make it easy for you. So, make it easy on yourself."

"So I'm a prisoner?"

"Don't be stupid, man." Flynn's hands resting on the table clenched, his knuckles turning white. "This is hardly jail. Out there, no one is gonna watch your back. We will."

"He's right, Mr. Furst. And I'll know before almost anyone if the Feds are coming."

Flynn leaned forward, inching toward me. For a second, I thought he would climb over the table. "Now, what's your real name?"

"Fritz Russell."

At that moment, the front door opened and a nun walked into the bar to another round of cheering and clapping. Obviously well-known, she began collecting money for some charity. I noticed no jingle of coins, but wads of cash, and not one-dollar bills. Flynn pulled cash from his pocket, as did Seamus and the cop. The nun didn't miss a patron, and as she headed toward us, I could see bills popping above the rim. A large movie popcorn tub doubled as her collection plate. I reached into my empty pocket, and remembered that I had given Kate all the money, even mine. When she reached our table and the others dropped the money in, she stuck the tub in my face. I looked up at her, and said I wasn't carrying any cash. The firm jaw jutted and the smile faded.

"And how were you going to pay for your food and drink. You don't look a pauper. Mr. Connolly, what sort of friend have you made?" Her brogue was as thick as his, and her face as serious.

"Sit down, sister. Join us for a pint." He signaled to Jane and circled his index finger for a round. "Sister Katherine, I want you to say hello, nicely now, to Mr. Fritz Russell. He's new to our family."

I glanced at him, thinking he'd lost his mind. He winked and turned to the nun.

"I guess you don't recognize me," she said to me, holding out her hand.

I looked at her face and shook my head. "Sorry, no. Should I?"

Jane plunked down the glasses around the table, laughing at me. Each of my companions wore grins that reminded me of Ashley.

"What?"

Flynn asked, "Sister, do you know where Kate's gone off to?"

"She'll be only a moment. Jane dear, would you lend a hand?" With her back to me, and Jane blocking the view, she removed the habit, and when she took her seat, a version of Cindy I hadn't seen before smiled at me. My stunned look set the place in uproarious laughter.

Flynn said over the noise, "Kate O'Hara, meet Fritz Russell." He then stood, and the room settled to a low din. He lifted his glass and said, "My friends. I'm asking you to bid welcome to Fritz Russell." The glasses rose as one, and "Slainte" filled the room.

"Drink up, boyo. They're feisty about their welcomes."

I lifted my pint and sipped. "I have to be at work, and sober, in a few hours."

Kate tapped my arm. "Enjoy it, Russ. Seamus will open and get things started." Seamus nodded when I turned to him. Then she took my hand and told me to come with her. "I want to talk to you. Alone."

Through the cheering and wolf-whistling, we exited by a back door to a small foyer with a locked, steel-reinforced door, and up a flight of stairs to a second door. The clang of heavy metal climbed the stairs behind us. When the door opened, two men jumped up, like they had been called to attention. "Kevin, Joe, meet Fritz Russell." I shook their hands, hard and rough, and saw the shoulder holsters beneath their coats. "Fritz will be here a while. Pass the word when you leave."

"We will, Kate," said the man named Kevin. "Your door is open."

"Thanks, boys," she said, and took my hand. The only other door led into an apartment that could have been a penthouse in upscale New York City, without the view. Hardwood floors, tasteful and coordinated wallcoverings and expensive furniture filled a large living room. Lace curtains were bordered by heavy floral draperies. On the right, a full kitchen, with a table seating eight and a granite-topped island with stools for six more left plenty of room for a cadre of cooks. On the front left, another door led to a bedroom, where she headed. "Make yourself comfortable while I get changed."

I walked to the window. Below me, a line of double-parked cars, two groups of three men talking and smoking, and the green sign reflecting off the cars and neighboring windows disguised a careful plan of defense. The slight blur of the light made me tap a thicker than standard plate glass.

"They're bullet-proof," Kate said, walking to a small bar. She poured us each a drink from the crystal decanters. "Sit down over here."

I took the proffered glass, and joined her on a couch, maybe the most comfortable seat I'd ever sat in. "This is your place?" She nodded. "It's like a fortress. Why?"

"That's a long story, Russ. And it goes back a long time."

I looked at my watch. "Then give me the CliffsNotes version."

"Not tonight. Tonight I want to know about you. You're a strange man, living like you do. I've watched you for a year and waited until you trusted me enough to talk. The cat's out now, so tell me."

"I'll make you a deal, 'cause I have a question or two myself. I'll answer one for one. How's that?"

"I may have some short questions in multiple parts. I'll start. Fritz Russell, that's your real name?" I nodded. "And where are you from, Fritz Russell?" I told her I was a Jersey boy originally and that before the portal, I taught history in Riverboro. "And you know the president, this fellow we just elected?"

"In my world, he's just about to leave office after two terms. He beat McCain back in '08. I met him the day I discovered the portal."

"And the president and the portal almost got you killed. And it's left you here for eight years. Doesn't sound to me like you got the best of the deal."

Before answering, I looked at her, legs tucked under, tight jeans and a form-fitting tee shirt. For a year I'd worked with her, with nary a clue that she lived a disguise. I examined her face. The lines and creases had all but vanished. Her daily routine of pulled-into-a-bun brown hair, now floated in a shoulder-length red. I shook my head.

"You're amazing. How long does it take to get ready every day?"

"Not long. A mask and a wig, and a little make-up. No one really notices. I'm a waitress. And until you came, we had no real regulars.

In the past few months, I've had to pay attention. It takes a little longer. Flynn's happy because the place is making money, finally."

"Why not just be yourself?"

"For the same reason that you don't. Random cameras, coincidental meetings. Too many people depend on me, too many lives would be in jeopardy. Tell me about your wife."

She changed course so fast, I thought of Jane, who always stayed three moves ahead. I guess I grinned so she asked again.

"When I came into this dimension, Linda and I would have been barely married. Most of the things that have happened only started a year or so ago."

"Your time or ours?"

"My time. This is hard to explain. In my time, Linda and I have been married just over eight years. So in this time, we were just getting used to being married in the year I showed up here. Before I got here, before I came through, we had a fight about the portal, or her father, or something. I never could understand it. But whatever, she left and I only saw her once in six months. She told me she didn't love me anymore. But I didn't, I don't, accept that. The portal changed our lives, the way we thought, what we did. I came here to end the people who had made life so awful. I accepted that I'd probably change things, but I had no idea how much."

"You've changed life here, for me. Do you have a picture?" I pulled out a thin and battered wallet. Not much inside. No money or credit cards. My driver's license for here, my library card and a small now-wrinkled photo of Linda, TJ and I.

While she looked at it, I said, "That's all I have left of them."

She handed back the wallet. "If you could find a way back, would you go?" Her dark eyes bored into me as I considered the query.

"Once upon a time I would have said yes right away. I made a mistake thinking that I was the only one who could handle Koppler. He had escaped again before I left. Now, I have no idea how long I've been gone. Inside the portal, time shifts. We had already learned that. But not how much. Like I said, I had no idea that I would cause time to blow itself up. So, I don't know what I'd go back to. Maybe."

"You didn't blow time up. I've been on this path my entire adult life."

"How old are you really? You lost twenty years from the time we left the shop."

"I'm thirty-seven, been married, he's gone. He didn't stay long enough for kids. So you and I could have met at Celibates Anonymous." She laughed. Despite the sense of humor, I sensed an underlying sadness.

"Why'd he leave?"

"Same reason I live here. The Feds and Interpol got very close. He didn't believe me when I told him about my involvement, and he tried to make me stop. Flynn had a long talk with him. I never found out what Flynn said, and he won't say, but two days later, Peter vanished. I've haven't seen him since. And how old are you?"

"I don't know. I was thirty-six when I left. It's the same year here. But I don't know if I lost years or if it's been added on. I could be eight years older. So maybe forty-four."

"You don't look it. In fact, you don't look any different than you did when I first saw you. Maybe you won't age here. That would be interesting."

As we talked, Kate sipped and I finally tasted some of the best whiskey I had ever drunk. "What is this?"

"Irish. Private label I bring back each time I go. Just for me."

I had lived apart, not just alone, and sitting here with Kate, began to relax and feel I'd returned from a long trip. "What were you collecting money for?"

"The Church of Saints Smith and Wesson." Her quick wit, engaging smile and off-center sense of humor explained why men so carefully protected her, men who couldn't miss her charm. I might be one. She reminded me of Ashley, which for me added both a joy and twinge of loneliness. "The boys were out collecting this week, and that's where those fat wads came from. We buy guns and food to ship back. We'll be sailing in a couple of weeks."

"We?"

"Aye. I'll be gone for a couple of weeks. I want to see my mother. And some others. If you'd like to join me, you'd be welcome."

"What about…"

"Seamus will run the place. Flynn and the girls will make sure all's well."

I straightened up as she leaned toward me. "Kate, I haven't…"

"Been on a vacation? Been out of the country? Been with a woman?" She kissed my cheek. As she leaned in, I wanted to grab her and hold her, and kiss her like tomorrow didn't matter.

"I was going to say, I don't have a passport."

When she laughed, her warm breath grazed my cheek. "Sure you do. Anytime you want one. In any name." She took my hand, and stood, beckoning me to follow.

"I don't think I should."

"Let me see if I can change your mind."

Chapter 13

Fritz

I CHECKED my watch. Nine o'clock. Sunlight streamed through cracks in the drapes, illuminating what had to be a formal country garden design. Alone, my little headache reminded me what I'd drunk. I readied myself for what lay ahead, not sure what that would be. Sleep had come fast and had stayed, longer and deeper than any I could recall. Kate had left a bottle of aspirin by the bathroom sink, whether for her or me, I didn't know.

"Probably both," I said aloud.

I took a quick shower, dressed, heading for home and then work. Two men stood up when I entered the hall. "Morning," I said.

"And to you, Mr. Russell. We have a message. Don't go home. Have breakfast downstairs. Flynn's waiting for you."

"Did something happen?"

"Flynn's waiting. I'll let him know you're on the way."

A half dozen heads turned when I walked in. Flynn waved me over, a cup of coffee already waiting for me. I hadn't noticed the shamrock-covered table cloth last night, the only one in the place.

"Late sleeper, are ya?"

"Not usually. What's up?"

"Tim called. The cops are sitting outside your house."

"Why? Are they going to arrest me?"

"No. Someone called in, probably a neighbor. You've had a break-in. Someone watching you saw that you didn't come home. That's my guess. Who might that be?"

"No idea. I don't have anything worth taking. Unless a librarian wanted books back."

"I want you to go home. One of my boys will be watchin' for you. The cops will want to talk to you. Do whatever they ask?"

"What if they want me to go with them?"

"Then go. I'll know and I'll take care of it. Kate already knows you'll be a while. So don't worry about that."

"Is she all right?"

He looked at me, the kind of questioning look that I would use to analyze a student's excuse for not handing in homework. "She's fine. They showed up early. Told them you took the morning off. So have some breakfast and then you can go."

Spread on the table, the morning paper showed a picture of the newly-elected president, with a headline, "What Change Can We Expect?" Flynn saw me reading upside down. "So you really know this guy?"

"Know him? No. A different version of him. He and I were friends. In a different time. That president was a good guy. And he did a pretty good job, given the hand they dealt him. I can only imagine what he could have accomplished with a little help."

"Do you think this one will be different?"

"Don't know. He's not gonna have an easy time. The whole world is a mess, not just in the U.S. But I'm sure everyone's waiting to see if it'll be more of the same, or if he really has some plans to fix things, and if Congress will let him."

"Do you think they will?"

"Flynn, he's smart. But he's in a system that moves very slowly. People are scared, mostly for themselves. They think the government has forgotten them. They're looking for leadership, common sense, not handouts. They want what every society needs to function. Jobs that pay enough to support a family. Education and training for themselves and their kids. Adequate and affordable housing. Protection if they get sick. Laws that are just and fair, and justice that's even-handed.

"Now you sound like a teacher."

"Sorry."

"Don't be. You make sense. What else?"

"They want to know that government serves everyone. And they want to believe it will. Look at the turn-out to vote. Staggeringly small. But if he's like the guy in my dimension, he'll try to bring them back."

"Then it sounds like we ought to pay attention. Maybe I will." He pushed the newspaper over to me and said to eat and get home.

I arrived at the Cozy Kitchen in time to beat the lunch crowd. Kate smiled when she saw me. Seamus glanced up from the sink, still washing up from breakfast. Kathy and Jane were setting tables. Flynn sat at a table in the back, talking to a man in a suit I didn't recognize.

"You took your time," Cindy said.

"You're right. My time. But I'm here for the lunch crowd, and I have a new idea for a sandwich." She had her banter primed and ready, but a new menu item stopped her. "It'll mean we have the oven on through lunch."

"We'll talk about it after the crowd. Do we need to buy different food?"

"Some. I have a name for it too." Her forehead creases were pronounced. I couldn't get over the difference, now that I'd seen what she really looked like. "Blow Your Brains Out."

"Don't talk to me like that."

I snorted. "That's the name. And we'll put signs up or maybe a banner. Just "Blow Your Brains Out."

"You're pretty chipper for being half a day late. Get to work."

For a moment, I saw an image of my old kitchen table with Linda and Ashley as we traded barbs. "Yes, ma'am." The image faded but the moment passed like molasses. Despite no longer having a home, the memory made me homesick.

When we closed up, Kate asked what had happened to my apartment. She'd asked me to stick around to talk about my new sandwich. But she hadn't mentioned it.

"The police were accommodating. Someone broke into my place. Nothing of value could have been stolen. They messed the place up a little, but probably only wanted money. I never leave it around. I even turn coins to paper when I reach ten dollars. I gave you all my cash last night. I need to check more closely."

"About last night." If voices could blush, she sounded full-on magenta. "I'm sorry if I was a bit forward."

"Look, Cindy, we probably both had too much alcoholic assistance. I really don't have much of a memory about it. So don't even think about it."

"Russ, I'm embarrassed at my behavior. I've never done anything like that. And you were asleep before, well, you know."

"Really. No wonder I don't remember. Too bad. I wanted to ask if it was good for you." She scowled and I grinned back. "Do you want to know about my new sandwich?"

"Not really. At least now." She hesitated, and then said, "Would you like to come over for dinner?"

My heart did a flip in my chest, certainly not a reaction I expected. The idea of spending more time with her, with all of them, set off worry bells, but at the same time, inched me toward what I'd missed most.

"I have to go home and check if anything is missing, or find a clue to what they might have wanted. Why don't you come with me? We can grab a bite on the way back."

She shook her head. "Maybe another time. I need to finish some plans for the trip. I thought we could talk while I work."

"Then, another time it is. I'll take that raincheck."

"It'll be hard calling you "Fritz"."

"Then don't. Russ fits nicely. Fritz is some other guy I used to know."

Chapter 14

Ashley

A RINGING PHONE. The last thing I expected first thing on Monday morning. Not the quiet buzz of my cell, but the abrupt, heart-stopping blast of a wall phone in the kitchen. I ran to pick it up.

"Hello?"

"When did you start answering your phone?"

"Natalie?"

"Who else? I expected to leave a message, but since I have you, have you looked outside?"

"No. Why?"

"It's raining. The weather report is afternoon thunderstorms. Are you going to try your portal?"

"I don't know. I won't know until I get to school."

"If you can open it, call me. I want to go with you." I told her I would call only if the portal might open. Otherwise, she wouldn't hear from me. "Call me," she said, and hung up.

With two weeks remaining before Christmas vacation, pleasing Natalie took a minor position in my priorities. If she could help, I'd call. But I'd much rather explore on my own. When I reached my classroom, I touched the doorknob, and when nothing happened, I went in. Sitting in the middle of my desk, a book about the Lost Generation in Paris dared me to check the paperclips on its pages.

I draped my coat over the chair back and turned to the pictures Sandy had selected. She'd picked people–Hemingway, Joyce, Fitzgerald. Even a group photo with Sylvia Beach in front. But the exact picture of Shakespeare and Co. that Fritz used before waited patiently for its own clip. If the weather cooperated.

While I thumbed through the book I'd not read, Sandy walked in. She asked me if that would work. I showed her the picture I wanted to use, and began piling her paperclips on the desk. She said, "I went to Shakespeare and Company the summer after my senior year in college. It didn't look like that."

"You weren't paying attention. This one is the original, but when the Nazis took Paris, it closed. The building is still standing, with a historic marker. I haven't looked at stories about the new one."

She said it didn't matter to her, and asked if I was ready to go. I told her I'd try it after school. Without saying a word, a skeptical look crossed the room. As she left, she glanced back and shook her head. I didn't care. She'd already shown her colors and I needed to find Fritz, not get her approval.

With the day almost ready to start, I took out my list of questions and selected the day's topic. "Are social issues important to governing or are they distractions from real problems?" I'd had this conversation with Fritz and Linda for years. I sat down and read the blackboard, looking forward to what my classes would think.

Starting with my first class, and the first hand up, the question hit the core of their relationship with the world. "Both, Mr. Gilbert."

"Fill me in, Jamie."

"Well, social issues are the things that affect our lives every day. When the government makes them issues, they become important to people who care about them."

"Like what?" Hands rose. I called on Glenn.

"Guns, abortion, religion, law and order," he said. "And whatever the government does, someone won't be happy. If members of government make those issues most important, the real work they're elected to perform, like the economy and foreign relations, gets ignored."

Debbie added, "That's why voting matters.

I can honestly say that I wasn't ready for the day to start that way. Nor was I prepared for another class to be so exhilarating. My students amazed me at how tuned-in they were, in light of what I'd witnessed of the lack of discipline in the hallways.

By the end of my next class, the kids had dissected the political parties, the government at all levels, and the election results, like political scientists would have. I wish I had been able to record all they said. Before they left, I said, "I know you aren't old enough to have voted, but if you could have, who would you have chosen. Raise your hands." I asked first for Republicans, then Democrats. Only a smattering, almost equal, but only half the class. I asked the rest who they would have voted for. The majority said no one.

"In spite of your discussion, you'd still not vote?"

"Mr. Gilbert, with millions of people in the country, couldn't we find better people to vote for?" The bell rang.

Between classes, I ran to the office. I wanted to grab my morning paper to see if the weather report, the political news and the sports page were consistent with my computer's news. At the moment, I questioned if maybe something else had changed, if Fritz had done something that altered the present again. I'd never, I mean never, experienced classes like the ones I'd just finished. Or maybe the portal worked here, just as Fritz had said in our other life. The bell and the first clap of thunder sounded together. I reached into my pocket to make sure I had my keys.

The next period, my first group of seniors had begun the discussion without me. "Don't let me interrupt." They didn't. I sat and listened to well-reasoned arguments about the Constitution, and how it applied to my question. Midway through, I asked my only question. "None of you has mentioned whether or not the constitution is cast in stone, and that only what the Founding Fathers wrote is permanent. Is the Constitution interpretable?"

"It has to be, Mr. Gilbert," said one student. "They included a Supreme Court and left room for change through history with amendments. They couldn't know what changes would take place in the world, but they made room for future generations to decide how government should run."

Another said, "The arguments that only the original document should be used are impossible. Even with all the historical documents written by the men at the time, we don't know, can't know, how they would react to inventions and growth."

"Keep going, guys."

They talked about a well-informed electorate, participation in the governing process, the importance of selecting good candidates, and how to reduce the influence of money in politics. After this class I would need to do my own research to provide more information. More homework for me, but they were giving me an opportunity.

When they left, I put my key in the desk, put Sandy's book on the left side, and walked out. I grabbed the doorknob and got a shock. If I opened the door, I'd be in Paris, so I pulled, peeked in, and shut it immediately. Shakespeare and Co. would have to wait.

After a few more classes, I really envied Fritz. I could understand why teaching this stuff became one of his favorite things. Only a few days had passed, and rather than fights in the hall, I observed students, when challenged, engaging in discussions, behaving more mature and serious than many adults. I put the key in my desk, and walked across the hall. Sandy waited for her next class, but I told her to come quickly. I tapped my doorknob. "We only have a few seconds, so let's go."

"I have a class now."

"Suit yourself." I pulled the door open. In front of us, my classroom. I walked in, ignoring her. But what had gone wrong, I didn't know. I needed to find out. She followed me in.

"I thought we were going to Paris." Again, I ignored her scoffing. "So what happened?"

"You have a class now." I opened the book, and looked at the picture. The paperclip had moved. I took one from my drawer and replaced hers. The new one had a different touch, a tingle between my fingers. The bell put our trip on pause.

I'll see you later," she said on the way out.

"Maybe. Meet me at the Eiffel Tower."

Paperclips. I had a clue. And a few minutes left after lunch that I could use. On my way to the caf, a crowd had formed in the hall, another fight. The lesson I'd been taught, not to interfere, didn't set with me. I shoved the kids out of my way, asked a teacher to alert the police, and I waded in. As I reached the inner circle, I saw the knife. It'd been ten years since I'd stepped into a knife fight and I had a long scar to remind me. I slid my jacket off in a flash and wrapped it around my arm.

"Drop the knife." I didn't recognize the attacker. "Drop it now." He turned on me, and slashed. Deflecting his blow with my jacket, I hammered my left hook to his cheek. He dropped to a knee, but bounced up to stab at me. A slice of jacket split as the blade kept coming. I seized his wrist with my left hand, swiveled and with my back pressed against him, slammed him into the wall behind us. Glancing around, I was on my own. His breath was on my neck, so I started to squat, and with the back of my head, smashed his face. The knife hit the floor as he reached for his nose. From the corner of my eye, I saw someone reaching down for the blade.

"Don't touch it," I yelled.

The soft baritone of Al Kennedy said, "Ashley, let him go." He picked up the knife. "I'm glad someone finally ignored George's rules. Now, all of you have somewhere to be. Get going."

"Thanks."

"Never figured you'd be in the middle of this. What happened?"

"No idea. Al, stop everyone from leaving. Teachers too. Let's find out."

Al collared two of the bigger boys and one teacher nabbed two girls. The rest of the crowd scattered.

"So what happened here?" I asked. When I got no answer, I asked them if they had ever heard of being an accessory to attempted murder.

"Murder, what murder?" George had arrived. I told him what had occurred and mentioned that I had been attacked.

"You wouldn't have been if you followed the rules."

"And if I hadn't, someone else might have been hurt. I can't believe you allow weapons in school."

"You don't make the rules here, Mr. Gilbert, in case you've forgotten. And now we have an incident. Insurance, police, newspapers. I think it's time for another discussion. You know what this means."

I looked around, expecting support. My colleagues it seems had no interest in confronting the principal. Instead, down the hall, Chief Shaw and three officers approached us.

I picked up my jacket, and looked for the knife. Al had fled with the rest. In fact, only one bloody kid, George and I were all that waited for the reinforcements.

"Thanks for coming so quickly, Chief," George said. "It seems Mr. Gilbert has a hearing problem. He attacked this young man."

"Now wait a minute, George. I broke up a fight. This young man, as you call him, came at me with a knife."

"So where's the weapon?" asked the chief.

"Al Kennedy picked it up. I don't know where he went."

"Now you're blaming a teacher."

"I am a teacher, George. A responsible one, unlike the cowards you've created. They could have stopped this. You could have prevented it." George's burn peaked. And I was alone. "Chief Shaw, you got here too late to see, but how can we teach if teachers are too afraid of rules to keep these kids safe?"

"We'll talk later, Mr. Gilbert. Right now, our job is to investigate the incident and file reports. I'll talk to you later. Will you be here?"

"Where else would I be?"

"I don't know. Paris?"

With that, a clap of thunder reminded me that I had another plan for lunch.

"Do you need me for anything else?" The chief shook his head, but George said he wanted to see me after school. "I have a meeting with a student after school."

"Then be quick about it. I have more important things to do than constantly disciplining you. And stop making faces when I'm talking to you."

"I'm not making faces. That's just how I look." He wasn't getting the last word this time. I glanced at my watch and hurried off. With fewer minutes than I'd hoped, I put the key in my desk lock. I walked back into the hall and peeked through Sandy's window. She looked back. I grabbed the door and pulled. Inside was a quiet street.

"Back again, Gilbert? So where's your bride-to-be?" Standing at the table, Ernest Hemingway grinned at me.

"You know who I am, that's good. I can't stay. The universe is upside down. Fritz is lost in here somewhere. I'm testing the portal to be sure I can use it."

"Sounds like you have a great story in the making."

"I wish I had the time to tell you the whole thing. Do me a favor, Hemingway. If he should show up, tell him to write a note and tell me how to find him. I'm sure I'll be back."

"It would be my pleasure. Say, how would it be if I come back with you now, just for a bit?"

I could imagine Sandy's face, being introduced to this man. I started to decline, but said, "Sure, but just for a moment." How much more trouble could I be in? So one more time, Ernest Hemingway stepped into Riverboro High School, but in a different world.

I asked him to hold the door, keeping the street scene alive. Sandy's annoyance flared when I opened her door and waved her to the hall. She stopped two steps out when she saw, not my desk, but rather a street with café tables and umbrellas. She looked at the man at the door and gasped.

"Ernest Hemingway, I'd like to introduce Sandy O'Connor."

"She's the one?"

"Nope. But that's a different part of the story. Maybe we'll get a chance to go through it all. I'd like your opinion."

"Well, you have to find Fritz soon. He may be sending some of those ripples backwards. The Germans are starting to get aggressive again.

Some fellow named Hitler is gathering a crowd, something about making Germany great again."

"You need to go, Hemingway. Classes are about to end and this hall will be full of kids. And I can't be sure I can get you back. So go now. I'll see you again."

"I guess I'm the one for whom the bell tolls. Nice meeting you, Sandy." I shook his hand and nudged him back to Shakespeare and Co. Just as he stepped into the bookstore, he waved. As I shut the door, the bell rang and thunder flickered the lights.

"Glad you could make it, Sandy. See you later. I have a class now." She stood statue-like in the middle of the hall.

With a rumbling background, my last classes were as animated as the earlier ones. My meeting with George lingered. Like a guillotine. My objective, finding Fritz, required a new strategy. Not getting fired now topped other priorities. Groveling would be an essential tactic. For a moment, I pondered Chief Shaw's comment. How much did he know? Had Sandy contacted him? A blazing flash and a tremendous crash shook the building and brought my attention back to my last class.

"You can start on homework. I'm going to the office. I want you all safe because tomorrow's question will be even better." Not stopping to respond to raised hands, I ran down the hall, as another rumble flashed the hall lights off. In my head, I could hear the admonition about not running in the halls.

With a mere few minutes until the final bell, I stepped into the lightless office. George guarded his doorway. I told him he might want to suggest that the students without a ride home should stay inside until they could contact a parent or wait in the gym. I told him that an announcement would show his concern for their safety.

"What is it with you? All of a sudden, you care about them." Another nearby clap of thunder made him jump. After a quick glance out the window, he turned his reddening face back to me. "Ms. Sweeney, please contact Coach Kennedy and ask if he will gather the gym teachers and have them keep the gym open until the storms are over." Turning to me, he said, "I'll expect you here shortly," and shut his office door in my face.

The lights returned as I reached my room just before the end of class. George's announcement just beat the bell. "Since when does he care?" one student commented to universal agreement.

"He just said how much he cares, in spite of how it might seem. All the teachers do, too."

"Yeah, right. Mr. Gilbert, you just stopped a knife fight, but all the teachers just stood around. You expect us to think they care?"

Next stop—George, but first a quick check of my doorknob. In spite of the storms, off and on all day, no finger tingle. As I walked to the office, how much more trouble I had brought on myself by offering to help the kids ran around my brain. And how did Hemingway know about our visits in other dimensions than this one? Ms. Sweeney said to go in. Chief Shaw sat in the third chair.

"Sit down," George grumbled. I did. "Why do you think I have rules about teachers avoiding fights between students?"

"Tell me."

"I can't easily replace staff," he huffed. "These animals don't care who or what they damage. If teachers are involved, I have reports, insurance issues, and explanations to the superintendent. I don't like any of that. And you make me do it all."

"George, I'm sorry. But that's the second fight in the past few days. We don't know when or if they'll turn on a teacher."

"Like they did on you today," said Shaw. "Mr. McAllister, I've stayed away from school politics, but this stuff has been happening since my student days here. I can't be here constantly and as fast as we arrive, a knife or God forbid, a bullet only takes seconds. Let's clean this place out and clean it up."

"How do I do that?" George barked. He leaned back, as far away from the chief as he could. He hadn't had time to turn red.

Shaw's eyes glowed with the chance to make a difference. "Get the kids and teachers on the same page. Let them all know—no more acceptance and no exceptions. Rally your staff. Tell them a new day has come to Riverboro High School."

George scratched his head, swiveling from Shaw to me and back. Shaw said, "If you'd like some help, I'm sure plenty of teachers will spread the word." I didn't volunteer because I hoped I would be home, and a flash outside made my wish even stronger.

He started to talk, but only a burst of air left his mouth, and he closed it again. The window rattled from another thunderclap. "Do you really think it can work? I've always run things the same way."

Shaw said, "Times have changed, Mr. McAllister. Kids are smarter, they get it, and they have technology I never had only ten years ago. Get started now, before the holidays, and you may have a whole different place for the New Year. Now if we're done, please excuse us. I have some further questions I'd like to ask Mr. Gilbert."

As Shaw and I walked to my classroom, he said, "You're an idiot, stepping into a knife fight." I rolled up my shirt sleeve as he gaped at the scar on my arm. I rehashed the story of my first summer, and the fight I'd stopped at the beach, in a different world.

"Twenty-six stitches," I bragged.

"You're still an idiot."

"Well this time, I had my jacket to protect me. But on a different subject, I think these kids can be turned, Jim, I mean, Brian. I've had only a few days, but I've never been this excited about teaching. It's going to be better." The hall became a tiled cave when thunder cut the lights, but a flash just outside lit the hallway. He proceeded to the parking lot, and as soon as he drove away, I tapped my doorknob.

The shock stung my fingers, but I didn't have much time. Thunderstorms in December offered a limited opportunity. Without company, I could test the portal later. The rain had started, and one step out the door and I was soaked. I glanced up to be sure I hadn't stepped under a bucket full of water. Sandy had seen me leave and pulled me out of the downpour. I had to choose to take her with me now or hope I could open the portal later that evening.

"Ashley, I'm sorry I didn't believe you. But you have to admit, your story is unbelievable."

Another flash and trying a trip now made sense. "Do you want to meet Robert E. Lee?"

"Ashley?"

"Forget it. I still have work to do. So if you want to come, I'm going now."

"Robert E. Lee? Where are we going?"

"Gettysburg. I think Fritz will try to connect with him. I want to let the general know, and find out if he's seen him." I set the paperclip, laid the book on the desk, and returned to the hall. I pulled and my desk stared out.

"No key." I jammed the right one in the desk lock. "Come on." This time, we stood at the door of Lee's headquarters, facing bayonets. The haze of an artillery barrage blurred our view. I asked them to tell General Lee that Ashley Gilbert requested to meet with him. "He's expecting me." I hoped that would buy a moment and prevent being shot. We were still almost two years before Fritz first met him.

When the door opened, a tired general stood looking at us. "Well, I can't say I expected you, Mr. Gilbert, but do come in."

"General, allow me to introduce Sandra O'Connor. She's also a teacher."

He ushered us to chairs and sat at a table covered by a map of the area around Gettysburg. "I'm about to begin a great battle, Mr. Gilbert. I don't have much time."

Sandy asked the only question that made sense to her. "Is this real?" The general chuckled, and asked me if she was a new traveler. I told him she had just found out, but with little time left, I pressed on.

"General, something's gone wrong with the portal. Fritz is in some other dimension. I'm looking for him. Have you seen him?"

"You may be correct. I have noticed that my planning is going awry. For some reason, time has become erratic. Why just yesterday, a coordinated advance was to begin in the morning, but we were unable to move until late afternoon. No one can explain why, as if time somehow jumped. But you're being here is strange since we don't meet until two years from now, and yet I know you."

"Fritz must have done something to scramble time, space or both. I don't know where to look, but I guessed he would come to you."

"No, not yet." He scanned the table top. "But he'll be at the McLean farmhouse in Appomattox when I surrender to General Grant."

"Do you know what's going to happen? Everything?"

"I do. I have for a few weeks. My dreams were at first disturbed. But now, waking, I can see down my life line. And if you get the opportunity, please give my regards to the president."

"I have so many questions. How did this happen?" Before he answered, his door opened, and Major Taylor said that General Pickett waited outside.

"I'm afraid that I am out of time, Mr. Gilbert. I have no idea what has happened. It is, after all, your portal."

Sandy stood like a sculpture, looking from my door back to me. I opened the door, this time to my classroom. I invited her in. As if in a trance, she took a seat.

"Was that real?"

"I don't know. He can see his future. But he'll see Fritz, so I have a clue. I just don't know in what dimension they'll be."

"Ashley, it's December, but I could feel the heat and humidity. Did you smell the air?" She took a deep breath. "Nothing now, but they all smelled like they hadn't bathed in months, even Lee. The stink of horses and manure and gunpowder hung in the air." She sniffed her sleeve. "It's gone now."

"You can't say anything to anyone, Sandy. If you do, you put us both in danger. The Ashley who you know can't open the portal. If I find Fritz and if we can return to my time, he'll be back, I think. You can get him killed. You can't even tell your husband. Promise me."

"No one would believe me."

"Someone would, and if they find out, they'll want to use the portal. They'll look for someone who can. I don't know if anyone else can or how it will happen. But I think each dimension has similarities, just at different times." I glanced at the other books while we chatted. "Do you want to come with me again? I have to keep looking."

"You've given me a lot to absorb. I don't know if I should."

"Then you need to leave. If these storms end, I can't open the portal. I'll have to wait until another one, maybe until spring."

"Where are you going next?"

"Appomattox." But Fritz didn't go there, not according to the books he picked. I needed to think, alone. How did he get there from wherever he was? Could he time-travel on a different time line? Did Lee really meet him there? The book Fritz had used to get to Lee's office and to Appomattox wasn't on the book shelves.

"Well, are we going?"

"Not yet. Not to Appomattox." If Fritz had caused this jumble of time, how would he do it? I picked up the book about Hitler.

"You're biting your lip, Ash. Why?"

"I wonder. If Fritz killed Hitler, that would have changed the world. The first time I saw Hitler, Fritz had already entered the portal, but I was still home. If Fritz went back, he would need to cross dimensions. That would mean he found another portal."

"Then, let's go look. I'll go with you."

"I'll be gone for a second. You'll be able to see if you hold the door." I put the book in place, checked the paperclips, and we went into the hall. Tapping the knob, I told her to hold the door but not to touch the doorknob. "It's still live." I didn't know if that would matter. I pulled the door and stepped through. As before, Hitler stood at the open window, looking up. When my footsteps disturbed him, he stared wide-eyed at me. He began speaking.

"I speak English," I said. In the little German that I had learned over the years, he said he didn't. But I continued, as he walked to the bars of his cell. "I'm looking for Fritz Russell. But since you're still alive, he didn't come here. If he had, he would have shot you." He repeated that he didn't speak English, but I didn't care. "Auf wiedersehen." I didn't, couldn't, see the look on his face when I vanished, but wished I could.

He hadn't seen me the last time I went. I'm guessing he didn't see Fritz either, but now he'd have an image to keep him company for the rest of his miserable life.

I told Sandy to shut the door, and the thought hit that I might have changed history just talking to him. He didn't speak my language, but he would know that someone who spoke English had just vanished before his eyes. "I better warn Winston."

"What do you mean?"

"Huh?" I'd been talking to myself, but aloud.

"What do you mean 'warn Winston'?"

"I spoke English to Hitler. He'll remember that I vanished. In that paranoid brain, maybe he'll think some English-speaking country has a secret weapon. He did concentrate on England, with the bombings and V-1 and V-2 rockets. And the submarines sinking all the supply ships from America. I wonder if my visit just now had anything to do with that."

"That's crazy. You can't blame yourself."

"Yes. Yes, I can. I've told you the portal is dangerous. But mucking about in history is even more so because we don't know what the effect will be. One more trip."

"Not for me. You travel all you want, but this is scary."

"You should be in my shoes." I chuckled at what I'd said. Fritz would be amused. I checked the time when Sandy left, both surprised and glad. Only four thirty. But the storms had weakened, so I peeked at the weather forecast on my computer. Storms ending late afternoon, it said. With not much time left, and maybe not again until spring, choosing where to go had to be deliberate.

I closed my eyes, hoping to glimpse a direction that Fritz would have taken. I walked to the windows, and looked at the nearby storm clouds, and the pink sky of sunset on the horizon. Looking closer at the thunderheads, I imagined a close-up of Churchill, sipping tea in the clouds. Fritz had once said he had looked for cloud pictures since childhood. "I'm getting to be him. This is SO weird."

Alone, and out of time, I put the Churchill book on the desk. The portal remained open, so I stepped again into 10 Downing Street. "Ah, Gilbert, I've been waiting for you. What's taken so long?"

"So long for what, Winston?"

"You'll need to address me as Prime Minister whilst you are here. Appearances, you know. The others won't understand. But to your question. You poked your head in a few weeks ago, and I've expected you to return. You have news for me?"

"That first. I'm here to warn you. I just spoke to Hitler, in English. When he was in prison in 1924. I don't know if that will focus him on England when the war starts, but I wanted you to know, to be prepared, just in case."

"Well, m'boy, whether it's because of you or not, that loud-mouthed paperhanger, that Nazi bastard, seems to have it in for us on our little island. But we'll survive. Did you know I'll be meeting Franklin soon. But of course you do."

"Prime Minister." I stopped as my words rang. Our first meeting, which hadn't happened yet, had been more glib, almost playful. My words carried more respect, more seriousness now.

"Well, go on."

"Sorry. You know we don't meet for the first time until 1949. How do you know who I am now?"

"I'm glad you brought that up." He flicked a two-inch ash from his cigar, puffed and blew out a long gentle stream of smoke. "Right after you were here before, I was informed that we had captured a German coding machine."

"The Enigma."

His brow raised, and the cigar moved to the ashtray, he nodded, a slow-motion up and down, as he appraised me. "It was then I believed we would win the war."

"But you already knew, from when Fritz and I visited."

"Yes, yes, but by then the war had ended. But something else. I had a vision of our own machine."

"The Turing machine." From his quizzical look, I had said too much. He knew me and about my visit with Fritz, but unlike Lee, who saw his entire life line, Churchill didn't know the present, although he remembered when Fritz and I had met him in his future. I had more to think about.

"The touring machine? What does it tour?"

"It's a man's name." I spelled it for him. "He'll be in touch with you soon, when the time is right. Winston, please don't ask me more now. I don't want to change anything else."

"Quite right, Gilbert. But tell me, what does this machine do?"

"It breaks the German codes. It will work, but you'll need to give Mr. Turing some help. But that's not why I'm here."

He looked at the clock and back to me. "Would you like some sherry, or perhaps some tea? You look as though you need some fortification."

"No. Thanks just the same. Winston..." He scowled at me. "Sorry. Prime Minister, Fritz is lost in the portal. Have you seen him? Has he been here? I believe he's changed the past somehow. I need to find him and turn things around. Otherwise, you may lose the war, or the U.S. will stop sending supplies, or maybe worse."

"That's quite a mouthful." He stood and walked to a decanter across the room. "If that is true, we'll have a toast to you being wrong." He handed me a small glass filled to the rim, raised his and said, "To history being correct." He downed his in a gulp, but I took only a sip. "Drink up."

"No. We need a different toast," I said. He chomped on his cigar to free his hands and refilled his glass. Turning back to me and raising his glass, he waited for me. "To finding Fritz and returning time and space to its proper state." I downed the rest. The heat radiated from my stomach, up to my head and down to my feet.

He saw my reaction and chuckled. In the gravelly voice the world would come to love, he said, "Good stuff, Gilbert. The best I can find here now. Now, I have seen Fritz, quite a while ago. Almost a year. Like you, he merely looked in. I was in a meeting, but I saw him. He smiled at me, nodded and vaporized. I think others saw him, from the ones who rubbed their eyes, but said nothing."

"But how do you know us if we haven't met yet?"

"That, Gilbert, is for you to answer. Perhaps you should engage this Turing fellow to assist you."

"That's probably a terrible idea. I'm not taking that chance, Winston. And you have enough on your plate as it is. So wish me luck."

"Still a cheeky one, I'm glad to see. See you in about nine years."

"Before I go, may I ask you a question?"

"Of course. I may not have the answer, but ask away."

"Why did you follow us? The first time we visited you."

He eyed me critically before he responded. "Gilbert, for most of my adult life, I have been called upon to make decisions, and to judge men whose character I would rely on. To venture into the past, as you did, required courage. You did not know what you would find. Yet you came anyway. Only a fool would accept your statements without a sense of who you were, are. I trusted from that brief assessment that you both were trustworthy. And your doorway was like nothing we have seen before. Knowing the world has a future gives me hope. You and your friend gave me the push to step forward. I wish you luck in finding him. Do come again."

"If you see Fritz, have him write a note to tell me where I can find him, if you would. If I can I'll pop by from time to time to see how you're doing. And Winston, KBO." He waved.

Chapter 15

Ashley

WHEN I RETURNED, the lights in my classroom were still on. That meant the custodians were probably still around. I tapped the doorknob. The storms over, the portal closed, and no closer to finding Fritz, I cleared my desk, grabbed my keys and started for home. Before I reached the parking lot, my phone buzzed.

"Where have you been?"

"Hi Natalie, how goes your day?"

"Where are you now?"

"Just leaving school. Why?"

"Stay put. Brian Shaw just called me. Sandy O'Connor had a car accident. She blamed you."

"Me? I haven't left here. Well, not the school property anyway."

"I'll be there in five minutes."

I walked across the parking lot to my, well, other me's, car. Intending to sit and wait for her, I saw it had been damaged, hit broadside. "Now what?" Obviously, someone had stolen it, had an accident and brought it back. Within five minutes, her yellow V-dub turned into the lot and pulled up next to me. She told me to get in, and in seconds, we were on a back street, headed where I didn't have a clue.

"Where were you?"

"Truth? Visiting Winston Churchill." She stomped on the brake and the car stalled. "I took Sandy to meet Robert E. Lee and we went to see Hitler in jail. Ask her."

"How did the car get smashed?"

"I don't know. I've been here."

"She said she talked to you. She told the chief."

"That's not possible. Unless … other me is back. But that shouldn't happen." I retraced our visits.

"You better come up with a good reason. She didn't mention your trips to Brian. He's got you leaving the scene of an accident."

"Wait. Be quiet for a minute. Let me think." Could I have set the pinballs in motion, or did Fritz do something? Did speaking English to Hitler change him? Did telling Winston about Turing alter the war? "I think I crossed into another dimension, and other me had nowhere else to go, so he came back. I bumped him back here, and I think he's gone again. We can't both be here at the same time."

She started the car and I asked her where she was going. To meet Chief Shaw at the diner.

Parked near the door, Chief Shaw leaned against the trunk of his police cruiser when the yellow car squeaked to a stop. She said to let her do the talking. She waved to him and climbed out. I stood by my door, not sure what to say.

"Mr. Gilbert, we need to talk. Frankly, I'm getting tired of seeing you. I didn't see you this much as a student." His laugh relieved some of my tension.

"Chief, Nat told me what happened. It wasn't me."

"I know. Sandy described what you were wearing and said you acted like you were disoriented, drunk or stoned. So I need to get the real story. Shall we have a cup of coffee?"

I glanced at Natalie, and she nodded, just enough that I would agree. "Sure, I'm buying."

We sat at the same booth where Nat and I had been before. They both sat across from me and the waitress had her order pad out as soon as we sat.

"Brian, you and I have talked about Ashley's comments already. I asked him what happened, and I think I'm right."

"Chief, this story is not believable, and I can't prove anything. I think I know what happened, and Sandy can verify some of it." In as much detail as I could, I explained my presence in this version of Riverboro, what had brought me here, and what had occurred that afternoon. I only stopped when the waitress placed the coffee in front of me, and when Niko stopped to say hello. "If Sandy will admit what she saw, that will prove I'm telling the truth."

"Mr. Gilbert, most people would think you were nuts. I don't. I've liked science fiction since the first Star Treks. The possibility of time travel has always fascinated me. But if it's real, then it's also very dangerous. But multiple dimensions? I never thought about that. So, all of us exist, at once, on multiple timelines. That's scarier than aliens—different me's."

"That's why I called you Jim. In my world, you are training to be a secret service agent. The president sponsored him. 'Other you' has been through the portal, helped rescue him from terrorists."

"Him? You mean her."

"In my world, the new president here, is just leaving office. She lost the election this year."

"Really. That's interesting. So you know this new guy?"

"I don't know. Maybe."

"So what do we do now?" Nat asked.

"Do you know if you have car insurance? If your other is as disconnected as he seems, he may not have bothered."

"I don't know. It should be in the glove compartment. Never thought about it. And he kept files of his bills and bank statements. Might be in the desk."

"Linda probably paid the bills," Nat said. "She is untidy about most things, but not money. And she was, is, whatever, always concerned to be above suspicion."

"Linda? Linda Miller? What does she have to do with this?"

"She was living with Ashley, the other one. She left a few days ago."

"Yeah, she didn't like this me."

"Let's go check your car. Hopefully, the insurance will take care of the accident part of this, and I'll try to find out about Ms. O'Connor's time travels."

"Probably be good if you ask her while I'm with you. That way she won't be afraid to admit it."

"Then I'll meet you at school first thing in the morning. Let's go."

We checked the insurance card, still good for a few months. I thanked Brian, and Nat and I sat in her car.

"How did he have a key?" I said, looking at my car. "I have my keys." I took them out, to be sure.

"You, he, used to have one hidden in the wheel well. Magnetic box. Driver's side rear." We got out again and checked. We found the metal container, but no key.

"This is getting crazier by the minute. And I can't go anywhere until we have another storm." I ran my hand through my hair. Natalie laughed. "What?"

"Some things aren't different. Other you did the same thing." She imitated my hand, through her hair. "So since you can't go anywhere now, I think you should buy me dinner."

WHILE I TALKED, Natalie listened. When we dated in my other world, she rarely shut up. When I wandered, trying to understand what had happened since I arrived here, she asked pointed questions to keep me on track. I also had the chance to talk about me in my other life. I told her about Jane, and all the other women who had died after dating me. As I dug deeper, I found myself telling her things I hadn't ever said to Fritz and Linda, or to Jane.

"You really are someone else, aren't you?"

"No, I'm me. I've told you before. The portal changes things. I think these other dimensions, other parallel universes, reflect different choices people have made. And their consequences."

"And if you find your friend, you'll be leaving. Too bad. Do you think if you go, that everything will go back to how it was before you got here? Here and where you came from?"

"I don't know. I think that we'll remember what's happened, but there won't be any proof. I think it'll be like déjà vu. Or maybe we'll remember exactly. If I can undo whatever Fritz did to start this, then maybe none of this would even have happened. We'll only know if I'm successful, or maybe we'll never know, because all this will be erased."

"That's pretty confusing."

"Yeah, it is."

I paid the check and she drove me back to my car. I asked her to wait until I got moving. I only had to drive a few feet to know the car needed repairs, so I asked if she would follow me home. I inched the car along, and when I safely reached my driveway, she asked if she could come in."

"You want me to give you a lift in the morning?"

"I get started early. Don't want to be a bother."

"Ash, what if you're here, you know, permanently?"

Her question had more than one meaning. I tried to sidestep with "I don't know." I told her that I would have a lot of decisions to make, and that I would need to mold my new life into one I could comfortably accept. In a number of ways, that had already begun. Especially at school.

"Can I have a drink?"

"Sure. Sorry. I should have offered. Soda or something else?" When I got up, she did too.

"You know, I can drive you to school easier if I don't have so far to go." In my other world, I found Natalie attractive, but annoying. Here she wasn't annoying. But I had a job to do and as George Washington had warned, avoid entangling alliances. I don't know where that thought came from.

"I have a guest room. That's the best I can offer you."

She smiled and shook her head. "Other you was easier." She took a step back. "Soda."

We sat at the kitchen table while I checked my plans for classes. I told her what I'd been doing, giving the kids questions to discuss. I asked her if she'd like to be a guest for my classes tomorrow. My question, I told her, would be pertinent. "What role should media have in politics?"

She asked if I could postpone that question, that she had other things to do, but could rearrange her schedule for later in the week. Since I had no particular plan, I told her to call me with the best day.

I thanked her when she left, told her I'd see her in the morning, and breathed a sigh of relief that I'd met the challenge. But, I had to consider the "what if" possibility.

Chapter 16

Jane

I WAS IN my PJs working on a report for the president. Koppler had skipped the country and his lawyer couldn't be found. After the debacle on Election Day, we had received a huge data dump from James Sapphire and to our surprise, from the Eledorian bank where so much of the Caballeros money had originated. As many times as the president had said that my feelings were scary, this information confirmed everything. Koppler had devised a plan for both enormous wealth and control of companies and governments. Fritz had continually asked why, and I could only conclude that only a massive egomaniac would go to these extremes. With all the money and power he had accumulated, what more could he possibly want? He wouldn't be able to spend it, with everyone hunting him. No one had benefitted except him, and from what I could tell, his massive wealth had accumulated, long before this all started.

I saved my report, closed the computer, and had reached for the light switch when the front door opened. Ashley took two steps in, looked around, went outside and glanced at the house number before coming back inside.

"Hi Ash. I'm in here." I was on my feet.

"Who are you? Where's Linda?"

I needed all my control to keep from getting my pistol.

"Ash, I'm Jane. Where have you been?"

"Jane? Do I know you? Why are you here? Where's Linda?"

"Ashley, sit down. Tell me where you came from. We've been worried about you." Ashley's constant head turning rattled me. This man was not my fiancé, but how did this happen?

"Whose Mustang is in my driveway?"

"Sit, Ash. Your memory is addled. Let's talk. Do you want a drink?"

"Yeah, bourbon. Neat. When did this place get painted?"

"You painted it a year ago, Ashley."

He was still on his feet, walked right by the kitchen to the bedroom. He opened drawers and banged them closed again. When he started to yell, I grabbed my phone, and dialed 9-1-1. When he started swearing, I told the operator I needed help and to contact Chief Dempsey and tell him his friend from Washington was in trouble. I heard a thud and a crash, and he headed back to me.

"Where's my stuff?"

"Everything is right where you left it."

"No, it isn't. Nothing is in the desk, or the box spring or my vault in the closet. My vault isn't even there. Who are you?"

"Ashley, sit down. You're acting like a crazy man. Just take it easy and sit. I'll get you your drink." When I stood, he made the mistake of grabbing my arm. In a flash, I had him sitting and rubbing his wrist.

"Take it easy, will ya? This is my house. I'm Ashley Gilbert. I had a stash of drugs which is missing from my bedroom. My girlfriend, Linda Miller, owns the bike shop and she isn't here. What the hell is going on?"

"You've just time traveled, and you're disoriented. Where did you come from?" I set a small shot of bourbon in front of him.

"This has to be a bad trip. But I didn't take anything." Adding to his distress, and mine, his tension increased when he couldn't figure out where he was.

"Listen to me, Ashley. The police are on the way. So tell me where you came from."

"The police. Shit. Why are you here? Who *are* you?"

"I'm Jane Barclay. I'm your fiancée. I work for the government. Right now, you need to get yourself together. We live here together or we did until you disappeared into the portal."

"Lady, I don't know you, and I sure don't know what you're talking about. What's a portal?"

The doorbell rang. I called out to let them know to come. Chief Dempsey said, "My guys have the house surrounded, so do yourself a favor, Ashley, and come quietly."

"This is MY house. I…" With a soft pop, he vanished.

"What the…?" Dempsey uttered.

"Chief, I'm not positive, but I think he's from a different universe. You know that Fritz and Ashley have gone missing in the portal. I think one of them has just done something to change time or history, or something."

"I didn't know they were gone. Are you all right?"

"I'm fine, but that was eye-opening. Fritz vanished on Thanksgiving and Ash went after him, I think. He didn't tell me when he left. Maybe something happened to him. You know that the man behind the attack on the school is still at large?"

"No, I didn't know that either. What can you do?"

"Nothing. Just wait and hope that they can put the pieces back together. But that guy was about as different from Ashley as I can imagine. A little scary. But not really threatening."

"Well, I'll have my guys sit out front tonight in case he comes back. Good luck, Jane."

"Thanks, Chief."

In spite of the late hour, I called Linda.

Chapter 17

Linda

WHEN JANE CALLED, my notes for a new writer's latest attempt were spread across the kitchen table. Although improving, she still hadn't captured the magic to make the story great. I'd worked with a few independent authors over the years, some very talented and creative. Most of them couldn't afford me, but when I saw possibilities, I worked with them to help develop their characters and plots. The ones that annoyed me most were the first timers who argued. They were short marriages. Others wanted to learn, so I gave them reading suggestions, and writing assignments so they could practice how to better use their words. I'd started back with my publisher again, easing in with a book at a time, while I began to set up the bike shop.

Mom took care of TJ, tested recipes, and planned decorations and meals for Christmas. Each week, we went out to dinner twice, and I cooked twice a week. She finally told me her secret about cooking for Daddy. Burn dessert, last thing he would remember. She said it helped keep her thin. As much as I wished Fritz were home, I enjoyed our time together.

I took my phone to the family room so Mom could hear. Jane said that Ashley had come back, but not our Ashley. Just a brief description of what happened set off my fear of the portal. Fritz had been gone a little more than two weeks. I asked her if this other Ashley showing up meant that another Fritz might be around here. Obviously she didn't know. How could she?

"Are you okay?"

"He startled me, but when I accepted that he wasn't Ash, I called the police. He evaporated right in front of Chief Dempsey. Just vanished. You need to pay attention around you, Linda. I've never paid much mind to science fiction, but I need to read up."

"Why don't you come for dinner tomorrow. We can talk more then."

"Thanks, I will. But think about this. We're not likely to see many more thunderstorms until spring. I think we need to prepare for a long wait."

Mom asked about Jane's side of the call. When I told her that Jane said no more thunderstorms, I started crying. "This is my fault, Mom. What if he can't get back?"

She answered so fast that she must have been thinking about the possibility. "You're alive, you're young, you're healthy, you're smart, you're attractive. Life is in front of you. He's only been gone two weeks. You left him alone for six months, and he made it. You have a son to care for, a business to get rolling. You pretend you're working. You don't need the money from those books. Get to work. The rest will work itself out."

Aside from the sting, my tears were gone in seconds. At that moment, I wasn't those things she said, but once again, she proved that moms are pretty smart.

The next afternoon, Lois McAllister called to tell me she had a contract for a store with plenty of space, and renters who lived above. She'd worked out the numbers, and the rent would pay the mortgage. She wanted to drop off the paperwork. I told her I'd buy it outright, so we could close anytime. I asked her how soon it would be vacant. She asked if she could come right over and we could discuss it then.

"See you in a few."

When the doorbell rang, Mom opened the door. The voice wasn't who I expected. "Hello, Emily. Good to see you again."

"Come in, Mr. President. Other than all that gray hair, you look a lot better than the last few times I've seen you."

"Feeling that way too. Is Linda home?" I was at the door before he hit the question mark.

"Hi, Mr. President. Come on in. Hi, Mel. What brings you here?"

"You still don't believe me? I like it here. That's why I bought that house across town. I'm here with a few of the guys at the airport to start planning the transition. It seems that an ex-president has to worry about his neighbors more than at the White House. I just left them to do their thing. Are you doing okay?"

"Not yet. But I will be. Lois McAllister is on her way with a contract for my shop."

"She's good. She negotiated my place too. She said I got a good deal. How's the bike business coming?"

"Mom gave me a kick in the butt, so now that I have a place, it should move along pretty quickly." He reached over and squeezed Mom's hand. The smile came right behind.

"Want a drink?" Mom asked them.

Mel refused but he said sure. Two sodas. Mel said she didn't want to be any trouble. He told her to put her training in the trunk. They were with friends.

When the back door opened, Mel already had her gun out. "Whoa, it's just me," Jane said. "Hi, Mr. President, Mel. Didn't expect you here. But I'm glad. I spoke to Tom Andrews a few minutes ago. They tracked Koppler to Paris. He's gone again, but he's left a strange story behind. He just left without a trace, literally. The agents followed him to a bistro, where he met with Arthur Salzmann. The waiter said when he brought their food they were gone. They would have been seen leaving, but nobody saw them. After last night, I think Fritz and Ashley are stirring things up in the portal."

Emily poured a third glass and brought them to the table. Brushing behind his left ear, the president thanked her while staring into the backyard. "I've asked Tony if someone else could get inside the portal.

So many of us have been there, I wonder if any of it rubbed off. He didn't think so."

When the doorbell rang again, I questioned who else might show up. Mom answered again, and multiple voices floated to us. Lois came in first but Tony and Nat were right behind, both beaming.

Nat said, glancing at the full table, "Well, Linda, you saved us a bunch of trips." She held up a sparkly finger. "Hi, Mr. President."

The hubbub of congratulations, hugs and kisses woke TJ. An unexpected crowd again, warm and joyful at the news, bypassed me. I looked over at Jane, watching me. "Life goes on," she said.

When Mom carried TJ in, he started to chatter almost as if he had missed having company. Mom put him in the swing so he could see everyone. I hadn't noticed before how quiet he'd become. He wasn't now and had everyone smiling. I wished I shared his joy.

Mom must have figured that with all the good moods, she had a perfect opportunity because she invited everyone to Christmas brunch. She hadn't said anything to me.

"I know you probably can't come, but Mr. President, you and your family are welcome too. Eleven sharp."

"Thank you, Emily. Let me mention it at home and I'll let you know. It's a little busy around my place. Regardless of what the news is reporting, I am still the president." Laughter filled the room.

Chapter 18

Fritz

WITH ONLY A couple more weeks to Christmas, and because Kate would be gone in a couple of days, I did what I had avoided for years—I went shopping. Since I'd refused her offer to join her going-away party, buying a small gift impressed at least me as appropriate. I had seen an attractive shop in one of the upscale areas of the District, and headed over before going home. Only after I had parked did I realize I had company. Tim McNamara pulled to the curb and called me over. I didn't know what role he was playing.

"Get in, Russ. We need to talk."

"About what?"

"You. Get in."

"I'm going shopping. A Christmas present for Cindy. Before they close."

"This won't take long. Just a couple trips around the block." After a frustrated exhale, I slid into the passenger's side and he pulled into traffic.

"You should go with Kate. The news stories of her arrest had a picture of you. An enterprising young Fibbie has been playing with facial recognition and every photo in the news. Took him a while to get to yours."

"So they're after me, and know where to find me? If I go with her, neither of us is safe."

"You need to disappear and going with her serves two purposes. First, she really wants you to come. Flynn told me. The second is that we can plant sightings of you elsewhere."

"That only delays things. They don't have evidence of anything. The gun is long gone. I left no prints and you guys can set me up with a good lawyer."

"After the Inauguration, things will get back to the usual. Besides, she'll make Christmas fun. You'll be gone until late January."

"What about the 'Kitchen?' I have regulars."

He snickered. "I'll have to do without your waffles, and the extra five pounds. But I'll let Flynn know your concerns."

He slid back to the curb, and pulled out a roll of bills. "Flynn said to buy what you need, for both of you. When you're done come up to the bar for dinner. Buy yourself a change of clothes for tonight. You'll want to look nice, but comfortable."

"I hadn't planned on going. What's so special?"

"You ask too many questions. You'll see. Flynn said to be there by six-thirty."

He barely waited for me to get out. I had to jump out of the way when the door closed. I pulled the wad of cash out and thumbed through the bills. I didn't count it, but the denominations weren't small. I stashed the roll in my pocket, checking to see if anyone saw. The next car that passed had a face watching. I nodded at Flynn as the car drove past.

I found a bench and sat. Were they watching me, or watching out for me? I didn't have a passport or any idea how to pack for an Irish Christmas. Strange as it might seem, before the semi-kidnapping, I had been heading to an Irish boutique. I had planned to copy Ashley—a nice scarf. But now that I had marching orders, I figured I'd ask what would be appropriate for the trip if I changed my mind. I'd think about going later. First, the things on my list.

The store had a simple name—Irish Lovelies. When I walked in, the door tripped "When Irish Eyes Are Smiling" in bells. At the counter, a "lovely" young woman, with dark hair and deep blue eyes glanced at me, stood up and smiled. "May I help you, sir?"

"I'm looking for a gift, or gifts. And do you know anything about the climate in Ireland this time of year?"

"I think I can help you on both counts, but I'm afraid we'll have to hurry a bit. I'm closing early today."

"This your place?" She flashed the proud smile of successful ownership, not a lot different than if I'd asked, "Is this your child?"

"Are you looking for something in particular?"

"Just some nice things. I have a friend who's going to Ireland for Christmas. She's particular, and I'm clueless."

"Then let's look around."

As we stepped into the merchandise, I asked, "What's your name?" She told me she was Mary Connolly, and that almost everything in the shop was Irish-made. Twice a year, she visited on buying trips. As we walked from rack to rack, and shelf to shelf, she handed me sweaters, scarves, shirts and jackets. I'd grown up near New York City, and my mother had taught me about clothing and quality. Although most of the garment industry had long ago fled the City, quality retail shops lined the streets. The feel of the linens and wools begged me to touch each piece to my cheek.

"Do you have a size in mind?"

After so many years of spending nothing, my stomach tightened at the prices. I looked at her. "Pardon my staring. Comparing."

"I understand." Then she slowly turned around, modeling herself. "Does this help?"

"She's about your height." She kicked off her heels. "Now she's a little taller than you. And a bit older."

"I'm afraid that's not going to help." She placed her hands under her breasts. "Bigger or smaller?"

I'd worked with Cindy for a year and really hadn't paid much attention until she changed into Kate, with jeans and that tight tee. "Smaller, I think."

She lowered her hands to a narrow waist, and raised a questioning brow. Kate was slim but I had no way to know. "Probably a little bigger, but I'm guessing just because she's older. But not much." She nodded and put her hands on her butt. "I don't know. She's on her feet all day, she can get away with jeans that are form fitting. Mostly, she wears loose and comfortable, stuff that's probably easy to wash. She owns a restaurant."

"I have a sense of what will work perfectly." She took me to a rack of plain white blouses, pushed a couple aside, and held out the softest, smoothest piece of linen I had ever touched.

"I'll take it. It's lovely." I smiled at her. "Can I return it if it's the wrong size?"

"As long as it's still in good shape. This is hand-sewn, so it's one of a kind, not a mass production number. Now how about a sweater? More for lounging than fighting the outside." She walked me to the rear and handed me a red cardigan, with a cable-knit kind of design. The buttons looked like snowflakes.

"I'll take it. I like that. It's a little different."

"Would you like anything else? I have some lounging pajamas that are perfect for those cold and damp nights."

"Sure, let's look." The door music jingled. She looked at her watch, and then the door.

"I'll be right with you," she called, and told me to look through the ones she pointed at. "I'll be right back." I watched her walk away, still barefoot and I looked out at her new customer. Kevin, one of Kate's bodyguards, held up his wrist, and wiggled his watch back and forth as she approached him. They were everywhere I went. I didn't like it. I grabbed a set of green lounging pajamas and walked toward them. Kevin stopped talking when he saw me.

"Hello, Kevin. Are you following me, too?"

"No, Russ. Flynn's waiting for Mary. We have some other stops to make."

"You obviously know each other," she said, taking my selections. Then, one eyebrow raised as the other lowered. "Wait. Russ? These are for Kate?"

"Yup, and Connolly, so your related to Flynn?"

"Yup," she mimicked. "Baby sister. And you have a discerning eye, Russ. Exact sizes for her. Kevin, tell Flynn to come back for me. I'm not finished yet. These things need to be giftwrapped. I'll be another fifteen minutes."

"He's not gonna be happy."

Grinning at me, she said, "Frankly, my dear, I don't give a damn." I understood the connection, and her subtle humor. I grinned back. Kevin shook his head and hurried out.

"Kate's going to love these, Russ. Really. But I do need to hurry. Flynn doesn't have much of a sense of humor. Do you want anything for yourself? I have some lovely sweaters to brave the winds off the ocean."

I said no thanks, with a twinge of guilt paying Flynn's sister with his money. I didn't want the kind of debt that Flynn could hold over me, so I'd skip shopping for myself, stop home, and get my own money. I'd be a little short until payday but I still had a few presentable pants and shirts.

Mary returned with three colorful packages, wrapped perfectly. She rang up the bill and as I pulled out the cash, Flynn walked in.

"Don't bother, Russ. She's just gonna give it to me anyway."

"That's between you two. I pay my bills. You should know that, Flynn. And I'll have yours later. These are from me. If you want to buy Kate something, here's a lovely scarf." As his face darkened, I thought of George McAllister, again. Flynn's wild red hair crackled with electricity. I handed Mary five one hundred dollar bills, picked up my packages, and thanked her. As defiantly as I could, I grinned at Flynn as I walked by.

I drove home, showered and changed, still with time to spare. A quick stop at the ATM, and I was on my way, in time to beat traffic. When I arrived at McNamara's, cars were double and triple-parked. As I pulled closer, a man I'd never seen waved me forward. I rolled down the window, as he lowered his face. "Valet parking tonight, Russ." I asked him his name. "Mary's cousin, and Flynn's, a'course. Tommy Connolly." I reached out and shook his hand. "Out now, and don't forget your packages."

The music blared through opening and closing doors, and through the window, I could see a crowd on its feet clapping a beat to someone I couldn't see. I checked my watch to be sure. Only a quarter past, I'd managed to arrive on time, early even. Whatever the reason, this party started early and showed no sign of ending any time soon. As I opened the door, air conditioning at full blast balanced the oncoming and unseasonably warm night outside. In full skirts, frilly white blouses, and pointy shoes, Mary Connolly and the sisters Sullivan, attached to three enormous smiles, ushered me in. In a far corner, a Christmas tree, with more decorations than I'd ever seen, blinked green. I noticed the absence of a topper.

My seasonally-wrapped gifts matched the merriment, as Mary made a path to Flynn's table. She offered to take the boxes, but I said I would keep them with me. I wanted to give them to her myself. With the table unoccupied, I put the gifts on a chair, watched and waited. Jane pushed her way to me, with a mug of porter and a shot of an amber liquid. I sniffed the whiskey. Kate's own special. Jane clicked as she walked.

"Don't drink the whiskey. But the porter's on the house. Actually, Russ, everything is tonight."

"What's this all about?"

"It's a special night, and a Christmas party, bon voyage and all that. You'll see." She clicked back toward the door.

Standing under an overhead light made me self-conscious and aware that people all around were glancing back at me. I sipped the porter and moved away from the still-empty table. I couldn't see through the packed room, but from the rear entrance to Kate's apartment, two men entered in costumes of green jackets and white shirts, carrying violins, each tucked into their left shoulders, and bows over their right, almost marching, as the cheering crowd cleared a lane. Out the window, a gathering throng pushed to get close enough to see in.

Somewhere in a corner, a drum beat began a slow, tenor tap, tap, tap and sped up as the noise inside built. I imagined a balloon filling with sound, loud enough to blow out the walls. Again, George came to mind, his hands over his ears in the Riverboro High auditorium. A spotlight lasered in on the rear door and the drum beats rolled and roared, introducing an upbeat melody from the fiddlers. When the door opened, a leg stretched into the room, a long loose skirt sliding up, as the hoots and hollers reached a crescendo. With a hop and a tap, Kate stepped in. Long flowing red hair swung below her shoulders as she tapped her way to what had morphed into center stage.

I hadn't seen them until now, but Jane, Kathy and Mary followed behind, stopping in front of the bar simultaneously. In a second, each was joined by two large men, one on each side, and in an eye blink, they were lifted to the bar. The music began slowly, and the tapping of the step dancing picked up speed with each drum tap. With Kate on the floor in front, all of them put on a show the likes of which I had never seen. I couldn't see more than brief glimpses of Kate until the pack separated in front of me, leaving an aisle between us. She pointed at me, wiggled her fingers in a 'come hither' command, and the crowd tugged me toward the front.

"I can't do this," I yelled over the cheers. She just smiled, and as the music continued, she danced around me, twisting, turning, taking my hand, our eyes locked. Then she stood next to me, urging me to follow her steps. Awkward, and in shoes unfit for the task, I tried to mimic her basic steps, not well, but, I'd said many times, 'fake it 'til you make it.' She was magnetic. With a massive audience clapping and shouting, the tapping on the bar and music no one could ignore, I joined in.

In a moment, I'd run out of steam. The women continued for what must have been twenty minutes non-stop. I stood sweating, doing almost nothing. Kate had hardly begun to glisten. When the fiddlers stopped, she reached around my neck, pulled hard and kissed me. And I kissed her back, to the roars of the people around us. She took my hand and led me back to the table, now fully occupied, except for two seats side by side.

"Thanks for being a good sport, Russ," she said.

"I feel a little foolish. With two left feet. You're quite a surprise." She leaned over, kissed my dripping cheek, and said she had surprises to come. "I have a couple for you, too." I scanned the nearby floor. Flynn had been eyeing me all along. He said the boxes were upstairs. I nodded my thanks.

Fresh glasses of porter were passed around the table, and Flynn stood up. The raucous noise instantly drifted down to approaching a whisper as fast as you can draw a breath.

"Welcome all," he began. "We're here tonight to celebrate, and to remember. Katie's takin' our love and best wishes home with her for our friends and loved ones, along with some more substantial offerings." Cheers rose, and ended as soon as Flynn raised his hand. "We have news. It seems that Her Majesty the Queen..." Boos filled the room. With a smirk, he said, "Don't boo, vote." The laughter even caught me. I noticed their new president used that phrase often. I missed him too. Flynn said, "She's agreed to a cease-fire and withdrawal of all troops by the middle of next year." Someone in the crowd yelled, "We'll withdraw 'em sooner 'n that." Again the room filled with boisterous laughter. He held his glass up, again quieting the crowd. "So, to Katie, bon voyage, travel safe, and happy hunting. To us all, Happy Christmas, and most important," he hesitated to be sure he had their attention, "to freedom." The deafening roar even rattled the windows enough for the crowd outside to step back. "Slainte."

Glasses were raised, the toast echoed, and then he raised his hand again. "Now make room and we'll eat and drink and think happy thoughts for those who can't be here with us." He swallowed the porter in only a couple of gulps.

Before his glass hit the table, a new one had replaced it. He turned to me, and lifted the shot glass and signaled I should do the same. I had the only other shot, and all eyes were on me again.

He said, "You found Mary's shop without anyone telling you." I nodded. "You've made the Cozy Kitchen a profit. And you've made me trust you, Fritz Russell. While I've asked others to bid you welcome, this night I'll do it for meself. So with no more speechifying..." He held the glass out to me. "Welcome to our family, Russ." I tapped his glass and we each drank.

"Thanks, Flynn." Kate put her arm around me and reached up and kissed me again.

I've been to wakes and weddings, bar mitzvahs and parties of all kinds, but never anything like this. Kelly must have cloned herself in the kitchen because so much food, and of so many varieties, constantly arrived on the long tables. I hadn't noticed, but three kegs had been placed around the room and people helped themselves. After so many years, being a part of something again brought happy feelings. Even without the booze, it would have been intoxicating.

Before the night ended, Flynn had them quiet once again. "As you know, Katie will be leaving day after tomorrow. And as you know, we have an angel watching us all. Since Kate won't be here, tonight we summon the angel to look over us now, and while she's gone." A drumroll began, and a little blonde girl was carried to steps by the tree and lifted to the top. She put the angel topper in place as the cheers resumed. She waved as the assembly clapped and waved back. Flynn said the angel would have waited until Christmas Eve, but we could all use a little of her special help even now.

Little by little, the street emptied, some coming in as others left, some giving up and going home. They had all been invited, I found out later. Flynn said they were all part of the family. When I had a chance to catch him alone, I handed him his wad of cash. All of it, I told him. He said he'd been rarely caught off guard, but "You're a revelation, you are."

"I taught kids for ten years and I tried to tell the truth. I've had to lie about everything for the past eight. I hate it. But if lying gets me home faster, know this. I'm gone. As much as being part of a family, yours, entices, I'm not safe and none of you are safe around me. You have your own lives, here. And as much as I'd like to make a new life, as much as I think Kate and I could have something special together, this isn't where I belong. I can't go to Ireland and I shouldn't stay here."

"Then don't go upstairs, Russ. I'll get someone to take you home. Seamus will take care of the Kitchen from now on. Stay away from Kate. If you change your mind, you have until tomorrow night. After that, I don't want to see you again. Understood?"

"Perfectly." He told me to stay put and went outside to find someone sober enough to drive, poked his head in to get me, and in a half hour, I sat down at my kitchen table. For the first time in years, I cried.

The banging on my door jolted me from a bad dream, where I'd been chewed little by little by a dragon. The sun peeked over the apartments across the street and in through my window. Sleeping with my head on the table made my headache worse. My neck stiff, my shoulders sore, the banging on the door increased the throbbing.

"Hang on. I'm coming." I opened the door which was kicked wide open. Tim McNamara and his partner pointed pistols at me. "What's going on?"

"Russell Furst, you are under arrest for the murders of William, Thomas and James Koppler."

"That's nuts. You woke me up. I have to go to the bathroom and then I'll do whatever you want." The partner read me my Miranda rights while I peed, with the door open. I asked if I could at least get some clean clothes. While I changed, I pondered that I'd been waiting for this moment for a while. As much as I regretted the circumstances, I had prepared my strategy. I asked if handcuffs were necessary.

"Procedure."

"I have a hangover. I'm not going anywhere."

"Damn right, you aren't," said the partner. I'd never felt as controlled as when he pushed me into the waiting car. Three patrol cars sat in the parking lot. Neighbors were scarce because of the time, but a few resumed their own commutes as I stared out the back seat window. One television station had a camera on me the whole time. A single picture from them would take facial recognition to one hundred percent.

Lost in my thoughts, the police did their paperwork and stuck me in a room, handcuffed to a gray, scuffed table, and left alone. I waited, my headache subsiding, thanks to the aspirins I'd popped while in the bathroom. The room looked like one from every cop show I'd ever seen. A small glass mirror which I presumed to be two-way, a couple of chairs on the other side and one against the wall completed the scene.

I anticipated what the process would likely be. Charges, an arraignment, and then a turf fight between the locals and the Feds. Then some kind of move to somewhere else, maybe a different arraignment. I'd tell the judge I didn't have money for a lawyer and I'd get some overworked legal aid newbie. For now, I'd just sit tight. I had nowhere else to go. As I had expected, the process played out exactly, except for the part where the cell door clanged shut. That part I'd overlooked.

Perhaps for the first time in these past years inside the portal, I had plenty of time to ponder all that had happened. I figured I'd be here, or some other cell for a while. I had nothing. No money for bail. No friends to help. I only really wanted a pen and paper.

By mid-morning, the good cop, bad cop routine started. Men I didn't know started the questioning with why did I kill the Kopplers? They asked my true identity, where I came from, all the basics. I wasn't afraid of them, just continued to repeat my name, job title and my Social Security number. They never grasped that all I gave them was name, rank and serial number. I didn't care. When the yelling began, I leaned forward, looking from one to the other and said as softly as I could, "You have the wrong guy." When they finally gave up, for that round at least, I chuckled a little. So far, they had done nothing more than turn my years of planning into reality.

In a few minutes, the good cop entered, in the person of Tim Mc-Namara, with a tray of coffee, smokes and some papers in his hand.

"Coffee?" he asked.

"Thanks, officer."

"Smoke?"

"Later, if that's okay."

He placed a few sheets of paper in front of me, the first, the report of facial recognition. He told me to take a few minutes and read through them. Then barely moving his lips, he said to cover my mouth when I talked. A slight nod toward the mirror confirmed my suspicion.

"I assume that this room is well-guarded. So how about taking off the handcuffs, so I can walk around?"

"Can't do it." I shrugged.

"Well, thanks for the coffee."

"You can see that we've got you. Exact facial rec. So why not just tell me what happened?"

Rather than a conversation, I returned to my original approach. He already had more information than what I intended to tell him now. He'd been included in the time travel story. Neither of us would mention that.

"So what were you doing last night?" I told him the truth since he had been present.

"I went to a party. My boss is going on vacation, so some friends were celebrating Christmas early. She invited me. I didn't have anything else to do."

"Do you usually hang around with terrorists?" Whose side was he on? Did Flynn know? Or did Flynn set this up?

"Terrorists? You have to be kidding."

"Where are the guns?"

"You have one under your left arm. Are you a terrorist? Should I be scared. Ooooo." He didn't take kindly to my mocking him.

"Okay, wiseguy. If you won't talk, read. I'll wait. You'll talk eventually." He sat back and crossed his arms.

The first couple of pages were the investigative reports from eight years before, with my picture taken from a side angle, probably from a cell phone. The early models weren't very clear and I had been moving, so the picture was blurred. A couple of shots had been taken from across the street from the Cozy Kitchen. And a single frame from the morning's TV video.

"Well, I'll admit, you work fast. That TV shot is me." The next page caught me by surprise. A note from Flynn, apologizing. It said the Feds were moving in, and by letting Tim get there first, they could tie the process up for weeks. He said he would have a lawyer appointed from legal aid who knew what to do. I glanced at Tim, but I didn't react.

"I'll have that smoke now, if you don't mind." He handed me a pack, and he lit it for me with a Zippo lighter. On its face was a shamrock, like the one on the sign outside McNamara's. "Thanks."

I turned to the next page, put the stack down, leaned back and took a long drag. The sheet of copy paper, eight and a half by eleven, contained a handwritten letter from Kate.

Chapter 19

Ashley

THE PORTAL HAD provided surprises but thus far no real clues. As I had promised, I'd saved my media question for a day Natalie could join me. The day before I'd told George and waited for him to consider saying no, until he registered that she reported for a local newspaper.

"I don't know what's happened to you. You're like that young man I hired ten years ago, not the one you've become."

Natalie chatted with my next class when I walked in. Seniors, with a lot of attitude.

"So, we have with us, as you already know, a person who is well-qualified to do battle with today's question. Natalie Johnston works as a reporter for the paper here, and has serious media credentials including magazines and New York newspapers. Let's get started. The First Amendment provides for freedom of the press. Newspapers were common at the time of our Constitution's writing, and the only way news spread other than by letters. Today, newspapers and letters are almost extinct. From those little tiny boxes you all carry around, you have instant access to all the information that has ever existed. How many of you have apps for newspapers like the New York Times?" Two hands. "What about the Riverboro paper?" No one. "So how do you know what's going on in the world? Don't answer. Let's answer this." I pointed to the blackboard. "What role should the media have in politics?"

"You mean the lame-stream media?" We were off and running. I asked, "Will you tell me what the lame-stream media means to you?"

"My parents say the reporters are all liberals, never tell the truth, and never report both sides."

"Ash, let me take over. This is my territory." I told her to go ahead. "There aren't always two sides. There may be differences of opinion, but not of the facts. And opinions differ depending on what point of view you hold. Here are some examples of facts. The Japanese attacked Pearl Harbor. The Nazis murdered six million Jews. The U.S. put a man on the moon. Now let's take the stories for the first one. America imprisoned thousands of Japanese-Americans. Tell me if that has two sides."

"They could be spies," one student said.

"It was morally wrong," said another.

Nat held her hand up. "Americans are supposed to have the right to a trial and to be proven guilty. Didn't happen. No Japanese-American was proven to be a spy. Homes, businesses and lands were confiscated. The government created laws so they could seize the property." She turned to the second student. "Wrong is a value judgment. That's your opinion. Let's move on. The Nazis murdering Jews. Two sides?"

"Some people say it never happened, that the press made it up."

"That's ridiculous," came a response from the back. "Pictures and movies prove the holocaust happened."

"They could have been photoshopped, or whatever they did back then. The German people didn't know what was going on."

"That's stupid. How could they not know?"

Nat stepped in. "Let's move on again. America's space program put men on the moon, not just once, but a dozen times. What's the other side?"

"Moon, New Mexico." The class laughed but Natalie stopped them.

"Think about these examples. I can give you plenty more. But what are your responses? They're not logic. They're opinions. You repeated things others told you or have been taught to believe. You've bought the idea that news and opinions are the same. Reporters don't interpret. They report research and observation. What the news means often gets twisted with lies and half-truths, and constant repetition until it sounds like it must be true. What is important is that you learn how to distinguish facts from news and opinion. You need to read sources that have earned a reputation for accurately reporting. And you need to compare what you read with what you personally see and hear and experience. Let me give you another example. Is welfare abused by people who could get a job?" No answers. "Yes or no. Raise your hands. Yes. About half the class. Are the rest of you 'no's'? Up, up, up. So half and half. Let's try another. Most welfare payments go to black women who have never been married and have lots of kids. Raise your hands if you think 'yes'." Close to three quarters. "Here's a fact." She stopped and looked around. "The majority of people who receive the majority of the money we call welfare are white, or children, who live in rural areas where jobs are almost impossible to find. Most of the others are people who actually have jobs, but because they live in or near cities, they don't make enough because the cost of living is much higher. Those are facts."

"What about the women they call 'welfare queens?' " Larry asked.

"Good question. Be honest now, did you ever cheat on homework, or a test? Even a little bit." Larry blushed a little, but didn't answer. "People everywhere cheat a bit. On taxes. Running a red light. Finding extra coins in a change slot. Welfare has cheats, too. But it's hard to do, and eventually they get caught, most of the time."

"It's a lot of money we have to pay for people who aren't contributing."

"The majority of welfare recipients have jobs, but wages are too low to get them above the poverty line. Even if wages stay the same, inflation over time leaves less spendable income. Does anyone eat tuna fish?" She waved her hand to tell them to raise theirs. "Have any of you looked at the size of the cans lately?"

"They're smaller, but the price didn't go down."

"Right. That's inflation. You get less for the same amount of money. My father told me that when he was your age, he could buy a candy bar for a nickel, gasoline cost less than fifty cents a gallon, and he could buy a pair of sneakers for less than ten dollars. Not that long ago."

I sat at my desk, entranced. Natalie had them all listening, and I could tell they were thinking.

Another hand went up. "But aren't you part of the media? Aren't you saying what anyone would say if that's their job?"

"Good question. I am part of the media. And I take my responsibility under the First Amendment seriously. We're done for today. But if you take anything from what we've said here, it should be read, analyze, discuss, and form your own opinions. Remember, everyone has opinions, but not all opinions are based in reality. Be as smart as you can."

The most amazing thing happened then. They started to clap, and then one by one, stood up and continued clapping for the short time until the bell rang. I asked her if she'd ever had a standing ovation before. She said only once, when she did a striptease at work, and then winked at me.

Just as lively as the previous class, the kids in the last period did all the talking. And arguing. One student said the news always slanted politics. She opened a book with campaign signs and slogans, mentioning both Honest Abe and Honest Ape, the Republican gorilla. Another said that the press was important when they asked hard questions. Even terrible answers were good ones because it helped people see the character of the candidates.

"Mr. Gilbert, I remember hearing last fall that only 5% of the people were undecided about who they would vote for. If that's true, then all that time and money seems like a waste to me. And it was all pretty nasty."

"Throughout our history, most presidential elections have been close," I said. "More than once, the man with the most votes didn't win, because of the Electoral College rules. Which gives you a head start to prepare for tomorrow's question."

"What's the question?"

"Think about it." The bell rang and before they were all out, Sandy walked in, scowling.

She said, "My car is going to cost me $2000 to repair. Your insurance doesn't cover enough."

"Not my insurance, Sandy. The other guy's. Sorry. I wasn't involved. After you left, I went to warn Churchill. Anyway, I may have bumped the other guy back here. When I came back, I think I bumped him somewhere else. I don't think both of us can exist in the same dimension at the same time. Make you a deal. I'll split the out of pocket with you. It might be my fault that he showed up."

"This is so strange."

"You should be in my shoes," I said, and grinned. *Fritz, where are you?* "I'll have a check for you next week. Okay?"

"Thanks Ashley. I've overspent for Christmas already. That really helps."

"It might take a couple of days dressed as Santa and ringing bells, but I'll get it." She shook her head and left.

School ended on Thursday with Christmas three days later. On Christmas Eve day, not having planned to be here, I went shopping. I bought a small turkey, mostly to have sandwiches, some instant stuffing and canned cranberries. I expected to have a chance to study where to go next and maybe watch some football. With a week off, I thought about what else I could do, besides waiting for spring. The toot from the yellow Beetle changed my plans.

I told Nat my plan, although I planned it for myself alone.

"I'll help you, and we'll both have something to do tomorrow."

Her offer sounded more like a demand and turned my quiet holiday at least a little noisier. She said she had to work on Monday, so going home wasn't possible. The twelve hundred mile ride to Chicago cost too much for a day trip, by car or plane.

I had to admit that this version of Natalie differed pleasantly. I wondered if I actually scared her off in my time, like Linda said. Another thought for another time. And I did owe her, way more than just a Christmas dinner.

"You got a deal." I unpacked what little I'd bought and she asked what else we'd be eating. Her suggestive grin teased and this time that's what she intended—teasing. "That's all I had planned."

"Good. Then I didn't shop for nothing." She walked out to her car and took out four plastic bags. My counter soon filled with sweet potatoes, marshmallows, mayonnaise, a loaf of rye bread, pumpkin pie and heavy cream. "You have powdered sugar, don't you?"

"No idea."

One bag contained vegetables for enough salad for a week, and she'd picked two different dressings.

"Were you planning this?" I asked.

"No, just hoping. Besides, we need to work up a plan. We should be ready when the next thunderstorm arrives. No reason to be hungry while we do."

"So do we cook the turkey tonight or tomorrow?"

"Tonight. That way we can decide on a meal at the table, or sandwiches and a game."

"Game?"

"Football, Ash, but if you have another in mind, you might need to teach me the rules." This time she wasn't teasing.

We got busy, put everything away and loaded the turkey in the oven. Without stuffing, the sixteen pound bird would take a couple of hours and I didn't have anything else for dinner. I told her I didn't feel like cooking, but we couldn't go anywhere until the turkey finished roasting.

"Duh. Really? One thing has crossed dimensions, Ashley. You don't plan very well. Good thing I'm here. So this is what we're going to do." She said she'd run to the store and she'd make dinner. But she needed to hurry. "It's Christmas Eve, you know."

"Duh. Really?" I had a feeling we were going to have a fun Christmas.

In a half an hour, the signature putter of her car shut off. I went to the door and she waved me out.

"Need some more hands," she purred. "I got a case of beer."

"Just the place for my hands."

"Well, one of the places." I just shook my head.

While the turkey cooked, she took out two pads and sat across from me. "Let's start with a timeline. What brought you here?"

"You know the story."

"No, we should write all the details, not from before, just here. That way, you'll know how to get home when you find your friend."

"Let me get the books."

When we were settled, I started to explain. I could see almost everything. "Since coming here, I've seen Robert E. Lee, Hitler and Churchill. Before the change, I went to see Wilbur and Orville Wright. Fritz had been there. They asked about the future. When I spoke to Lee, he said he could see his entire lifeline. I went to Churchill, and he remembered me, and said he'd seen Fritz, but he couldn't see his timeline, and I went to him after Lee." She wrote, but I stopped talking. Why could Lee know, even that Fritz would be at Appomattox, and Churchill not know? "I've changed the dynamics. Not a lot, but enough of a bump to bring other me back here, and change Churchill. I wonder if I've made a change that affects Fritz."

"What happened the day you got here?"

"On the drive to school, the sky changed, the radio shut off, the car stopped. Then moments later, it started again. Something happened at that moment, I'd bet on it. I parked in my usual place, and when I grabbed the handle on the school door..." I looked at my hand. "The door buzzed like it does when I open the portal, and I couldn't let go until I stepped over the threshold. Nat, that's it. That's when I got here. Exactly when. The door to the parking lot is another portal."

"Didn't you say that a door-shaped light forms when you're in the portal? Is there one?"

"No. I didn't choose the change either. I just walked through." When she started to talk, I held up my hand. "If there's no rectangle, then..."

"Then you have no way back." I raised my eyes from the pad to her. She told me that I should take a deep breath, and close my mouth. "You still have your worry ruts, Ash."

I leaned back in my chair, my bottom lip between my teeth, and looked at the kitchen, as it had been before Jane changed the way I looked at my life. Would Natalie be act two? I picked up the beer bottle, still almost full, and stood. "I need something stronger." Since my arrival, I hadn't purchased any liquor, and hadn't even looked for any.

"It's in the cabinet on the right above the sink," she said, when she heard the doors open and close. "Get me one of what you're drinking." I poured two small glasses, half way, with Irish whiskey. A couple of ice cubes, and I sat down again.

"Slainte," she said.

"Yeah, that," and I took a sip. "And Merry Christmas."

"Ash, come back. Figuring this out is even more important now. You can't change anything right now, so while the turkey cooks, let's keep looking for clues." I met her eyes, and I thought she might gouge mine out. "Stop it now. Stop feeling sorry for yourself. We have work to do and you being a crybaby won't help. You've only started the story. You've been here for a month. Face it. Thunderstorms are going to be scarce. So get it together." She stopped shouting and smiled. "Besides this could be funner."

"Fritz said that. Funner. Maybe you're related."

CHRISTMAS EVE passed quietly. We hardly left the table. Nat broiled up some hamburgers, sliced a tomato and put chips between us. Soda replaced the beer and booze. I talked, she wrote. We agreed that I'd said or done one or maybe more things that altered history, and made things worse. Not Lee. His change happened before Sandy and I arrived. Hitler and Churchill were the targets. At least one because other me had come back.

"Let me look for time travel on the computer," I said. "Maybe there are some articles that try to explain other dimensions, alternate universes, beside Star Trek reruns." When I got up, so did she.

"Ash, we need to talk." She picked up the empty plates and carried them to the sink, so I couldn't see her face.

"That's what we've been doing." I dodged the fact that she meant something else.

She wiped the trash into the can, and rinsed the plates, before turning to look at me. "I can make a lot of excuses, it's late, we'll be busy tomorrow, but you and I have never had this kind of closeness. Your doppelganger has a different personality. I'd like to stay the night, but you need to be comfortable with it. If I do, I need to go home and get some things."

I didn't know if she was testing me, but I was definitely testing me. If I couldn't get home, she would be a fun companion, maybe even more down the road. I hoped I could trust her, a critical component now. But I love Jane, I reminded myself, knowing I might never see her again.

"Natalie," I began, "I don't want a one-night stand or a casual fling. Being here is difficult enough and you're already wrapped up in it. Like you said before, I've only been here a month. In a normal world, I couldn't be more flattered or more interested in exploring our relationship. Really." Her face changed emotion with each sentence. "You're welcome to spend the night. But we should let this take some time."

Taking a deep breath, she slowly smiled. "That may be the nicest, most genuine refusal ever. I can't lose what I never had, but other you cared only for himself, regardless of how much time I spent here. When I introduced him to Linda, we were done. I moved out a few days later, and Linda moved in that day. They are too much alike. It showed. He's mean and she's self-centered, and they get along great. Perfect together." She pursed her lips, making some kind of decision, and looked up at me. "I'm going home and maybe I'll be back tonight. Let me think about it. Don't wait up. I still have a key." Before she could get by, I hugged her, and I could feel her shaking. I held on for longer than I should have, as we adjusted to the comfort of our embrace.

"I'll be back by morning," she said. The door closed and the VW started down the street.

Not knowing when she'd return, I quickly cleaned up and went back to our notes. I read hers first. She'd set up an outline for each event, like Fritz did with yellow pads. Fact, then detail, like she had discussed in my classes. She put stars next to where she thought I'd changed the past. She titled a page that said, "Finding Fritz," with a list of questions. Two struck me. Could I bring him back here from a different dimension? He couldn't get back either. The second asked if I could bring him here, how would either of them, us, get back if I didn't know what had started the jumbled history in the first place. I read a little farther to the last question. "If you've changed history, can you change it back?"

I added questions after that. If you can change history back, does the change happen in all dimensions, and at the same time? Will that, in turn, change everything back to the point where the change began?

The possibilities flew at me, and I wrote furiously to keep up. Did our trip to Shakespeare, or anywhere we went, become the starting point? Was Fritz even the cause, or could it have been me? Was simply materializing or talking enough, or was the change caused by an action? I tried to remember what Tony had said. What if what we changed happened before we were born, and if we changed it back, would we then no longer exist? Would we live, but in that time?

Assuming I could even find Fritz, would I change things beyond repair? Would I be better off just leaving things as they were? I'd never considered any of these questions until now. I wondered if Fritz had.

"Thanks, Nat." Her spotless analysis meant we'd have time to fill in more details as we went. I looked at the clock. Quarter past one. "Merry Christmas." I leaned back and surveyed the house. Only a year had passed since my party, when I gave Jane the ring. It felt much longer, like a lifetime. Painting the place would make it look more like home. Except that I had to do it myself. I didn't have those extra checks from the president. I stretched, then walked from room to room. I missed the clutter of all my books, which snapped another idea. Where were the books? A teacher should at least have textbooks, but wherever

I looked, none, anywhere. I flipped on the basement light, and piled one on another, cases of books jammed half the floor. I opened the closest box, curious to see if other me had the same tastes. Since we were now history teachers, I expected a different sort of collection. At least partially, I had guessed accurately, based on what I found. Books I'd never read, or even bought, began to stack on the floor. Some authors I'd never heard of. Not history or literature, but science fiction, time travel, physics books, none of which I would have in my library. I put them back and carried the box upstairs. Painting had just been postponed.

Chapter 20

Jane

I SPOKE TO the president last evening, only in part to wish him a good holiday, his last in office. Sadly, I hadn't made it to their Christmas party. I asked him what he planned to do about the portal, the airport, and me. His answer surprised me. He said he hadn't yet figured that out, nor had he briefed his successor.

"Jane, the transition team has been subtly inquiring everywhere about time travel. The official response is holding them back—that I had evened things with the press after eight years. Those who do know laugh at the question. I'll have to let them know eventually, but with both Fritz and Ashley inside, right now I think I would only decrease their chances to get back. As far as you're concerned, I'll give him a recommendation, but not draw attention, if that's okay with you."

"Mr. President, what matters to me, besides getting our boys back, is ending the Caballeros. The portal has done its own damage, but we haven't caught Koppler. He's already ruined the lives of good men, not to mention the ones he's killed. I feel badly for Florian."

"Don't. Florian made a choice."

"I think that you can blame the portal changing things as much as Koppler's threats. I have a feeling that he truly wanted to help you in the development plan, and not for the money. And I don't think he expected that Koppler would sink his big ship. Koppler got to him later."

"Maybe, Jane, but he didn't let us know. He could have. Jim Beech is devastated. He brought me his resignation yesterday, effective January first. He said he no longer trusts his judgment and wouldn't want anyone else caught in the mess. He also asked me to thank you. He said his greatest challenges and most fun came from working with you. He asked you to give him a holler from time to time. But he's taken his wife on a cruise until New Year's."

"Are you coming to Linda's on Christmas?"

"Not this time. If we could use the portal, I could get away unnoticed. It's hard to believe it's been a year since Ashley's party." That thought had run circles around my brain for the past few days. "Sorry, Jane. I forgot."

"I hope next Christmas we might be able to do it again."

"Me too. I still have a bet to win." I appreciated his trying to cheer me, and I couldn't ask for a better gift than seeing the two of them play basketball. Ashley would be home.

"Merry Christmas, sir, and to your family. I'll talk to you again soon." I didn't wait for a response before I disconnected.

I still had an hour, so I poured a cup of coffee. I rubbed my back against the chair to stop the itching. There were still places that hadn't healed completely, and I missed having Ash here to tend them. The medics at the airport had been gracious but they were gone now. I longed for Ash's gentle touch.

Despite all the good that the portal had made possible, it had left misery behind for those of us who were involved. I didn't need to cry. I'd done enough. I hoped that my knowing Ashley would be back would be more than wishful thinking. After all, my mother had worked so hard planning to make our wedding perfect.

Before I dressed, I stuck my head out the back door. Not too cold yet. Christmas snow had been predicted. So even though I didn't want to, I put on a pair of jeans and a soft, cotton blouse, and headed to Linda's.

The battle had begun before I walked in the back door. For a change, Tim had some unrelenting opposition. Linda's brother, Joe, and Natalie, were tag-teaming him with every outrageous thing he said. He received, and deserved, the worst in return. I wished them "Merry Christmas."

"Am I late?" I asked. "Am I the last?"

"No, Jane dear, you're just fine," Emily said. "We were just discussing the elections."

"I must have missed something." My sarcasm surprised even me. "Didn't the investigation show the machines were tampered with, and then the power failure?"

"Who are you again?" Tim asked. "Oh, I remember. You're the girl friend. I thought you were shot."

I stopped the others from reacting. I could take care of myself. "That's me. And then I was mistaken for a side of beef. They tenderized Linda at the same time." She looked shocked that I would take him on, but at that point, I didn't care. "You remember Thomas Koppler? The guy who tortured Linda. He's still loose, and thanks to you, he knows about us now." For someone who never gets mad, hitting him sounded like a great first step. I stood up and faced him, unbuttoning my blouse. Above the hushed stillness, Emily laughed softly, the only sound.

As the last button opened, I held my blouse open and slid it off. I held my laugh at the look of distress on his face, but after he'd had a moment to stare, and then look to his wife for help, I turned around. My back was lined with vertical scars. Linda watched in silence until I unhooked my bra and let him see all the damage. She took off her tee and stepped next to me. She still could only wear loose fitting tops. Even the skin grafting didn't disguise the beating she'd taken.

The most inappropriate laugh broke the quiet. Emily said, "Okay, girls, that's enough of Tim's gift. He may have lost his appetite for now, but I, for one, am hungry."

At that, TJ chirped what sounded like "Go, Nana."

Later, Natalie said we'd put on quite a show, but she had never imagined the extent of the wounds. She had learned almost the entire history of the portal, in antiseptic form, and had notepads galore with the details. She knew we'd been kidnapped, but not the lengths to which Koppler had gone. "I know he didn't do it himself, but that's sick."

"We were lucky, Nat. We made it out alive. I can't guess how many didn't."

"Well at least it's one more piece of the puzzle. I have nineteen notebooks. Did he say anything that might provide an idea where he could be?"

"He didn't know about the portal until my father told Jim Sapphire. And he hadn't tied it to Fritz or the school until he snatched me."

"Nat, could I read your notebooks?" I asked. "You may have picked up something that we haven't. Like you did with the suits."

"Any time, Jane."

"How about this afternoon? Sorry, Linda, but I'm not in a sociable mood."

"Tony and I had plans, but I guess that can wait."

"I'll take them home to read. No need to change plans. I'll take good care of them."

"Do you think you'll find something?"

"Maybe. I know things you can't know, Nat. You might not be able to tie things together."

Chapter 21

Ashley
CHRISTMAS MORNING

I was snoozing on the couch when Natalie opened the door. A book lay on the floor, a napkin acting as bookmark. The title, written in orange on a photo of the Milky Way, announced quantum physics as the subject. As she retreated to the kitchen, I said, "Merry Christmas. What time is it?"

"Six thirtyish. I'll make breakfast. Learn anything?"

I told her that I had thumbed through and read a few parts. The author had hypothesized a minimum of twelve connecting dimensions, complete with calculations, scientific discussion, and social proofs. He had included déjà vu, the Bermuda Triangle, and pyramids built around the world. "It sounds like nonsense, except for the reality. Some of what I read has to do with energy displacement. I need to read from the beginning."

"You want eggs and bacon, pancakes or waffles. Thanks for setting up the coffee."

"Right now, I want to wake up. Make what you like. I'll eat anything."

"That's one more strange thing. Other you would have said exactly what he wanted. Never asked me."

"The author said that the beings in different dimensions absorb energy from everywhere. Energy can't be destroyed and, when displaced, floats in the universe until it's reabsorbed. He explains virus mutations as just one example."

"Are you going to shower? Do you want a cup of coffee now?"

From my couch, I could hear the unsubtle sounds of pots and pans clanging, as she began her quest. From my doorway view, she had a waffle iron out on the counter.

"I didn't know I had that."

"Bottom shelf, right hand cabinet, next to the stove."

"It looks new."

"I've used it a few times. I bought it for him last Christmas. Coffee?"

"No. Shower."

I took longer than I needed to clean up and with a towel wrapped around me, I was shaving when Natalie opened the door. She grinned and said, "Too late. Oh, well. Breakfast in two minutes." I ran the blade across the last soapy spaces, rinsed, and dressed in time to see the first waffles hit the plates.

"I'll make more if you want them, but let's eat these first." My stomach thanked me. Last night's burger was all I'd eaten the entire day. When she asked, I told her another, to go with the finally-cooked bacon, sounded like a winner.

"So how did you sleep?" I asked.

"I didn't, much. You're an enigma. I've never been so forward, or cared about it less. At the same time, our search guarantees that if you succeed, you'll be gone, and some other you will be here. From what you read, do you even know which one?"

The edge in her voice and the redness in her early morning eyes told me she hadn't slept, and that she had cried while considering what was happening between us. I pondered the mystery a bit, not having absorbed the ramifications as yet. "If I can undo everything, then the other guy should be back, I think. But if I undo everything, I could set off another collection of earth-changing, no, universe-changing events. Then who knows?"

"You're a wealth of no knowledge."

"A fortune teller probably could guess better than I can right now."

We cleared the table and left the mess for later. Returning to her notes, she began asking about Fritz's books. I explained the order I had found and that I'd checked out all but the last two. I still couldn't decide if Fritz stopped at a specific spot.

"What's out of place?"

"More than one possibility, based on where he put the paperclips. But one of them puts him in the tiger's cage, which makes no sense to me." I pulled Koppler's book from the pile. "This one. I can't fathom his going there."

"Do you think he would know that's what you would think?"

I stood up and after a short walk around the living room, came back and opened the book to the paperclip. I had scanned the picture of a party numerous times, the Koppler brothers standing on a wide lawn.

"I'm getting my computer. I want to check something." James Koppler had been an important political advisor, so plenty of stories should be available. When I had the list of sites to choose, I checked for a date for the picture. On the second page, the date in the book and the headline matched. "Take a look at this."

She stood behind me and leaned over to read, none too subtly. I didn't move as she leaned in, and I didn't ask her if she wanted to sit down. She pressed on my shoulder even harder reaching for the mouse, and opened the Washington Post story.

"He's here, Ash. Says an unknown assailant killed two and shot the third, who remained in a coma. The dates match."

"He's picked one that's going to be hard to undo. If he's the shooter."

"Well, we can start planning. Now you know your next stop."

The sun through the windows had the slant of approaching evening by the time we took a break. We looked at every detail about the brothers we could think of, the house, the back gardens, the family. For eight years, James Koppler had been in a coma with only a sister to care for him. But how to find Fritz now, how to stop him, and how to get him home, these questions remained.

Chapter 22

Ashley

I TURNED ON a football game for a little background noise and a change of pace. From the kitchen, Natalie asked me to make a salad and set the table, while she pulled the sweet potatoes from the oven. I stood by as she added almost a whole bag of marshmallows to cover the top.

"That's a lot," I said.

"Yeah, I know. I like it that way, and the marshmallows will be nice and brown." She looked over her shoulder. "Get to work." She took out plates and glasses for the table, carved the white meat off the bird, enough for both of us. And a few strangers.

"Expecting company?"

"This will keep for a while. I'll clean the rest off later. Is this enough for you?"

"Yup. Plenty." The salad built itself as I cut and chopped, enough for us, for a week, while she prepared all the rest.

When she'd finished prepping, she said she would shower while the marshmallows melted, and asked me to keep an eye on them. Never having cooked sweet potatoes, I wore a path between the TV and the stove. Her shower lasted for only a couple of minutes, and she sashayed into the kitchen wrapped in a towel, grinned at me, and bent over to look at her concoction.

"Nice," I said. She wasn't trying to hide much under the towel. "I mean the sweet potatoes." She knew what I meant. She placed the pan on a trivet, smiled, and pecked my cheek when she walked back to put on some clothes.

The football game continued while we ate, but neither of us paid attention, even to the touchdown replays. Rather, we continued discussing a plan to get Fritz back.

"First, you have to find him. Then you need to figure out how to get him here."

"Then, we need to find a way to change history back. And then find the portal that gets us home."

"We should map a plan. If he's in this universe, or if he's in a different one, you have to know exactly what to do, so you don't get lost." I studied her face, wondering if she'd thought of that just then.

"I wonder if I should stop him first, in 2008, or try to find him in our present."

"Ash, what if Fritz didn't cause the change? Only he knows what he did. If you can find him before he changed history, do you think he'll know what to do?"

"I'll have to find him first and ask. And if I've changed things too, I have to figure out if I should try to change them back, and how. Right now, I'd like to punch him."

"He's not here. It's just you and me." Then, with an alluring grin, she added, "I bet we could find better things to do than punching."

We discussed where to go to find Fritz, and I avoided the complications of where she and I might be headed. A couple of times I caught her gaze, knowing that we approached an uncomfortable time of the evening. When we ran out of ideas, I got up, and broke her magnetic hold for the moment. One thing I believed to be certain—spring thunderstorms might not come soon enough.

Nat stayed Christmas night. She had agreed that my guest bedroom could substitute for her apartment, but in the middle of the night, I woke as she climbed in next to me. When the alarm rang early, she ran from the bedroom, a small bundle left behind. My morning fog lifted, and by the time I put my feet on the floor, she bounced in and said she'd see me later. To make the bed, I uncovered the bundle and removed her pajamas, still warm, her scent clinging. I had another addition to my list of things to think about.

The week off until after the New Year gave me time to plan the next semester's classes, which I found completed in other me's filing cabinet. I couldn't avoid teaching for a full term, so I spent part of the days reading his notes, the text, and some of the references he listed for assignments.

I devoted at least one hour each morning to reading time travel books to fashion my plan. Would there be discussion on crossing dimensions, my main obstacle for returning home? More than once during that week, I asked if Fritz had considered the complications. And having to wait for spring to find him only increased the pressing urgency to be ready. After all, I didn't have Tony Almeida or the president to help.

"Tony." I said it out loud. There had to be another Tony. I didn't remember telling Nat about Tony, just that she existed there, as I did here. I made a note to discuss him with her. As I planned the week, my urgent tasks were identified, the ones that took up the days. The nights presented a very different challenge.

As I worked my way through Monday, the television provided company. A winter-stormy five-day forecast looped most of the time until the sun winked good-bye. The more I had considered Tony, the more urgent a search for him became. Just before five o'clock, the tell-tale putter outside trumpeted Natalie's return.

"I'm glad you're home," I said. She cocked her head to my greeting like she gathered it from the surrounding walls.

"I like the sound of that. Home." I didn't try to change the word, or clarify my meaning. I liked the way it came out, and her reaction. "How was your day?"

With my notebook in hand, I told her not to take her coat off. We were going out for dinner. "There's a storm coming and we may be here for a while, so let's eat and stock up before the store is empty."

"Airport? Where?"

"About twenty minutes from here. If it's here. It's well-hidden, but not secret in my world. Easy enough to find out."

I planned to take her to a nice place at a later time, maybe, but a quick diner dinner served the comfort food we both needed, and offered enough quiet to talk in privacy. She told me she had spent the day researching previous inaugurations, and that her contacts had informed her that heightened attention permeated all of official Washington. I told her that in my world, both inaugurals for the first black president had been cold and completely non-violent.

"That's your world. This one is different, as you've already seen. Knife fights in school, you're a drug dealer. I hope you're right."

I told her I wanted to look for the airport, looking up at low, rolling clouds reflecting the light from the ground. The whipping winds carried the cold air across our noses, as we breathed the distinct smell of snow.

"Nat, I've been working on a strategy. I think I should find Fritz before I go anywhere else. I need to be able to get back here, with or without him, to start. If I can discover what he knows, then we can decide what to do next."

"What the next step is, in my opinion, will be to ask every question now, based on what his possible answers might be."

"You mean before I find him?"

"Yes. So we need to ask ourselves the questions and respond with any possible answers. That way, when you find him, you'll be able to act immediately. You said you never know how long the portal will be open."

"Once the portal was open, we never lost the exit while we were inside. But the connection can be disrupted or closed when we come back. Even then, the generator kept it connected. We took so much for granted. I can't believe we never really talked about all the consequences."

I found the airport road, more concealed than I recalled. Not more than a dirt track, weeds and shrubs grew right to the edge, and trees hadn't been removed for large vehicles. It looked more like a place kids would go to make out than a hidden government facility.

"Should we walk in?" Nat asked, with the quiet tone of 'let's not do this.'

"I have a flashlight in the trunk."

Both doors opened to waist-high grasses, opportunist saplings, and piles of leaves blowing across our path, as the larger trees were lashed by the approaching storm. I reflected on the previous winter when Mel Zack made the trip out of here in a Suburban, but deep snow here would be impenetrable. That road had been wider, and fairly straight, but this one faded to the left in the flashlight's beam. Fifty yards down and we could no longer see my car.

"Are there any animals back here, Ash?"

"I imagine, but nothing native should be a problem. Look at all the signs." I flashed the light on the 'No Trespassing' signs warning that we were on a private road. "Violators will be shot" caught our attention, as did the snowflakes that had arrived.

"We should go back, Ash. There's nothing here."

"I want to go further. If there's nothing, fine. But we're still close to the car."

Reluctantly she agreed, and side by side we pressed further into the woods. We'd walked almost a mile. The track widened, but with no indication of regular use. Surrounding us, the trees gathered closer and shook leftover leaves on our heads as we invaded.

"Do you feel like we're being watched?" I asked.

"Yes. Like the Ents in Lord of the Rings or the apple trees in the Wizard of Oz."

I pointed the flashlight into the shadows, scanning the trees for signs of surveillance. If the owner was serious and shot trespassers, then talking trees weren't our problem. We didn't dare to leave the road, but we kept going.

"Ash, turn off the light." As quickly as I did, a light far ahead froze our steps. "We should leave."

"Not yet. Let's see where he goes."

The light continued toward us moving side to side, looking for someone or something. I couldn't help but feel we were the target. If we left now, the sound of crunching leaves would give us away. So I took her hand and we waited.

Chapter 23

Jane

My phone rang. I closed the busy-work file. I'm not cut out for meaningless paperwork, and that's all they're giving me. My work with the transition promised a serious review of all the connections we had made, where the successes needed future commitment. I've been asked to clean out files of historical data that didn't fit with the new president's worldview. Which meant pretty much everything.

"Hi Jane. I want to talk to you. Not here. I'll be in Riverboro for the end of the year. I want to consider how to handle the portal when we leave."

"You already know, Mr. President. Without Fritz and Ashley, we're stalemated. If they get back, then you'll have to ask them."

I was right, he said, as far as I went, but for a little while more, he exerted the full power of the presidency, to bring to bear on … on what exactly? Without the portal, the full power flexed a lot less muscle. "Jane, the portal exists, time travel is real. We need to find it."

"Mr. President, I've been studying the quantum physics materials. Fritz found the portal by accident. Ash can open it because of another accident. We already know the ingredients. I've talked to Tony. We agree that we need a catalyst, something from the natural world."

"That's why I want to talk to you. I'm responsible for this, and I need to fix it."

"You didn't make Fritz choose as he did. Don't carry that load. We don't know why he went or what he went after. We may never know, but if anyone can find him, it's Ashley. I'll be happy to talk to you more. But I think this is out of our hands. Call me when you're in town. Oh, and Happy New Year."

* * *

Ms. Crispen announced that an insistent stranger wanted to speak to him. "He knows your private number, but won't tell me his name. Only initials, IM."

"I'll talk to him." He stared at the phone and another interruption.

"I assume you have a report for me."

"I followed him as you know, but he was gone. I've checked all previous addresses, in case of activity at any of them."

"Keep looking, and keep an eye on where he left from. I have a feeling that he'll show up again."

The president walked around his rebuilt office, alone. Surrounding him, all the closed doors stifled the noise of the handoff to the next occupant. With less than a month remaining, the pressure of his office had not lessened. He remained the leader of the free world. Only a few days before, the changes that would soon take place stormed to the forefront, when the new guy threatened to defund his development plan. The outrage registered by the leaders came to his desk. The temptation to use the portal to show what he could do, would do, was useless with both Fritz and Ashley gone. Finding a way to convince his successor of the wisdom to continue had become part of his daily plan. But a public disagreement would only generate animosity, so he considered strategies that might work.

His trusted advisors and friends were almost all gone. His wife had told him just the day before to call Jane Barclay and to get General Beech back from his vacation. Most of the cabinet had departed for the holidays, and those remaining were, like him, preparing to leave.

"Ms. Crispen, contact General Beech for me, please."

"Mr. President, may I ask a question? 'IM?' Wasn't he the one who fell from the building in Abu Dhabi? A Caballero?"

"Let's not use that name here. Not as long as Koppler is still loose. We already know he had ears in here. We don't know if we found them all."

"Sorry, sir."

"Now that you know, when he makes contact, just let him through."

"Is he the same guy?"

"Need to know, Carolyn. Sorry." He hung up, knowing she would continue to search for an answer. What she gave away in nice, she more than made up for in smart. She hadn't yet become her predecessor, Lily Evans, but he wished he had convinced her to join his staff, post-presidency.

Focusing again on the portal, he envisioned the desk and the paperclips, and his trips through space and time. He had accepted the portal's use as a tool, but hadn't explored the realms of physics that had been proven. Limiting knowledge of the portal hadn't protected Fritz and Linda, his priority. A soft tap interrupted his thoughts. *Doesn't it always.*

Ms. Crispin stuck her head in, and held a cell out. "Mr. President, the general."

He thanked her and walked out to the garden. "Sorry to disturb your vacation, Jim. I hope you'll come back now. We have our own Caballero."

When he disconnected, he surveyed his view of the South Lawn. *No matter what happens, I'll never have an office with a view that matches this.*

Chapter 24

Linda

I'D BEEN ENJOYING watching the snow falling through the family room window when a car door closed. A young man headed up our walkway. Not recognizing either the car or the young man, I opened the door as he took the four steps two at a time. I hadn't had a visitor in a while, and certainly not someone I didn't know. I opened the storm door and asked him what he wanted.

"Ms. Russell, I'm Eric Silver. Mr. R was my history teacher. I'm home on break and I want to talk with him about a project I'm working on."

I told him that my husband wasn't at home.

"Will he be home soon? I can come back later. It's about time travel, Ms. Russell. I've found a way to create a new portal."

I remember those words clearly because my knees buckled and I grabbed the door frame to keep from falling. Eric pulled the door open and reached in to steady me.

"Are you okay? You do know about the portal, don't you?"

I told him I did, too well, and after regaining my balance, I invited him in. When I opened the door, snowflakes beat him inside. As I had so many times with Fritz, we continued our conversation at the kitchen table. I offered him a drink and he said he'd have one if I did. He didn't want to bother me, he said. He couldn't have known how little a bother that would be.

"Is diet okay?"

"Sure. Anything."

While I poured, I looked him over. He was as tall as Ashley, with a comfortably short length of blondish hair. His golden-glow tan spoke of time spent outdoors. I handed him the soda and sat down across from him. I asked him to tell me what he'd found.

"Well, Ms. Russell, I'm not sure where to start. I'm in my freshman year at MIT, and just getting a general sense of what school is like. Boston's a great area to go to college."

"It is, Eric, but I meant about the portal."

"Do you think Mr. R will be okay with me telling you? The president made me take an oath not to talk to anyone but Mr. R about it."

"If you feel uncomfortable talking about it, just tell me in general terms."

"Well, it all started in September. Walking back to the dorm, my lab partner and I witnessed a spectacular meteor shower. We sat down and watched it, and began talking about what it must have been like before TV and telescopes. And all the bright lights that interfere with a clear view of the stars. We talked about the imagination those primitive people must have had. "Orion, that's my favorite constellation, glimmered low in the sky. For me, it's a welcoming of winter. All the summer stars are hidden and Orion's Belt dominates. Sorry, I'm getting sidetracked."

I understood. Fritz and I had talked about the artists who could look up at scattered stars and draw pictures and create stories that have survived through history.

"Mr. R told us something like that too. We were studying the Civil War period, just before the storm when the lightning hit him. He told us about the Underground Railroad, and he played a recording of…"

"Follow the Drinking Gourd," I interrupted. "The first time he gave that lesson, he played it for me too. And talked about the story he had prepared for his classes." I could feel my eyes well up.

"Are you sure you're okay, Ms. Russell?"

I wiped my eyes and told him to keep going. He said that he spotted the Big Dipper that night and he understood that he'd continue along that road, until he discovered how time travel worked. "If I succeed," he said, "I'll be one more in a line of people who have followed the stars through history."

"So what happened that brings you here now?"

"A few days later, a storm flooded a lot of the campus. A large puddle blocked our way into the lab building, so we waited. My shoes were new and I didn't want to wreck them. I would have to step through it eventually, but not at that moment. My lab partner picked up a stone and tossed it in the middle, and we watched the waves scatter. That gave me an idea. So…"

"Eric, I don't mean to interrupt, but you said you found another portal. Did you get inside?"

"Not exactly. I had seen Mr. R open the portal and how the paper-clips worked. I watched Mr. Almeida hook up the doorknob to the generator, so I did the same thing. I used a picture of my room in my parents' house. I opened the door and the room materialized. So did a younger me, as a kid. I just shut the door. Ms. Russell, really, I don't want to be rude, but I promised I wouldn't say anything. My lab partner thinks we discovered something new. I didn't even tell her."

I asked if he had the president's permission, would he tell me the whole story? When he said sure, and asked me not to be angry. I told him not to worry, that I might have a quick solution. At this point, I called Jane and told her she should come over now. I told her that Eric said that he'd found a way into the portal.

Chapter 25

Jane

"**HELLO, ERIC,**" I said. "We haven't actually met but I know about you. MIT, last year's valedictorian. Linda, Eric is the student who put together the play last spring." Linda said she understood the play had been successful, but she hadn't seen it.

"Linda was finishing up with her MBA, Eric. Otherwise she'd have been there."

"That's okay. We had sell-outs for all the shows. Mr. Gilbert missed it, too. We made a video and gave it to him."

"I've seen it. You did an awesome job. Now, what's this about the portal?"

Eric told me the same story he told Linda, and that he wanted to honor his word to the president. That didn't surprise me. The president needed men like Eric around him, the kind of person who put value to his word. I told him I thought I could arrange that permission for him.

"Mr. President, sorry to bother you, but I'm at Linda's, talking to an old friend of yours, Eric Silver. It seems he's found a way into the portal, but without your okay, he's trying to figure out how much to say. He said he made you a promise."

The president said he had one thing to take care of, but he'd be here within the hour. I told Eric what the president said.

"Look, I didn't mean to upset everyone's schedule. I can come back another time. I'll be here for a few days."

"Mr. President, did you hear all that." I laughed a little at his response. "He said he'll be here in a half hour."

While we waited, Eric told us about sitting under the stars, night after night with his lab partner. He said they talked about the universe, and the possibility of multiple universes and multiple dimensions. He told us she expected to major in physics and wanted to work for NASA.

"One night, she asked me if I thought time travel was possible. Since I knew the answer, I just said yes. Then she started to talk about how everything is connected. Even if time travel wasn't real, she said energy was." Eric scratched his nose, gathering his next set of thoughts. "Energy can't be destroyed, we know that. And the human brain runs on electrical energy. From synapse to synapse, every thought, every idea, becomes energy. If we can't destroy it, then it takes some other form. Imagine multiple dimensions and energy flowing through all of them. That means we are all interconnected through time and space for all of time. From dimension to dimension, universe to universe, it's all floating out there."

At the time, I thought, "wow, and he's only a freshman."

Chapter 26

Linda

THE DOORBELL ENDED Eric's soliloquy for the moment. The president and Mel Zack walked into the kitchen. He hurried to shake Eric's hand.

"So how goes college?"

"I'm enjoying it so far, Mr. President. I want to thank you for my scholarship. I haven't seen you to tell you in person. I hope you got my letter."

"Eric, I haven't actually seen it, but I'm sure it's in a file I'll get to eventually. I'm sure I won't be as busy not being president as I have been." A warm smile filled his face. "So I understand you want to talk to me?"

Once again, Eric explained his dilemma. The president listened and patted Eric's arm. "I appreciate, more than you can know, that you've kept your word. So, if I give you my okay now, will you tell us the whole story?"

Jane pulled a yellow pad from her satchel while I poured sodas. Mel slid into a chair in the corner as Eric began his tale. He started with the storm and the puddle. His lab partner, Lenore Green, said that they should measure everything. "So we weighed the stones, we measured distances and we hooked up an oscilloscope to measure the waves. We tried it with two stones, then more. We dropped them in different places. She even threw a big one into the middle. We timed the waves until they reached the edge of the puddle. And we took pictures of the patterns. We recorded everything and tried to see if it had any useful meaning."

"So what did you come up with?" the president asked.

"Our first conclusion was that the waves travel at different speeds depending on where you watch them. Time was relative."

"Einstein," Jane said.

"Right. Second, we concluded that if the waves were interfered with, they would change directions. Visualize this. Drop a pebble into a full sink. The waves go smoothly to the sides. Drop a second one, there's disturbance of the waves, and maybe some splashing when they collide, but at the outer edges, it's still smooth. Now add a big stone and everything gets churning like a giant pinball machine."

"I see where you're going," Jane said. "The larger the impact, the bigger the change. So let's talk about time travel, which you'll be getting to in a minute." I looked around the table. Everyone was concentrating, and so far waiting patiently. "When Fritz went into the portal alone, he would create almost no impact. A small pebble. Even constant use would still be small. But as soon as the impact is more significant, like interfering with the present, the greater the danger of changing the future."

I said, "And if you do the same in the past, you change our present."

"That's what we think, Ms. Russell."

"But add another piece," Jane said. "You're talking about incidental contact with time and space. If something changes in history because you made it change, you set the ripples off in a new direction." She directed her comments to the rest of us. "Eric's been talking about two dimensional or three dimensional movement. What if other dimensions exist that we don't know about. Scientific theory postulates more. As many as ten or twelve, that I've read about. Could that one act change time and events across dimensions?"

"You mean string theory?" Eric asked. "I just scratched through a reading about it. It's like a foreign language."

"So you think that time waves are similar to those in the puddle?" asked the president.

"I was skeptical too, Mr. President. I don't blame you. That's when we began to design an experiment. I discussed the wave theory with Lenore and she said that made sense. Since I met you, Mr. President, and found out that we can time travel, I've kept a journal about everything weird that's happened. I've been reading books on quantum physics, and even though I don't understand most of it, Lenore is teaching me. I can't talk to my professors. They'd have me kicked out. Or committed. Ms. Russell, that's why I'm here. I thought Mr. R would have run into some of these questions and he might have some answers."

The president looked at me. "Have you told him everything?"

"Only that Fritz isn't home yet."

"This might be a good time, don't you think?"

So I told Eric that on Thanksgiving, Fritz went missing in the portal, and a couple of days later, Ashley had followed, trying to find him. And now, with a new president, we wouldn't have access to opening it. We needed thunderstorms, I told him, but even then, none of us could open it.

When I finished, he had a sad, sympathetic look. "So neither of you have seen them for weeks. And I'm yakking away about an experiment. Wow, I'm really sorry."

"Eric, tell us more about what you've done," said the president. "It could be important, even vital, in getting them back."

"The day I met you, I noted everything you all did, especially Mr. Almeida. It's in my first journal. My lab desk is metal. We moved it to an empty room. I bought a generator and one of those blow up kiddie pools. I almost electrocuted myself the first time we tried it because I didn't hook up the generator properly, and touched the water. Believe me when I tell you that I must have sailed ten feet across the room. Water and electricity don't mix too well."

Jane said, "No, not well at all."

Chapter 27

Jane

"**WHY A KIDDIE** pool, Eric?" I asked.

"Well, you know that Ben Franklin first experimented with the kite in the thunderstorm. We considered the stream of electricity, and how water is the best conductor. In my journal, I described exactly how we set up our experiment and why I think it worked the way it did."

"Did you bring your journals?" I asked him.

"Just one. It's in the car. Why?"

"You probably don't know that I have a doctorate in physics. But I've never had the time or inclination to do battle with the portal. Knowing it existed satisfied me enough, being able to time travel, and using it to make a better world."

"That's just it, Ms. Barclay, or I should say, Dr. Barclay. You can't, I don't think. Using it changes the patterns of time. I don't know what changes take place, or how, but that's how I made the connection to the waves. I believe that use is cumulative, even over time."

"Ripples," Linda said.

"If the portal is used, even with no immediate change to the past, it sets off a chain reaction that scrambles reality as we know it."

"What about the paperclips?" Linda asked. "Fritz thought that only those that were in his desk when lightning hit the school would work."

Eric paused. "I don't think they matter, Ms. Russell. But they need to be exact where they're placed in order to make the connection work. I don't know for sure, but I had a box that I'd brought from home and they worked."

I took notes and recorded his every word. So far, he had explained a theory, in abstract. Linda was fixated on his description, and the president leaned on his hand, a pose I had seen for years. He wanted the whole story. So we listened.

"I think I've discovered a wrinkle that will let me go across those dimensions, and maybe even see things that might have happened but didn't. Like what would have happened if Lincoln hadn't been assassinated, or if we hadn't dropped the atomic bomb." Eric looked at each of us, while taking a slow drink. He gently set the glass down, as if not wanting to move its contents. "The day the lightning struck the school, track practice had been cancelled and I was about to take off my track shoes. They had metal cleats. When the lightning struck, the building shuddered. A wave, like a light beam shot across the floor. I didn't get a shock so much as a tingling feeling that ran up my whole body. Then it just went away. I had the same feeling when I opened my lab door and saw my younger self."

I asked him if he had gone in again.

"I can go into a portal I've created. I haven't tried outside my lab. I did go in. Twice. The same place both times." He looked me in the eye, his eyes mere slits. "With two different results."

"Where did you go, Eric?" the president asked.

"Ford's Theater." Eric put his hands on the table and made two fists. The president patted Eric's shoulder and asked him what happened. Eric slowly shook his head, reliving the moment.

"The first time, I saw when Booth fired and then jumped. I watched from the stage wings. He ran right past me."

Ashley had told me about one of Fritz's trips and how John Wilkes Booth ran by him. I asked Eric how he managed to have the same thing happen. He said that when Fritz had explained how the portal worked, he used the Ford's Theater book to show him about the paperclips. "I bought the same book. And I guess it carried the same energy because I had the same experience as Mr. R. I didn't know that before."

"And the second time?" the president asked. I noted the urgency in his voice. He wanted to hear the story all the way through, but he held his impatience in check. That wasn't new to me either.

"Before we tried it, we put the generator into the kiddie pool. I'd learned the lesson already so nothing was plugged in. The generator acted like a big rock, so we adjusted it until the power level produced only small, smooth waves. When I reached for the doorknob, the shock was stronger, and I couldn't let go. I pulled the door open, but this time, President Lincoln leaned out of his box, standing next to a soldier, and Booth was lying face down on the stage. Lincoln had spotted him and grabbed the gun. Then he and the soldier threw Booth all the way to the stage. People were running up the stairs and a crowd was forming back stage, so I just left. Someone said to get a rope."

"So the water in the pool took you to an alternate history," Linda said. "That means that someone in that universe changed their past, or present."

"Maybe," said Eric. "What if our history has been altered and Lincoln was supposed to live. Like I said before, I don't know what changes take place, or how they show up, but that's what I saw. I haven't tried since then."

Chapter 28

Linda

NO ONE COULD better understand Eric's obvious fear than I. Fritz never understood how much I dreaded something going wrong. And now, no doubt remains. Whatever had happened, Fritz and Ashley were lost somewhere in the past. Judging from the silence at the table, we were all processing Eric's story in our own ways. Jane and the president were staring out the window. Eric reached for his glass but only twisted it in its spot.

"I guess we have only one real question," said the president. "Eric, would you be willing to help us find them?" Eric raised his head and tilting toward the question, said he would, but he only had a few days and he wanted to know everything we had already discovered.

Jane repeated the story of the Thanksgiving search.

"Where are the books now?" Eric asked.

Jane told him that Ashley took them, wherever he had gone. But she had made a complete list and took pictures of the paperclipped pages for backup. "I didn't expect to need them."

"So no one here has the books?"

Jane continued her part of the story. She told him that when Ashley's disappearance was certain, she found copies in book stores and online and bought them. "I have them at home. Well, at Ash's house."

"Do you know what order they were in?"

"Yes. And the paperclips are outlined as close as I could make them to where they were that day. Should I go get them?" She asked Eric, but looked at the president.

He nodded but as she stood up, Eric said, "I can't do this now. My parents are taking me out, a sort of welcome home dinner. Could we do it tomorrow?"

"We can't use the school until later," Jane said. "But we can plan what you think you'll need to do."

"I want to look over the books before we do anything. I don't know if I can help or how long it will take. Today's Wednesday and I have to go back on Sunday."

"Then what's convenient for you?" I asked.

Eric suggested that he pick up the books first, and we could get together after school. "That way I can work out what I'll need when we go." Jane told him to follow her home and he would have them to browse when he had the time.

Chapter 29

Jane

I'VE BEEN DRIVING Ash's Mustang since he left. The new car smell has long been gone, but I can smell his presence, feel his warmth, as I sink deep into the leather seat. As I slid into the driveway, his "Home Sweet Home" rang in my memory. Yet, without him to say it, all I saw in front of me was another house. Eric parked at the curb.

In the past year, so much has happened. We've spent so much time apart, I almost wish I'd never said yes when he proposed. And now, I wait and wonder if we'll ever reach the altar. I'm not mad at him. How could I be? As important as my aunts' planning my wedding is to my mother, so is finding Fritz to Ashley. He wants, and maybe needs, Fritz to be his best man. Ash told me he was determined to find Fritz, or at least try, before the wedding. Twice now it's been postponed. Strange as it may seem, I'm really not worried. I have a feeling. When Ashley makes up his mind, things happen. So now, I'll wait until he comes home. But, I really miss him.

The tap on the passenger's window, Eric's face watching me, ended another day dream. It's only a few-minute drive from Linda's house, but I never cease to be amazed at what a brain can do in such a short run. We went inside to the stack of books on the kitchen counter.

"Let me get the file with the page pictures," I said.

"Dr. Barclay, before Mr. Gilbert went after Mr. R, did he tell you anything about how these books might tie to where Mr. R might have gone?"

I said, "We had had two long days of scouring the pages and recording his visit into the maze that Fritz left behind." I told Eric briefly what Ash had said, and his conclusion—Fritz didn't want to be found.

Chapter 30

Linda

CHRISTMAS HAD BEEN a bust. Other than TJ, the spirit of the season dissolved after Jane's strip act. With all I've seen with the portal, even that fit, although I'd have never guessed that she would do that. At least my father stopped arguing in front of her. I suspect Mom had a short and pointed chat with him.

Having Christmas here with my family might have been a bad idea. Mom hadn't been back home for a month. Daddy looked awful. He'd lost weight, and I'm sure the house needed work. But mostly, he didn't like being forced to confront his stupid comments. Jane put the final touch on Christmas morning but he'd started the fight, first with Joe and then everyone else.

Joe reminded him that Fritz had kept him out of prison and that if he'd kept his word, nothing would have happened to me. At home alone with him, I had said that the portal had affected everyone who encountered it. Joe had convinced me that I was wrong about Fritz. It made me sad when he left, but when Mom told me she'd be leaving, I felt abandoned. Instead of saying she'd be back, as she climbed into the car, she snarled, "Get to work."

I completed editing the books I'd been sent and told my publisher I'd let them know when to send more. Just after New Year's Day, Lois and I inspected the vacant shop and closed the purchase the next day.

To keep TJ close, I borrowed Ashley's duplicate swing and playpen, and told Jane we would be at the store most of the time. I hired a cleaning company to get the place ready for the contractor, and told them I planned to be open when February began. I had designed the sign years ago and the sign maker said he could have it ready. When TJ and I couldn't be on site, I followed my plan from home and ordered every item I needed. By the middle of the month, I began to set up the workshop. All my tools were where I had imagined they would be. Since high school. When the dream began to take shape.

Chapter 31

Ashley

"**THAT WAS WEIRD.** And you scared the hell out of him," I said. "And you followed my lead perfectly. The business card and 'call me in the morning.' I hope that was your cell. You're not going anywhere today."

Overnight snow had only begun when we reached the car, but with the wind, drifts covered major roads with more than a foot, constantly shifting, and falling more heavily now. But the coffee was hot, and we had nowhere we could go. The plows hadn't even attempted the side streets.

Turns out that the light we saw was a signal and we couldn't have been luckier to be where we were. Startled is too limiting a word to describe the light that lit us from behind. A man with a helmet-mounted spotlight and an automatic rifle told us not to move. We didn't.

When he walked around us, I didn't believe my eyes. Not a farmer chasing us off, but a soldier, fully armed, pointing his rifle at us.

"Tony, you're just the man I'm looking for," I said. He lowered his gun and pointed the flashlight.

"Do I know you?"

"You're Tony Almeida. Engineer. You're interested in time travel. I've come looking for you." I wished I could see his face, but the light in our eyes stayed put.

"I know who I am. Who are you and how do you know about me?"

"My name is Ashley Gilbert. I'm a time traveler and I need your help. This is Natalie Johnston, a writer for the local paper."

I had struck a chord. It took a minute while he processed what I'd said. "I don't know you, and almost no one knows about my time-travel interests. But you can't be here. My partner will be here in a minute." He pointed a thumb over his shoulder.

"Here's my card," Natalie said. He reached out to Nat and put the card in his pocket, turning to look behind him. "You'll see when you read it that I'm who it says. Call me in the morning."

"Why are you here?" he asked.

"Where's the airport?" I asked.

"How do you know about that? They haven't built it yet."

I grinned at him. "It's built already in my world. You are part of a team of time travelers who work with the president. You guys keep the world from going to war, save flood victims. That kind of thing."

"I exist in another world?"

"You're a hero in my world. That's why we came looking. I need your help."

"Look. You can't be here. I'll tell my partner you were out for a walk. But you have to wait until he's here."

"How did you know we were here?" Nat asked.

"You've crossed half a dozen signals. We spotted you at the entrance when you drove in. You passed infrared cameras all along the road."

In spite of the wind, the crunch of footsteps on the dead leaves was impossible to miss. Tony stepped to his partner, and we listened to their hushed voices.

"We'll take you back to your car. Don't come back. This place is hazardous," Tony's partner said. "We have your pictures. You only get one warning. If you come back, you'll be on a milk carton."

Although the comment sounded rehearsed, I had no doubt that he would be carrying out an order. I didn't ask if he'd ever had to make good on his threat.

"When do you think he'll call?" Natalie asked. All the way home, she asked one question after another. I shouldn't have been surprised. She asked questions for a living. When I got tired of saying that I didn't know, that fact registered. Thinking back to my previous relationship with her, my impatience with her simmered because she constantly asked one thing or another. Finally I understood why. And marveled at the way her brain worked.

I checked the time. I said he would probably wait until he could call without anyone getting suspicious. "He'll wait to call until it's likely you're at work."

"If all the roads are covered, he won't expect me to get to work until late, or maybe not at all. What should we do with him?"

"I don't know. Invite him here?"

"Want my opinion?" I told her I did. "Until we find out what he's all about in this world, meet him in a neutral place. The diner. Niko will put us in a quiet spot. Make it off-hours so we're not likely to be spotted or overheard."

"I'm concerned we'll be watched and then followed. I don't think it's safe to trust him yet. And we can't tell who he might have with him."

"I could ask Brian Shaw how to spot someone."

"We could meet him at school and use my classroom."

"Maybe Brian could keep an eye out for someone just hanging around. This is getting complicated."

"Ya think? And it's just getting started."

While we waited for the call, Nat showered and I made breakfast. While the bacon crisped, I glanced at my list. Maybe Tony had studied the real physics and could explain the best way to go after Fritz. When the toaster popped, Nat walked in, barefooted with red polish on her toes, her long brown hair wrapped in a towel, wearing a bathrobe. Mine.

"You're blushing. That's so cute," she said.

"You don't make it easy." She flashed a vixen grin, so comfortable in making me uncomfortable. I wished I could find out if I would be here permanently. I told her to eat her eggs.

I showed her the list I'd made up the day before, and she asked if I had a white board and erasable markers. How would I know? I asked. She pushed away from the table, the bathrobe barely covering, and bounced from the kitchen, the terrycloth flowing over her like a waterfall. She said she thought other me had one, and headed down the cellar steps.

"The board is here," she called as I joined her. "Where are the markers?"

"I think I saw them in the desk." I carried the board, and she picked up an easel. I went upstairs and in the desk were four different colored markers. What she had in mind I still didn't know. When I reached the bottom of the steps, she was on her tiptoes, holding the board and twisting something. I hadn't looked closely before, in either world, and I admired the picture of long legs and the lifted hem of the bathrobe. I cleared my throat, but she twirled and grinned.

"Go get dressed, Nat. Then you can tell me what you want with this thing." I had started to say "what you have in mind," but I didn't need that answer.

In seconds, she returned, glasses on, a pen in one hand and a notebook in the other, dressed in only her smalls. When she saw my grimace, she said, "I never wear clothes at home, so get used to it. Besides, it'll shut you up while I think." She began to draw boxes on the board, the options of what to do if I found Fritz. Although I read as she wrote, at eye-level, interfering with my direct view, a pair of light blue panties moved continually as she wrote, exercising a pair of shapely legs beneath a nicely rounded behind. Like she said, I kept quiet.

As I read her drawings, I grabbed my own notes to compare. She had left out one thing, the one that mattered most to me. How to open the portal home.

"Sorry. I couldn't call sooner, but other ears have been too close." Noon had passed a few hours before. "I'll be free but we're snowed in here." Tony had taken the bait.

Nat suggested we wait to meet until the roads were open, and asked if he had any days off. Friday all day, he said, starting at five o'clock Thursday afternoon.

"Friday is New Year's Eve," she said. "Do you have plans?"

"You mean like a date? Nah. Some of the guys are going to a place called The Mill, but I haven't said I'll go."

"Guys night out. I know the place. Doesn't sound like much fun." She mouthed 'The Mill' to me. "More storms are coming, so we need to be flexible. Call me back on Thursday when you're free. Do you have a car?"

"Not mine. I can walk to the main road once the plows clear it. Not the road you came in on." She wrote directions to his exit route and said she'd pick him up. Her car would be obvious. "Where are we going?"

"You'll see. Make sure you are not followed" Then, laughing, she said, "Or you'll be on a milk carton."

Snow threatened by week's end, but an efficient Riverboro road crew cleared my street by morning. Even the driveway entrance was unblocked.

"The same guy who works the street sweeper and picks up the leaves drives the plow. Other you gives him twenty bucks and a bottle of good rum every year so he doesn't have to shovel."

"I have to remember that."

"That'll mean you're still here."

"Here or there, it'll be worth it."

"I'll see you later." She reached up and pulled me close. "I hope you're here." A real kiss, which I didn't back away from, and she ran out the door.

With a couple of days left until we met Tony, I studied each of my options on her board, asking the 'what ifs' and finding new unanswered questions. Where did I think Tony would fit? If I explained what his twin in my world did, could he duplicate the connection? I needed to ask about his access to planes, but I had never asked how he had determined the altitudes or how many planes produced the necessary turbulence. Thursday morning, I bought a generator and a heavy-duty electrical cord. A long one. In the afternoon, I returned to reading the time-travel science, still searching for ideas on how to get home. I'm sure that what I read must be a fascinating discussion, but to me, completely foreign. One idea constantly popped as I tried to make sense of my quantum reading. Every article, every discussion, started with my old friend, Albert Einstein. Based on what my travels in this dimension had shown, Einstein would remember me, and maybe could help. But I needed a book about him.

I glanced at the clock, wondering if I had time to hit the bookstore, when the front door flew open. Wind blowing in tossed my notes around the living room. Nat held the storm door, her arms filled with packages and plastic bags.

"There's more in the car," she said. I started past her, but she pushed my chest, and said she'd get the rest, that I should open the door for her. I'd been so engrossed in my reading I hadn't noticed that the outside world had taken a stormy change. I opened the door as a gust yanked it. I stepped to the landing and pulled it shut behind us.

"The radio said gusts could be up to sixty miles an hour, bringing in two to three feet more snow by tomorrow night. I went shopping just in case."

"Did Tony call?"

"We're picking him up in an hour. We're not going to have a lot of time if the weather's changing."

I told her about my reading while we put the groceries away. She listened without comment, even when I said I had met Einstein. Something perturbed her.

Finally, she lifted only her eyes as she looked up. "Is there something wrong with me?" The insecurity of the question shown in her eyes, her long lashes framing the pretty brown eyes taking aim at me. My instinct to laugh vanished.

"No. Why?"

"Because you back off no matter how I approach. I just want to know if you find me unattractive."

This conversation required a serious answer, one where we took the time to talk, without a pending appointment. I told her to forget the groceries, and took her hand, leading her to the living room sofa.

"I don't have enough time to tell you everything now. But I promise we'll take all the time we need later. But let me get started so you can think about this." I told her she and I had dated in my time, and I had found every excuse to end it. "I'll tell you the whole story later, but Nat, there's nothing wrong with you. I sleep comfortably with you next to me. You're smarter than me, and I really enjoy seeing your mind at work. I can feel my blood racing when you prance around here in your underwear." She grinned, happiness glowing in her eyes. "I have a story to tell you when we're back. But you have to believe I mean it when I say I'm going home. And for that reason, I don't want a fling. I'll have to live with myself either way. And I don't want to hurt you. Or me." I helped her up from the couch and our hug tantalized. "And you have a cute ass. Now let's get Tony."

We arrived at the end of a long road that ended in a wooded backdrop. He paced at the side of the road, head down, a red scarf encircling his face. We'd taken both cars, so he'd recognize the yellow VW, and wouldn't be crammed into the back seat. I followed her to the diner and parked on her passenger side so he could see me as he got out.

His likeness matched the Tony I knew. Broad shoulders filled his coat, curly hair cut short but not too close to the scalp, intelligent dark eyes, and large hands, hidden within large gloves. I lagged a few steps behind as we all ran for the door.

"Hi, my name is Ashley Gilbert." I reintroduced myself and held out my hand. With a piercing stare, he looked me over before taking my hand. I'd been right, his large hand enveloping mine. The squeeze hurt a bit, but I think he could have broken my hand if he'd wanted. "Weightlifter?"

"Some. I bench..."

I interrupted. "Two twenty-five." His eyebrow arched, but he nodded. "So does your twin."

"What's this all about? You need my help?"

"Let's eat and then I'll show you. You don't have anywhere you have to be, right?" He repeated that he had Friday off. "Is anyone expecting to hear from you?" I watched his eyes. Without guile or deception, he said no.

"Good. Nat knows the whole story and we'll tell you everything."

"But you have to promise you won't tell anyone," she added. He looked closely at her, and I watched him scan her features. I thought, *typical guy*, but didn't blame him.

"For now, I'll promise not to mention you. But, when I know more, I reserve the right to change my mind."

She glanced at me. "Good enough. What you learn will depend on how smart you really are. What you say won't matter because nobody will believe you." Then she smiled and touched his hand. I didn't know if that made me jealous, but my blood heated up.

I paid the bill and stepped into a gust that made me take a step back. Nat and Tony walked around me and he took her arm to steady her. For once, the weatherman's prediction got it right. I followed the yellow blur, as Nat sped up and flew through a yellow light, as I hit my brakes. When I caught up, she had parked in the nearest spot to the school door, still blocked by snow.

Again, I parked beside her, and walked to the rear, and asked Tony for a hand. The generator wasn't too heavy, but cumbersome to lift. Before I could reach in, Tony grabbed it and set it in the snow pile.

"What's this for?"

"I'll explain inside." I reached for my keys, and he carried the machine. "Want help?"

"I'm fine. Just open the door." Nat grabbed the cord and shut the trunk, as I ran ahead and held the door. I told him to take it to the fourth door on the right and set it down. Snow from our shoes tracked to the door and melted in a small puddle.

We were set to begin, and I ushered them into the classroom, my classroom, Fritz's classroom. Tony took a seat, pushed the chair back, and demanded answers. "What's this all about?" he repeated.

I began, knowing full well that if I wanted his help, I needed to find out if he could help, and I needed to convince him that impossible was real.

"So here's the deal," I said. "I'm going to tell you my story, all of it. I'm going to ask that you keep an open mind because it sounds crazy. I'll also explain the mechanics of how it works. Then if you're on board, we'll find out if you can help. If not, I'll find another way."

"How what works?"

"That door, in the proper circumstances, opens a portal to the space-time continuum, and to multiple dimensions, I think. I've tried reading quantum physics and string theory, but I don't really understand it. Even the explanations for dummies are a foreign language. Math isn't my best subject." I read the doubt on his face. "So let me tell you the story." I started when Fritz first met Robert E. Lee. I skipped a few things, especially his friendship with the president.

Nat took notes as I told them what the portal had done, all the people we'd met, and finally how I came to be in this dimension.

"Not a different dimension," he said. "String theory is a great, though not total, explanation, because it leaves out the concept of multiple parallel universes. Einstein theorized time moving in waves. And that time can also reflect, like a mirror, the components of mass, because I think time is also energy. Wait, did you ever see sheet music?"

"Yes. Of course," Nat said. I nodded.

"Treble and bass clef. Ten parallel lines." He got up and drew them on the blackboard. "You can play individual notes, but when you combine the notes, and timing, on all the lines, you get Beethoven, or Chopin, or Mozart. Harmony. I think that's how the universes work together. And that's why we exist in different universes, different, like different notes, but also the same. The same note in different octaves."

"Do you imagine different universes in treble and bass clef?"

"I don't know. I've never thought about it."

I told him he should. When he thought about harmony, I asked, did he mean balance between good and evil, or just that everything fit together? Good question, he said. Then we discussed the mechanism, how the generator had recreated Ben Franklin's thunderstorm.

"Let me show you how we set it up."

We returned to the hall. I told him about needing an electrical connection to the doorknob and the air turbulence the planes caused to imitate the storm. Tony checked out the generator's output and its connections.

"Do you have jumper cables?" I didn't know, but Nat said she did. He plugged in the generator and when she returned, attached one cable to the neck of the doorknob, and tapping the other on the frame, sparks jumped. He touched the doorknob, but pulled back quickly.

"You'll need a buffer. Too much power here. You'd fry."

"Pull the plug, Nat," I said. "Let's get out of here, so we can talk."

With the school behind us, the generator back in my trunk, what to do with Tony headed the 'what's next' list. Snow blew sideways in a harsh wind. I asked Nat if she wanted me to drive Tony home. "We can talk on the way."

"I think I'll drop him off and then go home. I'll call you later."

As they drove away, I could feel snowflakes melt in my mouth, with a sour flavor.

New Year's Eve day, and Nat hadn't called or come by. Snow continued to climb anything it landed on, with more yet to come. I started to dial her up, but set the phone down. Now that Tony proved insufficient, I asked myself why I'd bothered. I'd been as kind to her as I could, while hoping this nightmare would end. And maybe connecting her and Tony here would mirror my world. The least I could do.

Returning to the lists, I hoped that spring would visit early and give me a head start. But a possible three or four more months prolonged the agony. I opened a calendar on my computer, looking for I didn't know what. With my search engine, I checked for any special events that might spur an idea. School began on Monday. Then, in a large headline, Inauguration Day.

On a new pad, I mimicked the computer and wrote January twenti-eth–first Black President. As strange to me, after the past eight years, as it would be to this world, I reminded myself to add the change to January as a discussion topic for my classes. I jotted a note to ask if Nat had a story in mind.

I read through the search listing for 2017. Anniversaries of historical events, births and deaths. We'd just passed the seventy-fifth anniver-sary of Pearl Harbor. We would mark the one hundredth anniversary of US entry into World War One, and a hundred and fifty years since the start of Reconstruction. I had a lot of reading to do. At least, other me had been thorough at some point in his career. I had his notes.

Before dressing to start shoveling, I opened a weather site to see what outside my igloo looked like. With more bad weather predicted, shoveling now meant less strain later. Dressed for the worst, I stepped on my front porch. In my world, the snow shovel would be leaning against the house behind the evergreens. The drifted snow covered the ground, leaving no sign of the shovel. I shook the snow off the bushes, and pushed the snow away, but still no shovel. I went to the basement. Not there either. Nat would know, so I called her, and got her voicemail.

As I hung up, the sound of a plow pulled me to the door. I watched it block my driveway. Then as the truck backed up and pushed it aside, I waved to the driver. He waved back and kept going. The scraping of the street, the sand and salt combo shooting from the back, opened a path for the putt-putting of Nat's car, turning into my driveway. Tony Almeida sat in the passenger's seat.

Tony climbed out and high-stepped around to help Nat through the drifts. I held the storm door, and apologized for not clearing the way.

"I don't know where the snow shovel is."

"Other you pays kids to do it. He couldn't be bothered. He walked through it if he had to go out. So relax, take your coat off." She grinned in a way that I hadn't seen before. "Make yourself at home." Tony had the same kind of grin.

Nat shook off the snow and took off her boots. Tony wore the clothes he had on last I saw him. Matter-of-fact in her next comment, she said that Tony had spent the night. The roads weren't cleared, so they went to her place.

"I thought you were going to call."

She glanced at Tony. "We got talking and all of a sudden, it was really late. Sorry. But we're here now."

"I noticed."

"We talked about how to hook up the generator so you don't get a jolt."

"Without the turbulence, the planes, it won't matter. So we'll have to wait."

Tony interrupted, which annoyed me. "I'm in a place where I may be able to get the real storm analysis, and maybe I can calculate the natural turbulence you need. If we can bypass the electrical part artificially, with the generator, maybe all we need is a windy day."

"We?"

"Yeah, I'm in. Even if it doesn't work, the possibility that it does is too tempting. I've speculated about time travel all my life. Natalie convinced me that you're on the level, and she said you had been looking for me specifically."

"Maybe I'm wrong."

"Ashley, only my sister and her husband know that story. They think I'm nuts. Never told anyone else. You two are the only ones, and you already know that I have some role in this adventure. So, I'm in."

Good thing we had food because the snow deepened. We spent the day reviewing the notes, the white board, the books, and I told him Fritz's story. By early evening, they were both filled with the entire portal history.

"You guys are real heroes," Tony said, after asking about the president and who they were going to see for the next four years. "I hope he doesn't need you here."

"Me too."

When the plow came by again, Nat opened the door and told the driver to wait. She grabbed her coat and boots and stomped out. While she was gone, Tony asked if she and I were dating. He said he didn't see a ring, but he didn't want to butt in.

"I think she's gorgeous, and smart, and funny," he said.

"Right on all counts. Truth be told, I'm not sure what our situation is. But I'll tell you this, if you're interested, you better do something about it. 'Cause if I'm stuck here forever, I'm grabbing her first."

"Well, I am stuck here, so all's fair."

"Then may the best man win. If I find a way home, be sure to watch out for my other self. He's not a nice guy like me."

When Nat came in, she said the main roads had been cleared and sanded, but the plows would be back when the snow started again.

"Tony, get your coat. Happy New Year, Ash. I'll talk to you tomorrow." They ran to her car, and waited for the plow to turn around. Nat had told the driver she would follow him out to the main drag.

I guessed my relationship with Natalie had reached the end. I spent what survived of the evening gathering her belongings, packing her carry-all, cleaning out her cosmetics from the bathroom. I assumed she'd want it all back. New Year's Day I parked in front of the TV and watched the bowl games until I hated football, and then read. The sun returned and so did the kids looking for snow to shovel. I didn't care that they wanted sixty bucks, only that my driveway was open, my walks free of snow and that I could finally get out of the house. Nat hadn't called.

New Year's night, as I scanned my notes for the next day's classes, a soft tapping on my front door lifted me from the kitchen chair for the first time in a few hours. Sheepish and embarrassed, and even though she had a key, Nat waited for me to ask her in.

"Hi."

"Hi, Ash."

"I packed your stuff. I figured you'd be needing it."

"That's not why I'm here. I want to explain."

"You don't have to. Tony may not fit into solving my dilemma, but he seems smitten with you. Maybe I've done something right." Her quizzical look called for an answer, but I doubted I had one adequate enough.

"So you're dumping me?" she asked.

That caught me off-guard. "You haven't called or texted me. I figured you had left. Dump you? I guessed that you'd decided that I wasn't a risk worth your time."

"You're an idiot."

"So I've been told."

"Ashley, you said you had a story to tell me. Tell me now."

Another surprise, another direction. A brief thought ran through my mind. *Wimmens.* I shook my head. I led her to the sofa and began the uncomfortable history of the me she didn't know. When I finished, she gripped my hand, and whispered, "You know, you're doing it again. Walking away."

"Nat, I don't expect to be here, and I don't want a guilty conscience when I get home."

"What about what I want? It's not like I don't know the risk. What if I'm willing to chance it, in case you don't get home."

"What about Tony? He's certainly interested."

"We had a couple of long talks. I tried to find out how far we can trust him. He's nice, he's cute, and he's easy to manipulate. But I can't see him being any help. He can hook up the generator, but that's about it. He has no access to the president or the air force. So we're on our own." An endearing smile met my eyes.

Pajamas on the floor and coffee waiting began my trek through Monday. I looked out the living room window at the heaps of dirty snow the plow had left at the curb. At least, I didn't need to shovel first, so I stood awhile admiring Mother Nature's gift, a white blanket covering the spring flowers that would visit in the not-too-distant months ahead. As a kid in New England, winters rarely meant school closings, but always meant snowmen, snowballs and skiing. I shook off the nostalgia, and hurried to school. George was waiting for me when I walked in.

"Just wanted to remind you that you have Rachel and Nicole to deal with today. I've put them together in all their classes, and told their other teachers to come to you with any problems they cause."

"Thank you, George. I'm looking forward to it."

He began his hike to redness, and said, "It'll be your head, not mine. By the way, I looked at their records. They both get high test scores and good grades, in spite of how they act. Surprising."

"Not to me. I'll let you know how it goes. But I'm doing it my way. It's my head after all."

I had spent part of the holidays looking for a way to keep my classes animated, while I met George's requirements. The questions on the board had worked, so I kept them going, making them specific to each class. Then I added homework. My first class let me know I struck the right note. They hated the idea. The first question on the board was "When did the end of colonialism begin, and what factors made colonialism last?" Most of them didn't know what colonialism was, so we started with Gandhi and India.

"Now you know why you have more homework. You'll need to read about Gandhi and tie him to Europe and the American Revolution. And, by the way, we'll have a quiz every Friday. So do the reading." 'If looks could kill,' the saying goes. I'm sure they'd be unique in the ways I would die.

Second period, my first encounter with Nicole and Rachel began with attitudes. I smiled when I told them they needed to come back after school. A certain glee found its way around the class, after having been disrupted by the two girls.

"I have a doctor's appointment. I can't come," said Rachel.

"Not anymore. I spoke to your father and told him you'd be here."

"You knew you were giving me detention?"

"Let's say you didn't disappoint me."

Nicole was smirking. "I can't come either. I have..."

"No you don't. It's been cancelled. I spoke to your mother. So I'll see you both after school. No more than three minutes after the last bell, or you'll be here tomorrow. Understand?"

They looked at each other, grimacing, realizing they were both in the same boat. Shooting bullets from their eyes, they left, no doubt wishing me dead. When the final bell ended the school day, I sat at my desk, which I hadn't done all day. Before I had a chance to look at my next day's schedule, two teachers walked in.

"Don't tell me, Rachel and Nicole."

Joe Rosenberg nodded and Barb Lucas grimaced. She said, "George told us to see you, Ashley. That this was your idea."

Joe said, "We've all tried to avoid them for four years, but both, together? We'll have a war."

"Stick around. They'll be here in just a minute. You'll see. I have an idea, and maybe we can gang up on them." The door opened again, and this time, Shelley Rapstein and Ben Cumber walked in, followed by their nemeses. "Right on time, girls. Good call. Take a seat."

"You didn't talk to my father," Rachel said.

"Or my mother," Nicole added.

"Good. They did what I asked. They didn't know anything about it, did they?" I chuckled, just enough to make them curious.

"Ashley," Ben said, "I needed to talk to you about them." He pointed his thumb over his shoulder.

"You all do. So let's not waste any of your time. They're mine now. Rachel, Nicole, for the rest of the year, you and I will be spending a lot of time together. But before I tell you what we're going to be doing, your teachers will tell you why they're here right now. Ben, tell them why you need to speak to me."

"This should be between us."

"Why? The problem is with them. You have a captive, and I choose that word specifically, audience." He almost cowered, as if he'd never confronted a student before. "Did they disrupt your class today?"

"Yes. We were discussing Hawthorne. The Scarlet Letter. We ended up in a discussion about women's rights, and how horrible a writer Hawthorne is, was."

"He's terrible," said Rachel. "Why do we have to read that crap? With millions of good books, Mr. Gilbert, all we did was say that the book portrayed women as criminals, not as victims of the male society norms at the time. Hester Prynne would be a suffragette in another time. She'd probably be an abolitionist, and a feminist. That's a pretty important discussion, if you ask me."

Nicole chimed in, "And if you want to teach about romantic literature, why not read Jane Austen instead. She's no more boring than Hawthorne."

"Because the curriculum is American literature and that's what I'm supposed to teach," Mr. Cumber answered. "Do you think teachers always like the material? We don't have a choice." He shouted the last sentence.

I turned to Ms. Rapstein. "What about you, Shelley. What do you want to say to them?"

"Only that they shouldn't make fun of people who have trouble with French words. We don't use it every day, so tenses and even pronunciation can be difficult."

Nicole jumped on her. "Jack didn't do the reading over vacation, and Gail doesn't ever do your grammar homework. Ever. She's only taking French because her parents made her. She wanted to take Spanish, so she can work in Acapulco next summer. And we have to put up with that." She stood up and, in clear, fluent French, told her teacher that her class was dull, and that the work wasn't worth the reward. Ms. Rapstein put her hand over her mouth, and I couldn't tell if she was shocked or angry, or both, because I had no idea what Nicole said.

"That sounded like French to me," I said.

Rachel answered, translating, her teacher's hand remaining over her mouth, firmly in place. I asked how she knew. She told me she had a language program on her computer. "So do I," said Nicole.

"Which one do you use?"

"Fluenz."

"Me too. What one are you on?"

"Level four."

"Me too." The two enemies quietly eyed each other, while we teachers watched, furtive glances passing between us. I asked Barb Lucas if she had something she wanted to say.

Still mesmerized by the previous exchange, she said, "Only that I wish you would both stop talking in class."

"Ms. Lucas, I'm sorry about that," said Rachel. "I was arguing about the formula with Bob. Until you told us what it was. Then I stopped. I was right and he got mad."

"Joe, do you have something you want to say?"

"Just that when we're doing experiments, I want everyone to stay seated. Some things are dangerous in the lab."

Nicole looked at the ceiling. "Mr. Rosenberg, you really should watch what *your* students are doing. I hit Tom because he was turning the gas on and off when you were writing on the board. Steve was about to light a match, so I pulled the box out of his hands. I don't know about you, but I didn't dress for an explosion today."

Rather than wait for Joe to respond, I asked the teachers if they wanted to say anything more. They all said no, so I said I'd see them tomorrow. When the girls stood up, I said, "Not you. We have more to discuss." The door closed behind the teachers and I asked if they wanted a soda. Nicole shrugged and Rachel said sure, so I told them to follow me. Behind a bush just outside, I had left a small cooler, out of sight and buried in the snow. A couple of steps in and out, and now I had them without interruption. I took cups from my bottom drawer, and told them to sit.

"You won't need ice. Let's talk about what you can do for me." I asked them about themselves, about what they're plans were for college, and why they had such bad reputations among the teachers and staff.

Rachel went straight to the point. "Mr. Gilbert, school's boring. Half the time, no one does homework, or participates. When so much is happening in the world, you'd think the teachers would talk about some of it. I think I know more than they do. At least about some things, but they all seem to get lost with the kids who don't care."

"I've been taking classes at the community college. Since last year. Stuff I can't get here. I could teach the teachers some things about computers, and all the new apps that we can get on our phones. It pisses me off not being able to use phones in class. They think we're not paying attention. Think of all we could add to discussions if we could." Rachel's frustration reflected on Nicole's face.

"Then explain to me why you two tried to kill each other only a couple of weeks ago."

"That's personal," Nicole said, glaring at Rachel.

"Bullshit. You were trying to steal my boyfriend."

"Bullshit, yourself. I was just talking to him."

"He told me what you said."

I stepped in. "This isn't why you're here. But we'll get that straightened out too."

Nicole asked, "Then why are we here? I want to go home."

"Me too."

"I need two seniors to be my assistants. I want you both to help me. I hand-picked you because I know that you're both smart, and that you have a lot of influence, good and bad, on a large number of kids."

"Doing what?" Rachel asked, her belligerence mixed with curiosity.

"Class preparation, test grading, liaising with teachers and Mr. McAllister, and coordinating a major project, and we don't have much time."

"What project?" Nicole asked.

"The history baseball tournament. This one needs to be a success. I need more questions, I need to get the kids and teachers involved. My tenth graders need guidance to organize, in and out of school."

"They started over vacation," Rachel said.

Nicole said, "A bunch of stores downtown refused to display their signs. I heard they tried going door-to-door to raise money for a scholarship, but that didn't work either."

"I'll have to check into that. Look, I'm not asking you to volunteer. I'll pay you both a hundred dollars a month until graduation, but you'll need to work together. If one or the other doesn't do it, neither of you get paid. Now, do we have a deal?"

"What if I say no?" Nicole asked.

"Are you testing me?" She looked at my face and could tell I wasn't kidding. "If you say no, you can expect to be in detention every day until the end of school. That work?"

"Both of us?"

"Five of your teachers were here only a few minutes ago. Do you really think they won't join me? Do you both think you can behave so perfectly every day that one of us won't find a reason? Think about it."

After a minute of silence, where they glanced back and forth, Nicole said, "You drive a hard bargain, but here's my offer. Instead of paying me, pay me each week with weed."

"Not a chance. That guy is no longer here."

"I'll do it," said Rachel. "Come on, Nicole. We already run this place. Between us, we might get something done." Then she looked at me. "Mr. Gilbert, do you think we might be able to get something done about what they make you teach?"

"I don't know, but I think you'll have a lot of fun trying, and you'll make some people very uncomfortable. I might know someone who could help you. Now go home and tell your parents I said thank you."

Chapter 32

Fritz

CHRISTMAS BEHIND BARS, but almost certainly not the only day. Kate had left, all except her words, which I could recite from memory. I shoved the note out of my conscious mind. Because of the holiday, my lawyer, who'd been promised, hadn't shown up and no one could decide what to do with me. The Feds wanted me, but McNamara, or more probably, Flynn, had created a tidy jurisdictional snafu, keeping me here. I'm not sure why, but I trusted Flynn, my wild-haired, red-headed guardian angel, to look out for me. The image of him as a tree topper brought a momentary smile.

For most of the eight years I've been here, I've ignored Christmas. With no concept of time in my other life, I had abandoned all contact, but my mind still held the memories. I only remember one Christmas with TJ but he'd grow up comfortably. Tim Miller would see to it. I put him back in the vault and locked it. A quick glimpse of Linda and she went with him.

Over the years, I'd worked as many holidays as I could. Avoiding happy people had helped. *I should have gone with Kate.* Just as I had found a new life, with friends, my past caught up. *Put it away, Russ.* Down the hall, the clang of a cell door opening helped. The footsteps were too many. Tim McNamara and another man stared in.

"Merry Christmas," the man said. Tim opened my door. "My name is Michael X. Corcoran. I'll be your attorney." The short and balding man stepped past Tim, who grinned at me, as the cell lock clicked back into place.

"Nothing better to do?"

"I'm Jewish. So, no. Flynn Connolly asked me to look in on you." He handed me his business card. Removing a yellow pad from his brief-case, he said, "Tell me in detail who you are. Flynn's already told me his version."

"An Irish Jew. On Christmas. What could be more ironic? What do you want to know?"

He pulled the chair over from the corner, sat and leaned in to whisper. "Flynn wants you kept away from the Feds until after Inauguration Day. After that, the heat should die down. I need to know every-thing, so I can have a plan for court tomorrow. Judge Sweeney and I have crossed paths many times, and I think he'll be cooperative. But he's hoping for a bump to a Federal court, so I'll have to be persuasive."

"Get ready to write. I've got a long tall tale to tell. My name used to be Fritz Russell. I'm a time traveler."

"That's a good start. Your name now is?"

"I use the name Russell Furst."

"Ah, so you're 'Russ.' I've been told a lot about you. Flynn's tale lacked specificity. Now tell me the rest."

For the next couple of hours, I talked and he wrote. He got Tim to bring us sodas and sandwiches, and he continued to write, the pad resting on his thighs.

"So did you really shoot the Kopplers, or is this a very imaginative story?"

"Take your pick, counselor. You saw the picture of me. They say it's me, but I don't seem to look any different, eight years later. The weapon doesn't exist. I doubt the so-called eyewitnesses could identify me. But no matter, I'm stuck here, in this cell, in this universe. And I can't be like E.T. and call home."

"Do you want to go home?"

"I left home to put an end to the Kopplers. They were the worst kind of animals—ruthless, deadly and above the law. I didn't expect to go home. But I didn't expect I'd change the world either."

"You didn't answer my question."

"A few weeks ago, I might have said yes. Now, I'm not sure."

"And Kate is the reason?"

"Yup. And Flynn. And the rest. It's like I've found a new family."

"And maybe a woman who cares about you?" I raised my head to see him staring. "She does, you know. I had a long talk with her before she left. I always go to the airport with her. Just in case. But don't tell Flynn."

"I don't expect to be seeing him. Don't worry."

"You'll see him tomorrow. He'll want to know what the judge decides and he'll be ready to do whatever he needs to do. Kate will want to know."

"So what am I supposed to do?"

"I'll be back early tomorrow with my suggestions. My goal is to keep you here. We go to court at 11 AM."

"What about bail?"

"If you get bail, the Feds get you the minute you step outside. I'm sorry, but there's no other way. But we need to convince the judge. I'm sure that between Flynn and me, we'll succeed. Do you want anything? I'll see what I can do."

"How about some books. Paper and pen."

"What books?"

"How about this week's New York Times best sellers, three or four. Or a Civil War book."

"I'll try. Maybe one at a time. I'll talk to Tim."

"All right, counselor. See you tomorrow."

"Call me Mickey. After all, I am Irish."

With nothing more to do after he left, I started making a list, of course, outlining the activities available to me. Never having experienced the luxury of jail, accessible distractions came to me slowly. I tried to remember all the movies and books about prison life I'd seen or read. Even the Count of Monte Cristo and Cool Hand Luke had other people around. I didn't know if I did.

"Is anyone else here?" I thought I heard a grunt. "Hello?" The clank of a key in a lock vibrated down the hall, preceding Tim McNamara's arrival. "Is anyone else in here, Tim?" He shook his head, and handed me a legal pad, and a felt-tipped marker. "You're kidding, a marker?"

"Rules. No sharp points. You can't attack or kill yourself with that."

"And you think either of those is likely?"

"Probably not. But we don't take chances anymore. A long time ago, one of the academic intelligentsia killed himself with a pencil. Stabbed himself in the neck and laid down on the cot. The pillow absorbed the blood. We found him too late. Since then, markers."

"I'd never thought about that."

"Neither had we. He was a writer. We didn't consider him a threat. Dinner will be along shortly."

"You got anything up front I can read?"

"Besides the girlie mags? I'll look around. Sorry, Russ. It's just how we do things."

The smell of cigarette smoke wafted in. I hadn't had a smoke for a couple of days, so I asked. He shook his head again. I had quit, the last time, before Linda and I got married. Another place, another time. Maybe this time I could do it again.

After what could have been a frozen dinner of holiday portions of turkey and gravy, stuffing, peas and carrots, with some kind of berry-topped cake, I began to write my list. With nowhere to go, an exercise regimen would at least keep me busy, and perhaps put a little tone back in my body. I hadn't done push-ups or sit-ups in years, and I could walk and run in place. All my time on my feet made my legs less of a concern, but they hadn't been pushed hard either. Without a watch, I couldn't time anything, so I decided to do as much as I could for as long as I could each day. At least I had a plan.

Once dinner had settled, setting a baseline occurred to me. First, push-ups. I did eighteen. Sit-ups. Twenty-three. I did forty leg thrusts.

I counted to two hundred running in place. Dinner didn't like any of it, and told me so.

When day one of my new workout ended, and my dinner resumed its position, I sat with the pad, thinking about writing something, anything, to kill time. In my former life, I'd started to write a history book, but my life had changed. Instead of a history teacher, I'd graduated to jailbird, a prisoner of my own misguided passion. Maybe an autobiography? I couldn't help but chuckle at the twist, a true story that would be read as fiction. At that moment, I wanted a book. Just to have an idea of where to start. Tim came by again to announce lights out, blessing me with the almost-dark that carried me away from my dubious literary future.

I rose early and waited for the lawyer. The cop on duty ignored my questions, my requests to take a shower. He wouldn't even tell me the time. I remembered from the movies that jail time was slow. Doing nothing made it sloth-paced. I thought of exercising, but moving reminded me that I had abused my body, first by not exercising, and then by trying to get in shape in one night.

The bang of cell doors opening and closing, then footsteps, had me at the bars straining for a view. Another face preceded Corcoran, Flynn Connolly in a three-piece suit and dour countenance. When they were in and the cop had left, I asked to hear the plan.

"Russ," Flynn began, "sorry for this. I am. I had no time. At least, we can control things better."

"Not now, Flynn. We need to get him prepped," Mickey said.

"I need some food, some aspirin, a smoke, and a shower." My nose wrinkled at my smell. "And a watch. What time is it?"

"Seven," said Flynn. "We have clothes for you up front."

"We'll get to that," Mickey said. "We don't have a lot of time, and you need to get cleaned up. They will move you in two hours, and then we wait."

"I do a lot of that."

He flashed a silly grin and said, "Here's the plan."

I arrived at the courthouse shortly after nine. Soon after, Mickey joined me in a holding area. "The judge is grumpy this morning. He's moved you up on the schedule. He wants your case processed before the reporters are awake. The prosecutor is a new kid, and she'll be trying to score points. You have to do exactly what I told you."

"Tell them the truth, I know. I don't know what they're talking about."

"Then I'll move for dismissal. We won't get it. Then I'll ask for bail. We won't get that either. Then he'll set a trial date. But no matter, you have to follow the script."

Rows of unoccupied benches greeted my arrival in the courtroom. Not like the movies, with all the seats full, everyone on edge. In the back row, three elderly women chatted. I thought the judge must have his own groupies. My handcuffs were removed, but as I shook the circulation back in my hands, the officer slapped the cuffs on again, attaching me to the table.

"Is that necessary?' Mickey asked.

"Judge's orders." I glanced back and forth. Mickey shrugged.

The bailiff called the case, the judge returned to the courtroom, everyone stood, and he stared at me. He read the charges and asked how I would plead. Mickey elbowed me and whispered, "You're on."

"Your honor, you have the wrong guy. I'm innocent. I wasn't even here when those men were shot."

"Mr. Corcoran, this is inappropriate."

"Sorry, your honor, but he has a point. I've seen no evidence other than a blurry picture. I move to dismiss."

"Not quite yet, counselor. Mr. Furst, how did you come to be in this situation?"

"Your honor, I'm a time traveler, and I'm stranded here, unable to get back to my universe."

The judge gave a snort, holding back a laugh. "Mr. Corcoran, Miss Wellesley, approach the bench."

"It's Pennington, your honor. I went to college at Wellesley."

"Whatever." He waved the lawyers to the front.

"Mr. Corcoran, did you tell him to say that?"

"No, your honor."

"I'm not dismissing. That was the wrong answer."

"What about bail?"

"Your honor," said Wellesley, "this is a capital case. The people request you deny bail."

"The guy's a fruitcake, not a murderer, your honor."

"If he's a time traveler, Mr. Corcoran, he's a flight risk," The judge said, holding in his amusement. "No bail. We'll have him see a shrink. I'm setting a trial date for the end of March."

"Yes, Your Honor."

"Thank you for seeing our position, sir," said the prosecutor.

I hadn't noticed the young man with the notebook until he headed out after the details made the record official.

"Who's he?" I pointed as the man reached the door.

"A reporter," Mickey said. "He's got a scoop. The police have arrested a time traveler." Then he laughed.

"What's so funny?"

"We got what we wanted. You stay here. The judge will keep the Feds away. You just need to be patient for a few months."

"Are they going to put me somewhere else?"

"Probably. You'll be safer with people around. I'll arrange, or rather Flynn will, for a comfortable environment, with people watching out for you. And I'll be there to see you regularly. The prosecution doesn't have a case, so you behave, and you'll be fine. By March, they'll have other things to do."

"Can I have visitors?"

"You mean will Kate come see you? I'll have to talk to Flynn."

They moved me that afternoon from the local lockup to a small county jail, with about a hundred prisoners and a cell to myself. When the powers that be learned of my background, I found myself assigned to the kitchen, where I quickly made friends among the prisoners and the guards. In only two days, they asked if I would make waffles for the guards.

"Get me what I need and sure, no problem."

The jail population, my roommates, had been subjected to institutionalized crap for breakfast. After a few days of waffles, I convinced the guards to let me improve everyone's mood. So instead of oatmeal and runny eggs, I revised the menu, enhanced the oatmeal, added French toast and cooked-to-order eggs. I spotted a handful of potential helpers, guys who knew their way around a kitchen, and cooked and taught my way through the meals. Breakfast became the best meal of the day.

When the warden showed up on the sixth day, he invited me to join him. A nice gesture, I thought. When I sat down, he said, "I hear good things about you, but you're killing my budget. So I'm moving you out of here."

"If I may, sir, I can show you a way to make the costs go down. If you look at how much food ends up in the trash at night, because it's lousy, that's where your budget can be tightened. I'll bet you have less trouble with the prisoners during the day already. A good meal to start the day, and something to look forward to at night, that'll keep things calm. That's what you really want, isn't it? Look, I've begun training five guys at breakfast who will be able to find real work outside when I'm done. That's got to be a good reflection on how you run this place."

He put his hands together, his fingertips touching. He licked his lips, while I waited for his answer. He lifted his right eyebrow, creasing his forehead. Until that moment, I hadn't noticed how quiet the hall had become. Two guards sat next to me, two on either side of him. A short glance around revealed that all eyes were on me. Only a few men were even eating.

"Your waffle's getting cold. Would you like another?"

"You're an enigma, Mr. Furst. I'm usually able to tell when one of you is BSing me."

"I'm not." I surprised him when I turned to the kitchen and pointed to the warden's plate. One of my helpers nodded and in moments, a new plate, with small pitchers of melted butter and syrup were placed in front of him.

"I don't like my cooking to go in the bin. So what do you say? Do we have a deal?"

"I'll give you two weeks. I want a full accounting of costs, man-hours, and what goes to waste."

"Can I keep my guys and get some more?"

"I'll talk to Mr. Roscum. Don't know if you've met him. He's the supervisor of guards. He'll come see you." He grinned in a way that reminded me of Shawshank, and I wasn't sure I liked what he said. "And I want to give my wife you're recipe."

I returned his grin with a subtle snarl. "If everything goes as I expect, I'll give you the recipe when I leave. But you can eat one anytime. Just let me know."

"You think you're negotiating? With me?"

"No sir. I'm making promises." I stuck my hand out. He stared at it, glanced at me, and then shook it. I hoped I could get my guys a better life. "Anyone else want a waffle?" The four guards looked at the warden. With an almost undetectable nod from him, all four said they did. I lifted my arm, and drew a circle in the air with my index finger. The clank of plates and silverware, and four waffles emerged within seconds. The guards even said thank you. I was as close to home as I could get.

I met with the warden twice in the following two weeks. The first time, I showed him my training program plan. By adding men to the kitchen, I had the help I needed, and the jail had fewer men with idle hands. I gave him a list of price differences from the food suppliers. The vendors told him that they were told to sell better quality goods at a lower price. I didn't tell him that Flynn had visited each company. I hadn't asked how he had persuaded them.

At the second meeting, I showed him a detailed report of everything that I'd accomplished. I handed him a letter from Mr. Roscum, who mentioned that his labor costs had decreased, with less overtime and fewer absences.

"What happens when you leave?"

"Each day, you get newbies. Give them all to me for a couple of days, and let me sort them out. Warden, most of these guys are kids, and minorities. Have you looked at the kitchen lately?"

"No."

"They start each meal in clean whites. The guys in the laundry want them looking good, so the food stays good. The place has probably never been as clean, or polished. I have an assistant in charge of each meal. They all know you're watching–I keep telling them."

"And?"

"And most of them haven't eaten this well in their lives. Good taste, good nutrition, variety. They're working as a team, helping each other. They've bought in. None of them want a newcomer to screw it up. And I keep reminding them to check computers for short order cooks and chefs. They see the money they can make outside. No one's ever tried to guide them before."

"And you think this will continue when you're gone? I doubt it."

"This is a transient population. Some of these kids are headed for hard time. I'll do the best I can to keep them moving along. But you could help too. Help them in the courts with good reports. Help them get jobs. Get the schooling and skills they need when they're out of here."

"You're a dreamer. This is supposed to be punishment."

"It can be rehabilitation. Turn them now, make them productive. Give them a reason not to want to be back here."

"You really are an alien."

I'd been working seven days a week, from 5:30 in the morning to 9:30 at night. Only the new guys didn't know me, and pretty soon, everyone did. Even the toughest, hardest characters would give me a nod or a wave when we passed. As the population turned over, I even got hugs, guy hugs, from my crew as they left. I asked them all to let me know where they landed. And I asked Mickey to help where he could.

Winter had been long, and spring took its time getting here. We had a new president, and one of my crew even got a job in the White House kitchen, thanks to a letter one of my guys had sent to his cousin. But my time here had an expiration date.

The first rumble of thunder and a lightning flash brought me back to that day two years earlier by the calendar, when Ash and I were playing hoops. For me, almost nine years had passed. I drove those days out of my head. I'd been so busy, so absorbed that even Mickey's visits went on with him talking and me thinking about my work. When he arrived with a suit, a white shirt and accessories, I began to worry about leaving. I'd had no visitors, not even Flynn. Just Mickey.

The suit didn't fit as it had in December. My exercising had put muscles back, and my waist must have shrunk. I didn't remember when I last needed my belt on the last hole. The jacket pulled tight in the arms and across the back.

"You look good, Russ. Jail agrees with you."

"Not funny." But he had a point. I hadn't left yet, but I would miss the guys, and the routine.

"Let's see if we can end this nonsense today. The Feds are drooling to get their hands on you."

"Still?"

"Apparently, the new president is interested in time travel."

Chapter 33

Ashley

I SENSED THAT I'd nearly reached the top of a high hill, about to see into the distance, to know how my journey would continue. Or end. School slipped into familiar routine that made waiting tolerable. I had succeeded in changing my new world to suit my worldview. If I were truly and forever stuck here, life wouldn't be so bad, except that a possible abrupt end still lingered. The girls had proven to be assets, as well as great organizers. It occurred to me that possibly some traits were ingrained, no matter what universe people lived in. Even George remarked how the atmosphere had changed.

Despite record-setting snowfalls, winter loosened its grip. The poet said, "Can Spring be far behind?" And the day came when the hint of green arrived, replacing the no-longer-welcome snow. My focus each morning became the weather, not the news. Two problems continued at the forefront. Finding Fritz came first, which undoubtedly would bring new issues. The other, Natalie, who had remained steadfast in her support and her lack of demands. I couldn't argue, even with myself, that she had been a welcome partner in almost all our daily routines. Only nighttime pushed my resolve, often to outer limits.

By mid-March, the weather began to turn in our favor, everywhere else, but not in Riverboro. Evening or weekend storms provided the only safe entry, but only for short periods. At last, on the day before Saint Patrick's Day, we had a chance to try it out.

As soon as night cleared the streets, Nat and I headed for school. By the time we reached the parking lot, the skies had opened full throttle. No way to avoid a soaking, we ran across the lot and waved to the police car. Nat had called Brian Shaw, telling him we were coming and that he should keep the parking lot secure. He said he'd take care of it himself.

Satisfied that all the talking, reading and analyzing led to one conclusion, I put Koppler's book on my desk, checked the paperclip to be sure it took me into deep foliage, and I tapped the doorknob. Nothing.

"Did you do everything?" Nat asked.

I looked through the window. My keys glinted at me from the desktop. "No. Keys." With the one last step complete, I tried again, and a weak buzz tingled my fingers. Used to a bigger zap, I worried that the connection wouldn't last. I explained that I would inch inside and look around.

As soon as I crossed the threshold, a pulse ran through my body. I was in the right place. The three men who had been shot were standing less than fifty feet away. I double-checked the portal. The fluorescence glowed weaker than any I'd seen, but I knew Fritz had to be near.

"Fritz, where are you?" A rustle of bushes to my left led me to an answer. What I saw made me want to run in the opposite direction. A translucent figure, Fritz's ghost, moved toward me.

"What are you doing here?"

"Looking for you. I know you intend to shoot them, but if you do, you change history across dimensions."

"I know. You're looking at me in my past, like a memory, in a different universe."

"I came to get you out."

"You can't do it here. Not now. I don't know how you found the bridge between universes, but that's the only way you could have found me. You need to come to my present."

"You can see your timeline?"

"From here I can. If you get stuck now, everything will change again. You need to move the paperclip. March 2017. Look for newspapers in Washington DC. A story about arresting a time traveler named Russell Furst. Now get out of here. Now! Go!"

"Good to see you, Fritz. Hopefully soon again."

My abrupt arrival in the hallway, my face pale, started questions. Chief Shaw had joined Nat, so I asked them to give me a chance to think about what had happened.

"You found him, didn't you?" Nat asked, sitting in a chair in my classroom.

"Yes and no. This is going to be more complicated than we thought." I closed my eyes and related my trip, as close to word-for-word as I could. When I finished, a click from Nat's hand turned off her recorder. Having a record made telling the story easier. "I think we need Tony's hookup to keep the portal live once it's open. The storm makes the turbulence to replace the planes, but once I'm inside, I think we can keep it open if we keep it electrified."

Rumbling in the distance told me I might have a chance to go again. We needed to figure out where. I thumbed through the book. At the time of publication, the Koppler brothers were alive. Fritz knew where to go, but where in the book would the paperclip need to be placed? I told Nat and Brian that the next step might take a few tries. And the storms were still far away.

"It's still early, Ash. We can wait. The weather system has rows of storms all night, according to the radar. We need to get to the next step."

"I hope Fritz knows what to do. I found him in a different dimension, or universe, and I don't know where he needs to be in order to change things back. What makes this harder is that everything is moving. The planet, the solar system, the universe. And time."

"What did he mean about 'bridges'?"

"A theory speculates that bridges exist from one universe to another. You have to be exact to cross them. I don't know if they stay in one place or move. There's no description of them, or any instructions on how to find them."

"That's helpful," Brian said.

"I found one, from here to there. I need to do it again. Precisely. I have no idea how I found it. So let's start thinking of what we need."

Nat made a list of everything we'd done, including forgetting my keys. She noted the Doppler as the storms slid around us. While we waited, I checked my computer for anything unusual in March, 2017. Natalie asked if I needed to be specific now. She suggested that any Washington Post report would get me to the right place, and if I could get a newspaper, we could check for stories. I said that might work, if I went to the proper universe. We discussed how I would know if I had found the right place. She said we would look for stories about the new president. A story about anyone other than the first woman president would be the right place. A female president in the other dimension would require more investigating.

"Good idea, Nat. You really are smarter than me. I'm glad I don't have to figure this out alone. Thanks." So, with my trusty computer, we looked for Washington Post editions for around the time Fritz had said. I found a story about gentrification in the District, apartments converting to condos, and printed the picture. I don't know why that sounded right, but it did.

After two hours, I said we were wasting our time and we started for the car. In the parking lot, a flash right above us and a downpour forced us back inside. I put everything in place again, and when I tapped the doorknob, a spark jumped into my hand. I pulled the door and stepped through. I found myself on a sidewalk in a quiet urban neighborhood, filled with old apartment buildings and street level businesses. Which universe I'd stepped in, I had no clue. As long as the portal glow remained strong, I would be fine. So first, find a landmark and then a newspaper. Not wanting to go far, I took a few steps toward the street, both sides lined with parked cars. Nat and Chief Shaw watched me through the open door. "Keep the door open. I'm going down the street. There's a bar. Maybe they'll have a paper."

I walked into a local pub. St. Patrick's Day decorations covered everything—Irish, of course. I asked the lady bartender if she had a newspaper.

"What are you looking for?"

"The story about the time traveler. He's on trial soon."

She lifted a newspaper to the bar, and pointed to a story at the bottom of the front page. "Next week. Are you a friend of his?"

"Yeah. We go back a lot of years."

She looked at me, suspicious of my comment. "You've known Russ for a lot of years? You should stick around. A few people might want to talk to you."

"I wish I could. I'm only here for a short time, but maybe I'll get back again." I asked if I could keep the paper. When she said I could, I said, "Thanks for your help. What's your name?"

"Jane. What's yours?"

"Ashley Gilbert." I waved as I headed for the door, but a cell phone was at her ear. As I walked to the portal, two men ran out of the bar, chasing me.

"Hey, Mr. Gilbert. Come back."

"Sorry. I'm late," I shouted over my shoulder, as they closed the distance. I looked at them, a mere glimpse, and stepped through.

"What happened?"

"Let me catch my breath." I needed to process what had just happened.

"So, they know Fritz? And were chasing you? Why?"

"I didn't stop to find out. But I need to get back here in a week, in their time."

"Do you know what their time is?" asked the Chief.

"I got a paper, and the bar was decorated for St. Patrick's Day."

"Ash, were they like ghosts, too? From here, everything seemed a little blurry."

"No, as solid as you are."

"Does that mean you found another bridge?"

"Or made one?" the chief added.

"What do you mean?"

"Maybe where the paperclip takes you isn't random," Shaw said. "Maybe you follow some kind of stream in time."

I didn't know, but I needed time to examine the clues. But now I had a newspaper.

"I have to leave," said the chief. "I'll have my guys keep driving by."

"Then call me in the morning, Brian. I'll fill you in if we find out more."

"If you do, call me tonight. Anytime. If I don't see you again, Mr. Gilbert, good luck."

The possibility hit home, to both Nat and me. "Thanks, Brian. For everything. But I think you'll see me again. Me, not the other guy."

When he left, Nat had another question in her eyes, but I skipped past the emotion. For the present. "You're done for now, Ash," she said, looking at her cell. "No storms until the middle of the night." I wasn't sure if that had more than one meaning.

I expected her to start bombarding me with questions as we headed home, but she told me not to talk, she wanted to think. I had the paperclipped printout and had marked the last place with a pencil. A lot of information had been collected in just a few minutes and not talking made it easier to begin sifting through it. One thing stood out for me. Seeing Fritz again made me happy. But if we could change things back, would I remember any of what had happened. Or ... I glanced at Natalie.

Before I could get my coat off, she said, "You're really going home, aren't you?" Two tracks lined her cheeks. I wrapped my arms around her and pulled her close. I didn't say anything.

Chapter 34

Fritz

"**ASH, ASHLEY. WAIT.**" I woke up. On a cot. In a jail cell. The strangest, most realistic dream I'd ever had lingered as I regained my bearings. Dawn had to be close. My brain grappled with the arrival of my friend, missing so long, and trying to reconstruct the conversation. Where were we? Had he actually found me?

MICKEY TOLD ME not to expect any miracles on the first day. Most of what they did would be procedural. He had asked for a jury trial, so we had that ahead. The government, no one, had any hard evidence, no gun, no DNA, nothing. I added "waiting" to my daily exercise regimen.

Two cops escorted me to the defense table at the front of a packed courtroom. Flynn sat in the first row, next to a nun. Kate smiled at me. The first day lasted a half hour, with jury selection to start the next morning. I glanced back as I reached the side door. She nodded. Twenty minutes later, a crowd blocked my cell door.

"What's going on?" I asked Mickey. "I need to talk to you."

"Later. Now you have a visitor." I focused on the group of people, and said, "Hi, Mel." She looked back attempting to draw a memory of when she had seen me before. Without another step, my visitor's identity had been clarified.

As I walked into my cell, he stood, hands to his side, and a Secret Service agent between us. "Mr. President, nice to see you. I'd offer you refreshments, but I haven't been shopping lately."

"Mr. Furst, I'm here out of curiosity. But now that I see you, you seem familiar. Like we've met before."

"Sir, I assure you that we haven't met. Not you and I, not here."

He rubbed behind his left ear, as he met my look. "I'm not sure exactly what that means, but I think you have a story to tell, more than what the newspapers report."

"You think that, do you?"

"I do. And I'd like to hear it."

"Mr. President, you have more things to be concerned about than me. And my story is keeping me here, with all the comforts of home." I smiled. I'd seen his expressions before, but I didn't know this man. He frowned, trying to guess if I were kidding. "I've been informed that my testimony will either put me in a mental institution or prison. Telling you denies me my day in court."

"Can you time travel?"

He asked, not willing to banter with me. I glanced at Mickey, his unreadable look offering no help. In my previous life, I wouldn't hesitate to talk to this man. "My lawyer should say something at this point, but since he's being quiet, let me say this. You and I are surrounded by witnesses, all of whom are subject to the rules of the court, and as witnesses, can testify against me. I'm protected against self-incrimination by the Fifth Amendment. As you know. So let's make a deal. I'll tell you my story, one on one, if you pardon me now, so I can return to my life."

"Without any information? You expect me to agree?"

"I do. And here's why. If time travel is possible, you want to know if you might make use of it to make the world a safer place. You recognize that manipulating time is also a danger. Both options exist side by side. You wouldn't be here unless you thought I was for real." Our eyes locked while he fashioned his response. I didn't wait long. He stood up, reached out to shake my hand, and thanked me for my time.

As he turned to leave, I said, "I'll take that as a 'no'. Too bad. It's a fascinating story."

"I'll read about it."

When the crowd finally left, I told Mickey that I wanted to see Kate. He told me that wasn't possible now. Especially after talking to the president as I had.

"Did you expect me to tell him?"

"You were a bit rude. And aggressive."

"You didn't say anything. So I figured I had nothing to lose. In my other world, we were friends. I saved his life more than once. We actually time traveled together. But I'm stuck here now, and I don't relish spending my life in jail. I had to take a shot."

He shrugged. "It doesn't matter now. We start with the jury tomorrow. Be ready."

Chapter 35

Ashley

THE THUNDERSTORMS COOPERATED. We were soaked again before we reached the door. Still trying to understand all the connections, our plan, meticulous in its detail, was about to be tested. Tony met us at school after dark. Brian Shaw waited again in the parking lot.

Tony had fashioned a buffer to connect to the door, a description I'd given him. With the generator hooked up, I poked my head in to ascertain my location. Same place as yesterday. Confident I had more time, I entered the pub.

"Back again, Mr. Gilbert?" the lady bartender asked. "He's in court today." She handed me the morning paper. The picture of the courthouse and the headline of "The Time Traveler's Trial" jumped off the front page.

"Can I have this?" She said to take it. "Thanks, Jane." I ran out and through the portal in seconds.

"Did you find him again?" Nat asked.

"Not yet. But this will get me closer." I showed them the picture. "I'll go here. Find out where he's being held, follow him and get another picture."

"Will the portal stay open that long?"

"Let's hope so."

I sat in the back of the courtroom, the portal well-hidden in the shrubbery. When Fritz fell, it looked like he'd fainted. I hoped that my stay would shorten, that the judge would end early. The little bald guy sitting with Fritz had spoken to the judge, who nodded. Fritz sat, his head hardly moving, as the jurors were selected quickly. Both the prosecutor and Fritz's lawyer asked if anyone had a problem with time-travelers. The judge banged his gavel to stop the laughter.

I left the courtroom, and followed the handful of men carrying cameras. I asked one where they would take Fritz. Only a few blocks down, he told me. When he asked me what my interest was, I said I wrote science fiction and I could smell a best seller here. I asked his name and told him I might make him a character. He offered a ride, and with the clouds looking full, I accepted.

He parked in a perfect spot, directly across the street. Old trees lined the one side and the jail building looked like many municipal buildings from the '50s, red brick fronted by concrete steps and patios. I snapped off a couple of photos, as the thunder rumbled, and then headed back to the courthouse to beat the rain.

"I found him," I said, removing my suit jacket. The rain had fallen in buckets a block before I reached the portal. My shoes were soaked and muddy. "He's at the jail."

"Now what?" asked Nat.

"I'll get him out later tonight. Just like we planned."

Chapter 36

Fritz

THE COURTROOM BEGAN buzzing when they brought me in. Kate wasn't among the spectators, at least not that I could see. Flynn stood just behind the defense table in the front row. No one reacted when I stepped over to him.

"Where's Kate?"

"Working. She has a business to run, and a new cook to train. We had a visitor yesterday. A guy says he knows you. Name of Gilbert." All of a sudden, I was surrounded, being lifted to a chair. As I refocused, Flynn's sharp eyes burned into mine.

"Are you all right?" Mickey asked. "What happened?"

"I don't know. A little dizzy, I guess." But I did know. I wasn't dreaming. Ash had found me. The rest of the time in court passed in a blur as I concentrated on what his presence might mean.

Not long after returning to my cell, my visitors arrived. Flynn pulled up the chair and Mickey sat on the cot.

"Sit down, Russ."

"I've been sitting all day."

"Sit down. I need to tell you what happened, quietly." Flynn pointed to the spot next to the lawyer. "Who's Gilbert?"

"A friend from my old life."

"Old life. So he's a time traveler? Kevin said he vanished through what he said looked like a neon doorway."

"That's the portal. I thought I dreamed it. When did Kevin see him?"

"Last evening. Early. He came into the pub looking for a newspaper. A story about you. You really are a time-traveler?"

"You didn't believe me?"

Mickey held up his hand to stop Flynn, as Tim McNamara stopped outside the cell. "There's a guy wanting to see you, Russ. Says he's your lawyer. Ashley something."

Heads swiveled from the bars to me. I looked at Mickey hoping he would have the right response. "He's from my office, Tim. Would you bring him here?"

"You know this is irregular. You shouldn't be here either. I'll take him to a visitor's room. Then I'll come get all of you."

When Tim could no longer hear, Flynn asked, "What's he want? What's he doing here?"

"I haven't seen him in more than eight years. How would I know?"

"Is he here to get you out?"

"Flynn, he can't just walk me out the door. I don't know what he has in mind until I speak to him."

"Are you going home?"

Home. I thought about the word. Four letters. Vague faces. At that moment, I wasn't sure I wanted to leave here. I had a new life. I'd dismissed my past, never expecting to return. "Flynn, I don't know."

Tim handcuffed me to the table. Ashley sat across from me in a blue suit, white shirt and a red, white and blue paisley tie. That tie proved he was the genuine article. He eyed my companions.

Mickey said, "Don't shake my hand. You're supposed to know us."

"Who are you?" Ashley asked.

"I'm his lawyer, and Flynn here is a friend. We don't have much time, so tell us what you want."

"I'm here to find out how to undo the changes in time that Fritz set in motion when he came here. I need to get him out of here so we can go home."

"You're just gonna walk him out?" Flynn sneered. "Are you nuts?"

"Here's my plan." He looked only at me. "I need a picture of you in your cell, so I know where to go. I have a phone for you. Take the shot and send it to my phone. I'll print it and get you. Then we can figure out what to do. I'm in a parallel universe, too. We need to find a way to stop you from shooting the Kopplers."

"I have no place to put the phone. Give it to Mickey."

"If I take it," he said, "I'm an accomplice to your escape. I won't do that."

Flynn said, "Kick off your shoes. Tim will let you put them on. Palm the phone and slip it into your sock. Now, let's get out of here. When we stand up, slip him the phone. Russ, kick off your shoes. Do it now."

Mickey signaled they were ready to leave, and as they stood, Tim came in and released the handcuffs. He looked at the shoes and told me to carry them. With the shoes in my left hand, and Tim standing on my right, I reached over to shake hands. Ashley dropped the phone in a shoe.

Chapter 37

Fritz

I SAT IN THE quiet and waited. The ugly paint job on the cinder blocks jogged a memory from years past. My old classroom. I'd sent the selfie to Ashley. But who knew what would happen, when he might come. And then what? I wasn't ready to go back. Not yet. But not being in jail appealed to my comfort genes.

While I waited, the anticipation of leaving fought with the desire to stay. Not in a cell, but here, with people who had become friends, almost family. I thought about the difficult decisions made by the millions who had chosen to leave their homes over the centuries seeking a new life as immigrants to a new world, America and elsewhere. Funny, but I hadn't thought those things when I had decided to end the Koppler conspiracy. I stepped through the portal from one world, expecting to step back where I'd left, and then go find General Lee. That plan hadn't quite worked.

I wrote a note with my marker, thanking my hosts for their hospitality and telling them to let the president know that time travel was real. I'd give them something to remember me by. I even autographed it. All my random thoughts and time wasting activities diverted my imagining about going back. If Ashley did show up again, I'd have barely a moment to decide.

Lights out. Evening had gone, night descended in full gloom. Only some of the lights went out. I'd only seen pictures, but thought about what life must be like in the northerly countries when the sun never set. Did they have blackout curtains? Did they ever get real sleep? More random speculation while I waited. Totally awake.

I had only a sense of how much time had passed when the familiar rectangle light lit my cell, leaving almost no room for me to stand up. Ash poked his head in, and whispered for me to come through. I left the note on my pillow and stepped into the hallway on the other side.

When the door clicked shut, I looked up and down the corridor. Before I could utter a word, Ash hugged me while Nat and Tony looked on. "Let's get out of here. We have a lot to talk about," he said.

"Wait, Ash. Give me a minute. I haven't been here for eight years. Let's go in and sit down."

Nat said, "You must be Fritz," as she extended her hand.

"Yeah, I still am, Nat. Hi Tony."

"I'll explain it all, but not here." Besides the uncomprehending stares, I rubbed the ugly yellow wall by the door. "Fritz, you haven't met Nat or Tony, or rather they haven't met you before. We're in a parallel dimension. This isn't home."

"I need to go back, just not to jail. I have people I need to see."

"I can get you back, but not now. Trust me on this. We've been here too long tonight already." Like my most recent lodging, I had no place I had to be, so I agreed. After eight years of adjusting and adapting, I followed them out into the rainy night. Sitting at the curb, a police car discouraged the curious, as well as overly hormonal teenagers. The driver stepped out.

"Chief, this is Fritz Russell. Fritz, meet Brian Shaw."

I looked at the cop, then stared. "Brian? What happened to Jim?"

Shaw answered immediately, shaking his head. "Ashley, I wasn't sure I believed you. Fritz, is it? Nice to meet you."

I wanted to get away from the weirdness. McNamara's summoned, an ideal spot just then. Safe and familiar. "Ash, get me out of here."

We climbed into a strange car. Nat sat in the passenger's seat, and Tony sat next to me. The tennis courts and open fields behind the school, dark and empty, flashed years of memories through my head.

"Where's the Mustang?"

"Home, I hope. Fritz, I'll explain it all once we're home."

"This is just so weird."

"You should be in my shoes." He was looking at me in the mirror. The police car led the way down streets I had forgotten.

Ashley drove past the parking police car and the yellow Beetle and into his driveway. Before he got out, he turned to me. "I'm glad you're here. You didn't make it easy."

"Good to see you, too." I could visualize the books I'd left on his desk. "I didn't expect to see you again."

"Come on. We've got work to do. Then we can fill in the blanks."

"Ash, I want to go back where you found me. I have unfinished business."

"Let's figure this out first. I can't get home from here now. You can at least help me. And don't forget, you promised to be my best man."

I'd forgotten about that. I climbed from the back seat and followed the rest into the house. The white-walled starkness made me squint. No mess, no book piles, a black stain on the old blue carpet spoke in stark contrast to my instant memory of his living room.

"I like what you've done to the place."

"It's not mine, but I'll get to that."

Nat asked if anyone wanted a drink. I told her I did, and asked if she had any Irish whiskey. The rest asked for soda. When she delivered the glasses, everyone sat, with me as their focus.

"For more than eight years, I've been wandering in the portal. I ended up in D.C. where you found me."

"You took off at Thanksgiving," Ashley said. "I've been looking for you ever since. You've only been gone about four months."

"I've lived every day of eight years, Ashley. I hope you'll forgive me, but I have a lot more adjusting to do than you."

The man I had known as Jim Shaw asked what I'd done that changed everything. I told them I'd planned to shoot all three Koppler brothers to stop them from ruining lives if left on their own. When I entered the portal, two of them were already dead. If they were all killed, I figured that would bring back all those they had killed, and prevent them from carrying out the damage done by the Caballeros. I should have known that I'd turn things upside down, but I hadn't thought it all through.

They listened as I told a brief history of my time in the portal, as if they knew all about me. With a police officer sitting and staring, I carefully sidestepped an admission that I'd shot anybody. I told of my travels from coast to coast, using my cooking skills to find work, what books I'd read. My pointed discussion of time-travel literature and physics generated the desired effect—boredom. By midnight, the stifled yawns morphed to full-blown groans of fatigue. Although my energy had drained, their departure would let me talk to Ashley alone.

He said, "I hate to break up this party, but I have classes to teach in the morning. You're all welcome to come back tomorrow, but I've got to get some sleep."

I was actually surprised when they all headed for the door, and even more so, when Nat whispered something to Ash and kissed him. I thanked them for helping to rescue me, and shook hands with all the strangers I had known so well.

"We have a lot to talk about, Fritz."

"I know. But not tonight. Go to bed. I'll sleep on the couch. I want to think about what happens next."

"I need to know how we get home. I've figured out some of this, but you know more than I do. Especially about what we've done to change history and how to change it back."

"Give me something to write on. I'll make some notes."

Without an audience and with total solitude, I plotted the events that I had started. When I first stepped into the portal, I'd set the books, so I could step out, and go directly to Appomattox. If I was going to be stuck in the past, General Lee would be a perfect companion.

My first target was the surviving brother. In my time, the last one, Richter/Richemartel, had been the most elusive and the most deadly. I shot him first, then the others. When I ran back through the portal into the hallway, the generator was gone, the window wasn't broken, and the ache from my stitches had stopped. When I went to the parking lot, my car had vanished.

I went back into the classroom, but another teacher's papers were on the desk. My books and my plan were up in smoke. I had made sure not to have my phone or any identification when I started, only a little cash in case nothing worked. I looked for a reference point, anything that would give me a sense of where I was. The teacher's files on her desk top were arranged by class. I began to scan for names and dates. The names gave it away. Some of her students had been in my classes, except they had graduated already. In the third folder, unreturned essays were dated, November 22, 2008, and all contained some lesson learned at the forty-fifth anniversary of President Kennedy's assassination.

No car, little money and a world I'd just changed chased me out of the school. Now what? With no other choice, I walked home. The rude awakening came with the "For Sale" sign in the front yard. Linda and I had bought the house the previous year, so who lived there now clearly wasn't me. The perfectly trimmed shrubs, a line of boxwood, still green and seemingly healthy warned me that I didn't live here. I'd dug up the dead bushes when we first moved in. Against hope, I rang the doorbell. I asked the woman who answered if Ms. Russell was home. No one by that name lived there, she said. Then I walked here, to Ash's house. I figured my reception would be similar from the tan Camry parked in the driveway.

As I walked, the weather turned on me. I had worn a jacket, but the clouds began to spew little white puffs with a promise of more to come, and guaranteed that I would be stranded. I hitched a ride to downtown, bought a newspaper, and searched for Hoffmann's, for a cup of coffee and a little warmth. I found neither. When I finally saw a Starbucks sign, snow covered the sidewalk.

The newspaper helped. Black Friday. If I could get to a store, I could get a heavier coat, and work out where to go. What public places would remain open where I would be unnoticed? The idea of heading to warmer climes rolled around the story of record warm temperatures in the south. The best way to get there would also be open, so I headed for the train to Philly. Exiting on Market Street, I walked toward City Hall, looking at sale signs in all the shop windows. The fifty-percent-off sign vacuumed me into the outdoor gear emporium. Ten minutes later, I left with a parka, and the first of many backpacks I would buy over the next eight years. I took the next train to the Amtrak station, bought a ticket for Florida, and said goodbye to the life I had known.

My travelogue paused when the front door opened. Nat hung up her coat before noticing me at the kitchen table. Over her shoulder she carried a bag large enough to hold the Library of Congress. She reached in and placed a notebook across from me.

"So Fritz, wanna trade notes?"

"I haven't gotten far, mostly been thinking about how this all started."

"Do you know how to get home?"

"No. I haven't been near the portal for quite a while. I'm not even sure where I am now. I do know this isn't home."

She asked if I thought I'd be able to figure it out. I told her that I honestly didn't know. We had only travelled in our own dimension. "So Ash and I need to have a chat."

She pushed her notebook across the table. "We've been recording everything we planned, thought and did for months. Tonight is the only missing episode."

I thumbed quickly through the pages. I told her that tonight the universes, or dimensions, were connected. The most important aspect, exact detail, might identify what differed from other nights. She said she'd been taking notes of everything since they had left home tonight, even while I talked. "I don't have to be anywhere early, so we can talk more in the morning. Good night."

I wrote a reminder to ask Ashley about their relationship, and returned to my notes.

Not knowing if I'd be a suspect, I'd kept on the move. With each move, I found a local library and a free computer. Find a job, make some money, move on. For the first year, I worked my way west. When I reached California, I stayed between LA and San Diego, changing jobs regularly. When my employer or fellow employees started to get friendly, I found a new place to hunker down. After a couple of years, I started retracing my steps and aimed for the East Coast.

When my eyes finally told me to quit, I started for the couch, but changed direction to the bathroom. I looked into the extra bedroom, made up, but empty. The tempting available bed beckoned, more than the couch. I sat, laid down, and before I could think a word, sleep attacked.

Ashley's banging around early woke me, so I joined him for a cup before he left. I had my work awaiting. He had found a bridge between worlds, but not one to get us back to ours. I read Nat's journal that morning. They had planned while winter passed, and needed a storm to activate the portal. I could feel the answer but couldn't put a finger on it. Not yet. I began to retrace my steps. I had left my world and after the shootings, planned to step back, but instead, found myself in another universe, without the portal. When Ash came after me, he jumped into a parallel dimension, also without a way back. So, we needed to get back to our world to stop me from shaking the universe. Sitting now in the world I'd first caused, Ash had found me in a different universe. The portal slowly returned to my conscious thoughts. For us to get home, we needed to open the portal and find a bridge to that universe that would allow us to cross. I would need to stop myself from taking the first shot. We would have to return before, find me and stop me. Or maybe Ash had to stop me. I couldn't be in two universes at the same time. Or maybe I could go back to when I first went in, and change my mind and leave. Then none of the past eight years would have happened.

Another problem crossed my mind. I changed universes twice. At least. The second time happened while I was driving east on an empty road somewhere in Ohio. The sky rumbled, like a time-lapse picture. It seemed like only moments later that I found myself sitting in a traffic jam on the Interstate outside Pittsburgh. At the time, I thought I had been so engrossed in driving I'd missed Ohio completely. From the notes, Ash may have changed history and we might need to change that first. Maybe then the bridge back would show itself. But, the portal only opened to the past or present. To get home, time would have to be in sync. Having the quiet of an empty house allowed me to explore the alternatives, and to weigh our options. In the middle of my solitude, a nagging thought joined me. Did I really want to go home?

Chapter 38

Ashley

I CERTAINLY WASN'T in the mood for teaching. All I wanted was a long talk with Fritz. Home, really going home, had become a real possibility. Yet what about all the changes I'd been able to coerce from George, and what would happen when other me came back?

My question that day, more for me than them, asked, "Is time travel possible? Where would you go?" Most of my seniors were taking physics, so the concepts of time travel might not be foreign. Second period, they neither disappointed nor gave me reason to change the questions. Most of the day, the students treated me to remarkable ideas. From earth-shaking events to poignant personal revelations, the students stuffed each class with delightful, inventive stories that would make the great science fiction writers proud. By the end of the day, the topic had word-of-mouth distribution. My last class ended when one of the kids said he would visit his dad, who'd died when he was a baby. Usually by that time, they were noisy and anxious to be gone. Even the bell didn't signal the start of noise as they packed up, a few stopping for tissues on the way out.

I found Fritz where I had left him. A yellow pad with pages flipped indicated that he'd hopefully spent the day developing a plan for what to do. When I settled across from him, he collected whatever thoughts he'd accumulated, and started by saying that the one thing he couldn't understand was why I was here.

"I came after you."

"I know. But why are you the only one affected when time changed, when I shot Richemartel?"

"I don't know that I am. I've been trying to find you, but I know that Linda is different. I know George is different. So is Shaw and Tony, and Nat. I haven't seen Jane."

"That's only for the people here, but I think we're the only ones. We're the only ones affected by the portal."

I'd seen Fritz think about the portal since the first day he found it, but we'd never really discussed all its possibilities and consequences. We'd never considered other dimensions or universes, or just how much our using the portal might really impact our own futures.

"Maybe. Did you figure out how to turn things back to normal."

"I don't think we can." He told me that in order to change things back, we needed to get home first, and that would require someone in our home world finding us.

"No one but us ever opened the portal. So what do we do now?"

He pushed away from the table. One thing had changed in just the short time since I'd last seen him. His hair was graying and the forehead wrinkles and frown lines no longer vanished. The chiseled face, and a frame that had lost twenty pounds would be unrecognized if we got home.

"You can open it to where you found me, right?"

"Uh-huh."

"And you can go to the places in the books?"

"Yes."

"Where did the books come from?"

"I had them with me when I changed universes." Fritz rubbed behind his left ear.

"You still do that."

"What?"

"Rub behind your ear."

"Hmm. I don't think I've done that in years. Must be you. Anyway, the books are from our time. And from the notes, you met Lee and Churchill from here, but they were different. They remembered things that happened in our future. You said, or Nat did, that they could see into their futures."

I interrupted. "Lee could, but I'm not sure about Churchill. He could see to when we met, but not the near future, the war."

"Let me finish this. To change history back, you need to figure out what you did, and we need to see if we can change things back from here. If we can, then we'll know that we can change them at home. We need to get these universes back to normal."

"We may not have to," I said. "I've seen at least three universes. We're still surrounded by the same people we know. At least here. What makes them different is the question I've been pondering. If we figure that out, we may know what we need to change, and what can be left as it is now. But I wonder what I'll have to do at school. The other me isn't held in high regard. I've been working to change that. How can I alter what I've done?"

"Everything you did here had nothing to do with the portal. You convinced them. You alone. It's the history stuff I'm concerned about."

"Three places I think are possible, Fritz. Lee knew about you. He told me you would show up at Appomattox. I talked to Hitler in English, so he would be aware that some English-speaking country had a way to appear and disappear. I met Churchill right around the start of the war and told him he would need to help Alan Turing to decode Enigma."

"What do you know about Enigma?"

"I'm a history teacher here. But we saw "The Imitation Game" together. But that was in our home dimension. Do you remember?"

"Honestly, I don't remember a lot about that world. It's almost like amnesia, or a bad dream. Like I'm looking up from the bottom of the ocean, covered with barnacles. I'm disconnected. Ash, I've relived all those years. I don't even know how old I am now."

"I should feel bad for you, I guess. But I don't. You set up a puzzle when you left, so you had to know I'd come after you. Otherwise, why would you have left clues? And you had to know you would alter everything by killing someone in the past. We talked endlessly about that. And you left the mess for me to clean up."

"I didn't want you to follow me. That's why I set the books up the way I did. To make it too hard to find me. I figured you'd take one look and know you shouldn't pursue it. I thought I could just come back and then decide where to get lost. I had no idea you'd be sucked into the void. You said it took a few days before the changes happened. That's actually interesting. I went in on Thanksgiving and the changes didn't happen until the Tuesday after. I wonder why it took so long. And you didn't set the portal up. It just happened."

"I don't care. I want to go home."

"Sorry, Ash, really I am. But we should look for a clue there too. Maybe we've fooled around with the portal enough that all those ripples added up."

"You remember the ripples?"

"Yeah. I can see Tony say it and Linda getting mad."

"Linda's home, Fritz. What really happened with her father finally hit home. She had no idea that he broke the oath, or that he had met Richemartel AKA Koppler. TJ needs his father, and I think they both need you. And I want my best friend home, too."

"I haven't thought about them in a long time. Or I've tried not to remember. I didn't expect to get back. I need time to adjust, and I still have to find a way."

"*We* have to find a way. It's not just about you, not now. Not anymore."

"What are you going to do about Natalie? She's not going to give you up willingly."

"I told her up front that going home was a possibility, and I've kept her at a distance even if she has made it difficult. But if we change everything back, she'll have no recollection because none of the changes will have happened."

"Don't be so sure. I'm not. And if we can't get back, then what?"

"Then, old friend, I'll have to decide what happens next."

"Ash, before we go back, I have a couple of stops I want to make first. Unfinished business in a world I don't want to leave. At least not yet."

"Then let's be ready for the next storm."

We talked about the places that I might have changed history, and how that needed to be fixed first. Fritz said he wanted to go to McNamara's before we changed anything.

Chapter 39

Linda

THE TULIPS WERE undressing, leaving a kaleidoscope blanket in the beds. All of Fritz's plantings of two falls ago brought brightness to my dismal mood. It's been four months and change since Fritz and Ashley disappeared. Thank heaven for the store or I'd be a complete basket case. Business hasn't been great, at least not for new bikes, but I've kept busy with repairs as the warmer weather approaches. Charlie told me to expect a rush when the weather changed.

Mom had been right on target, although I shouldn't be surprised. She said to take care of the house, TJ and the shop. TJ comes with me every day, so I can kill two birds with a stone. My editor would kill me for using a cliché, but for the past few weeks, getting up and running is where the rubber meets the road for me. And to make things easier, Mom has been in Riverboro more than home, so the house has been cared for.

But I'm waiting for spring for a different reason. Eric Silver will be home for his spring break, and hopefully he'll have some new ideas on how to get into the portal. At Christmas, he had studied Ashley's notes and Jane's comments, and tried to open the portal at the high school. His swimming pool with the generator sitting in it had failed to do more than create shocks, but he said he would keep trying in his college lab. I've been tempted to call him for a progress report, but Mom said we'd see him soon enough and not to put pressure on him.

I seldom see Jane. She moved back to Washington and comes here every three or four weeks. When she is here, our conversations have been tepid. She's not involved in the activities of the new president, who doesn't know about the portal. I think she misses the action. When she's here, she spends a lot of time with the, I guess I have to call him former, president. He's concerned that the Middle East plan isn't getting more support. Many of the leaders have asked if our commitment is going to last. Projects are moving ahead, but more slowly than expected. The new president has said publicly that we should be spending money to build our military instead.

Eric will be here in the next few days. I checked the weather forecast earlier. The usual spring thunderstorms are late in starting this year, and I don't know if we'll need them to open the portal.

Chapter 40

Jane

I MISS ASHLEY. I didn't know how much until my job took me back to DC. I have plenty of time to miss him because I've been shuffled into the revised Homeland Security operation. Immigration, the border, airline travel and reheated rhetoric has generated the need for new reports on the same old, same old. A new crisis in North Korea has everyone's attention except mine. No one wanted my opinion, in spite of the analysis I'd prepared for the newcomers. So I do nine-to-five, go to my parents' place most weekends and wait for news from Linda.

The waiting has always been hard. Even with the portal, waiting in the school hallway was the worst. When we were making a difference, I could tolerate waiting. And I had Ash right next to me. My mother asked me if I'd started dating again. Although I told her no, I have to admit that I've thought about it.

I go to Riverboro less often now. I keep the house ready for Ashley's return, and keep the Mustang running. I'd cleared out the garage after Christmas, so it would have a safe winter. And every time I go, I read our notes, searching for that elusive clue, or a missed idea, that might help get him back. I'd thought about all the families of servicemen and women, how awful their lives had to be with their loved ones away for so long. I wish I could get a letter or a phone call.

The president is doing the same, I think. Keeping busy waiting. He isn't in Riverboro often. Before I go, I call him. If he's free, I stop by. He knows I miss being involved. We've even talked about whether or not he should tell the new guy about the portal. Always the same conclusion: no point if we can't show him. I'm not sure we should even if we could.

Last time I went, Nat and Tony had gotten engaged. Then Tony got transferred back to the Energy Department, so I don't know how that's going to work out. Nat said she liked her job. Good to know someone does.

Eric Silver will be home for spring break soon. Hopefully, he'll have some new ideas.

I miss Ash.

Chapter 41

Fritz

I TOLD ASHLEY that as soon as spring storms begin, I need to go back where he found me. I can't leave Kate, or Flynn, or any of them, without an explanation. Ash reminded me that I did exactly that when I left home. For the next couple of days, I tried to explain to him what had changed, my emotional connection to the only woman who had taken me into her family in eight years. He argued that I didn't know how long I'd been gone, and how much more damage I could do using the portal for my own selfish—his word—reasons.

"Your relationship with her, in *your* time, was only a couple of months. You've been married for eight years. And you have a son who needs his father to help him grow up. So you need to grow up first."

"All I want to do is say goodbye and thank them. You can come with me. You'll see why I need to do it."

"Are you going to break her heart? Or yours? Don't be stupid. That's never been why you've used the portal. Don't forget we need to figure out what we need to fix."

"How can I forget? You won't let me."

"Then let's get the next steps ready, so when we can, we just go."

While I studied Natalie's chart, the front door opened. When I lifted my head, standing in the kitchen door, Linda scowled at me.

"Where's Ash?"

"At school."

"Who are you?" I told her my name. "Is that your real name? You never know with him." I nodded, more from shock than anything. "Do you know when he'll be home?"

"After school."

"A smart-ass, too. Tell him I want my bike parts and my money."

I checked the clock. "He'll be back around three. You can tell him yourself if you want to wait."

"You tell him. I'll be back." She reached for the door as it swung open. "What are you doing here?"

"I should ask you that," Natalie said.

"Not your concern." She turned to me. "Tell him." She left as fast as she'd come.

"What did she want?"

"Bike parts and money."

"What's wrong with you? You're as pale as a ghost."

"Maybe. You know I'm married to her in our universe. So maybe not a ghost, but I'm not sure how to describe what just happened."

She stood at the doorway, staring. "I didn't know it was her. Ash told me I'd introduced you to your wife, but I didn't make the connection. I introduced her to the other Ashley, too. That her, the one that just left."

"Natalie, none of that matters. Your map is great. I have specific questions for each stop that should tell me where the changes happened."

"Like what?"

"I have a feeling that if we go in reverse, he'll erase what he did. By disconnecting the bridges. Then I can do the same, just not doing or saying what I did. Take Hitler. Ash spoke to him. If he goes in and says nothing, and leaves, that might get us disconnected from that dimension."

"He did it in this dimension."

"But something he did here pushed me across to the other dimension. So, for each time he entered, I need to see if I can get back. If I can't, that will identify a place where he's disrupted the dimension. That's where we'll need to concentrate in order to turn things back. All your detail of each entry he made is critical."

At three-thirty, Ashley opened the backdoor. Before I could ask why he'd come in that way, the front door banged against the door stop. Nat and I were in the crossfire. Linda, at the front, her oil-stained hands on her hips, entered with a battle plan. Ashley, carrying a stack of books, stopped and scowled. Linda started the shouting, and Ashley held his response until the steam ran out.

"The bike parts are in the shed. The drugs are in the sewer system, and I don't know what money you're talking about. You are, however, trespassing. So unless you would like to tone it down," at this point, he was almost whispering, "and would like a soda and a civilized conversation, please leave. And give me the key."

Her jaw dropped, her balloon punctured, clearly, at least to me, unsure of what more she could say. Without a word more, she slammed the door behind her. Ashley ran to catch her.

"You forgot the key." He held his hand out and waited. She had stopped midway down the walk, found the key and slapped it into his outstretched hand. "Thank you. Now would you like a soda?"

I knew the answer before he completed the sentence. She almost barked "no" and he stayed at the door as she sped away.

Nat said, "She'll be back. For the bike stuff."

"I don't care. I don't want the bike parts. That shed needs to be cleaned out anyway."

"Sit down. Nat and I have made some progress."

For the remainder of the afternoon, we worked backward from the spot before he'd found me. We'd left Koppler's book alone, and the newspaper articles, too. I'd need them to see if reviewing the order of entry worked. More, and I didn't say it, I was going back to McNamara's, despite Ashley's admonitions.

"How will you get to Appomattox?" Nat asked, after Ash said that Lee had known we would meet there.

"That's a good question, Fritz. None of the books you picked took me there."

Since I had no idea how Lee knew, I guessed. I picked up Longstreet's book and flipped to the rear pages. "You used this one when Lee told you, right?"

"Right. Do you think if we change the clip, we stay on the correct timeline?"

I read the pages about Lee's retreat from around Richmond, General Grant's message about surrender, and the meeting at the McLean house. Longstreet joined Lee at the surrender, so a possible connection existed.

While Natalie wrote, I asked questions about Ashley's pathway through the books. He hadn't spoken to Lincoln, hadn't stayed long at either the artillery barrage on the third day at Gettysburg, or in the rain on the Potomac. He only observed the Kopplers. He'd spoken to the Wright brothers, Hitler, Franklin, and Churchill. Dealey Plaza lasted only a moment. Reversing the stops with no contact should be easy.

"Can you tell me about the school, the buzz on the doorknob, anything that might have an effect that you noticed?" I asked.

Ash closed his eyes. He tried to see each stop, and spoke a description as he worked down the list. He mentioned the accident with Sandy's car, and his double maybe showing up while he spoke with Churchill. "I didn't pay attention to the time. Each time in the portal seemed longer than the actual amount of time I'd been gone. I never timed it. I should have thought about that."

"We already know that time moves differently inside."

"But we're in the portal now, Fritz."

"No, we're not. You were when you came to get me. Right now, we're in a different dimension. Our time is moving the same through this world." When I said it, I knew I had the right answer, although I had never had the thought before.

"Have either of you considered how long this reversal might take?" Natalie asked. "If time plays catch up from dimension to dimension, it could take months."

She had a good point. If that were the case, we couldn't go fast, in and out, and get an answer. We might be able to hurry through the places where Ash had just looked, check the next place going backwards where he'd spoken to someone. But then we would have to wait.

"Is it necessary to go in order?"

"We won't know until we find the first change. And until we have a storm, it won't matter."

Chapter 42

Ashley

I COULDN'T HAVE been happier to have found Fritz. But being together with my friend was little different than living with a stranger. I went to school each day, to his classroom, teaching his subject, and running his activities. My tenth graders had worked hard to get the history baseball tournament in motion, but by the start of spring training couldn't generate enough interest among the students, even with Rachel and Nicole using their unique style of pressure. Teachers had no interest in being involved, and the kids had not convinced local businesses to become sponsors. At the start of February, Susan Leslie, with tears of frustration, told me they were giving up. I told her what people said for years about the old Brooklyn Dodgers—"Wait 'til next year." In another moment, in a different setting, I would have worked harder to make their effort successful, but finding Fritz and going home had filled my dance card. And teaching a brand-new subject without years of notes and plans, including the ones in my desk from other me, filled whatever extra time I could carve out. I had to remind Fritz more than once that I wasn't his entertainment. Once the initial burn cooled, he gave me time when I said I had something else to do. I considered the possibility more than once that he had changed during his absence, and maybe Linda had a reason to have left.

As mid-April approached, we routinely watched the Weather Channel, checked weather websites and began the countdown to thunderstorms. April was slipping by, drier than it had been in years, and May flowers might be behind schedule.

Because I'd changed my routine before Christmas, and had continued the question-of-the-day at least once a week, I reached the end of the Civil War at the end of the month. I asked Fritz if he had any interest in guest lecturing. Instead of an immediate decline, he asked if we might have a storm he could borrow.

"What? You mean take them to meet Lee?"

"You still have that book, don't you?"

"I had to buy a copy, but that's a bad idea."

"I know. But he may be able to help."

"We're going to find him anyway. No reason to subject the kids to our problem. Not when we're so close."

"So close? So close to what?"

"Skip it. Sorry I mentioned it. I thought you might want to see the inside of a classroom again."

"I don't think I'll ever be in one again. Sorry, Ash. I'm not sure going home will make things better."

The Appomattox classes came and went, without Fritz, and without a thunderstorm. As tensions built between us, and we had less and less to talk about, the clouds rolled in, with the promise of putting our plan to work. The first storm arrived on a Tuesday. As we had planned, I stepped across the threshold to the telegraph office, where Lincoln spotted me. When I stepped into the Pennsylvania State House, Franklin saw me, but I left without a word or a wave. Next, a rapid entry to Dealey Plaza, and out as quickly.

"Okay, I'm next," Fritz said.

"You only have to find McNamara's. Then come right back."

"I know the plan," he snapped.

Although a quick look down the street would suffice, Fritz walked through and aimed for the pub door. I debated going after him, but remained in the doorway. Not a long wait. He came back in less than ten minutes.

"What happened?"

"I knew them, but they didn't know me. I didn't cross over to the other dimension." Downcast, Fritz turned away from me.

"Does that mean you've reversed that dimension?" Nat asked.

"I don't know. Let's go."

We lucked out with the weather. Three days later, another storm blew in. Friday night. Nat had alerted Brian Shaw that we were going to try, and needed the school parking lot watched. She also called Tony and I brought the generator. With long days, even with the clouds, we hit the hallway at ten. The storm threatened, nearly overhead, though the rain fell in a drizzle.

I tested the door and Tony hooked up the power source. Fritz and I had discussed having only a part of the equation, and he thought if the storm were strong enough, the generator should keep the portal open for quite a while, even after the storm passed.

Our only stop was Churchill. I'd seen him more than once. And spoken to him. This time, a step, a glimpse, and out. I'm not even sure he saw me. Then, Fritz's chance came again.

"Let's move the clip to a little later. If the place is busy, I may jog memories, or even better, cross the time bridge."

I told him to do whatever he thought would work. With a flash of lightning, the rain finally started. Before Fritz tried again, Brian Shaw ran in, and tracked the rain down the corridor, dripping like he'd brought the rain inside.

"Can I watch?"

"Sure," I said. "Look in the window. See, it's a classroom." I grabbed the doorknob, and Fritz walked past Shaw and into the portal. A car drove by, and I pulled him back. "That was close." Another flash and Fritz ran toward the green neon. I let the door close.

"Now what?" Shaw asked.

"Now, we wait." I'd forgotten those long minutes, waiting for Jane to come back. All our adventures flitted through my heightened memory until Fritz returned.

"They knew me," Fritz said, a smile of both happiness and relief.

"You know you've just set the tumblers in motion again. And we'll never know for sure if what they do changes things here."

"At least, I know that option is still open."

"Why this time and not the last?" Nat asked, wiping the collected footprints from in front of the door.

"I think it was the lightning. Last time, I went in before any nearby flashes."

"Time to go," I said.

"No, Ash. Let's go to Koppler's. That's where you found me. Let's change the clip to forward in time, and see what's there."

"You can't be anywhere near the door, Fritz."

"Fine, but let's check it."

A minute later, I stepped through, again behind the shrubs. On the ground, surrounded by swarming party-goers, three men lay helter-skelter. Three others, no doubt security guards, headed toward the greenery not far from me, so I left. I'd been gone maybe ten seconds.

"What did you see?" Fritz asked.

"A party. Not enough time to see anything else." Brian Shaw had been read in about the portal, and even why I'd been looking for Fritz. He didn't know I'd just seen the men Fritz had shot. "Nothing's different. Now, let's go."

When we got back to my house, Fritz and I sat in the kitchen. I contained my shouting, and got a drink instead. "I'm not sure how we'll know if we've reversed things, especially if you jumble them. I'm beginning to doubt you want to get home."

"I told you before, I hadn't planned to go home. I don't know if that's changed. At least, I know I can get back there."

"I can't make you want to go home, even though I think you should. But, Fritz, I want to go home."

Chapter 43

Fritz

THE SUN ON Sunday kept us home, so I helped Ashley clean out the garden, all the while working backward. What had he done that pushed me across dimensions? The key that triggered the bridge had also brought his doppelganger back here. Then I remembered he had visited all those places more than once. I leaned the rake against his holly bush and told him to come inside with me. He didn't argue.

"Let's go over the timeline again."

"Why? We've done this a dozen times already."

"You went back and forth, more than once, to all the books. But, only twice did you cause my dimension to change. The second time you brought me back. But I've lived in that dimension for three years. So whatever you did happened later than sooner. Even if time changes speed, it remains relative."

"Einstein will love to know that."

"Let's do the arithmetic. I've been gone eight and a half years. You say it's only been five months and a few days. Where do they match up closest? What trip would have been at roughly the same time? Ash, if we can graph this, we'll know which entry is the tripwire."

"That will close access to that dimension, but we're no closer to getting home. We still have to undo the Kopplers."

"I'm getting to that. You found me, as a memory, at the party after I shot them. You had to move forward in time to find me in today. Moving paperclips can take us backward."

"So, first, we close the dimension, then from here, you go back to 2008 and just leave."

"No. It's more complicated. Even if I go back sooner, I have a mission—kill them. I need to be stopped."

"So I have to come too."

"No. You have to enter after me, and stop me. And I'm going to put up a fight. Trust me. I'm right. It's on you to make this work."

"Will that get us home?"

"I don't believe it will. But it should eliminate any obstacles."

"In other words, we're stuck here, unless we can find a bridge home."

"Yup."

We spent the rest of the afternoon studying the exact times that Ash had entered the portal, where he'd gone and where they fit on an eight-year timeline. When he reached Hitler, the time he'd spoken to him, the answer jumped out. Or one of them did. Either Hitler changed his future strategy and war against England became primary, or Ashley's chat with Winston provided the catalyst.

"How do we tell which it is?" Ashley asked.

"Not sure. It may not matter. Our objective is closing the other dimension. You made all these trips from here. So we keep going backwards until we reach them all. Then we'll see."

"Fritz, I can't be sure, but my visit with Churchill stands out. Right before, when I saw Lee, Lee could see his future, but Churchill couldn't. What if meeting him in his future and sharing the same information both in his past and his future, blocked his view?"

"But you said he remembered you, and our future visit, just not the rest of the war. And that's when the other Ashley showed up, that car accident with Sandy. Maybe you shoved other you into the next universe. We need to find out."

I wrote a paragraph to outline what our next step needed to be. If his chat with Churchill was the key, then that would close us into only this dimension. Lee would still see his future and I wouldn't be able to see Kate again. I didn't mention that to Ashley, but the plan now required care.

"This complicates matters, doesn't it?" he asked.

"We'll figure it out. But I don't want to be stuck here."

His response hit me, hard, when he sat up and said that our goals differed. Ashley almost never loses his temper, but he shouted. "We're at cross-purposes. I know you, Fritz. You don't want to go home. If you want to stay, fine, but figure out how to get me back first."

When I didn't respond, he pushed away from the table and walked out the front door, retrieving for me a memory of the same empty feeling I'd had when he was shot. I had always known that he had never lacked courage, that I couldn't have a better friend. I'd always sensed that Linda liked him better than me. *Don't be stupid. She married you.* I had to consider what going home would mean. But that would have to wait. The weather people predicted another storm for Monday.

As expected, the rain came. But we couldn't try the portal until evening. We went alone, just the two of us, and waited in Ashley's classroom. The storms were scattered and predicted to continue through the night.

"Here we are, waiting again," said Ashley.

"And proving one thing. We've forgotten what we recognized from the start. The portal is dangerous. Playing with time isn't a game. Tell me what will happen if I go home. I can't see it anymore."

"Like I told you before, Linda came home as soon as she found out you were in trouble. I didn't have enough time with her to know her reasons, but the portal scared her, from the start. She told you that. You, we, never really considered the problems we were creating. We ignored every sign."

"We did some good things with it, Ash."

"Enough to make wrecking our lives worthwhile?"

"I don't know."

"I do. It was. I'd never have met Jane if you hadn't found it. But we abused it. All those trips to the past, talking to dead people. Telling them, showing them what their futures looked like."

"How do I go home? She said she doesn't love me."

"You remember that? She's had her life jumbled, just like you. Maybe she was more susceptible to the changes. She warned us. You'll only find out if you go home. Remember why you're here. You wanted to prevent all the bad things the Caballeros did. And we can't go home until you undo it all. Fritz, none of what you've done or seen is real. Not for you. Not for me. We're just actors in this play."

A distant rumble caught our attention. If we could be travelling, it would be soon.

"Here's the plan if we go," I said. "We do the two Gettysburg trips and then Hitler. He has to see you, but you won't say anything. Then, Churchill. One of them will close the other dimension." Those words halted me. Ash had been pacing, and stopped.

"So this is it. Fritz, if you're right … you need to decide now."

I stared past him, at the ugly walls. My worlds were intermingled, and only one could survive. I stood at the windows, watching the trees bending in the storm, and swaying back in retaliation. Then a final thought made it to the surface. "Ash, if we succeed, will any of this have even happened? Will we remember?"

"I don't know. I guess it depends on where we go back to. If we can."

Rumbles and flashes passed nearby for two hours. The rain had been steady, but neither of us could open the portal. As midnight approached, we agreed to try with the next storm.

Chapter 44

Ashley

FRITZ GATHERED THE notes and I grabbed the books. We walked toward the car as the rain fell harder. Natalie's VW turned into the lot. She parked right at the curb in front of us.

"I thought you'd be here. Any luck?"

"We were just leaving," I said.

"Don't go yet. I came when I saw the weather report. A line of thunderstorms is coming fast. They even put up a tornado watch. Stick around for another half hour and see."

As if she'd ordered it, a crash overhead opened the spigot. She climbed out, and in the twenty feet back to the door, we were drenched. Hurrying to the classroom, we were chased down the hall by a blinding flash, and rattling lockers welcomed us back. We set up the trips just as planned. When the next flash came, I grabbed the doorknob—nothing. Fritz said to open the door, let it close, and try again. Still nothing.

"You have to go in, so let me try." After the next flash, Fritz grabbed the doorknob, nodded and pulled. I stepped through, into the rainy hills above the Potomac. A glance around, a gust of wind, and I returned, as wet as I'd been minutes earlier. Fritz opened the door and flipped through the next book, Longstreet's memoir, and clipped it, while I dripped in the hall.

"We're making a mess again," Nat said.

Fritz said, "We'll get it later. We don't have much time." He pulled again, and the billowing smoke on a warm breeze hid my steps. Longstreet held his binoculars at his chest, staring at me, and two soldiers were taking aim just beyond him. I nodded and made a most hasty exit. Two bangs on the closing door must have been musket balls chasing me.

"That was close. Last time, Longstreet didn't see me. He did this time."

"That may be helpful later, but let's finish this," Fritz said and replaced Longstreet with "Mein Kampf." He looked at my soaked clothes and asked if I was ready. I told him I was, but before he opened the door, he said, "Wait."

"Why?"

"If Hitler is the change agent, when you come back, that closes the dimension. Lee saw his life in the future. Maybe we should do that first." For most of the time since he found the portal, I had trusted his choices. But closing the route to that dimension prevented another trip that he wanted to take.

"Why does that matter?"

"If he can see his future, maybe he can see how we cross dimensions. He might be able to help us get home." His logic made sense, but his voice lacked its usual passion, especially when going to visit Lee.

"Fritz, we both know that we control the portal. You will see Lee again. He said so. We can set that up. But if we don't close that connection, we can't undo the Kopplers."

He licked his lips, deciding how to respond to me. But he looked away. Something else held him back. In the moments he hesitated, his eyes began to cloud and tears trickled from the corners. Then he looked at me squarely. He had made his decision.

"Let's get you home."

He reached for the doorknob. Hitler looked from the cell window, his back facing me. As much as I would have liked to stay longer, I stepped backward into the school, watching him until I could no longer see him.

At the next stop, Churchill paced his office, reading from a handful of papers, talking to himself. I lingered a bit longer, listening as he prepared a speech. As he started to turn, I stepped out of the portal.

"Okay," Fritz said, "one last stop." Unless I had done something I couldn't remember, the Wrights would be my last trip. As I stepped through, Orville looked right at me. He told Wilbur that I'd returned. But I had returned to Riverboro before he got a response.

"Wait, we missed Lee. We need to go see him. I went with Sandy, in this dimension. That's when he could see the future. I don't know which dimension I was in, but that's the same day that other me came back. We have to make sure I didn't bump him."

"I can't believe we forgot that. Then we'll do Churchill again."

"Will the order matter?"

"We'll find out soon enough."

In theory and according to our plan, we had now reversed all we could. But out of order. We waited a week for another storm, and Fritz's last check of McNamara's. I hoped our guessing proved correct. Fritz had moped for a week, hardly speaking to me. We believed he'd been right, and the dimension should be closed. Now, we had to work out reversing the Koppler mess.

"Let's try something different," he said. "Instead of McNamara's, let's go to the Cozy Kitchen."

"Why?"

"If the dimension is closed, I won't surprise anyone. Kate will know me if it's still open. We have that news clipping to connect us."

"Can you do this without changing anything?"

"I said I'd get you home. We need the lightning, but that should do it."

I never doubted that he'd find a way to see his lady friend again, but I agreed. A storm waited all day until evening when it finally rolled through. Not wasting time, we waited for a flash, and I opened the portal. I watched Fritz cross the street and turn down the alley. In about five minutes, he returned.

"It's closed."

"How do you know?"

"I went in the kitchen door. I set the time so I would go in during breakfast. Seamus was cooking. He asked what I wanted. I told him I wanted a smoke. He gave me two and told me to get lost. Kate was at the window. Neither of them recognized me." Fritz dripped tears as he spoke. "I've relived every day that I've known you. I'm not sure I can go back to what life used to be."

"No one said life would ever be easy. If you go home, to our real lives, maybe all you've been through will be just a vague memory. We need to get *home* to find out."

I've had hints, feelings, forebodings, that Fritz might not be entirely forthcoming even if I convinced him that we'd succeeded. Warmer weather promised that we'd have access to the portal, but no means to get home. We still needed to reverse the initial act that started all this. If Fritz crossed into this dimension when he shot the Kopplers, then getting out required a plan we agreed would work. Every day without a storm allowed time to be exact. Natalie's notes, and her objective analysis, kept Fritz from drifting. In the daytime, I prepared for the end of the school year, while he became progressively more remote.

By Memorial Day weekend, my classes were caught up, finals were prepared, the seniors had their college plans completed, and police visits had ended. Even Rachel and Nicole had found common ground. They helped teachers keep the peace, surprising the staff and particularly George.

At home, however, Fritz became a disagreeable guest. He'd stopped cleaning and cooking, shopping and cutting the grass. When I asked what he did every day, he said, "I took a walk."

Saturday brought a downpour. Waiting in the lot for our arrival, Nat, wearing a yellow slicker, leaned in the driver's window of a police car. She said we all should get out of the rain. Chief Shaw climbed from the car.

The four of us dripped a path to my door. Fritz placed the book on the desk, and I checked where he'd placed the paperclip.

"You don't think I know how to do this?" he growled.

"I want to be sure where I'm going. This trip ends the questions, so I need to be exact. I want this over, Fritz, even if you don't. So let's do it."

Natalie and Shaw waited by the door, side glances at the grumbling they had witnessed, standing in the small puddles we had brought with us. I tapped the doorknob. No buzz. Fritz said we had to wait for lightning, and so each with our own thoughts, we silently stood in the hall. Nat had been following the storm radar on her phone, and said the storms were going by to the north. After a few minutes of trying the door, I said we should go in the class and wait. Fritz growled that we were wasting our time.

"Do you have pressing business somewhere? Maybe a date?"

"Stop, Ash," Nat said. "That doesn't help."

"Sorry, but we can't fix this mess if we're somewhere else. Nothing," I looked at Fritz, "is more important. So we're gonna wait." My anger rose, but I didn't say more. My doubts increased that I could count on Fritz, something I had never doubted in our real life. He sat in a chair at the back, arms crossed, staring out the windows.

"We're making a mess here," Nat said. "Water everywhere. I'll get some towels." When she stood up, a crack of thunder jolted us. But still no lightning. I followed her to the hall.

"Nat, unless we get some help from Mother Nature, we should forget it for tonight. This will dry. Don't worry about it."

"According to my phone, there's a heavy band on the way. I'll get the towels. I think we should stick around a little longer. Do you think this will work?"

"I hope so. Fritz annoys me more each day, and he refuses to talk. Your notes are my only source of how to attack the problem."

She patted my cheek, and went to get the towels. When she returned, the three of us were back in the hall. The buzz tickled my fingers.

"Ready?" Fritz said he was. "Where's the gun?"

"I didn't bring it. I can't kill them if I don't have one."

"That's not the plan. I have to stop you."

"We only have to go in and step out."

"You're improvising. We've spent weeks on this, Fritz. Don't screw it up."

"Don't tell me how to do this. I know what I need to do." At that moment, the chance of going home dropped off the charts. I would be on my own.

Chapter 45

I WAITED FOR Ashley to open the door. Natalie tackled the puddle by the door and stopped to watch as the door opened. In front of me, the party materialized, just as it had eight years before. I took the step across, and surrounded by shrubs, watched men rushing to the piled bodies. A second later, a hazy figure appeared nearby.

"Go back, Ash," the other dimensional me said. "The paperclip is wrong. Time changed."

"No, that's not what happened. We're in the other dimension. Like when I first found you. I don't know how it happened. Can you see your portal?"

"Yeah, right here."

"I'm leaving. You should as soon as I'm gone."

As soon as he exited, I met him in the hallway and closed the door.

"What happened?" Nat asked.

"The other dimension isn't closed, or we just re-opened it," Ashley said. "Do you know?" He was talking to me, but the tone wasn't questioning, but accusing.

"We jumped to the universe where you found me. I thought the lightning caused the bridge, but another variable must be in play. If that's so, then I'm not sure closing the other dimension even matters.

But I need to be in this dimension to reverse the killings. So let's try again."

We went to the desk and I looked at the paperclip. We needed to enter earlier, but not much, so I nudged the clip. When Ashley opened the door, I could see the Kopplers alive again, setting my heart pounding, knowing they had ruined my life.

"Chief Shaw, Ash is right. Can I borrow your pistol?" He glanced at Ashley, who nodded. "I'll bring it back in a minute."

As if it had just happened, I could recall the hate that drove me at these men.

That hadn't changed. I waited in the bushes, concealed and safe for the moment. From where I stood, ten steps, three shots and I would be gone. I checked that the chamber held a bullet, and released the safety. Most of the security guards and secret service agents faced away, and were nowhere close. I held the pistol close to my leg, and took a step toward my targets.

From behind, my collar was gripped and I found myself airborne, weightless, until I crashed on my back. Ashley interfered, trying to keep me from killing those bastards.

"Let me up, Ash. I have to do this."

"You did it already. We're trying to reverse it. Don't you remember?"

I swung the gun from my side at his face. He blocked it, but my finger found the trigger. I pointed it at him.

"Back off, Ashley. I have to do this."

"Calm down. I'm not the enemy. Give me a chance to get up." He started to get off me, then dropped his knee on my right hand and punched me on the jaw. He squeezed the top of my shirt, and banged my head on the ground.

"Get off me."

"You need to come with me. The portal is making you do this. You don't remember why you're here now."

I'd never seen him so angry and I had never tested his strength. With no help from me, he pulled me upright, and in the same motion picked up the gun. The rectangle of the portal was in front of us, only a couple more steps.

From behind us, a voice said, "Stand still and put your hands up." A secret service agent pointed a gun.

Without loosening his grip, Ashley said, "We were just leaving, James. See you soon. Say hi to Lucy." As soon as James Williams leaned in for a closer look, with his gun lowered, we were through the portal. Before we stopped moving, Ashley slapped me.

I rubbed my cheek, feeling the welts from his fingers. "What did you do that for?"

"I want to be sure you're back to normal. Do you know what just happened?"

"Yeah, I just shot the Kopplers. For ruining our lives. You should thank me."

"Brian, take this." Ashley passed him the gun. "How many shots have been fired?" The chief switched the safety back on and sniffed the barrel.

"Hasn't been fired at all."

Ashley grabbed my shirt front again. "Did you hear that? You did what we planned. You tried. I stopped you. Now we have to find a way to get home."

"Stop yelling, Ash. You'd think I'd killed somebody."

On the way back to Ashley's house, my left cheek burned. I gently touched it, but the sting held on. He saw, and said he had to slap me to get me back.

"Back where?" I asked.

"You don't remember?"

"All I remember is stepping into the portal, and you trying to choke me in the hallway."

"Interesting. Do you recall our plan?"

I wanted to say yes, but hesitated, trying to recall what I'd gone into the portal to do. I could see the three men, and I tensed as my anger rose.

"You stopped me from killing them. I wish you hadn't."

"Listen to yourself. The only way to get home is to reverse exactly that. You started this by killing them. Two of them were dead already. We may have the third to deal with when we get home."

"What do you mean?"

"Fritz, you need to get a grip. Richter, Richemartel and Thomas Koppler are the same person. You killed James Koppler. Jim Shaw killed the other brother. Have you forgotten all we did with the portal?"

"I think we need to talk about it, about home. It's all a blur. But it's been so long ago my memory hasn't caught up. Ash, going home is going to be hard."

When I said that, my emotions swirled, like a full bottle being dumped in the sink. Living in this world offered nothing. And what my former life had available did nothing to make me want to be there. Ashley turned into the driveway and sighed before opening the car door. He told me to come inside. Our long talk had waited, and the time for it had now arrived. Natalie went to get dinner and would be back soon.

"I want her to hear this, Fritz. She'll take notes so you can keep reading when I'm not here. Nothing can be normal again until we get there. Both of us."

"Fine. If you think it will help."

Once at the table he poured us each a shot of whiskey. I took a couple of sips to calm myself, but not enough to dull understanding. He began with when we'd first met. The only interruption, Nat and dinner, didn't stop his monologue. Nat served the food, but had her pad filling almost before she hit the chair.

Lights burned into the early morning. Ashley had introduced me to someone I had forgotten, who lived in an alien world. Me. Slowly, as he detailed an alternative timeline, I began to remember. I'd known all this, of course, for eight years, yet each new story elicited memories, feelings and images that could have been a movie, a novel, or a dream.

"Ash, I know everything, but it's like I have some kind of a cloud veiling my memory, but only from going into the portal today."

"Good. At least you remember. If you do, and you lost it when you planned to kill them, then the trauma from your original entry reactivated by repeating the mission, the reason for doing it. Do you remember what happened to me when we rescued the president in Geneva? Dr. Dutton?"

I had to admit that dredging up memories took me longer than either of us expected. The memories were like the bottom of a three-layer cake, trying to get through the filling, the top layers and the icing. They existed, but were mixed with each bite, hard to separate.

"I get it. I burned my past in another universe. Until now, my memories weren't real. Thanks, Ash. Now we have to figure out what's next."

"Fritz, I've been over all the entries, especially the ones into the other dimension. Other than getting home, this is the last obstacle. We've missed something. I don't know what it is. We're solving an equation for an unknown. "X" equals what?"

Chapter 46

Ashley

WE'D REACHED MEMORIAL Day, Fritz and I, marooned in lives not our own. Every waking minute, we talked or thought about how to get across to our world. Even puttering in the yard, one of us had notes at the deteriorating picnic table. Natalie came and went, mostly running errands for us, reserved and reluctant to interject a comment about an outcome she hoped wouldn't occur.

With less than a month of school remaining, I had avoided extra visibility, with the kids or the teachers. Sandy had bluntly asked if I had started using drugs again. When I asked her why she thought that, she said I'd been aloof and uninvolved. I said I had a mission to complete, and then I'd be gone. In spite of what she'd seen, she shook her head.

George cornered me on Thursday, as June began and the combination of spring fever and senioritis spread virally through the halls and into each class.

"Ashley, I want to let you know that you've been named "Teacher of the Year."

"I'm flattered. But I'm sure you can find any number of others who are more deserving."

"I agree, but I didn't choose you. The faculty voted, with some assistance, I understand, from Nicole and Rachel."

I grinned at the arm-twisting I could imagine. "Thanks, George. Give it to the runner-up."

"I can't. You won unanimously. The teachers saw those two troublemakers and what you made them into, and voted as they were told. I have that information from multiple sources." Then he laughed, and slapped my arm. "I'm glad you haven't time-traveled away."

That evening, with another late storm on the horizon, Nat and Tony joined us for a quick dinner. Finding Lee at Appomattox provided our next challenge. We discussed which books to use.

"You said Lee would meet Fritz there," Natalie reminded me. "If Lee saw you at Appomattox, you can't meet him if you don't go."

"I still don't understand what he can tell us that fits this puzzle. Which dimension will we be in?"

"From all I can figure," Fritz said, "Lee met you in this world, so this is the one we need to be in. But that's not a problem now."

"Maybe."

Appomattox. Where this nightmare began. I found my copy of the book Fritz originally used and thumbed the pages to Lee's arrival at the McLean house. Fritz and I planned to go together and see if we could arrange to meet the general for a private conversation. We needed to be visible to him, and obscured from other eyes.

Nat invited Brian Shaw to join us. She explained that if we were successful, we might not return. Tony hooked the generator to the door to give us an escape if this plan didn't work. As I stepped to the door, Natalie grabbed my arm.

"You need to tell Brian what to do if your old self comes back. Her eyes told a story of their own, one that had nothing to do with Shaw, other me, or Lee. Tears tracked her cheeks.

"Don't cry. You have a different future than you think. If this works, you may not even remember these last six months." I circled her with my arms, and pulled her tightly in. I didn't dare kiss her properly, so I pecked her cheek. "When we step in, the door will close but the portal will remain open. If we're coming back, one of us will let you all know within an hour. Don't leave until at least then. Brian, if we don't return, expect that another version of me, the one you know, will likely be back. You remember what you said to me when I first got here?" He nodded, recognizing the possible finality of our relationship. "Tell him the same story. He'll be disoriented, and may tell you that he believes he time-travelled. Tell him what's happened here. I can only speculate, but I have a feeling he'll straighten out."

I thanked Tony, hugged Natalie again, and pulled the door open. Fritz led me through the woods to the far side of a house, around which horses waited and soldiers milled, all eyes wandering to any movement or sound near the front door. When the meeting finished, Lee mounted Traveller and with hat in hand, returned the salute of the blue-clad men who had removed their hats. When he turned to go, Fritz pulled me to the road, the exact location we needed. Lee spotted us, nodded his recognition, and with his hands on the reins, gently waggled his fingers, pointing for us to follow.

We walked at a leisurely pace, not wanting to draw attention, until no one at the house could see us. Then we sped up until we enter the woods. Waiting just out of sight, to the left of the road, Lee sat on a tree stump.

"Good to see you again, General," Fritz said.

"And you, Mr. Russell. Mr. Gilbert, I see my visions have been real."

"As I told you, General, we're in a different dimension, a parallel universe."

"So there are multiples of me. Do I win the war in any of them?"

"We don't know, but for some reason, we were supposed to meet you here. At Appomattox. Do you know why?" Fritz asked.

I added, "Can you help us get home, to our real world?"

"I'm afraid I am unable to tell you more than what my visions have shown me."

"Other than meeting us here, would you tell us what more you've seen?"

"Straight down this road, my men await me. They will want orders and my report. I must make haste. Follow me, if you will, and keep to the road. I will send horses for you. We will have opportunity to speak in a short while. I'll prepare a pot of tea for your arrival."

Chapter 47

Linda

ERIC'S SPRING VACATION began yesterday, according to the MIT website's student calendar. I'd called Jane and asked her to let the president know. I'd also emailed Natalie and asked her to tell Tony. Lois McAllister visited the bike shop earlier and I asked her to let George know we could all be at the school off and on during Eric's time off. Once more, with all the pieces in place, we waited for Eric.

On Saturday evening, Mom told me to sit and watch a movie, or take TJ for a walk because, she said, the carpet couldn't take the beating any longer. I'd expected to hear from Eric, or Jane, or at least Lois by now. So I raced full speed to the door when the bell rang.

Standing on the top step, Mel Zack reached for the door handle. I touched the handle, like Fritz did with the portal, and three more cars pulled up and parked, and a red Mustang pulled into the driveway.

"Mom, we have lots of company."

"Wonderful. Ask them if anyone's hungry. My lasagna is done."

When Eric hopped up the steps, just ahead of George and Lois, he had a smile for me. The first real crowd in almost a year, I sat them in the dining room.

"Emily, good to see you again," said the president, when Mom carried a pan in and set it on the table.

"Hello, Mr. President. You better be hungry. You all better be. Natalie, dear, will you help me. Jane, get drinks, Linda set the table."

"I can help too," said the president.

"You stay there. You're the second guest of honor." She ducked around the corner. Plates and silverware clanked and clinked, glasses pinged, as Emily cut the lasagna. As fast as the plates arrived, Mom had a portion on each, large enough for two appetites. Once everyone had a plate and a drink, eating began in earnest, except Mom, who looked from plate to plate.

"Linda, as usual, this is delicious. Maybe better than the last time." The president looked at me and grinned, then filled another forkful. When I started to speak, Mom tapped my hand. Like a crew of mutes, only the scratch of silverware on stoneware preceded the gentle melody of enjoyed food. After two or three tastes, each eater complimented me on my latest masterpiece.

"I didn't make it. This is Mom's version of my recipe. She made a couple of changes, and I think it's better than mine."

"Emily, it's fantastic," the president said. "Sorry, Linda, but I think you're right. Not by much, but she's got you beat."

"I'm glad you like it. I never appreciated how much work Linda did to make one. Now I do." Mom blew me a kiss. "But now that you're fed, it's time to hear from our first guest of honor. Welcome home, Eric. What news?"

"Let him finish, Mom. Those portions are enormous."

Tony said, "They were the exact right size. And anyone who can't eat it all, send it my way. Ms. Miller, Emily, this hit the spot. I'm glad I skipped lunch."

"How's the shop, Linda?" the president asked, giving a sideways glance at Eric's plate.

"Still quiet. It'll get busy once the warm weather gets here. Or so I've been told."

Mom interrupted. "We can talk about that later. Eric, I'll wrap up what you have left, and I have some you can take home for your family, but let's get down to business. Tell us what you've found."

Eric laid his fork down and pushed his plate away. "I've opened my portal a few times now. I've bought all the books. I didn't find Mr. R or Mr. Gilbert, but I do know that they both went to the places, at least some of them. I only spoke to two people. The first, Orville Wright, told me that he and his brother had spoken to Mr. R and Mr. Gilbert, but that had been a while ago. Mr. President, Winston Churchill asked me to give you his greetings. He told me Mr. Gilbert had recently poked his head in, but he remembered meeting them both. So I know I'm on the right track. I think I need to use the school to fine tune my search."

"Then we should go now," said George. "No one will question us if I'm there."

Eric said, "That's fine with me. But I have a list of all the variables I could think of. If it's okay, I'd like to use Mr. R's classroom, and I'd like to start where the portal first opened. Dr. Barclay said that Mr. Gilbert believed that Mr. R wanted to go see Robert E. Lee. So I want to go to when my class met him. Maybe Mr. R will be there. At Appomattox."

A half hour later, Eric had everything set up. George brought buckets from the cafeteria to fill the pool. Eric selected paperclips from Fritz's desk drawer, no longer containing a lock.

"The desk may not work, Eric," Tony said.

"It's still electrified. Mr. McAllister, do you have the key?"

"I've been carrying the master since Election Day. It's not his key, but it will open all school desks. Ms. Sweeney hadn't yet left the day the lightning hit. Will that work?"

"I won't know until I try."

George handed him the key, and he laid it in the drawer in front of where the lock should have been. He selected the necessary book from the bookcase, clipped the page, and everyone cleared the room. With the generator hooked up, Eric pulled the door open. To Fritz's classroom.

I can't describe my disappointment, but I didn't have time to say a word.

"Planes," Tony said.

"I can't help," said the president.

"We need a thunder storm," said Eric. "I couldn't get through in my lab without them. Sorry. I thought we'd have the planes."

I asked the president if he had any ideas. He scrolled for numbers on his phone, dialed General Beech and explained the situation. The general said he would make a call and be back to us shortly.

While we waited, we sat in Fritz's room. Eric described all he'd seen on his other portal trips. He said he avoided exposure, only looking in, not talking to anyone else. I asked if anything unusual caught his attention.

"The scariest spots were Hitler and Dallas. Seeing Hitler and knowing what he would become, I wanted to get a gun and shoot him. The emotion surprised me, almost as if the portal gave me feelings I'd never had before. I opened the portal to Dealey Plaza, just as President Kennedy came around that corner. I watched and listened for shots. An echo amidst the screaming made it impossible to tell if more shots came from other places. Then I shut the door. When the shock wore off, I wiped my face. I'd been crying. That surprised me too."

Jane asked, "Do you think the portal influences our emotions?" Eric started to answer, then paused and nodded. He reminded us of his first conversation at Christmas. Jane repeated that he thought energy changed forms. All thoughts, including emotions, flowed through all dimensions. "If that's true, at least to some degree, our relationship to the portal is as strong as our relationship to each other. And maybe stronger between those we know best. That explains why you left, Linda, and also why you came back."

The president said, "Fritz and I went to see my mother, and we had no trouble making the connection, or convincing her I was her son."

"It may also help to explain why it's been so easy to convince figures from the past that we're not really aliens," Mom said. "When I met Ben Franklin, I felt like I'd known him for years. I can't explain it, but it's like the portal communicates its own good and bad, depending on where it opens."

The president's phone rang. The ringtone sounded like "Ready or Not." I couldn't be sure. He grinned when I looked at him. The only part of the conversation we could hear lent promise to our wait. "That's good. Thanks, Jim."

He said the general had arranged for the pilots who had worked with us before to join our newest adventure. I wouldn't have picked that word. He said the general would make arrangements for special duty and would send phone numbers to text the pilots. But he couldn't put it together until tomorrow. The code word would be "history."

Eric said he'd be home all week, and he could be here early if we wanted to have a full day of trying. He said that he'd also checked the weather. The 10-day forecast called for possible storms later in the week.

"That's good," said the president. "I don't want to overuse our welcome."

For me, Sunday couldn't come soon enough. I invited everyone back for coffee and dessert, but only Jane and the McAllisters came. Eric said he wanted to check his notes and visit with his parents, but we agreed to meet at the school at ten the next morning.

Chapter 48

Jane

I ENJOYED MY time with Linda on Saturday night. She acted like her old self again. And Emily kept us all laughing with her stories about Tim, Ben Franklin and life in general. I think she shocked Linda with a personality that had been disguised. I can't recall the number of times Linda said, "You never told me that."

When I got back to Ash's place, the hominess had fallen off a cliff. I hadn't been there for a few weeks, and unless Ash got back now, my new job limited my freedom of movement. My mother asked what I would do if Ashley wasn't home soon. I had told them about the portal and all its history because I needed to get her off my back. As always, the president helped, stopping by one weekend in February to get their oaths. My father has said repeatedly that the president's visit and our story would be a highlight of his life. No doubt.

I arrived at Riverboro High early by fifteen minutes, the last to show up. Everyone's anxiety surfaced. The president paced the hallway. Eric had his pool set up, the planes had been called, and George had a pink hue. Greetings were subdued, waiting for Eric to open the door.

"Dr. Barclay, these are my notes from last night. See if you can spot any mistakes." I read them quickly and marked from the details that he might have a photographic memory. He even remembered our dinner conversations.

"Nothing I can see, but I told you before, I haven't really looked at the physics angle of the portal. Just try it and see."

"Does anyone want to come with me?"

"I met Lee a couple of times," said George. "Most of us have." He glanced at the faces and nodding heads. "Why don't we all go?"

Eric said if Lee was alone, we might frighten him. He might not have met anyone yet. "Then I'll go with you," George said. His color returned to normal and his warrior demeanor shone like armor. "Open it, Eric and let's see what we have here."

Dirt and grass replaced the classroom, trees and the strange mixed smell of spring flowers and sulfur wafted into the hall. George took a stutter-step and crossed the threshold, Eric on his heels. The door clicked shut.

As I've said, waiting is the hard part. Fortunately, we didn't wait long. Eric reported that the general had asked if he had forgotten something. So he acknowledged that Fritz and his classes had been there, but didn't know George or anything else about the portal.

"I didn't want to say too much. I don't want to change something that will make it harder to find them." He wanted to explore the places in the books again from here rather than his lab. Different starting points might have left a trail.

"I have an idea," Tony said. "Mr. President, I have my detection rods and my recorder with me. But no one knows I've kept them. I know I should have told someone, but..."

"Where are they?" When Tony said they were in his car, the president said, "Go get them. We'll worry about the protocols later."

Eric asked what he was talking about. Tony said he'd explain once he could show him. The story of how Tony had been able to detect images of people in an empty space based on electrical residue amazed even those of us who had been included.

"We can go inside and see if I can capture images of where Fritz stopped showing up. That way we can find where he actually ended up." Ashley had mentioned Tony's "gizmos" before he disappeared.

Now I understood what he meant. I suggested that we replicate the entire scenario, which meant transferring to Ash's classroom.

"I've had a substitute teacher in Ashley's room since November," said George. "Will that matter?"

"It shouldn't unless she's done something to his desk."

"She complained about the indelible markings, said it disturbed her to have a messy desk. Ashley's desk is in another classroom that nobody uses."

"Good thing we're doing this now, but we can't keep moving it every time we're here," said Tony.

I told them that Ashley and Fritz had experimented with the desk and Fritz said it was the desk not the room.

"I remember. He was coming to get me," the president said.

Eric listened and made some notes. He said if we could use it once, today, he'd try to get everywhere Fritz might be. "Can we store it nearby?"

"Across the hall. The Summit room, I call it," said George. "I haven't changed it, but we've used it for meetings. We can keep Ashley's desk in there for now."

When we finally had all the pieces on the chess board—I know Ash would appreciate the analogy—Eric and Tony began the search again. Eric skipped the Wright Brothers and since Hitler was still alive, he moved on. I held the door when they stepped next to General Longstreet and slammed it shut as soon as they ran back. The general hadn't seen them come through, but Tony waving his long wands had attracted guards who yelled. I held the door for the next entry, and they stepped into a downpour, the retreat from Gettysburg. Both were soaked and dripping, but the weather allowed Tony to take his time. While they dried off, Linda wiped the floor, seeing George get agitated with no clean-up crew available.

Eric set up the Koppler book next. In spite of Linda's efforts, he still tracked water into the classroom. When I opened the door, shots rang through the opening. I shut the door before they got in. Eric said to open it, that he would be okay. The view became clear, that of three bodies on the ground. Tony waved his sticks, and they both returned, again leaving tracks at the doorway.

"That was weird," Eric said. "The portal got foggy, like a haze or a cloud. I wonder if that's important."

Tony said, "I could swear I saw another portal rectangle just as we were leaving. Over behind some bushes."

Linda asked, "What do you think that means?"

"I need to think about all of this. It didn't look like that the last time I went in. Let's keep going."

When he opened next, Winston Churchill looked squarely at me. "They've both been here. Mr. Gilbert said Mr. Russell was lost. I presume you are searching for them still. Hello, young man, I've seen you before. Would you all like to come in?"

"We're tracking Mr. Russell's last known location," said Eric. "If you wouldn't mind, just a couple of minutes and we'll be gone."

"While you perform your experiments, may I offer you all some tea, or perhaps something a bit more lively?"

"Thank you, sir," said Tony, "but we're trying to avoid any contamination or interference. More bodies would mess us up."

"Mess you up? I must remember that, for a speech. Interesting turn of phrase. Oh well, some other time. Do give your president my regards."

"I'm right here, Mr. Prime Minister. Good to see you again. So you've been elected again, I see."

"Not yet. Officially, you and I haven't met. But whatever you've done, I'm able to see a bit of my own future."

"We're done, Mr. Churchill," said Eric. "Thanks."

Churchill waved, and as they stepped toward the portal, he said, "Good luck. And KBO."

When the door closed, I asked what had happened. "How could he know you if he's not met you?"

"What does KBO mean?" George asked.

The time to discuss what had just happened needed to occur later. First, Eric wanted to finish up this round of the search. He opened the door again. Tony saw the crowd, brandished the wands and vanished from Dallas, aware he had been spotted by what he assumed to be secret service agents.

"If Fritz came here, he wouldn't have gone far. Too many people would have seen the portal," Tony said. Linda agreed. She said that a picture like the one from the Ford factory the day Fritz found the portal might become the latest JFK assassination conspiracy news.

The portal next opened to Ben Franklin's house in Philadelphia. Franklin's surprise evaporated when he saw the president in the doorway. "Welcome, Mr. President. I've just arrived home from New Jersey. I have nothing to offer you, I'm afraid."

"We'll only be here for a moment, Dr. Franklin. We are looking for Mr. Russell and Mr. Gilbert. Have you seen them?" Franklin said he hadn't seen Fritz since his last visit with the president. "I've been away for many years."

"Then we'll leave you to recover from your travels, sir. Good to see you again."

When the door closed, Tony said the last trip wasn't necessary. Fritz hadn't seen Franklin so Lincoln could be skipped. The president asked if Eric would be willing to go to the last trip anyway. He said he'd like to see Lincoln. Eric said he would, but Tony said that he would be tempting fate in case something went wrong. The president let out a sigh, but agreed. Tony then said his next job was to analyze the data.

Before we left, we made sure everything was back in place for school the next day. Although we had been at the school early, we left at mid-afternoon. Linda invited everyone to her house, where Emily welcomed us with lunch.

The questions flew at Eric and Tony like a swarm of bees. To me, the most pressing one continued to be where did Fritz go? I had a feeling that wherever he was, Ashley would be nearby. Eric took his notes to the sunroom to compare these portal trips with his lab, and consider what differences there might be.

I went to him and asked if the hazy portal might have been another universe. And Churchill knowing his future, did he cross one of the bridges between dimensions?

"I can't prove it, but that seems reasonable. What I'm trying to figure out is what we did to trigger it. And if it is another universe, how will I ever find them?"

"Let's ask Tony. This is his bailiwick too."

With a room full of listeners, Tony and Eric discussed possible inter-dimensional travel as the answer to what we'd witnessed, but Eric said he didn't know why it happened here and not in his previous trips. Tony said again that he saw another fluorescent rectangle, which he believed had to be Fritz. No one had any new ideas, but agreed to try again if the storms came later in the week. Since Monday was a work-day, I hoped I could get back to Riverboro in time.

Chapter 49

Linda

WHEN THE HOUSE finally cleared, Mom and I sat at the kitchen table and talked about how close we were to finding a solution. I'd asked Eric to stop by the shop after he'd studied his notes. He said he'd see me tomorrow. I asked Mom what she thought I could expect if Fritz came home.

"What happens will be up to you. You know what's happened here, but you have no idea what he's been through. If you're sure you want him back, then you'll have a lot of apologizing and making nice to do, maybe for a long time. You both will need to get to know each other again."

"What if he doesn't want to?"

"Cross that bridge then, Linda. Worrying serves no purpose. You have work to do now, TJ, the shop…"

"And the house. I know. Thanks, Mom."

The storms came as predicted on Thursday evening. Jane said she would try to come, but a required meeting on Friday might make her trip impossible. She said what I was also thinking—we both wished we had the portal to use.

Tony didn't have the same restrictions, and had spent the week studying the local nuclear plants, for what he didn't say, and I didn't care. As long as he was here. He said he'd completed his analysis of the trip he and Eric took. We all met at the school, as the first rumble passed overhead.

Eric said he wanted to try a couple of places, especially where General Lee and Fritz might be together. He also suggested we keep our cell phone cameras ready to download pictures. He said he thought if we got them to a printer quickly, we could preserve the images. Tony and he had discussed the electrical effects, which were consistent with the image results Tony had detected.

Before going in, Tony said the data convinced him that Fritz entered the portal at the Koppler book. Fritz stood out more in this one image, and better defined than in the others.

"So why go anywhere else?" I asked.

"He would have used his portal to leave. But I don't know where he went after that. Remember Jane's visit from another version of Ashley. We're dealing with more than one universe, I'm sure."

Eric agreed. "That's why I want to follow the trail you and Dr. Barclay believe is most likely."

My phone interrupted the explanation. Jane asked if Eric could use his portal to come and get her. "I'll send a picture to your phone. Can you print it at the school?"

George took us into a classroom that had a printer. Tony had brought his laptop to show us the images, so he hooked up the printer. I don't know where she was, but the picture was clear enough, so Eric set it on Ashley's desk, and in a second, Jane crossed to the hallway.

"Shut it. Quick." She sighed with relief when the door clicked. "I heard footsteps."

As she was greeting everyone, she backed into the pool and water sloshed on the floor. Eric pulled her away. "Water and power don't mix," he said.

"I'll get a mop," George said. "I might as well be doing something useful."

"Okay, Eric. Let's give it a try," said the president. The small crowd in the hallway anticipated Eric's next step. He reached to the generator to turn it on, slipped in the puddle and fell in. George returned with the mop and a package of paper towels.

"What did I miss?" Lois repeated the past few minutes. "You're all right, aren't you, Eric? I don't want to file an accident report." He waited for the deadpan faces he expected from his intended uncaring comment, and then he laughed. Lois rolled her eyes.

"Do you feel like doing this, Eric?" the president asked.

"I'll be okay. I'm ready." He reached for the door.

Standing at the door frame, we watched General Lee backing his horse from in front of a house. Darting from the far side, two men were recognizable, so completely out of place in 1865.

"Quick. Take pictures and print them." We saw Fritz and Ashley trail leisurely behind the departing Confederate delegation, until they sank below a hill. "I need to get to that hill. Get me a picture." He closed the portal.

"Was that really them?" I asked.

Jane said, "Who else could it be?"

"Did you notice the haziness?" Tony asked, passing a handful of photos to Eric, with the best one on the top. "No question it's them."

Seconds later, Eric opened the door to an empty road through the woods a short distance down the hill.

Chapter 50

Ashley

WE SHOOK THE general's hand and he mounted. As he reined Traveller back into the road, the image of the many statues I had seen crossed my mind's eye.

"I will send Colonel Taylor to fetch you. He already knows our story." He waved and rode away at a gallop.

Fritz sat on the stump vacated by Lee and we waited, Fritz lost in a thought I didn't want to hear. In spite of his willingness to get me home, I wasn't sure he planned to go back with me. Seeing Lee again presented another choice for him and dilemma for me. Would he change his mind? And by doing so, would he force me to remain? We had an open portal waiting for us, but I didn't know how long Tony and Natalie would wait. We had about forty-five minutes.

I had just finished this thought when the thumping of hooves came down the road. As good as his word, Lee had dispatched his adjutant straight to us, two horses galloping behind, their reins in his hand. We stepped into the road, and the colonel waved, as he slowed.

I had never ridden a horse, other than pony rides as a kid, so mounting was harder than the cowboys made it look. The colonel held the horses steady for each of us, chuckling at my awkwardness. Fritz climbed aboard like a seasoned rider, leaving me another question for later.

My driving habit, looking both ways, added another problem. "Fritz, wait. Look up there." Too far away to make out a face, a man stood at the top of the hill surrounded by a fluorescent rectangle.

"It'll be there," Fritz said, as he and Taylor headed in the opposite direction. I watched them go, but turned the horse toward the portal. Bouncing up and down got old fast, so I got off and walked, pulling the horse behind me. The rectangle seemed closer but I made no progress as I walked up the hill. Squinting to identify who stood on the hill, he was too far away. I waved. He waved back. But where had he come from? Floating from one universe to another made the possibilities not only numerous, but worrisome. Was this a way home, or had we jumbled the universe again. I kept walking, determined to know. I won't say things couldn't get worse. I knew better.

As I climbed, almost able to recognize the face, behind me a rider pounded down the road, calling my name. Another soldier who I hadn't met before pulled up next to me.

"General Lee said to look for you, sir. Are you able to ride?"

"I'm fine, but I need to find out who that is." I turned to the top of the hill, but the portal had vanished.

"Sir, did you fall? Colonel Taylor said you weren't comfortable in the saddle."

"It was easier to walk."

"What did you say you were looking at?"

"It was nothing. Nothing."

I climbed on the horse again. The soldier took my reins and I hung on, even though we didn't go fast. I looked back a number of times until the hill was hidden by tree branches. In front, spread across a field of tents, men busily collected what little they had. Down one road, and across the nearby fields, men and horses, all walking, headed in all the compass directions going south. Their war had ended. A line of soldiers stretched out of the opening of a large tent for twenty yards. Standing outside, Fritz shared stares with the soldiers in line, some barefoot, all wearing the tattered remnants of uniforms. I couldn't help comparing the men with their cause. Remains of what they had once been.

As I slid to the ground, and thanked my tour guide, I called Fritz. He waved me to him.

"Where were you?"

"I went to see the portal and who came through."

"Who was it?"

"I didn't get close enough. He closed it."

"We have a while to wait. These guys are saying goodbye."

"Something's wrong. Aren't they supposed to give up their flags and guns to Chamberlain? Take an oath not to continue fighting?"

"A lot more men are waiting in another camp to the south."

"We're in a different dimension, Fritz. Maybe things don't happen here like they did in ours. We should get back to our portal." I checked my watch. We still had more than a half hour. Time was slowing down.

The line dwindled, and when at last the men were gone, Lee emerged wiping the sides of his eyes with a cloth, decorated with a few red dots.

"Mr. Russell, Mr. Gilbert, forgive me. I didn't mean to keep you gentlemen waiting. But we will meet again, in better times, as you know." He turned to me. "Mr. Gilbert, my vision led you here. I am glad for us both. I have been haunted since Gettysburg, and now you've proven me correct. Thank you."

"I'm glad to see you again, General," Fritz said. "I have so many questions. I've been floating in another universe for the past eight years. And wished I could ask your advice."

"Mr. Gilbert informed me that you were lost. I have been alert for your return. But I doubted until today that our paths truly would cross. What would you like to ask me?"

"Now that we know we exist in more than one dimension, can I return to my real world?"

"Ah! A difficult question, yet not unexpected. When Mr. Gilbert first told me, the prospects of different lives enticed me to consider possibilities. Mr. Russell, how our lives evolve, as I will tell you again in your future, is determined by the choices each of us makes. Can you go home? That choice is yours."

"But we don't know how to open the portal to our time."

"Your way home will come to you. What remains is to decide which choice to make. Choices are sometimes difficult. Unless you can see the future. I assure you that foresight is neither a blessing nor a gift."

"Thank you, General. I hope we will speak again."

As I reached out to shake his hand, he said, "We will not, not in my lifetime, Mr. Russell. Our future conversations have taken place, in your other world, as we know. And sadly, my time with you here is now complete. You must excuse me. I have a war I must bring to conclusion."

I had remained a bystander, but with his last words, I reached out again for his hand. "Good luck to you, General. Thank you."

Lee smiled, with a twinkle, which might have been a tear. As he turned to Fritz, just behind me a soft pop sounded, a rectangular doorway materialized, and a young man stepped through.

"Eric?"

"Hi, Mr. Gilbert. Sorry to scare you. We need to get out of here. I think that if your other portal closes before I'm gone, I'll be stuck here. We all will be." I checked my watch again. Only three minutes remained to the allotted hour. "How do you know about our portal?"

"I saw it when I chased you. Before I went back to get here, I stuck my head in. The people are the same as home, but they didn't know me. Please, come now. While we can. Dr. Barclay is waiting for you."

"Fritz," I said, taking steps toward the portal, "we're out of time. Let's go."

"Give me a minute."

Eric stepped ahead of me and said I could see just as well from the school, and he crossed the threshold. I waited a little longer, hollered to Fritz, now with Lee's left hand on his shoulder, and both of his holding the general's hand, and I stepped through. Behind me, the opening turned pitch black. And solid. The portal had closed.

Chapter 51

Fritz

THE POP OF THE closed portal was the same sound as the time I thought I would be stranded in Lee's office. Lee turned to Colonel Taylor, and instructed him to take me back to the McLean house. "Take him quickly. His time is running down." He took my arm again, and said, "Godspeed, young man. I have enjoyed knowing you. But now you must hurry."

"Thank you, sir. For everything." I mounted my horse and dashed off with the colonel leading, through the woods, up the hill, and as close to the McLean house as the colonel dared. He pointed to the sparkling rectangle, as yet undiscovered by the men in blue. I dismounted as quickly as possible, eager to avoid detection. As I climbed the incline toward the portal, the fluorescence evaporated. I turned to see the dust of Taylor's gallop away from me. Once more, I returned to the road back to the general, the landing site I had planned when I first went after the Koppler brothers.

As I breached the view at the top of the hill, General Lee and Colonel Taylor, still holding my horse, faced me. I waved and picked up my pace.

"It seems that I am mistaken and we do meet again. Your portal has closed again, Mr. Russell. In my vision, I saw your exit vanish.

The colonel and I have been waiting for you. Come with us. We must discuss your future."

Chapter 52

Ashley

NO SOONER THAN my feet were across, the portal slammed shut. The crowd welcomed me home, but only one face stood out. She waited, anticipating a reaction, a word, so with my heart pounding, I took that step and, like the Red Sea, the crowd parted and I reached the promised land. I held her at arms-length, looking deeply in her brown eyes, and gave her a short, gentle kiss. I said, "More later."

The president stepped forward, patted my arm, and suggested we all sit down to hear my story. I told them I had more to do, the story hadn't ended. In as complete a version, and in as brief a time as possible, I outlined what had happened while I'd been gone. I'd be quick, I said, and asked them to save their questions, but 'late' came faster than 'finish', so the questions remained unanswered. Jane said she had to leave but would be back the following night.

"You're the reason I'm here. How can you leave now?"

"Ash, I still have a job. I don't have the freedom the president gave me. Now I'm just another bureaucrat. I'll see you tomorrow and we'll figure out what's next. Eric, will you get me home." She kissed me, and as reluctant as I was to let her go, we'd have more of them. Before she stepped through the door, I told her to call her mother.

"Get our wedding planned for as soon as possible."

Linda said she would give me a lift. As I reached Linda's car, I asked Eric if he knew where I live.

"Sure, Mr. Gilbert."

"Do you have some time tomorrow? I'd like to find out how you found us."

"I'm free until dinner. How early could I come?"

"How about eight?"

Linda's distress shadowed her, so I invited her in. Cold and damp, the house had no signs of life. I had some adjusting to do. I offered her a drink. When she asked for Jack and rocks, a long night forced its way through the door.

"Where's Fritz? How is he?" I should have expected that, but hadn't, and she wasn't the one I planned to tell the story to. No one would hear it until Jane had a chance to think it through with me.

"Physically, he's fine. In fact, he looks great. But he's confused, Linda. He turned the world upside down. We've spent weeks trying to undo the damage."

"Do you think we'll find him again?"

"I don't know. But I'm going to try. That's why I need to talk to Eric. He found a missing variable and I need to know what it is. We're dealing with multiple dimensions in parallel universes. Nothing like what Fritz and I ever discussed, or even considered. Trust me, it's weird."

"I told you it was dangerous, that you could change things."

"Don't," I barked. "This isn't the time for that little chat. You have no idea." I stopped. I could feel heat reaching combustible levels. I needed time on my own now, and I didn't want to say the wrong thing. So I changed the topic. "I just left Appomattox in April, from early June. What day is today?"

"March twenty-seventh. Eric's home for his spring break. Riverboro's is coming."

"Then I need to get back in classroom shape. I've been teaching history in the other universe."

"History?"

"I told you. Weird."

Linda wanted more of my story, but I checked the house to see what I needed to do. It had been morning when I left Fritz, evening when we went through the portal. My internal clock was screwed up. All the activity guaranteed that sleep belonged on the back burner. A yawn, as artificial as I could make it, hinted that she should go home.

"I know you must be tired, Ash. And I'm really glad you're here. But can you tell me one thing? Why did the portal close when you came through? Does Fritz want to come home?"

"I can't give you a simple answer. And now's not the time. I'm going to bed. So I'll tell you this much. I found Fritz in a time warp eight years ago. He's relived every day, had to make a life for himself to survive, with no hope of being found and no means to get here. Sometimes I thought he was back to being himself, and other times, I talked to another, different person. He's changed. But I also have no idea what he'll be like, if I can find him again. I can answer one question that concerned us. Will everything go back to the way it was? So far, no. I remember everything. But we won't know for certain until he's here."

"Did he ask about me?"

I didn't want to answer her, or leave her the option to continue asking questions. I told her that we had talked about what life would be like if we made it home.

"But…"

"Linda, I told you that the story isn't ready to be told. It's complicated and right now, I'm too tired to unravel the details. I've been gone since Thanksgiving. I'll tell you more when I figure it out. Now go home and know this. I went after him once, and I'm going after him again."

She left, disheartened. I wiped away her tears, gave her a long hug, and walked her to her car. I couldn't help but feel a touch of anger, a gut reaction that she deserved the uncertainty. And then my remorse kicked in. I feel her pain. I had Jane back. She still didn't have Fritz.

All my months of notes stayed behind, so I needed to recreate the other worlds. Jane had put the house in order, so I had to look for a notebook. For the past decade, outlines have served me, better than lists. Once I started, details and images flooded the pages. As if I were looking at photos, I wrote all the details Natalie had recorded. When an out-of-order thought popped in, I added it to a different book. I found myself writing paragraphs under outline headings, not bullet points. When the coffee machine turned on, the first noise in hours, I stopped writing. The light of morning flooded the windows, showing an overcast and possibly stormy day. Eric would arrive in a couple of hours. Sleep wasn't an option. I hadn't eaten since 1865, a thought that brought a chuckle, so I poured a cup of coffee, and skimmed my night's work before showering.

Nothing says domesticity or woman like a bathroom. While the hot water came to life, I inspected the exceptionally clean room. The few cabinets and drawers brought a feeling of warmth. Jane's touch, her things, shared the space. Even the linen closet had her scent. But she wasn't here. That fact struck me. She was in Washington. I had months to tell her about, but had no idea what had happened here in the interim. I'd need another list, this time of questions.

I love my shower, and didn't realize how much I'd missed it until the hot water beat on me, warming and relaxing, and fortunately, waking me up. My clothes were mine again, and I could see how much time Jane had spent making sure everything was in its place. It shouted "when he gets home, things will be perfect." Close, with only one missing person.

With an hour to spare, I had time to make it to the doughnut store, which started my stomach rumbling. I grabbed my keys. My keys. Exactly where they should be, I made another note. I'd had my keys the day I crossed over. What were these? I checked my pants pockets, the pair I'd changed out. I didn't remember removing them, in either universe. But they were mine.

I opened the door. The usual red of morning, my Mustang, was gone. Too soon to accept that I'd been through this already, I examined the keys. Ford, not Toyota. So where was the car?

I refused to do the most logical thing, call Jane. I didn't want to hear a stranger's voice or a wrong number. My phone, which I had carried since I went after Fritz, and which I'd charged overnight, had other numbers. I sat at the table, and looked at the names. Who could I call and be certain I was still home? Logic fought back, so I dialed Linda. My relief came instantly.

"Hello, Ashley. So glad you've made it home. Come for breakfast."

"Emily, is that you?"

"Who else would ask you to pick up bagels?"

I could only laugh, and I said bagels would have to wait. I asked if she had any idea where my car was.

"You should put your toys away instead of making Jane pick up after you."

"Is this a riddle, or are you just being difficult?"

"A little of both, I would say. So where does a car go to sleep?"

"In my driveway."

"Beep. Wrong answer. Would you like to try again? The prize is smaller for the next guess."

"You know what, I'm not sure I missed you."

"Of course you did. It's in the garage."

"I'm not going to ask."

"Jane cleaned it out. I think she took better care of your car than you did."

"I'll see you later, Emily. We'll do breakfast maybe tomorrow."

Time returned to its regular speed and I didn't have enough of it before Eric would show up. So I backed the car to its normal place in the drive, inspected the garage, and noticed the new edition to my backyard. A storage shed. Custom-built, I guessed. I'd never had one. The garage was all I needed.

Although the shed added to the list of things that I needed to thank Jane for, it occurred to me that I hardly spent any time in my backyard. I didn't have a grill or a patio or a picnic table. Not much landscaping. I had a feeling all that was about to change.

I poured another cup and shuffled my papers into an order of sorts. Eric's arrival would mean detective work, and a new notebook. He'd found that bridge to another dimension I'd read about and I needed to know how.

For now, that question alone required an answer.

"I thought you might be hungry," Eric said, handing me a box of doughnuts. Great minds.

"Come in. If I seem out of it, that's because I am. I've been working all night to have my notes ready for you." I told him he was free to read, but he couldn't take them. I hadn't yet had time to fill in the details and every new thought jogged another.

"You mean you have more details than this?" He turned page after page. "There's a ton of stuff here, Mr. Gilbert."

"I had to get it down in case we find Fritz and everything changes again. Besides, you have a new skill which we need to dissect. I need to know how you found us. So I can go get him. Again."

"I didn't stay up all night, but I went over everything myself, until around four o'clock. I brought all my journals since I left for college. You can have them for now. But, I don't know the answer. I hoped that together we could figure it out."

"Me too. So let's get started." I pushed my papers to him and began reading his. We agreed to not ask questions until we were done, but I did give him a notebook to write his questions for later. Reading took less time than writing, but by the time we finished, it was almost noon."

"Let's take a break," I said. "I've missed some things since I left. You want a sandwich?"

"Sure. And I have a bunch of questions."

"I don't have anything here, and pastrami from the deli just called my name. Let's go see Mr. Hoffmann."

Chapter 53

Linda

THE BRUSH-OFF FROM Ashley left me only Mom to talk with about what had happened. She had stayed home with TJ intentionally, I think. She said she'd only be in the way. I think she wanted to avoid me in case we didn't find Fritz. But I had stood by the door each time Eric opened the portal, and I saw him, a blurry version of him anyway. I told Mom that I had a million emotions knowing he would be back in minutes.

When the portal closed on its own, I had as many questions as feelings. Why had he waited instead of running to catch up to Ashley? What happened with the portal? I wanted to go to Ashley's this morning and talk with him and Eric to find out what they know. Ashley's answers weren't heartening. Some had a bite. Mom said to go to work, that I'd find out when Ashley was ready.

The cloudy day promised a slow one at the store. A new shipment of models had arrived, so I had some building to keep me busy. With TJ crawling around, I had time to work, and talk to him, as I waited for the evening storms. But Eric would be gone on Sunday, so we only had today and tomorrow to find Fritz.

By mid-afternoon, I'd built two bikes, but trying them out would have to wait. Even if the rain started, that wouldn't stop me. But I had no one to stay with the baby. I took a break and TJ and I stood by the front window. When a black Suburban pulled up, and a man in a suit and sunglasses climbed from the passenger's side, TJ pointed. Mel Zack came around the car to the store entrance and when the president hopped out, Mel opened the store door. TJ said, "Da" when the president entered the store.

The president grinned at him and patted his head. His first visit surprised me, but he said he'd driven by a few times, and wanted to see for himself. TJ and I gave him a tour. I showed him the back workroom, complete with the two I'd finished and one with the parts spread across the floor and bench. "These just came in. Top shelf racing bikes. I have one of these at home. I don't get to ride it much but it has a great feel."

He ran his hand across the handlebars, and along the frame to the seat. He rubbed the tire tread with his palm. Then he asked me if I had something that would be fitting for a family outing. I led him to the showroom, and to a bike that Charlie had said was his best-selling family bike.

"Does it come in different colors?"

"Six, last I checked."

"Good. I need to get some exercise, and let the folks know I'll be around. A bike seems like a useful diplomatic tool. Besides, I think my girls would prefer not being stuck inside when we're here this summer." He scratched his cheek. "Are they all men's bikes."

"Most are unisex these days, Mr. President. We do have the traditional models, but it's not like the days of fat tires and wicker baskets."

"I'll be back when I can take one for a ride. They won't let me ride without a crew, so I'll be ordering a few."

"Bring the girls and the First Lady. I'll check what's available and send you some ideas. Leave me your email address."

I'd seen his glances at the accessories and began to plan what he would need. Before he left, I asked if Ashley or Eric had spoken to him. He said they hadn't, but would see me later.

Later. The word floated through my thoughts for the next few hours. Hurry up and wait. Where are you, Fritz? Would he be home later? I put the next bike together quickly, saving the final tune-up for later.

I shut the store and took TJ home for lunch and a nap. I could come back to finish later. Later.

Ashley called at six. He said he and Eric planned to be at the school at eight-thirty. I asked if they had figured out how to find Fritz. He said they had a couple of ideas, but he'd explain later.

When it's all said and done, I guess I didn't realize how much I want Fritz to come home. I want to share all this with him. Now. I've never thought of myself as an impatient person, but I think I hate 'later'.

Chapter 54

Jane

AS I WALKED to my car, I called Ash. As if I'd interrupted him, his brusque response worried me. I asked if he would come for me early. He said he'd open the portal at eight-thirty when everyone would be at the school. He didn't want to spend more time than necessary when we were so exposed. I asked him how the weather looked. Overcast, but not stormy, and the forecast wasn't favorable.

"Ash, you don't sound happy to hear from me. Is something wrong?"

"We need to talk. The pieces aren't fitting together and I can't figure it out. I wish you were here. Are you going back again tonight?"

"I have to be back on Monday. Should I drive instead?" When he didn't answer, I said, "I don't mind, but I can't get to Riverboro until later. I have to go home and pick up my stuff."

"We only have the planes for thirty minutes. The president called. General Beech said the wrong people are asking questions. I don't know if I can get you back by Monday. Do you have some time off you could take?"

"Let me see what I can work out. I'll see you later."

Until I look in his eyes, I won't know for certain what's bothering him. After almost a year apart and only crises bringing us together, we need time together before I call my mother. If Fritz isn't home, I'm sure he'll postpone the wedding. I need to find out if the postponement is permanent.

I'd left some clothes and cosmetics in Riverboro, so packing took no time. The strange thing about choosing what to bring had more to do with Ash's tone than the best fashion selections. He'd been back for less than a day, and we'd spent less than an hour together. Maybe his time away changed how he feels. Maybe I should have taken today off. He's right, we need to talk.

At quarter past eight, I sent a picture of my living room to his phone. Twenty minutes later, the rectangle emerged from out of nowhere. I grabbed the bag and stepped through into the hallway. Without a word, I put my arm around his neck and kissed him hard, in spite of our audience.

"That's enough, you two," Lois said. "You'll have to get a room."

Ash sucked in air and said, "Hi."

"Hi. What's going on?"

"We have time for two tries. I'll tell you what's up when we're done." He set the portal to Eric's last entry, where they had last been, and opened the door. Instead of a field full of tents, a paved road ran past, with cars travelling in either direction. On the left, we could see houses. Ash walked down the road, stopped to read a sign, and trotted back to us.

"It's an historical marker," he said. "We're in modern day. That doesn't make any sense." He and Eric checked the paperclip and reset it. "We're running out of time." He pulled the door, this time opening to a yard full of uniformed men and horses. "This won't work." He shut the door.

Ashley's forehead jutted, but he ignored us all and ran to his desk, Eric on this heels. Once again, nothing said, he pulled the doorknob.

"Fritz and I were in those woods, just off the road. I'll be right back. Keep the door open." He plunged into the portal and ran down the hill. I couldn't tell how far he'd gone, but he stopped, looked left, and started back immediately. Questions flew at him as soon as he approached us.

He shook his head at the questions and held up his hand for them to stop. He waved Eric into the room while we silently watched. Tony's phone broke through the quiet.

"Yes, sir. I'll pass the word. Thank you." He grimaced and shook his head.

"Don't you make us wait, too," Natalie said.

The frown on Tony's face said it all. The planes were leaving. "Unless the storms show up, we're done."

Ashley asked, "Do we have time for one more try? You could tape the door." Tony dug a roll of electrical tape from his supplies, and told Ash to open the door. The classroom. He tried again. The portal was closed.

We crossed the threshold taking care not to affect the portal, although the likelihood was zero. Ashley and Eric stood by the desk as we took seats. Natalie pushed buttons on her phone and announced that the storms had dissipated. No new ones were likely until mid-afternoon the following day.

"So what happened, Ashley?" Linda asked.

"Eric and I have gone over all the details. We believe that the hazy view you saw was the bridge. Lee knew us. When Fritz and I first started to experiment, way back when, we visited and I met him. Fritz reset to a time before that, and he didn't know me. Yesterday, before he'd met either of us, he remembered us both. Something here caused the bridge to match up."

"How did you connect to present day?" George asked.

"The paperclip touched an advertisement. We printed a map from the internet. We didn't use the book. But none of that matters. Fritz is in another dimension."

"Why don't you do what you did when you went there?" George suggested.

"That's the problem. I didn't do anything," Ashley said. He told us about his first cross-dimensional episode and not having a portal in order to return. Whatever Eric had done opened a bridge and they had traded ideas because whatever Eric did, Ash must have done the same to reach Fritz. "We're dealing with three separate universes. Look, this story has more twists than a good spy novel, and I've been awake since I got back here. I was awake for a day before going in the portal. I'm out of gas, and I need to think."

"Ashley, if you tell us more, we might be able to help," said the president.

"In order to do that, I'd have to tell the whole story. Right now, I'm too tired. Tomorrow would be better."

"Then how about breakfast at my house?" Linda asked. "If the storms aren't due until afternoon, we have all morning. Say ten. That should give you time, as well as some sleep."

I worried from that point. He grabbed my hand, and without another word, we left. Even in the car, he said nothing at all. When we walked in the kitchen, he went straight for the coffee. Still without a word, he lifted a stack of papers and notebooks and laid them in the middle of the table.

"Hi," I said.

He looked at me as if he'd just seen me. Then he kissed me. "Sorry, I'm not sure where I am anymore. But I need to tell you the story before we go again."

"Can it wait until morning?" I didn't say, but he looked like coiled steel, and I wanted to feel his warmth next to me.

"Jane, I love you. I've missed you. But I need you to help finish this."

"I thought you were tired."

"I am, but this is too important. If you're up to it, we'll go until we can't. I didn't want to tell the story until you've had a chance to analyze it all."

So he talked and I read until we emptied the coffee pot. When he completed the story, his return, I filled him in on what had happened here, including his doppelganger's arrival here. Just as I had imagined, he and Fritz disturbed science, and proved the theories. I watched and listened, never doubting a word. I'd seen it. But bubbling to the surface, I questioned him whether or not he wanted to make his story public.

"We can ask the president if he thinks we should keep all this as part of the oath. Ash, Koppler has escaped again, and he's still out there. If you tell the story, from what you've said, the news becomes part of universal knowledge. At least in this dimension, people won't handle it well. Before we go to Linda's, we need to edit this." I took his hand, stood up, and kissed him. "Morning will be here soon. Let's call it a night."

Banging on the front door startled me from a dream. Eight o'clock felt like only eight minutes after I closed my eyes. When Ashley opened the door, Natalie's voice said her morning began a while ago.

When I greeted them, half a pot of coffee remained. I asked her why so early. In response, she said she'd been up writing a detailed description of everything that had happened since Eric's first visit. I got a cup, listening to her version. While she talked, Ashley followed her in his notes, scribbling if she hit a point he hadn't considered.

"Will you leave these for me? I want to read them myself and compare. Between us, and Eric, the answer is here. I just don't see it. Yet. Fritz thought lightning did it, but that's not it. And Eric leaves tomorrow. Let's go eat. I'm hungry." When he got up, he made my day with a real hug and a kiss that made my legs shake.

Chapter 55

Ashley

THE OVERCAST HADN'T changed. I asked Natalie if the weather forecast had improved. When she said scattered storms were in sight and the predictions for clearing made hanging around the school a likely waste of time, but we couldn't afford to miss them. Today would be the last chance with Eric here. We arrived at the school as we had planned. Sitting on the curb, in animated conversation, Nicole and Rachel waved to the approaching cars.

"Hi, Mr. President," they said in unison, as we crossed the lot. When they saw me, they ran up to me. Or so I thought. "Hi, Jane," they said. They had another party for their chatter, and they ignored me, walking with Jane, captive between them. They joined us as we entered the school.

George elbowed me. "Looks like we don't count anymore." I agreed, but a pervasive sense of no longer being on their radar made me lonely. Maybe more had changed here than I thought. "Should we let them stay, Ashley?"

"They know the drill. So why not?"

"Should we get set up?" I said I would talk to Eric and then decide. I wasn't hopeful. I didn't want to stay any longer than necessary. The big breakfast must have landed on my eyelids. All of a sudden, sleep became a logical next step.

Eric said he was leaving for Boston first thing the next morning, but would continue to search for the answer if we failed to find Fritz today. We agreed to wait another half hour. If the storms came later, we could come back.

While we talked, the president had spoken to General Beech. No planes would be available. When we joined the others, my belated greeting generated the smirks and laughs I had missed. "Hi, Mr. Gilbert."

Rachel asked if they could help. "Jane said you were going after Mr. R."

"We can help you look," Nicole said.

I thanked them for the offer, but it could be dangerous. The portal had malfunctioned, I said, and they could get lost, too. The president asked if they would like to help him sort through his papers. "I have my library to put together. You can work for me until you go to school in the fall."

"Cool, Mr. President. Summer jobs. That will be fun," Nicole said.

"Can we start today?" Rachel asked.

Amidst the grins at their enthusiasm, he said, "Give me your phone numbers and I'll set it up. I know I can trust you, but we'll need to get you clearances and background checks. Mel will get everything started."

"Will we be spies, too, like Mr. Gilbert and Mr. R?" Nicole asked.

"We'll see." The president reached out and shook their hands. "But we have a deal."

The storms disappointed everyone, Linda most of all. When she invited us back to her house, I declined. Tired, and with no ideas to share, Jane and I left them to shut down.

"Jane, we need to talk," I said, when I roused from my nap. "I'm not waiting for Fritz to come home. I want to marry you. And I don't want to put it off any longer. But without the portal, we need to decide where to live. I don't think we can do a long distance commute."

Instead of an answer, her long distance stare filled her face. She said she wanted to think about the logistics.

"Does that mean you're not sure?" I asked.

"No. What it means is we have a lot of work to do, and some serious decisions to make. My mother will want to plan the wedding properly. That's important to me, Ash. And we need to discuss the job situation. I'd like to talk to the president and get his opinion. Maybe he'll have some suggestions."

"Let's get married now. We can do it again when your mom's done her thing. We don't have to tell her."

Jane stared at me. I've never been able to read that look. Some people might call it a blank stare, but I could feel the probe, like an electrical charge travelled through my brain, grabbing data bits. I put my hand at the back of my head to check for a hole.

"Ashley, I'm going to say no to now. When you left in November, I believed that you'd find Fritz. And I know you want him at your side. You may not care, right now, but you will. I know you're going to find him."

"It might take a while. Again."

"I'll wait." What I missed most, when I thought she was dead, and while I was in the portal, flew at me. Her smile. Everything would be okay. "But we need to figure out what I'm going to do tomorrow. I hate to go, but until we figure out what we're going to do, I have a job."

"Then call the president now. At least, he'll have a chance to think about possible options."

We talked about the people I'd met in the portal. She questioned what I had seen. The lack of negative response, the willingness of those in the past to believe and accept the notion of time travel amazed her. I told her what Churchill had said, but I believe that's only a part of something more.

"If everything has an electrical component, and we know electricity flows, when we make contact, especially touching like shaking hands, we share those charges. We've observed that there is a universality across the dimensions that allows us to influence each other," she said.

"I can't prove it, but from what I've witnessed, the desire to travel through time to the past and the future isn't limited to us. I think that the wish even explains a lot of philosophy and religion, the things that bind us as a species. It's weird, but I think I'm right."

"That makes sense to me. I need to let it soak in. I know you've written all your adventures on paper, but will you put them in the computer?"

"I can. Why?"

"I'd like a copy. Your idea of interconnection jogged my memory of something I read in grad school. I'll see if I can find it. As I recall, the piece was philosophical, no practical application, no proof. You may have the tangible next step."

"It may take a little time to type it all. I have to figure out where Fritz might be and how to get to him. How about if I send you the whole thing in parts as I get them done? That way, we can both try to see the connections."

"That works for me."

Chapter 56

Linda

APRIL SHOWERS HAVEN'T bothered. Eric left three weeks ago, and Ashley has avoided me. He told me he had typed his notes and I suggested that I could edit them, and maybe get a better picture of what he'd been through. I think he doesn't want me to know.

Mom delivered a cryptic blow. She said my absence from my home and family should make me sympathetic to Fritz, and to Ashley. "He went after Fritz, you left him." When the remark hit, I recoiled as if she'd punched me. Then she went shopping.

At this point, my frustration has risen to a peak level. It's hard to keep busy with what I need to do when every minute reminds me what I can't do.

I stick to Mom's mantra—the house, TJ, the shop. The president ordered ten bikes, so I've been building them, and with the stormless days, customers stop in more regularly. I asked Mom if she wanted to go home for a while, but she said she wanted to invite Dad and Joe to come for Easter. She said I should ask the rest of the crew, including the president and his family. She said I could make what I wanted, but she was making lasagna.

Joe said he had a project to complete. Natalie said she and Tony had already made plans. The McAllisters were going to see one of their kids. The president wouldn't be in town. Ashley said Jane's parents had invited his parents, and they would all be in Virginia. When I told Mom I felt like a pariah, she just shrugged. "I'm still making lasagna." So, as April moves ahead, I spend more and more time wondering what life will be like if Fritz ever comes home.

Chapter 57

Ashley

"**MR. GILBERT, I** think I figured out how to cross dimensions."

Eric called me as Jane and I were loading my car to come home. My parents went home on Tuesday after a welcome visit and lots of chatter about the wedding. Jane's mother had once again invited the world, but my folks handled the challenge. We've been here for a week and I plan to return to work on Monday. So leaving tonight makes sense. After dropping Jane in Washington, I intended to head home tomorrow, Saturday.

Eric's call changed our plan.

"Lenore and I, she's my lab partner, we changed one thing that made the difference. It was so obvious I can't believe it. We..."

"Eric, that's cool, but what is it?"

"Water."

"Could you be more specific?"

"When I connected to bring you back, before I opened the door, I fell into my pool. You might remember I was soaking wet, and made a puddle by the door. I stood in water, and when I opened the portal, the image was hazy. Or blurry."

"Did you find Fritz?"

"No. Not yet. We tried a couple of places, but mostly to see if we could keep getting the hazy image. I didn't actually go into the portal. But the storms here are clearing, so we'll have to wait."

"Write it all down. I'm not home now, but I will be tomorrow. You have my email. Type it and send it." I needed to review every trip with the water in mind. I was soaked myself when I was chasing Fritz. Another clue. "Thanks for letting me know."

Jane had her phone out. "Riverboro weather calls for scattered storms on Sunday."

"Then I'm going back tonight."

"We're going back."

"What about your job?"

"I'll worry about it later. They didn't miss me this week, or they would have called. I certainly didn't miss them."

We arrived in Riverboro a little after midnight. Jane brought her copy of my notes and before unpacking, we sat at the table, reviewing the trips while I tried to remember the weather, and in which storms I'd walked through the rain. For certain, my trip to DC, the courthouse and the jail, I'd been saturated and left puddles by the portal entrance. But which times, which other ones, had taken me across the universes?

We slept fitfully and were back at it early Saturday. I had an erasable board in this universe, too, so we listed the trips in order, and next to each, I wrote the rain conditions. If the rain dates matched, then Eric was right about how obvious the crossing was. But reconstructing the scenarios to be sure which ones actually crossed dimensions wasn't easy to remember. All I could think about was the water, but I still had no idea where Fritz had gone from Appomattox. He could still travel, and what made matters worse, he could set off the universal tumblers. I hoped he remained predictable.

Jane and I reread every entry, and we agreed that Eric had found the missing link. Now the only remaining question—where did Fritz go? My original thought continued, that he went in search of Lee. Since that's where I left him, he would be in friendly company. But a nagging reminder of his reluctance to come home kept tapping for attention. That he could time-travel, create portals of his own, complicated matters. I believed the portal where I found him remained open. He might try to go back. The reason made no sense to me. But I hadn't lived his life for what he believed was so long a time. I asked Jane if I should call Linda. She said we should find out if we could replicate Eric's findings first.

"You don't know where Fritz is, so telling her won't help find him," she said. "And if you go back in, you need to be able to get out. You know how to open the portal to the other dimensions. But you can't stay unless Eric can track you. He's found a variable, but according to physics, more than one bridge exists."

"Do you know how to find them?"

"Not exactly. But I have a theory. We all float on a timeline, here, and in the parallel worlds. The bridges are formed based on individual connections. In other words, if I could time travel, my bridges would connect to significant events or people, like magnets, in my life. Your connection to Fritz is a very powerful one. So you will open to places you share. That's why you met our friends in that dimension, went to your home. And that's why I believe, why I'm certain, you'll find Fritz. Wherever he is."

Chapter 58

Fritz

NOW I'M WEARING glasses. I don't have any idea how old I am. The necessities of my previous life are wishful thinking, things I took for granted. Lights with a flick of a finger, indoor plumbing and toilet paper, controlled heat and air conditioning. If you've never had these things, you accept improvements with Five Star ratings. When you know what's coming, but can't change things, suffice it to say that I would trade places in a heartbeat.

Since Appomattox, I've followed Lee around like a puppy. When he was offered the job here at the college, he brought me along as an instructor, which at least gave me a chance to face classes again, with an entire century I didn't have to teach. And for the past four years, my skills as a cook haven't gone unnoticed. I have however had to learn how to cook with less than ideal products. Supermarkets and convenience stores are only a dream, so I plan ahead. And now I understand why so many recipes had "a pinch of this, a handful of that."

General Lee and I have daily conversations about the politics of the day and about the future. I think he prefers discussing the future as an escape from the deprivations of Reconstruction. I see first-hand the damage to a once proud, if arrogant, society, and we've argued more than once that what has changed is the hubris of a society based on slavery continuing, succeeding.

Lee is adamantly opposed to Negroes voting. I've come to know a different man. When I told him a Constitutional amendment would pass soon, he asked if I thought slavery would have ended on its own, and none of the disruption would have been necessary.

I told him that question will be discussed for years to come, but that if the rest of society progressed as it will, slavery will stop being economically feasible in an agrarian economy. I said that just as the cotton gin made slavery's expansion feasible, other machines such as motorized vehicles would replace the need for so much labor. Whether that labor would be converted to industrial use within the same culture, I didn't want to speculate.

"Motorized? Like your automobiles?"

"Exactly. A tractor will be able to plow and furrow acres in a day, and harvest crops by the ton. Take cotton. Large versions of Whitney's machine will clean the bolls from an entire field in a matter of hours. After other machines have harvested the crop. Other inventions will prevent depleting soil of the nutrients needed to grow a variety of crops."

"So if the North had known slavery couldn't survive, we could have avoided the war."

"No, General, I don't think so. Both sides saw slavery as the underlying cause. Enslavement of other human beings couldn't survive moral scrutiny, and the South didn't use the economic argument, only that your slaves were inferior and each state had the right to decide what law prevailed. All the other arguments merely deflected the real reason."

Lee's eyes bored into mine, as he considered my response, "Do you think if we agreed to emancipation by some year in the future, say the turn-of-the-century, the Yankees would have agreed?"

"I don't think the north wanted war any more than you. Secession ended the chance for discussion and reconciliation. And for more than a century and a half into the future, the ramifications of the war still resonate in my world."

We often discussed the portal and how tampering with time could change the present and future. He asked me to relate the details of how I ended up here with him. Each time we spoke, I noted the topic and any item that might give me an idea on how to get back. He offered encouragement, reminding me that I had been stuck in his office once before. Leaving him, he said, would inevitably occur, that I belonged to a different time. Patience would have its reward.

After almost four years, I prepared my lectures in my little office down the hall from the general. A soft tap on my open door turned my attention to the general's smiling face.

"Come with me, Mr. Russell. I have something to show you."

I placed a paperclip where I'd stopped. I had purchased some of the earliest ones available. I stepped to his side, but he gave me no clue why. He stopped at his door, an almost sad grin passed to me.

"Is something wrong?"

"Yes and no. Please come in."

Sitting at his desk, his back to us, a rather tall young man stared ahead, not turning to see us.

"Mr. Russell, I believe you are familiar with this gentleman." As I entered the room, a glowing rectangle sparkled just out of sight of the door. The man stood and turned.

"Hi, Mr. R. I've finally found you."

Chapter 59

Ashley

TWO WEEKS AFTER he'd called, less a couple of days, on a Wednesday, Eric called me again. He said he'd found Fritz. I asked, "Is he with you now?"

"No. But I know where he is and how to get back to him. He's with General Lee. At the college."

"Can you get him now?"

"If he'll come. I think he will. At least, Lee thinks he will."

"Where are you now?"

"In my lab, looking through the portal at the general's office. By the way, he said to tell you hello. Mr. Gilbert, he remembers me, from when Mr. R found the portal. Weird, huh?"

My mind raced. I couldn't go to help. How to get Fritz back here ran through my head. I told him to hang on, and borrowed a phone from a student.

"Linda, what's your brother's phone number?"

"Joe? Why?"

"I'll tell you in a minute. The phone number."

"Is it Fritz? Have you found him?"

"Linda, yes and yes. Give me Joe's number."

When she calmed enough to answer my question, I said I'd call back within the hour. I disconnected as she began to shout.

"Eric, write down this number. Linda's brother lives in Boston. Get Fritz out. I'll call Joe. He'll help. Tell the general I said hello and thanks for his help."

"I'll call you when I'm done."

Chapter 60

Fritz

"**ERIC, THAT'S YOU,** isn't it?" I looked at the portal opening and the young woman holding the door.

"Mr. R, I can get you back to our dimension. If you have anything you need to bring, get it now."

Lee said, "I believe your patience is now your reward, Mr. Russell. Although I will miss our conversations, you should go with Mr. Silver."

I ran to my office, gathered my papers and placed them in my saddle-bags. Like my days with backpacks, I had my emergency getaway only a few steps away. In moments, I returned, had parting words with my old and new friend, General Lee, and as I reached the portal, Lee said as he had before, in my past and my future, "Godspeed, young man."

I expected to be in the hallway at Riverboro. Not the case. I let my eyes wander, but had no idea where Eric had transported me. He introduced me to his lab partner, Lenore Green. Judging from her penetrating gaze, in her mind, she was something more. Although stunned at what she'd just observed, she led us to an office. Eric made a call. To Ashley.

"I've got him, Mr. Gilbert." He held out the mobile to me.

"Hi, Ash."

"It really is you?"

"It is. I wondered if you all still remembered me." When he asked why, I worried I might be in another universe. I told him I'd been in the past for almost four years.

"Fritz, it's only been a few weeks here. It's only the end of April."

"Well, I'm back in our universe. Thanks for not forgetting about me."

"Give Eric the phone. Joe is coming to get you. You're in Boston, at MIT. Eric will fill you in."

I handed the phone over. Eric called Joe and explained how to find us. I asked for the phone. "Hi Joe. It's Fritz. I'm back. Ash said you could come and get me home."

"Glad you're back, but like I told Ashley, I'm short of time right now. I can get you later and you can stay at my place, but I can't drive you home until the weekend."

"That's okay. We'll figure something out. Eric can arrange where to meet and I'll see you later." I handed the phone back, and walked away. I'm back, I thought, but not sure I'm glad.

More importantly, Eric had a portal, not in Riverboro and without being hit by lightning. We had lots to talk about.

"Mr. R. He said he'll pick you up around seven outside my dorm."

"I have enough questions to fill the time. Can we sit somewhere? Before we leave, I'd like to see what you've found. But do you have a change of clothes? You're soaked."

When he grinned and said he knew, the story began.

"So, water and electricity do mix," I said. "And everyone knows how this works?"

"Nobody knows. Except the three of us. The only difference I could find was falling into the pool. But I felt ... not wet, but, I don't know how to say this ... like Superman breaking through a wall. The door required an effort to pry open. Then some force on the other side exerted a counter pressure, and just like that I could see in. Then the force just disintegrated, like smoke in the wind."

Lenore listened as intently as I did. She said Eric hadn't told her the story before. Eric said he didn't want to tell her, that he had promised the president. I wanted to ask about all those people in Riverboro, but I had another trip I wanted to make.

"Eric, Ashley found me in another dimension and brought me back. If that bridge is still open, the universe is at risk. Do you think you can get me there? I couldn't go from Lee's office. I need to be in the current time."

"What book would I use, Mr. R?"

"All the time I've been gone, I've collected anything that might be important. I've held on to it, first in a backpack, and now in here." I opened the saddlebag to a stack of notebooks, labelled with times and dates. Pressed between the pages of my writing were the precious items that would transport me. "I've carried these with me everywhere, every day, in a pouch I made to fit my coat pocket. Ash doesn't know I have these. I'd appreciate it if you didn't tell him. Or anyone else."

I selected the notebook with my most recent days in Washington and the article Ashley had used to find me. I handed one article to Eric, showed him where to place the paperclip if I got stranded, and told them both what to do in an emergency.

"So, let me get this straight. To get here, we need to punch through one dimension and then another. And still keep the portal open? That's a lot of power, Mr. R. I used up most of the generator just to find you today."

"Do you have a heavy duty electrical cord?"

"Not heavy duty enough."

"Let's give it a try. I won't cross the bridge if the power gets strained."

"I think the strain will be greatest when you open to the second dimension bridge. It's really strong. It's like being pushed and pulled at the same time. I wish you would wait to get home to try this."

"No time like the present, Eric. That bridge needs to be closed. I'm the only one who can do it."

Eric didn't need to know what I had in mind, and he agreed to help. Joe wouldn't be here for at least two hours. So we set up. Eric said that both of us should be soaked, so we took our dips in the pool.

"Not enough water in here now," Lenore said. I didn't know how time would match up, and rued any added delays. But Eric insisted that following the precise steps made a difference. He asserted that I stand by the door and drip, and then get back in the water once more.

"Mr. R, maybe you can't tell, but you smell awful."

"It's the woolen clothes, Eric. They probably don't get as clean with lye soap in a barrel. I haven't had a dry cleaner. I bathed this morning. I can tell you that when they dry, I'm going scratch like a dog with fleas."

"Okay, let's go." Eric said that he would stay back, and hold the door after I opened it, and keep it open while I was gone. I said that depending on where the rectangle formed, energy could be saved with the door closed. He didn't need to know my destination.

A powerful jolt replaced what I remembered of the familiar tingle when I grabbed the doorknob. I pulled, harder than ever. When I had a crack, air rushed by me from the hallway, pressing the door closed. Eric helped pry the door, and we both fought the suction until the door fully opened. Then the closer I moved to the portal, a greater force pushed against me. I told them both to push me. And in a moment, a green neon sign flashed, lighting the street and buildings all around. McNamara's awaited.

Chapter 61

Ashley

TWO BACK-TO-BACK text messages from Eric sounded urgent. I pulled to the roadside and from his first words I had no doubt that something had happened.

"Mr. Gilbert, I didn't know what to do so I'm really glad you called."

"Calm down, Eric. Tell me what's wrong."

"It's Mr. R. He's in the portal again. He said the universe you found him in is open and he's the only one who can close it."

"Do you know where he went?"

"He had a newspaper story with him. It's about a trial. In Washington. About a time traveler."

"Dammit. I knew he'd do something stupid. Can you find him again?"

"He gave me instructions, but I'm not sure. I haven't tried."

"Just what I need. Can you come and get me?"

"I'm in my lab. I don't have any way to reach you."

I told him I'd call in ten minutes, once I arrived home. Just in case, I told him to call if Fritz came back. I hit the gas and pulled in the driveway five minutes later. Either the dimension had never been closed, which is what I thought, or the idiot reopened it, and the chase would resume.

I took pictures of my living room, sent them to Eric, and then called him. I told him to print the pictures, and once I arrived in Boston, we'd figure it out. He said it might take him a while. He needed to go to his dorm to hook up a printer.

"Go quickly, Eric. There's no telling what damage he's doing. Call me when you're ready."

Just as I disconnected, my phone rang and the door opened. "Hi Jane. Hang on. Linda's just walking in. We have a problem."

"Fritz?" Jane asked.

"Yeah. Hi, Linda. What's up?"

"Is that Jane?"

"Uh-huh."

"Good. I called her. I told her you found Fritz. Are you bringing him home?"

"Jane, can you hear all this?"

"Yes."

"Good. I'll tell you both. Eric called. Fritz went back in. I'm going to Boston and see if I can find him."

"Why did he go in?" Linda asked, her eyes welling up.

"I don't know. And until I do, we're guessing."

Jane asked, "Do you know where?" Yes, I said. "Did he go back to Washington like you guessed he might?" I told her yes again. "Don't tell Linda anything. Just go get him. If you can, come get me. I'm home. Either way, call. I'll get off. Wait, let me talk to Linda."

"Jane wants to talk to you." I went to get a drink, and she followed me, and handed the phone back.

"He doesn't want to come back, does he?" Linda asked, wiping the dampness from her cheeks.

"Do you want a drink?"

"No. Answer me."

"Linda, he said he thought the portal to the universe where I found him is still open, and he's trying to close it. That's what Eric said. I won't know until I see him."

"Take me with you."

"No. This mess is screwed up enough without adding more fuel. I don't know if he wants to come home, but if he has any more distraction— meaning you—I don't know what he'll do."

"I can help."

"No ... you can't. In his world, he's relived eight years and now four more with Lee. He doesn't know whose life he's living. So stay out of it for now. Go home and wish me luck. Maybe we'll see you tonight. I'll call. Now, go."

I'd just taken a swallow of soda when Eric called. Linda had been out the door for less than two minutes and I watched her wipe her eyes as she pulled away from the curb.

"Mr. Gilbert, he's not back. Lenore waited for him."

"Come get me. I want to see how he connected the paperclip."

Chapter 62

Fritz

FEW CARS PARKED on the street signaled a quiet night inside, and one glance in the window told me I'd be safe. At his table, Flynn and Tim McNamara talked, two almost full mugs of dark beer joining them. I'd never seen the place so empty. I walked in and waved to Jane and Kathy behind the bar. Jane called Flynn's name as soon as she saw me, and pointed in my direction.

"You can't be here, boyo. The whole world's looking for you." He said each word in beat with each step he took toward me. "And what's with the costume?"

"Flynn, I'm here now. I've been gone four years since I last saw you. I need to speak to Kate."

"Four years? You escaped the jail this morning." He wrinkled his nose. "You stink. And she's not here yet. She's at the shop with Seamus. He said she's been cryin' all day. I don't want you here when she gets back."

"I've just spent four years with Robert E. Lee. I want a chance to explain. I'm not going anywhere until I talk to her."

"Holy Mary! How could you be gone four years and have left this very day?"

"Because I've been tinkering with time. And believe me, you can mess up a lot when you do. I can explain it to you, well, most of it. But

I have something else to talk about with Kate. When I've talked to her, I'll leave quietly, if that's something we agree on. I'm being followed. So I don't have much time."

"Who's after ya now? Cops from the 1800s?"

"No. Ashley. You met him. He's in my world. He found me and brought me back. Can you call Kate and get her here?"

"Oosh," he sighed. "Take a seat. Jane, bring Russ a porter. He's driving me to drink. So bring me a fresh one, too."

Jane smirked. "Good to know you can count." He lowered his brow in a question. "One, two." She held up her fingers. "Bring me one, two." She laughed back to the bar.

As best I could, I explained. I told him that the many times I'd used the portal gave me a chance to pinpoint locations exactly, which I had never shown Ashley. For me, most of the guesswork had ended. Flynn asked the one question that concerned him most.

"After flyin' 'round the galaxy, why did you come back here? You could go anywhere, including home."

"I've never told you the whole story of why I left my world in the first place." So I did.

"Well, Russ, that's quite a tale. I've seen the truth of it myself, so you're not inventing it. But what does Kate have to do with it?"

"I couldn't explain before, and I'm here now to say how sorry I am. Flynn, you've given me a family again. I wanted to thank you, no matter how this turns out."

A familiar face saw me as soon as she opened the door. Cindy Frankfurt, an index finger raised, said she'd be right back. The metamorphosis would be quick, and Kate would leave the cocoon in minutes. I asked Flynn to get her a drink.

"If she wants one, she'll get it," he said. I shrugged and leaned back, keeping one eye on the back hallway. Seamus waited at the bar door, more a bodyguard than a patron. The metal door clanged shut as she stepped into the dim lighting. Her red hair sparkled as though she had sprinkled it with fairy dust. Flynn signaled for glasses. Kate carried a bottle, one I'd seen many years ago. I stood as she approached the table.

"You shouldn't be here, Russ," she scolded. "It's not safe."

"Look across the street." I pointed to my portal exit.

"I saw it when we parked. Just like you described. So you've found a way home?"

"Yes and no."

"Always a mystery man."

"Kate, Flynn said I left this morning. In my life, I haven't been home. I've been locked in the past for four years, waiting, hoping for a chance to come here again. I'd like to speak to you, alone, and we can decide what happens next."

"Alone, eh?" She glanced at Flynn. "First, a drink. I think I might need it." She poured her special whiskey for five, and waved Seamus to the table. She raised the glass. "To what happens next." She downed the amber liquid and poured herself another. I'd barely sipped mine, when she nodded to Flynn, and seconds later, we were alone. "Go ahead, then. What's next?"

I told her where I'd been, and Ashley's rescue, then my return to my time. "I came here to say I am sorry. I've thought about you constantly for four years. You've made possible the hope of return, redemption. I don't belong here, but I feel closer to you, to all of you, than anyone I've met in the past dozen years."

She smiled and took my hand. She said she hadn't expected to see me again, but had spent most of the day considering what she would say if we met again. She downed the second shot. "You're married with a kid. I'm a gun runner, not a home wrecker. So, can you take me to your world? We can meet your family and then you can decide what happens next."

In a list of choices, that one had never been a thought, not to mention a possibility. The ultimate confrontation. A bizarre panorama floated across an invisible screen in front of me. People I'd known, places I'd been, ending with Robert E. Lee's admonition to go home.

She watched, expressionless, no doubt assessing the impact of her idea. Interrupting my reverie, she asked what I'd been thinking.

"I've never been a hero, never been a boat rocker. Then I found the portal. Kate, if nothing else, and this is important, meeting you reminded me of what I'd missed. You proved to me that I could love again."

"But is it me you love? Or being in love? The person or the feeling?"

"I've known you for what seems an age, but it's not possible for me to measure time. Not anymore."

"Let me help. Here, you discovered me, Kate, not Cindy, a bit more than a few months ago. Not time enough for us to decide if it's love. Fritz Russell, I can't make this choice. It's not mine to make. But I will be frank. You're fascinating, a curiosity. You're an attractive man. But will I fall in love with you? I don't know you long enough or well enough to say. What happens to your portal if you stay?"

"It will remain open, but for how long is anyone's guess."

"So like this morning, one day you could be gone."

I had to consider that. More than once I'd been yanked into a different dimension, not by choice. I could set up to leave, but I had no idea where I'd end up. I had left my saddlebags in Boston, so any route out could lead anywhere.

"Kate, the simple answer is yes. But the actual one is more complicated."

"It's not, Russ. Not for me. For me, you're an alien that looks human. Listen." Music in the background reached my conscious. The lyric gave us both the answer. 'My life, my lover, my lady, is the sea.' "Go home, Russ. I'll always remember you. And we'll drink a toast to every weird happening in the world, knowing you might have had a part."

She filled our glasses, and raised hers. She turned to face the room, and said, "Jane, a round for all, and a toast." The small crowd moved to the bar, and when the front door opened, a familiar voice said, "I'll have one."

Chapter 63

Ashley

"**MR. GILBERT, AND** a guest," Kate said. "Two more, Jane."

"You're a pain in the ass," I said to Fritz, staring at her. "Let's go."

"Mr. Gilbert, I recognize you from your previous visits." She held up her hand to stop Flynn. "And you wouldn't be Linda, by chance. No. Wrong hair."

"Kate, let me introduce Dr. Jane Barclay and Ashley Gilbert."

"So this is Kate?" Ashley shook her hand.

"And Dr. Barclay? Are you a traveling psychiatrist? They could use one."

"No, Kate, I'm a physicist by training, and call me Jane."

"Ashley, huh? Gone with the Wind, too?"

"Too?"

"My full name is Katie Scarlet O'Hara. My dad, rest his soul, loved the movie. But he favored the fellas in gray. But your interruption may be timely. Everyone, to Russ, our time traveling friend. Slainte!"

The room echoed the toast, almost like the walls had joined in. Kate invited us to sit, but I said we should leave. Flynn reached out and shook my hand, and then Jane's. And then he said, "You should stay awhile."

Fritz motioned to the chairs, and said he'd tell us the story later. He took a step toward Kate and she, a step toward him. "If I leave..." Fritz began.

"When you leave," Kate said. "That's what happens next."

"Okay, when I leave, this portal closes for good."

"For good, or ill, you'll be gone, Russ. I wish you a happy life." On her tiptoes, she brushed his lips with a kiss, and pulled him into a hug.

"It's time, Fritz." I squeezed his arm. One long last look into Kate's eyes, and he released the hug. He hugged Flynn and shook hands with the gathered crowd, kissed Kathy and Jane at the bar. As he headed to the door being held open by Seamus, Kate said, "Godspeed, my friend."

Fritz took a long glance back at Kate and then I pulled him across the street. I stopped for a moment to glance into McNamara's a final time. Kate watched from the window. Jane stepped through, while I waited for Fritz. I told him to go first. He waved, blew a kiss and with a short step, and my push, we found ourselves in the hallway of a building at MIT, and a frowning Eric Silver, hands on hips, ready to unload.

Walking down the hall, a look similar to Eric's firmly sculpted on his face, Joe Miller hurried to join us. Lenore hadn't let the door close, so I stepped to the opaque opening, and started to reach in. My fingertips met a wall as hard as the ones in the hallway.

"It's closed," I said. I didn't know if I was surprised or not at the tears sliding down Fritz's face.

Jane patted his arm, and said softly, "You're almost home now, Fritz. We've missed you."

"Will someone tell me what's going on? Ashley, I thought you were in New Jersey. What do you need me for?"

"Joe, I had some unfinished business," Fritz said. "Eric and Ashley didn't trust me. So once more, it's my fault. How are you?"

"I'm fine. I'm glad you're back. Now, maybe, I'll have a little less drama. And maybe I still have a chance to get to my date since you don't need a ride."

"Thanks for being willing to help, Joe," Fritz said. "Come visit some time."

Looking at me, he said, "I hear that Ben Franklin does a great job at the Fourth of July party. Maybe I'll see you then. And Fritz, tell my mother to call my father. He's driving me nuts." He waved as he turned the corner.

"Okay, Eric. One more time," I said. "My house. You're welcome to join us."

"I've done enough portaling for one day, thanks."

"I'd love to meet Albert Einstein, Eric," said Lenore, a gleam of hopeful anticipation shooting from her eyes.

Once we were planted firmly in my living room, and the rectangle had vanished, I told Fritz to call Linda, but Jane said to wait. She wanted to ask some questions first, and wanted a drink.

"Kate makes coming home a difficult choice, doesn't she, Fritz? Tell me about her."

"You don't waste time. I kissed her a few times. That's about it. I worked for her for more than a year. But not really. She wears a mask, literally, during the day. But that happened long ago."

"I knew you would go back," I said. "You didn't close that dimension."

"Ash, I kept the clippings. They didn't dissolve, like your picture of Lee—I seem to remember that. I had to see her, to explain, to apologize, and to see if we had a future. I've traveled in a wilderness of time. I have memories of a life I couldn't have lived, but did. I hoped the bridge was still there."

Jane said, "The bridges will always be there, connecting us to our important life events. Ash found you, Eric could locate you, because your thoughts left a trail. Tony Almeida found your image inside the portal and pinpointed the places you stopped. The books provided direction. You and Ashley are so tightly interwoven that he could probably find you anywhere. I had a feeling he would."

"So what now?" Fritz sighed. "I haven't been here for almost thirteen years. My memories are intermingled. I don't know who I am, or even how old I am."

"Linda's going to want to see you," I said. "She's sent a handful of texts already. What's the matter?"

"I forgot about cell phones. You don't understand. A little while ago, I had a horse, and an outhouse. I ate what I caught. I even wrote science fiction stories about what happens in the future. They're in my saddlebags. Ash, you were the alien protagonist."

Jane jumped in. "See what I mean, Fritz. Even in your fantasy world, you and Ashley are connected."

Fritz sat back, licked his lips, staring at us. "What day is today?"

"April 26, 2017."

"Time flies, et cetera. I just left October, 1869."

"Fritz, what do you want to do?" I asked. "Do you want to go home now?"

Fritz checked his wrist, then reached into his waistcoat pocket and removed a watch. "No. I need some clothes and a watch. I probably need a haircut. Do you have a mirror?"

"You know I do. In my bedroom. Down the hall."

"Ash, I may have known once, but nothing is familiar. Give me some time. Do you have anything to eat?"

Ashley looked out the window when slamming car doors made him curious. "You don't have much time to adjust. Linda just parked. She's got TJ and Emily with her."

"What should I do?"

Jane said, "You can't avoid this. Ash, take him and get at least a shirt. I'll tell Linda he's here."

As thin as Fritz was, my pants were too big, but what he was wearing smelled like he had just mucked a stable. I grabbed a pair of old jeans and the first shirt I touched, a blue button-down. On me, perfect fit. On him, he could have passed for a ghost wearing a blue sheet.

"Ashley, I don't know how to handle this."

"She won't either. You'll both have to figure it out. Jane, Emily and I will help as best we can." I'd seen Fritz make decisions before, but never one so unnerving. He rattled me with his lack of confidence. Everything would work out, I said, but I wasn't sure.

Chapter 64

Linda

THE MUSTANG IN the driveway announced they were home. When Jane opened the door, I asked if Fritz was here. She nodded and greeted Mom, not me.

Turning to me, she said, "He's disoriented. According to his timeline, Ashley said he's been away almost thirteen years. Don't push. He may need some time."

"Joe called and told me a little. We'll take him home and then we can talk. Now that he's back, I'll help him get back to normal."

"His last memory of you is you saying you didn't love him. That's not going to be easy to overcome. He may not want to go with you. He can stay here. Ash will be here, and he may be better for Fritz than you right now."

I could feel my blood pressure rise. Fritz belonged in his own house and familiar surroundings. Mom was poker-faced, so the job of convincing Fritz fell to me. He is my husband, after all. The floors creaked in the hall, and I held my breath. I stepped to the kitchen entrance and smiled at a man who stared at me like we had never seen one another before.

"Welcome home, stranger." His frown yelled that I'd said the wrong thing, but he was indeed a stranger. I sensed Mom behind me with TJ.

She said, "Hello, Fritz. Glad you're home, but I think I'll need to feed you. You look a little scarecrowish. Come in and let's talk. Ashley, do you have any eggs in the house?"

"Yeah. I could use some pancakes, Emily. There's a fresh bottle of syrup in the cupboard." He tapped Fritz from behind, and they walked into the kitchen.

I started to go toward Fritz but Mom grabbed my blouse. I turned to see her shake her head.

Finally, Fritz spoke. "Hello, Linda, Emily. TJ has grown. That is TJ, isn't it?"

"Yes. Of course," I said.

Jane invited us to sit. I wanted to tell Fritz everything that had happened since November and tell him how happy I was that he was home safely. I wanted to ask all the questions that had filled my mind about where he'd been. I wanted to hug him and tell him how sorry I was. But nothing came out but "you look good in glasses."

"Thanks."

Mom and Ash quickly whipped up a stack of pancakes.

"I guess you want me to tell you where I've been," he said. "I'm not ready to do that." He avoided looking at me, staring instead at the activity at the stove.

"Start on these," Mom said. "I'll make another round and then we can talk."

I asked Fritz if he wanted me to fix him a plate, something he had usually done for me. As if he'd just noticed where he was, he nodded, shifting his gaze to me. It seemed silly to fuss, but I buttered four pancakes, passed the plate, and started to pour the syrup.

"I'll do it," he said. He stuck his finger into the flow, and licked the sticky liquid. He closed his eyes, as he spread the flavor around his mouth with his tongue. "That's good. It's been years since I've tasted maple syrup. Not since I cooked in Washington." He looked toward me, but again his glazed look passed through me. I doubted at that moment if he had actually seen me since we arrived.

Ashley finished and sat between Jane and Fritz, and Mom sat next to me. TJ dozed in the swing I'd brought with us. Fritz had eaten only a couple of bites when he stood and walked out the front door. Mom grabbed my leg when I started to follow.

"He'll be back," Ashley said. "Leave him alone. He needs time to adjust. He has thirteen years of memories we can't share."

"How can he get normal if he won't talk?" I asked.

"I don't know if he can. So don't make it harder for him. When he's ready, we'll find out."

"Linda, remember what happened when you finally came home?" Mom asked. "You said you couldn't believe you'd left. And you were gone almost six months."

"He's been gone that long now," I said.

Ashley interrupted. "I keep telling you, so pay attention, Linda. I've been to places in the portal where he's spent time. I've seen some of the people he's known. Not just in his mind and memory, he's relived years, day by day. Time has no meaning to him right now. He's been gone thirteen years, and you need to accept that. He has a lot of catching up to do. And a lot of forgetting."

After forty-five minutes, Mom said we should go home. She said that Ashley could bring Fritz home. Jane had been unusually quiet, but she said not to expect Fritz quite yet. She told me to let him find his world his own way.

"If he wants to come home tonight, I'll call you. Don't stay up past midnight though."

"What if he doesn't come back?" I asked.

"He'll be back," Ashley said.

Chapter 65

Ashley

WHEN LINDA FINALLY pulled away, Fritz had been gone for more than an hour. Jane and I sat down again. Each plate had uneaten pancakes and none of the second batch had been touched.

"What makes you so sure he'll come back?" Jane asked.

"I'm not. But Linda being here makes his transition back difficult. He's just been rejected by Kate. I spent a few months with him. The portal has changed him. But now that he's back in our time, our universe, and without a way to escape, we're the only familiar faces he knows, the only fixed place he can latch onto. If he's not back soon, I'll go get him."

"Do you know where he went?"

"Like you said, we're connected. He's walking, absorbing the Riverboro he may or may not remember." I checked my watch. "Unless I've guessed wrong, he'll be at Lou's Midtown around midnight. That'll be the only place open by the time he walks to downtown."

"Do you think he went home?"

"Absolutely. That's one of the first places. But he'll be cold soon. And tired. So he'll be inside. Do you want to come with me?"

"I should stay here in case he comes back while you're searching. Ash, do you think he and Linda can patch things up? I mean he hardly looked at her, or said a word to TJ."

"What you don't know is that he's carried a photo of them in his wallet all this time. TJ will be two, and has seen Fritz for less than a year. Coming home can't be easy. But to answer your question, Fritz and Linda are smart and resilient. They need time, each of them. When he remembers why he left in the first place, the pieces will begin to come together. I may need to remind him, but yes, I think they'll be able to patch things up."

At quarter to twelve, I grabbed an extra jacket, told Jane I wouldn't be long, and headed to find Fritz. Somehow, and I didn't know for sure why, Fritz would show up. As I slowed for a parking spot, I saw him, standing in front of Linda's store. At an open spot in front of the bar, I parked and adjusted the mirror to watch him. As I had predicted, he crossed his arms and rubbed each to get some warmth, then turned in my direction, and walked in the bar. I rushed in behind him and sat in the next seat. He nodded to me, like I was a stranger.

"I brought a jacket, Fritz. It's in the car." He glanced at me.

"Oh hello, Ashley. Didn't know you'd be here."

"Let's have a drink. Want a sandwich?"

"Sandwich?" He turned on the bar stool. "Lou's?" he asked.

"Yeah. Lou's. It's too late for something hot." I ordered two roast beef sandwiches and two beers. Fritz said he wanted a shot of Jack. "Make it two," I told the barman.

"Where have you been?" I asked.

"It's strange. I'm used to the smell of horse dung and country air. And you can't imagine how quiet nighttime is."

"Did you go to your house?"

"Walked past. After I went to the school. I looked into my classroom. Pretty much like I remember it. Do you remember going after the president when they took him hostage? And the Summit, taking Putin to see his childhood home?"

"I remember. Obviously, so do you. Little by little, Fritz. We can talk about all we've done tomorrow, or after."

The bartender placed our sandwiches on the bar, and slid the shots and beers in front of us. I lifted the shot glass. "Slainte," he said. We tapped our glasses and downed the golden shots. Between bites, he asked me what would happen next. Sleep first, I said, then we'd deal with whatever tomorrow placed on the table. As we left, Fritz turned right. I told him the car was in front of us.

"We met Rachel and Nicole here with Ben Franklin," he said.

"I remember. They exist in the other dimension, too. I had a few interesting, that's not a strong enough word, months with them. You spent time with me there too, Fritz. After we reversed the Koppler killings. Before you disappeared again with General Lee. I'll tell you more tomorrow."

Instead of a U-turn, I drove around the block, past other shops that might help jog his memory. On the way, he asked where I was taking him.

"To my house, for tonight. You need to find yourself and get your bearings."

"Good. I'm not sure what to do. Linda is a stranger right now." For the rest of the short drive, he looked out the window.

In all the years that we've been friends, he's been the stable, reliable one. I know that I've caused more than one sleepless night for him. But I would never hurt him or desert him. Our roles reversed as the portal took over so much of our lives. He became less predictable, and in retrospect, bolder, braver, and more erratic. He's my friend, so I've joined him in these escapades and adventures, but now, I feel like his older brother, trying to keep him safe. Not like I did with my own younger brother on that awful hunting trip. Seeing Fritz as he is now, well, it's a painful reminder of how badly I've done.

As I pulled in my driveway, Jane opened the door. Fritz saw her and asked, "Are you married?"

"Not yet. I've been waiting for you." I reminded him that he had agreed to be my best man.

Before he climbed out, he said, "That was such a long time ago."

Chapter 66

Jane

WHEN FRITZ WALKED in, I thought of Peter Pan and the lost boys. His puffed out shirt and pants belted tight, his jutting cheek bones over a sharp jaw reflected a man in need of care. His brown eyes were blank, and I would say unaware. Even walking, he stepped carefully, trying to avoid some unseen obstacle.

"Fritz, come in the kitchen," I said. Without a word, he shifted direction and sat where he'd been earlier. I asked him if he wanted something to eat. He shook his head. Ash sat next to him and said that tomorrow would be a better day.

"What are you going to do about work?" Ashley asked me.

I told him I would call and tell them I had a family emergency, or something. I had until morning to invent an excuse. "I have to talk to the president."

"Then let's get Fritz settled, and get some sleep. I think we're going to need it."

Morning came too quickly. Ashley's phone rang at six a.m. Linda wanted a report, which started an argument. Ashley told her that Fritz was asleep and that she'd awakened us. He listened to what she had to say but told her not to come here.

"Linda, I won't let you in. Give him a chance to acclimate."

By the time he ended the call, I had a towel drying my face. Cold water works wonders this early in the morning. Fritz had left the door open to an empty room. When I told Ashley, he sighed heavily, dressed and walked out, while I put on a shirt and jeans. Hearing them talking erased my concern. At least, Ash didn't have to chase him again.

"Good morning, Jane," Fritz said, as I showed myself. "Thank you both for letting me stay here." In front of him, a half-full bowl of puffed rice still popped, a milk carton stood in the middle of the table next to his coffee cup.

"You're up early," I said. His light-hearted cheeriness confounded me after his actions of the previous night. "Did you sleep well?"

"I'd forgotten how comfortable a mattress can be. But this is my normal morning time. At least, it was."

I anticipated a frown or a return of the fog in his eyes. That didn't happen. Instead, he smiled, his eyes twinkled, the bad episode having vanished.

"You look rested. Are you ready to take on the new world? How do you feel?"

"Like a different person. Not exactly myself, whoever that is or was or will be. But we have a lot to talk about."

So I poured coffee, while Ashley whipped up scrambled eggs, bacon and toast. Fritz talked. First, he led us on his previous night's journey, then he talked about mornings with General Lee. How he collected freshly-laid eggs, the bread he baked and would bring as his gift, and which Mrs. Lee made into a meal.

"You had breakfast with the general every day?" I asked.

"Most days. Then we would walk to the campus. In the beginning, I asked a lot of questions about how I would learn to live. He always said the same thing, 'Patience, Mr. Russell.' The second day, he said I would begin teaching the next day, and showed me my classroom, and the handful of books I had available. For the past four years, I've been instructing those young men."

"What did you teach?" Ash asked.

"History, government, civics, geography, current events. Current events presented a different perspective for me. I had only read about some of the things that my students experienced firsthand. With so few books and limited access to research, I had to rely on old habits. My lists, and copious note-taking. Just like the old days." He halted his story as the words struck.

"Which old days?" Ashley asked.

"You know, I'm not sure." Although the comment wasn't funny, we all laughed at the irony.

At quarter to eight, I called work and said I'd be out for a few days. My supervisor wished me well and told me to take as much time as I needed.

"I think I'm about to lose my job," I said.

"Why?" Ash asked.

"He told me to take all the time I need. I expected him to yell about leaving him with all kinds of extra work. I don't have that much to do, but he was too nice."

"Then you need to call the Man."

I sat down with another cup of coffee. I didn't want to call the president so early, so Fritz continued his tale. He said that he'd become comfortable riding a horse, and began to venture further away, looking for books, magazines and newspapers to buy or borrow. He said that after a few months, he rode to Richmond and collected as much material as he could.

"I bought a couple of copies of *Harper's Weekly*, and a copy of *Goday's Lady's Book* for Mrs. Lee. Did you know that the editor of Goday's, Sarah Hale, convinced Lincoln to proclaim Thanksgiving a national holiday? I also borrowed a copy of the *National Police Gazette*. That's what gave me the idea to start writing science fiction stories."

"Did you publish any of them?" I asked.

"No. But I've kept them all. Can you imagine how that would screw up time?"

"I think I can imagine it just fine," Ashley said.

I said, "I'd like to read them, but right now, I need to call the president."

"Hi Jane. Where are you?"

"Hi, Mr. President. I'm with Ashley. Fritz is here."

"Here, where?"

"Ash's house."

"Good. I'll be right over."

The abrupt end of our call cut short Fritz's history lesson. "He's on his way. Ash, make another pot of coffee."

Chapter 67

Ashley

IN LESS THAN twenty minutes, a black Suburban parked in front, and Mel Zack and two other agents hopped out. After a careful scan of the neighborhood, the door opened. Surrounding the president, they all came up the steps. I held the storm door open.

"Come in. But what's with all the security? This is Riverboro."

"That's why I wanted to talk with you. Hi, Fritz. Glad you're home. I'm going to need your help."

Jane asked, "What's happened?"

The president turned on my TV. The news reported that a North Korean, warhead-topped missile had exploded over Hawaii. "We don't know if the explosion was intentional or an accident. We need to stop a response until we know. Jim Beech called. The military is on the move. As a result, the Russians have heightened their defense alerts and are sending troops toward Europe. The Israelis have activated the Iron Dome, which has set the entire Middle East on a war footing. The Chinese are trying to open communication with North Korea. The Japanese have called for our help, so the Navy is repositioning ships."

"Mr. President, are you asking to use the portal," I asked. "The new president doesn't know about it, does he?"

"No. That's why I need you. He has no idea how to deal with this. The wrong decision can set off a nuclear holocaust. We have almost 30,000 troops in South Korea, plus civilians, in imminent danger. Mr. Kim has said he'll launch against the South if we attack."

"That didn't take long." Fritz's quiet voice filled the room. "What do you want to do?"

In one question, Fritz had calmed the obviously upset former Commander-in-Chief. "What's the damage in Hawaii? Could it have been accidental?" Before the president could answer, Fritz held up his hand to stop him. "We need to shut down the school, empty it, not a lockdown. Ash, get me a pad." Fritz stared unblinking at the far wall. I'd seen that same look on Jane's face plenty of times, so I ran and found a yellow pad and pen.

Fritz continued his list, so rather than hand him the pad, I wrote. He looked at me when he saw, and said, "We'll need to call George right now. Mr. President, we'll need General Beech here, and Colonel Mitchell needs to get his team here. Then you're going to need to visit the Oval Office. It might help to contact some of your Cabinet members." As the list started to take shape, I handed the pad to Fritz.

"Are you back with us," I asked him. This new version of my old friend rose taller and straighter than I think I have ever seen him. His immediate adjustment to this crisis added confidence to all of us listening.

He asked, "Have you tried to contact any of the people who were at the Summit?"

"I have no authority to act, Fritz. I can only offer advice, so, no, I haven't."

"The world saw what happens when you all work together. Call Putin. Tell him you're coming to get him. As I recall, the new guy likes him. We'll bring them to the conference room. And we may need to get some others."

"Do you want me to call George?" I asked.

"Yes, Ash. Tell him to get teachers to take the kids home. They can take three or four each. The kids who can walk don't need a ride. Have all the kids call their parents. George will say what we're doing is irregular. Tell George he's back on the team, and the team is about to take the field. Tell him he needs to call Mr. Chatham first, and don't ask, tell, the superintendent that he's closing the school and the rest of the town's schools should be closed, too. Tell George to keep Tom, Al, and Liz. And Rachel and Nicole."

"What are you thinking?" I asked. He raised his hand again.

"Tell George to keep Ms. Sweeney and Joe Pettinelli close. We don't have time for George to dither. Okay, do it now. Mr. President, can you call Putin from here?"

"No, but I can from my house. I'll go now."

"Wait. Jane, please copy the list. I'll need a handful. Ash's printer makes copies. Mr. President, we need the Australians, the New Zealanders and the Indonesians on this."

The president pursed his lips, and his brow furrowed. Fritz offered a brief grin. Both men were battle-tested comrades-in-arms. Jane ran to my office while I talked to George. To my astonishment, he told me to hold on while he wrote down each item. No argument, no questioning.

"Got it," George said. "I'll get started now."

Jane passed a copy to the president. He said he'd make the calls and meet us at the school as fast as possible.

Fritz said, "Tell Beech we need the planes. Where's Tony?"

"Washington," Jane said.

"Call him and tell him to get ready. We're coming."

"How are you going to open the portal?" I asked.

"What did you do with the stuff I left behind?"

"It's in the basement."

"That's how. Jane, do you have copies of the Summit connections?"

"With the rest of your stuff, Fritz. We cleaned out your desk."

"Good. Where's the White House brochure?"

I said, "I have it."

"Good. Okay, let's move. Hi, Mel."

Chapter 68

Fritz

NOTHING I HAD said required lots of thought. I could see every step. After so many trips through, what we needed was like riding the proverbial bicycle. "It's just past eight-thirty. Mr. President, if you can get me planes, I'll have the portal ready."

"Okay. Jane, I'll keep you informed. I have your number."

I asked if one of the agents could stay. I wanted to be sure we had the hands we needed to set up everything in the school.

"Jon Charles, nice to meet you," the agent said, as the president ran to the Suburban.

"Ash, get the stuff from the basement. I need to get dressed." A strange memory struck me. Quiet had returned and left. I'd been here before. The portal resumed its role in our lives. I looked in the mirror in my bedroom, and an older model of the skinny kid from North Jersey jumped out at me. My woolen pants had escaped from the mid-1800s. The baggy shirt made me look like a human parachute. I called to Ashley. "Call Linda. Tell her to bring me clothes. I'm going to grab a quick shower." A shower. I hadn't had one in years. Adjusting the water temperature, a bar of soap not made from animal fat in the backyard, thick, fluffy towels, were all reminders of how the world would change, or how it had changed. Lee had once said to me that we take so much for granted.

By the time I turned off the water, another voice came from the kitchen. Ash carried a bundle of clothing to my room and said that Linda had arrived. The mist of her existence had lifted. We had a lot to talk about. A lot to talk about. That phrase showed up attached to the back end of every thought and every person. But now, I had a job to do. I dressed, but my pants were still too large. Ashley had suspenders. How I remembered would come later. I asked. He delivered.

"Hi, Linda. Thanks for helping."

"I'm glad you're home."

"We need the portal." I walked to her and kissed her cheek. She hesitated to come closer, so I took her shoulders and pulled her into a hug.

"I like your beard," she said.

"Thanks. We're going to the school now. When this ends, we should talk."

"I'd like that. Good luck."

Ten minutes later, agent Charles and Ashley unloaded the Mustang. Jane called the president, and I stepped into Riverboro High School for the first time in thirteen years. The people I'd asked to hang around huddled in the middle of the hallway, still the pleasant blue-green tint that burst into my conscious memory.

"The planes are up, Fritz," Jane said.

"Which room should we use?" Ashley asked.

"Yours. I know it works." I connected the generator and attached the cord to the doorknob. Ash cleared his desk. I took the Summit files from what Ashley had saved, and thumbed through, flipping the pages, rubbing the proposal Jane had written. Everything felt familiar, and at the same time, newborn.

"The substitute's not going to be happy," Ashley said, as he stacked the books and papers on a student's desk.

"She'll get over it," said a voice in the doorway. "Welcome back, Fritz."

"Hi, George. Sorry to do this to you."

"Truth is … I've kind of missed it, all the action." Then he laughed. "Lois says welcome home, too."

While we arranged the files to fetch the foreign leaders, a rising noise announced the president's arrival. In his hand, he held the list and without waiting began to tell me what he'd accomplished.

"Mr. President, first things first. Tony."

"He sent a picture of where he's at. Here." I set a paperclip and we left the classroom. I told Ash to open the portal.

"Not this time. This one's your party." His gentle smile reminded me that I had a lot to thank him for.

I grabbed the doorknob. The tingle vibrated through my fingers, and caressed my arm like an old friend. I pulled the door open and Tony joined the crew. I shook his hand and received his welcome greeting.

"Check everything, Tony. We have a long day coming," I said. He tossed his jacket and one of Churchill's volumes on the floor, asked for a chair, and started to wiggle all the plugs.

"Next, let's get the general."

The president handed me another sheet of paper. The group of teachers and staff watched from a distance. Some had never seen the portal in action. Later. I set the portal and General Beech entered the hallway. I asked him if Colonel Mitchell had managed to get his team together. He told me the unit had been continued, so they were together and would be ready by now. He handed a package to Jane, and said, "These are for you, Colonel." She thanked him and excused herself.

I said, "Next, we'll get Putin. Is he ready?"

"He said to pick him up where we first met him when we captured the stolen nuke." I found the floor plan quickly and set the portal for Russia. The president and Mel walked across the threshold, while I held the door. The Russian president added to the growing throng.

"Nice to see you again, Mr. Putin," I said, expecting the scowl he saved for public appearances. Instead, he reached his hand toward mine.

"And you, too, Mr. Fritz." He grinned. "I do not always say the things I know."

"It's just Fritz. You don't need to know my full name." The cabinet members were spread out, but we could gather them later. Only SecState and SecDef were needed here now. He handed me two sheets.

In less than a minute, I'd secured them. I asked Ashley for the time. "Almost ten."

"Who next, Fritz?" the president asked. "The leaders are ready when you are."

"Okay. First, the British, French and German, then Chinese, Japanese and Australian. But this is taking too long."

Ashley said, "Left, right, center, Fritz. We've done this before." He removed each from the files. The president handed a sheet to Ashley, one for Australia. He had them for those who hadn't been here before. "Those calls took a little longer."

"George, take everyone to the conference room," I said. "Mr. President, Mr. Putin, stay here."

With three quick openings of the portal, Mel Zack ushered the first group to the conference room, only the German Chancellor not startled. Moments later, sleepy men from the other side of the Pacific joined their European counterparts. The last one to get, the South Korean leader, took a bit longer.

When the president returned with his colleagues, I escorted them to the Summit room to join the rest. I told Ashley to set the White House brochure. I asked for quiet and told them they would be going to the Oval Office next. Their objective was to stop reaction to the missile explosion, bring the new president through the portal, and then make a trip to North Korea as diplomats. When I asked if he had a report on the North Korean leader, the president said he was sleeping.

"We'll be able to pinpoint our arrival when we're ready," said the president. "Lady and gentlemen, our new president is not aware of the portal. Expect push back, but we'll bring him here. John, Charlie, you'll stay there. General Beech also. Coordinate with your counterparts.

Leaders, come with me. If we can't convince him, we'll scare the hell out of him. Mr. Putin, I'm counting on you the most."

The newly-formed invasion force gathered outside Ashley's classroom door. Jane had morphed into Lt. Colonel Barclay, and received instructions from the general. Colonel Mitchell and his team would destroy the missiles and nukes. She had the location maps in a folder. General Beech told her to contact the colonel and while they were waking up the Dear Leader, the team would enter North Korea.

"Can you keep the portal closed that long?" she asked.

"I'll take care of it, Colonel Barclay," I said. "Mr. President, are you ready?" When he nodded, I pulled the door open.

First one through, the president startled his successor. With an unexpected group of leaders and former Cabinet secretaries, his intense confusion galloped across his crimson complexion.

"What are you doing here? I didn't have meetings today."

Putin stepped forward. "Mr. President, we are here to advise you how to handle the North Korean situation."

"I didn't know you were in Washington. Looks like the fake media was asleep on the job."

"Not quite on the mark," said the president. "You are about to learn just how precarious the world can be."

"What are you talking about?" the new president said, his orange hair falling out of place.

The rectangle glowed behind the visitors. "When I announced during the campaign that we could time travel, everyone thought me either kidding or nuts." He glanced at his wrist. "Less than half an hour ago, Mr. Putin was in Moscow and these folks were all at home."

"Don't you know I have a crisis. I want you to go away. Now."

"Mr. President," said Putin, "we all have the same crisis. We are here to help you. We wish you to join us to plan what needs to be done."

"I won. I'm the president now. I don't want your help." His shouting brought secret service agents through his door. Mel Zack stepped in front.

"Mr. President, is everything okay?" Bill Sharp saw the dignitaries and Mel Zack. "Hi, Mel. So, the portal again?"

"Hi, Bill. Yup."

The new president scowled. "Agent Sharp, you knew about this?"

"Not this meeting, sir. But I swore an oath to protect the portal."

"Bill, we're asking the president to come with us," said his former boss. "We're going to end this threat now."

"Sharp, you're fired." The crowd laughed.

Putin sat down in front of the Resolute Desk, his smile vanished. "Mr. President, you are the only one in this room who can officially stop American action. You are also the only one here who doesn't know what is about to happen. If you come with us, you will be the negotiator who brings peace. If you do not, we will, without you, and you will never know how we persuaded Mr. Kim. But more, you will, for the remainder of your life, be unable to mention our visit. If you say time travel, your Congress will remove you, as insane and unable to perform your duties. You have ten seconds to decide." He pushed up his sleeve.

"Are you threatening me?"

"Seven, six, five…"

"Okay, okay. I'll go with you."

The president said that some of them would remain and asked that the new Secretaries of State and Defense come to the Oval Office. "And the Chairman of the Joint Chiefs. Charlie, John and General Beech will fill them in."

"I'll have my secretary call." He picked up the phone.

"Don't," said the president. "You make the calls. None of your staff or your family has clearance. You can decide later if you want to include them. Time is wasting."

The new president scowled at his uninvited visitors. He removed a list of phone numbers from his desk, picked up the phone, and placed the calls himself. When he stood, the group began to move toward the fluorescent rectangle by the Oval Office door.

"What is that thing?"

"You'll see in a minute," Putin said.

"I have to tell someone I'm leaving."

"That is not necessary. Come with us now."

"Bill, you come too," said the president.

* * *

I DIRECTED EVERYONE down the hall. The final arrivals, the former president, the new president, and Putin, stopped in the middle of the hallway. The new president asked where they were.

"That's not important now. North Korea is," said the president.

"Mr. President, while you were gone, Ashley and I brought most of the others from the Summit through. They're waiting for you."

"Here's the floor plan for Kim. His bedroom. It's just past midnight in Pyongyang. Get the colonel started, and then come join us." Major Barclay exited the room, leading the teachers and school staff.

I'd been away from this activity for years. Strangely, what to do flooded back to me. I welcomed Colonel Mitchell and Major Dolan as their men poured through into the school and took their places on both sides of the hall, as images of many other times leapt from memory.

"Fritz," Ash said, "the president wants you."

Surrounding me, my colleagues, fellow teachers for many years, quietly watched, and as I walked down the hall, each patted my arm, or softly welcomed me home.

As I opened the door, argument assaulted me. The president waved me over. The room hadn't changed. The round conference table elevated two steps up, the white panels which housed the video screens, the walkway around the perimeter, still the same.

"Ladies and gentlemen, this man discovered the portal. Our adventures together have been numerous, as some of you know. You may recall the surprise ending to Naria's nuclear program. Or the attack on the White House during the Summit last spring. None of the leaders were hurt because we were in here. And you will recall the attack in Palestine at the opening of the development project. We escaped catastrophe through the portal. In addition, we have the ability to travel back in time. Today, we intend to visit Mr. Kim. Our people on the ground have informed us that he has gone to bed, after a day of celebration. We have also discovered the locations of their missile storage and where they have hidden their nuclear arsenal. The explosion over Hawaii was due to a malfunction of the guidance system. The North Korean military has already made their report. So the celebration acted as a cover. But we must consider the range the missile traveled with a payload. That's what we must stop."

"Why don't I know any of this?" shouted the current president. "And why haven't I been told about this portal thing?"

The president began to answer, but I stopped him. "You don't know because I didn't want you to know. You're here now because you've got the country fearing a nuclear attack, and every major military throughout the globe is preparing for war. You don't know that because you don't believe your own intelligence agencies. You tweeted that this morning."

"Who are you? And where are we?"

I answered. "You don't need to know. You've been given a gift here. The opportunity is yours to ratchet down the fear, and to protect the world from holocaust."

"We need to go," said the president. "Mr. President, are you coming?"

"Where?"

Groans and rolled eyes filled the room.

The president said, "Our next stop will be Mr. Kim's bedroom. If we succeed, the North Koreans will be joining the community of nations. If not, they will wonder where he went." The president's head nod sent me down the hall.

At Ashley's classroom door, I asked the colonel for the maps he would use for his mission. He handed me a folder. I called Ashley over.

"We're going to do this together. I'm going with the president. I'll step out if Kim resists, and then you need to move fast. When you go, the portal will be closed for our exit."

"The first groups are already inside. The rest go when you're in. Then I'll reconnect the portal to you."

With the leaders gathered behind me, I told the colonel to keep some men right at their entry point. The fluorescence would vanish when we came back.

The president said, "Take out one site first. We should be back before you'll need to do more. Wait for us. Good luck."

I set the paperclip. The president said the intel was perfect. An agent was guarding Kim's door. I patted Ash's arm and he pulled. As quietly as possible, the leaders of the world entered the bedroom of the sleeping North Korean leader. A nightlight provided enough illumination to avoid mishap. When I stepped in, Ashley softly closed the door behind us. I opened the bedroom door, and the guard, who would serve as a decoy, came in.

At the president's signal, I turned on the lights. Kim jumped up ready to yell, until he saw the Chinese president, who told him to be quiet and listen. From the rear, a translation flowed through the crowd surrounding the bed.

The new president said, "It's an honor to meet you, Mr. Kim."

The Chinese leader said, in English, "We know you speak and understand English. We are here to invite you to join us. We wish to put an end to North Korea's isolation in the world community."

The president said, "We wish to introduce you to a technique we have discovered which has allowed us all to be here. Will you come with us?"

Kim sat still, his anger shifting from face to face. "My guard will have called soldiers by now. You will be prisoners."

The guard spoke from the rear. He said he had been surprised. No soldiers were coming.

"So you see, Mr. Kim, you have the choice of coming with us and finding a road leading to an end to our disputes, or never knowing when your sleep will be disturbed again." The president's warning kept Kim from responding. "You made a mistake today. You attacked the United States and celebrated. You made no attempt to warn us, provided no information that your attack was a technology failure. You have declared war."

"It was a mistake," Kim shouted. "The operators are in prison already."

The current president said, "The rest of the world interprets your action as a surprise attack on Hawaii. My advisers woke me when they detected the missile launch. We won't put up with that. So I am trying to save you. I said I'd invite you to my country. You should come now. We'll have a nice talk."

The Chinese president said, "You have only this chance to make yourself a great leader, like your father."

Stepping forward, President Putin sat on the bed next to Kim. "We do not intend to harm you. But our patience is limited, and our time is short. Join us now and see what the rest of us know. You have ten seconds." Repeating his earlier action, he put his watch in Kim's sightline and counted backward. When he reached 'seven,' the rest added their voices. At three, Kim said, "I will come. Let me dress."

A pair of pants, a shirt and expensive sneakers were passed from the back and dropped in Kim's lap. Putin told him to bring his clothes with him.

When we emerged in the hallway, I held the door. The leaders returned to the conference room between two lines of soldiers.

Trailing the others, Putin said to the president, "He is a bully—your word. I would not be so forgiving."

"Yet, you convinced him. Now he will see what the collective influence of the world can do, just as you have. He'll know what we can do and what we will do." The president signaled for the colonel to begin.

I told Ash to start, as the soldiers lined up for their mission. Jane's voice rang out, "Let's go." I watched Ashley as Jane led her team into the dark night of battle.

As the leaders took seats, the president told Kim to follow him. "Major Dolan, would you escort Mr. Kim to the bathroom, so he can dress?" While Kim was absent, he said, "On the screen behind me is a satellite picture over eastern Asia. I expect when Mr. Kim returns, we will show him the first detonation. We are prepared to finish his nuclear program if he objects."

The South Korean president asked, "Mr. President, what about us?"

"An alert has been sent to your people. I believe a message from Mr. Kim, broadcast from here, will shut down his military. If not, we'll show him this." A series of low-angle photos of short-range missiles, from Russia, China, Japan and Australia flashed across the screen. Shocked looks passed over the faces of the Russian and Chinese leaders. "Yeah, we know where they are. And we know you're ready to launch. That doesn't include our submarines."

"And ours," said the Chinese president.

Dolan returned a fully dressed North Korean leader. The new president walked to him and shook his hand. "We have a plan for you."

Kim listened to the brief comments, and then was shown the slide show. The picture changed to the satellite footage, as the room grew quiet.

Noise in the hallway disturbed us. I opened the door, and the sound of firing rifles raced into the conference room, as soldiers crawled into the hallway. "Hurry, Ash," I said. "That door needs to be closed."

Ashley told Nicole to hold the door and he ran into the portal.

"Everyone, stand away from the opening." I ran to the door, and pushed Nicole back. Three thumps behind me hit the opposite wall. "How many more need to exit, Colonel?"

"Three plus Ashley. I can see them, but a squad of soldiers is chasing them." He called his men to the doorway and ordered them to begin covering fire. Six rifles began shooting, two prone, two kneeling, and two standing. Everyone nearby had their ears covered. The remaining soldiers, Jane, and Ashley crawled out.

"I'm okay, Ashley," Jane said. Her left shoulder was bleeding. "It's only a scratch."

"You're accident-prone," Ash said.

"Shut the door," I said.

I returned to the conference room, in time to see an explosion on an otherwise dark screen. The president told Kim they had just witnessed the end of the North Korean's nuclear storage. He said the time had come to end the nuclear program, and to begin the process of North Korean entry into the community of nations. "With our assistance, you can bring peace, raise your country's living standard, and become a leader, not a dictator."

"And if I don't agree…"

"Then you will remain here and watch as similar detonations take place. Your weapons aimed at the South will be obliterated. We can return as many times as needed to stop you. Would you like another demonstration?"

"Yes."

The president nodded to the Japanese president. "You will see momentarily five missiles enter from about here. Their target is right here." He tapped the screen as the rockets entered view.

"This is war," said Kim.

"This is retaliation. And an end to war. If you choose." Five explosions showed on the screen. "We picked sites where you have weapons hidden, but few people in danger. Are you ready to join us?"

Kim exhibited a poker-face, offering a blank stare in response. Unable to discern his intentions, Putin said, "Do you need another example of what we will do?"

"If you say you want us to do it again," said the new president, "we'll do it. We'll take you home and leave you on the roof of your palace. You will have a perfect seat as the missiles fall on your house."

"How can I believe you? No one believes you."

"Who would you believe?" asked the Russian.

"Him." He pointed to the Chinese president.

President Xi said that if he chose to see, he could watch the rocket launch. The screen changed to the Chinese missiles. "I have a direct link, and the necessary codes. All four that you see are ready and aimed at your palace. We have shown you that we will not hesitate. Or you can make a speech, with us around you, apologizing to your people and the world. You will say that you have determined that the best future for North Korea is settling your differences and bringing peace and prosperity to your people. That's all you need to say."

From behind him, Putin said, "Ten," and was joined in the count-down again, by multiple voices.

The Chinese leader stepped to the control panel at 'five.' At 'one,' Kim said, "Wait."

Chapter 69

Linda

A BREAKING NEWS alert scampered across the bottom of the TV screen. A statement from Kim Jong-Un would be broadcast in two minutes. I called Mom to come watch.

"Fritz did it."

A clear picture came on the screen and world leaders arranged themselves behind Kim. He spoke in his native language, with a simultaneous translation on the screen as he spoke. North Korea would end its nuclear program, and end its military aggression toward the South. The new U.S. President spoke next and said that world leaders had agreed to begin shipments of food and supplies to one of the poorest nations on earth. As he finished, he said, "Together, I and the rest of these people, will make peace real, and we'll get peace everywhere. Soon. Believe me. Soon."

The screen went blank for a split second, and then the scheduled coverage resumed.

I didn't want to hear the talking heads. I went to the kitchen and poured a cold cup of coffee.

"You think Fritz set that up?" Mom asked.

"They were in the conference room across the hall from Fritz's classroom, Sandy Horton's old room. That's where the Summit was held last year. I recognized the paintings on the back wall."

"Well that means they're almost done, doesn't it?"

"I don't know, Mom. I'm going to drive up to the school."

"Stay here, Linda. Let's watch the news and see what we can find out first."

The news speculated about everything. No one admitted the meeting had been planned, or where the leaders were. As the world was informed what had happened, reports that leaders were missing further confused the story.

"I hope you never find out." I muttered.

Chapter 70

Fritz

THE PRESIDENT WARNED every participant to say the meeting had been pre-arranged, and the location would remain classified. "Have press conferences if you choose, but remember that travel through time and space is impossible, and any mention of it will be dismissed as insanity caused by the pressures of your office. The press tolerates me and they'll be very interested in my opinion. Mr. Kim, you'll go home first. We always know where you are. So we can help at a moment's notice."

I had a seconds' head start and ran down the hall. I set the bedroom plan on Ashley's desk. Kim shook hands with everyone. This smiling young man, about the same age as Ashley, had been shown the abyss and stepped back. Relief had relaxed his shoulders. He glanced at me, and bowed slightly, as I opened the portal. In front of him, his empty bedroom vibrated with banging on his bedroom door. Before he left, Major Dolan handed him his pajamas.

The current president was the last leader to depart. "Wow, that's amazing. I did good, I think. I like winning."

His predecessor said, "Then keep doing it. The world is too small, as you just saw, for this country not to play a big part in it. The Middle East needs you to honor our commitments. Have a nice trip home."

I opened the door to the Oval Office. The general and the secretaries walked out amidst gasps from their counterparts. The new president walked in and I shut the door.

"Good job, Fritz," the president said. "Thank you all. We didn't know what we would need, so I'm glad you were all able to help." Jane asked him if she could visit him later. "Of course. Are you okay?"

"Just a scratch."

"Fritz, let's get everyone else home. Thanks again, Colonel Mitchell." He turned to the line of troops. "Once again, well done, guys. I hope we're getting closer to not needing to do this anymore."

I set the portal to their base and moments later, only General Beech needed a lift. "Do you want to go home, General?" I asked.

"Yes, please, Mr. Russell. I think my part is finally done. Good to see you all again. I'm liking retirement. I've taken up painting."

"Maybe you should take lessons from Winston Churchill. We could arrange it," Ashley said. "He might like the company." The general asked if Ashley was joking. He wasn't. I set the portal, and only the president and we Riverboro people were alone again.

George said, "School is out for today, but I hope you'll be back in the classroom soon, Fritz." My colleagues echoed agreement.

"I'll let you know, George."

"Mr. R," said Rachel, "classes have been pretty dull without you. Nicole and I invested a lot of extra effort to make things interesting. The tournament was okay. Not as much fun. You did good though, Ms. Chambers."

"Thank you, Rachel." Liz laughed.

"Now what?" Ashley asked. He looked at his watch. "It's just past noon. I'm hungry."

Chapter 71

Ashley

THE ADRENALINE RUSH of the past few hours receded like molasses flowing uphill. The president and his agents prolonged their exit with hugs and handshakes. Fritz had slipped into my classroom, and I could see him through the window in my door, replacing our papers with the books and papers that belonged to the substitute. When he finished, he sat in my chair and ran his hand over the desktop. I didn't disturb him. Less than a day had passed and he found himself in the midst of another international crisis. But this trip into the portal had been very different.

Before leaving, the president asked to speak to Fritz. I told him that Fritz would call later, that he needed some time alone. All the while, I blocked the door. Jane asked the president if she could go with him, so finally they all left. Except Tony. From the outset of the portal missions, he was always the last one anyone thought about.

I said I would see her later, and asked Tony to keep an eye on Fritz. With the corridor finally empty of strangers, my fellow teachers had questions. Liz Chambers said that the president had sworn them to the oath, and said she would explain the portal history to Ms. Sweeney and Mr. Pettinelli. "What we want to know is where you and Fritz have been. Is Fritz okay?"

Rachel and Nicole stood in the background, but Nicole said, "He'll be fine, Ms. Chambers. Mr. R is a spy, so he's done all sorts of things, I'll bet."

"Thanks, Nicole," I said. "I'll take it from here." Not wasting words and wanting to get out, I told them that Fritz had unintentionally discovered parallel universes. He altered the past which changed the present. "I've been looking for him. We reversed what he did, so we could come home to our time. For him, he's been gone for thirteen years."

Joe Pettinelli said, "I've heard stories about what you guys were doing here at strange times. Kids talk. I know I can't say anything, but can I ask you questions, you know, like between us?"

"Sure, Joe. Everyone here can talk among ourselves. But today isn't a good time. You've seen with your own eyes another example of what we've done with the portal. But one thing we know is that the portal is fickle the more it's used. History doesn't like to be tampered with, and sometimes, it rebels. That's what happened to Fritz. Really, guys, I could spend hours talking about it, but we've been at this since dawn, and I want to get Fritz out of here. I'll answer your questions some other time. Sorry."

George asked, "When are you coming back? I need to know in advance, Ashley."

"When I know, I'll give you all the time you need. Okay? See you all soon."

I noticed the Dough Twins behind me as I walked to collect Fritz. I thought my delayed, but expected greeting was on the way. Instead, Rachel said that she and Nicole had news. While I was gone, they were both accepted to college. Nicole said they had been accepted at the University of Pennsylvania. "Together."

"I'm proud of you both. Well done. Now let me get out of here."

"Mr. Gilbert, are you ever going to marry Jane?" Nicole asked. Rachel said, "You should, you know."

Before we left, Fritz said he wanted to peek in his room. He walked down the hall and looked in the window. As he turned away, he tapped the doorknob.

"The portal is closed."

"For now," I said.

Chapter 72

Fritz

I HAD A FEELING that the day we'd had so far hadn't finished its unruliness. I sat in Ashley's kitchen, while Tony and Nat talked in the living room. Ashley said he wanted to take a quick shower, so I sat alone. What had just happened? I grabbed a pad and jotted some notes. As the conductor this time, even the president followed my orders. The only hitch in the entire morning, Jane's wound, fit our previous patterns. I had planned everything in my head and saw what would unfold. Everything happened as I envisioned, as it was supposed to.

I pulled out my pocket watch. We'd completed the mission, start to finish, in less than six hours from the time the president called. My only remaining doubts concerned two men, the North Korean and our president. I truly hoped the message had penetrated their pampered egos. If not, another trip to North Korea might be necessary. But our side of the Pacific concerned me more. The president had seen what we could do, and how easily. Without doubt, we would hear more from him. That fact didn't make me anticipate another meeting.

At the moment Ashley returned to the kitchen, the front door opened and the Dough Twins arrived, carrying boxes and bags.

Ash said, "Great. Let's eat."

The girls chattered about how they could set up a sandwich business at school for their dorm. As Ashley carried the wrapped sandwiches to the table, the door opened again.

"Looks like we're eating in the dining room," Ash said.

Jane, Mel Zack, and the president joined the party. Outside a voice called, "Hold the door." Emily, Linda and TJ walked in.

Ash said, "Girls, looks like we don't have enough."

Rachel said, "Mr. Gilbert, did you count? We have fifteen sandwiches. And here's your change."

"You got all this for forty dollars?" Ashley asked.

"Well, we told Mr. Hoffmann who it was for. He gave us a discount," Rachel said.

Nicole said, "So he didn't really give us a discount, Mr. Gilbert. We said you and the president and Mr. R had just saved the world. He owed it to you not to charge anything."

"Then he shook his head," Rachel said. "He said he would only charge us for his costs. Nicole asked him what his cost was for the potato chips. He gave them to us for free."

The laughter, as much in relief and happiness for our return and the end of crisis as the humor itself, surrounded them and brought everyone to the table.

"Fritz, join us," the president said.

Chapter 73

Ashley

I HADN'T EXPECTED a crowd and I sensed Fritz's desire to be left in quiet awhile. His extraordinary performance rated among the top feats I'd ever seen. Other missions paled in comparison to what we'd accomplished today.

Fritz had never sought the limelight, in school or with the portal. Now, with Linda here, and surrounded by our fellow portal warriors, he'd begun to slip back into the fog. Before I sat, I whispered to him to snap out of it, that everything would be fine.

"You did it, Fritz," Linda said. "We've been watching the TV. Do you think Kim will follow through?"

After seeing Fritz's face, the president didn't give Fritz a chance to answer. He said that he'd spoken to Putin already and the new French president. Both had received emailed apologies from Kim. "I'm sure some of the others have, too."

"Why don't we eat, and talk later," I suggested.

"Good idea," Emily said. "Do you have one of those pastrami sandwiches? Ashley, do you have any beer? I like them together."

"Mom, what's gotten into you lately?" Linda chided.

"We're celebrating. Fritz is home, Ashley is home, world peace at least for now." I handed her a cold bottle. "A toast," she said. "To Benjamin Franklin."

I looked around the table at this most unlikely gathering. Two high school seniors and the former president of the United States, secret service agents, a local reporter, an electrical engineer, a physicist who I love, my two closest friends, their son in the swing set I'd bought, and one very wise woman. And we all shared the portal. Around me, I could see my life returning to normal.

Then the door opened again.

"They said I'd find you here," said the former vice president.

"Come on in, Joe. We're just having lunch."

While the newest arrival found a seat, Jane said, "I have an announcement, if I may." The chatter stopped dead, like the mute button had been pushed. The president had offered her a job, curating his papers and helping to set up his library. "My boss accepted my resignation, and rather than having a hissy-fit, asked me for a job."

"Does that mean we'll be working for you," asked Nicole.

"Some. Until you leave for college."

"Where are you two going?" the vice president asked.

Together, with pride and confidence oozing, they said, "The University of Pennsylvania."

Tony said, "Nat and I have an announcement, too. The president has offered me a job, too, coordinating the tech in his house and making it run properly. So I'll be in charge, and that means I'll be here. But that's not the announcement."

Nat said, "God, you are so slow. We're getting married. That wasn't so hard. You sound more like a politician than a geek." She shook her head, but Tony kissed her when she turned toward him. "At least something will get you to stop talking," she said, taking a deep breath.

"If I may, I'd like to propose a toast," the president said. When he stood, everyone did. "To all of you with these wonderful changes in your lives. But most of all, welcome home, Fritz and Ashley. And Fritz, on behalf of a grateful, although unaware, world, thank you." Emily had the only proper toasting drink, so she made a point of clinking her bottle on everyone's glass.

Within an hour, almost everyone left. Emily took TJ for a nap, and she, Jane and I left Fritz and Linda free to talk.

Chapter 74

Linda

"FRITZ, I'M GLAD you're home safe. I know it's going to take time to adjust. I want you to know that even though I miss having you with me, you should take as much time as you need."

"Thanks. Today's events jolted me. I know I'm home, in the right universe, but I need to get used to things I'd almost forgotten. Time here hasn't passed, but for me, well, I've been away a long time."

"I know. I can't know all you've been through but when I came home..." He gave me a "who are you?" look. "Fritz, I can't tell you how sorry I am that I left. We've always been able to sort our disagreements. I don't know what happened."

"Ripples. You were right. The portal. It's changed us all. But even with the nicks and dings, our own basics are the same. That holds true even in other dimensions."

"Can you tell me?"

"Not yet, Linda. Maybe someday, but not now."

"As I was saying, when I came home, what I missed most surrounded me ... here. Except you weren't here. Us, our house, our dreams together. I'm glad I finally figured it out. Maybe the same will happen to you. Mom always knew Ashley would find you."

"That might happen," he said, "but I have some things to think about. If all that's transpired is to have a finale, Koppler must be confronted.

He's still a threat. It's up to me to end the destruction he's caused. Especially of our lives."

"I'll help."

"You may need to. What's happened here, neither Ash nor I know. I know this may sound strange, but I've learned how the ripples work. Eric Silver discovered the mechanisms, although he doesn't know it. I've had four years to map out the theory and its outcomes. I need to add in changes in this universe."

"Let me know what I can do."

I tried to hide the tears on the way home, and failed miserably. I told Mom that Fritz wasn't coming home yet.

"He'll get here eventually, dear. Stop feeling sorry for yourself. He's the hero I always hoped you'd find. Just make it easy for him. When he comes home, everything will be back to normal."

"What about Dad? He hasn't changed his opinion of Fritz."

"Dad? What happened to Daddy?" Mom said. I wasn't sure, but I think my mother was mocking me.

"Mom, I'm a thirty year old woman with a child, a husband, a house and a business. Don't you think the little girl thing is a bit old?"

"I've thought that for about twenty years. It's been annoying. Maybe you finally deserve Fritz."

Chapter 75

Jane

I HAD EXPECTED, I don't know why, that Fritz would go home with Linda. I wanted a little time alone with Ashley. I'd decided about the job without discussing what the change meant to us. The money would be less, the retirement went away, at least until I had a chance to negotiate. The president said he hadn't finalized where the library would be built, so Ash and I needed to talk about possibly moving. The wedding needed organizing. And now, finally, I could close up my apartment and move everything here.

But Fritz hadn't left. "Congratulations," he said to me. "Awesome job."

I thanked the president and said how much I relished being back working with him, and being with Ashley as a benefit. As much to myself, I said I didn't see myself becoming a bureaucrat. "No one listens. They're not interested. The new people have a different worldview. A lot of good people, experts in their fields, with established relationships, have left or they're updating their CVs. I'm glad to be gone."

"I'm glad you're okay," Fritz said. "I'm surprised Ashley didn't fuss more about your going through the portal."

"If General Beech hadn't brought my gear, I wouldn't have. But I'm still a soldier, Fritz. And duty called."

Ashley had been in the garage and came in the back door carrying a carton. "I forgot about this. Jane, it's your stuff from the Summit." All the files for the leaders, news clippings from the attacks on the White House and Camp David, the booklet she'd prepared. On top, an illustrated copy of "A Christmas Carol." I told him to leave it in the basement. "I'll go through it when I have my apartment cleared out."

"When are you doing that?" Fritz asked, surprisingly animated, more than packing usually makes people.

"Sooner the better. Ash, my sofa would be a great replacement. The colors match, and we can get rid of this broken down thing."

"Are you gonna say the same thing about me someday?"

I grinned at him, but made him wait for an answer. "Now that you mention it, probably."

"Tomorrow is trash day," he said. "We can go tomorrow, rent a truck, and be back on Saturday. Fritz, if you come, I'll drive the truck, Jane can bring her car and you can bring the Mustang home."

"Or I could just drive away."

"Welcome home, wiseass."

We planned to leave early enough to miss the Philadelphia rush hour, and in time to skirt the back end of the Baltimore beltway merge. We reached the District before noon and headed to my place in north-west Washington. Not far from Georgetown, I had lucked into the place when a colleague got married. Expensive, but comfortable, and an easy trip to work. One flight up, or ride a tiny elevator, time to get working had arrived with us. I opened the door into my spacious living room. Only then did I recognize the workload, and the amount of stuff I had. So did Ashley.

"I have two ideas," he said. "Trash bags and movers."

Fritz said, "We'll pack. See if we can find a mover who'll do it in the next day or two. It might not cost much more than a one-way rental. You find the truck, Ash. I'll get the boxes and tape."

While Ashley looked for a mover, Fritz checked the rooms looking at what I had and guessing how many boxes we'd need. He said he had a sense of what we would need, found a DIY truck rental that sold boxes, and said he'd be back in a while.

Chapter 76

Fritz

I WAS GLAD the rental place wasn't near, so I had time to do what I'd planned. I drove out of the ritzy neighborhood, and headed to my old job, Cindy's Cozy Kitchen in an offbeat residential-small shop section not far from K Street. I parked and ran across the street. With a deep breath, I walked in to the late lunch crowd. An older woman asked if I wanted a seat, as she swept a table clear of the most recent occupant's presence. I told her I was supposed to meet someone, but I was late.

"Are you Cindy?" I asked.

"There is no Cindy. She's long gone. This is my place. So what do you want to do?"

"I'll try to find my friend. Maybe I'll be back."

"What's your name? If someone is looking, I'll let them know you were here."

"Fritz Russell. My friend might say Russ. Thanks."

My next port-of-call, McNamara's, had a new name. So I kept going. In spite of the disappointment, I pushed back in the cushioned bucket seat. I thought in that second that I'd always enjoyed riding in the Mustang. It took less time than I remembered to reach "Irish Lovelies." Maybe Mary Connolly would still be there. In a posh shopping area of boutiques, the standout store was Italian leathers, not Irish linens.

The easy part, revisiting, ended with no conclusion. If they were still here, I'd have to really search. I didn't have the time at present, so I steered toward the rental place, bought what I hoped would be enough boxes and supplies, and headed back. As if some fundamental force of nature had drawn me, I passed a sign pointing to Georgetown University. I made a quick right turn toward the Potomac.

The security guard directed me to the main library, told me I would have to use the visitors' parking lot, and directed me to what would be a longer walk. When I finally reached the library, my phone rang. Ashley.

"Where are you?" His voice mixed concern with irritation.

Not being back kept us from packing, but my agenda included a few side trips. "I'm on the way. The first place didn't have enough boxes, so I kept going."

"Then, hurry up. I found a mover who says he'll take the job if we can load up tonight."

"I won't be long."

Once inside the Lauinger Library, I walked to the reference desk, and asked the young man behind it, a student I guessed, if they had records of former students. He said they had some, including yearbooks, university periodicals, theses and other material depending on how long ago.

"I'd be happy to help you. We have some pretty serious cross-referencing software. Who are you looking for?" His courteous customer service may have been real, but I couldn't help think that I had interrupted his boredom. A quick glance indicated a quiet afternoon. Next to me, a man about my age sighed. His casual attire was topped off by a stereotypical sport coat with leather arm patches.

In order to reduce attention to my presence here, I said, "This might take a while. Why don't you help this gentleman first?"

"Sir, give me the name, and I'll get the search started. Then, I'll help Professor McMillan." The professor gestured to go ahead.

"The name is Katie O'Hara."

Before the student had time to type the name, the professor asked, "You knew Katie?" The student looked up at us as I nodded to the man. He said, "If you have a few minutes, I'd like to talk to you. I'll be right back."

"Sir." The student got my attention back. "Some university news articles referring to a Katie Scarlett O'Hara. From about seventeen years ago. If you'd like to use one of our computers, here's the Guest ID code and the reference URL to find the articles."

I thanked him and walked to the computers by the Pierce Reading Room, where I'd be able to observe the professor's return. When he walked in, the professor spotted me and stuck out his hand as he reached me. He apologized for the delay, and told me his name, Sean McMillan.

"Fritz Russell. Nice to meet you. So you know Katie?"

"I did." He gazed past me, looked at his shoes, and then straight at me. "We were students here. She lit this place up. But why are you looking for a girl who's been dead almost twenty years?" I'm sure my gasp reflected my surprise and sadness. "Obviously, you didn't know? Why are you looking for her?"

"Long story, professor. I won't bore you with it." I started to leave.

"You won't bore me. For years, I've kept the story to myself. I was in love with her."

I wanted to learn more, so I told him I'd like to hear his story.

"Katie was a firebrand. The Troubles were over and Ireland was on the road to peace, but Katie wasn't ready to give up the fight for justice and caring for the poor, those who had suffered through the years of war. She told stories of her visits home, raised funds on campus, and online in the early days of computer marketing. But as riled up as she could make a crowd, she was that sweet and kind that nobody objected. And she was brilliant."

"What happened?"

"She went home to visit her mother at Christmas, the middle of sophomore year. A bomb, left over and forgotten, blew up a building where she was standing. She was killed instantly. We had a memorial service here when school reopened. I helped organize it. We filled the quad outside, the paths in were all filled. No one could draw a crowd like she could." He wiped his eyes. "Enough about me. How did you know Katie?"

A buzz in my pocket gave me a brief second to fashion my answer. "Hi, Ash."

"I thought you said you'd be here. Where are you?"

"Georgetown University. The main library. I'll be there soon. I'm not far away." He asked me why I was there. I said he'd have to wait until I got there, and I hung up.

The professor checked the time and said he had a class in ten minutes. "I wish we had more time."

"There's never enough time, Professor. We don't realize just how precious our time is, and we waste so much of it."

"Before you go, tell me how you knew her?"

"I was a short order cook at a place where she was a waitress. She had an endearing way to be a real pain in the ass. I'm only here because a sign to Georgetown popped out of a black hole in my memory. But I've got to go. Nice talking with you."

"One more second. Black hole. I teach physics, and I've been fascinated with the spacetime theories since I was a kid. Like time travel. What do you do?"

I told him I taught history. In New Jersey. But like him, I found time travel to be fascinating.

"Small world," he said.

"This one is. We Earthlings are self-centered. The universe is a big place. But I really do need to go." We shook hands and ten minutes later, I parked the Mustang.

Jane and Ashley had been waiting outside for my arrival, and they were clearly annoyed. He said the truck would arrive around five-thirty and we needed to be finished. He asked what had taken me so long. As if my journey had been normal, I said I had visited all the places I might find Kate. "In this universe, she's dead. Almost twenty years ago. Jane, you're sense of how we are all so interconnected must be right, almost eerie. I met a professor who was standing next to me when I mentioned her name to the librarian. He said he was in love with her. And he teaches physics."

Jane asked, "Did you get his name?"

"Sean McMillan."

She snorted and laughed. "Another interconnection for you. I know him." Ashley asked how. "Well, besides the fact he teaches physics, he's the one I told you about, Ash."

"Your high school prom date?" Ashley asked. "The one your mom fixed you up with?" The grin on her face answered the question.

"That's him. You know the saying, 'Nerds of a feather flock together'."

"And we all knew Katie," I added. "Sorry it took so long. I had to find out if she was in this universe too. The Cozy Kitchen is owned by someone else. McNamara's and Irish Lovelies are gone. The Georgetown sign sucked me in like a giant magnet."

"He's a scifi geek too. Good thing you didn't get him started on that. He used to teach a course in 'experimental physics.' He told me once that the administration never found out that the real text books were science fiction novels."

The movers, four burly men, were on time and had the truck loaded, covered, and tied down in no time and said they would be back to pick us up in the morning in time to miss most of the day's traffic, and still be back home for dinner.

"Damn," Jane exclaimed as they pulled away. "They took the vacuum. So much for my security deposit."

Chapter 77

Jane

MORNING CAME IN a frontal attack. The floor didn't bother Fritz too much, but my back rebelled, which kept waking Ashley, so we tossed and turned until we gave up when the sky brightened. Ashley went for coffee, while Fritz and I finished packing and loading my car with my papers and the last-minute boxes.

Shortly, the truck arrived and we were on our way. Ash drove my car, never allowing more than two cars between us and my things. Not far behind, Fritz cruised in the Mustang. As we took the slow lane up I-95, I guessed what the odds were of Fritz meeting Sean, each with a memory of the same woman in separate universes. As we passed the University of Delaware exit, I broke our silence.

"Ash, do you think Sean plays a part in this story, or is his connection merely coincidence?"

"Good question. I don't know. As for Fritz, I'm glad his curiosity about Kate is resolved. Getting normal just got easier."

We had just passed the Pennsylvania welcome sign when my phone rang. The president asked where I was. I told him we were about a half hour from home.

"Thomas Koppler resurfaced about twenty minutes ago," said the president. I asked where my torturer had been. He said he intended to find out, and finally end the Caballeros. "Is Fritz with you?"

385

"He's following us, about a mile behind. So we'll reach Ash's house between one and two. Closer to one, I think." Ash nodded. "We're following the moving truck."

"Call me as soon as you can when you get home. I'll have an update by then."

"This will complicate matters," Ashley said, when I lowered my phone. "I don't know who wants to shoot that bastard more, Fritz or me."

"Or me. Or Linda. But Ash, the president will want to arrest him. We need to plan this. We can't go in guns blazing. He may be with other people."

"I don't care. If he's in this dimension, he doesn't get away this time."

Chapter 78

Fritz

ASHLEY LOVES HIS car and I understand why. The Mustang purrs. If I'd hit the gas, I'd already be in Riverboro. I've stayed back to have some time alone, and just in case they might need me. The traffic on the interstate moved along at a relaxed pace. As Philadelphia came closer, science fiction distracted me. I was moving, the earth was moving, the universe was moving, so did Philadelphia actually come closer, or was I getting closer? Sometime, I'll have to ask Ash about my grammar.

Confined to the silence of a three hour drive enabled me to examine my present situation. I'd returned to my world, but I hadn't returned home. Renormalizing my life had yet to occur, although a residue of the abrupt departure from the nineteenth century faded faster than I would have expected. In my previous trips into the portal, I returned unscathed by the past. But prolonged time in another world slipped into memory despite the time I'd been gone. Maybe spacetime affected only my physical body, not my mind. Something else to consider later. But my memories of then and now coexist.

When we reached Wilmington, a plan finalized. I'd help Ash and Jane unload, and then I'd call Linda and ask to visit. I wanted the feeling of being in my house again. The time to go home had arrived. That decision came with less struggle than I had anticipated. I may never be able to explain my lengthy absence, even to myself, probably not to Linda. She's always been the pragmatic one. And just as I told Emily and Ashley so long ago, she did come home. I accepted then that somehow we'd work it out. I should have taken my own advice.

I snapped out of my daze on the downslope of the bridge and passed the Philadelphia sports stadiums without a horn blaring at me. I ignored my brain trying to make me envision my car accident. How long ago was it? Only a year and a half in this universe. That memory could remain forgotten, so a quick glance in the rearview mirror left that day behind.

Over the Betsy Ross, and a few minutes later, I pulled to the curb in front of Ashley's house. The truck had pulled into the driveway. Before I could climb out, Ashley had the front door open, and the movers had begun to unload.

Jane waved me over and opened her trunk. I started to reach in.

"That's not why I called you. The president called. He's located Richemartel."

I snorted and then chuckled. "I get home and all hell breaks loose. He must be bored without all the action. Where's Koppler?"

"He said he'd have information by the time we got here. I told him I'd call when the movers are gone."

"I want to call Linda before we do anything. She needs to know, too." I could feel the tingling of muscles in my neck and shoulders, foreshadowing the approaching danger. My memory of many things remained unclear, but the neck and shoulder muscles had a memory of their own. "We better hustle." I nodded to the sky. I grabbed a box and said, "Those clouds look angry."

The couch fit, the boxes owned the living room, and the movers took off. Jane's furniture filled the guest bedroom, the kitchen and some of Ash's personal space. Her careful labelling organized the final deposit locations, but until the boxes could be emptied, we hauled them to the basement. She said they could wait, but the president couldn't. When she called, he said he wanted to discuss exactly what he planned to do.

"I think we've got him," Jane said. "Tony's coming with him. He'll tell us everything when he gets here."

The Suburban pulled into Ashley's vacated driveway, and the president climbed out after a quick secret service scan of the area. Koppler had been spotted three days earlier in Paris, at the same place he'd vanished from in November. He told us that the informant said Koppler had arrived in a costume, acting disoriented, like he'd been awakened from a bad dream.

"That's when the dimension closed. When I got back," Fritz said.

"I was thinking the same thing," the president said. "Is it possible you sent him somewhere else and he only came back when you did?"

"Without questioning him, I can't be sure. But it fits. I'd say, even probable. Another Ashley showed up here. I know we have twins in the other universes. Where is he?"

"Paris. A penthouse apartment. I'd like to go after him, but I have the same problem as before. No planes." He couldn't ask the French for help, either. "We either ask the president to cooperate, or rely on today's forecast to be accurate. I want to confront Koppler personally." My frown prompted him to add that he would have the agents with him, and another intermediary to secure the contact.

"So all I need to do is get you to Paris? What are you going to do with him? He's dangerous." I said.

Ashley's anger boiled in an instant. "He's killed people. He's responsible for what happened to Jane and Linda." He said the man needed to answer for what he'd done. I've seen Ashley mad, but he spewed like a dragon spitting fire.

The president held his ground. "I'm no less angry than you. But I can't arrest him. There's no chance of extradition. He knows his money will win. Too many campaign chests owe their expanse to him."

"Then why do you want to see him?" I asked.

"I still want to know why."

"Does it matter?" Ash asked. "He's a murderer, a predator, and an accessory, at the least, to everything the Caballeros did." Ashley strained not to yell at the former commander-in-chief. "More likely, he planned it all."

The president said, "What he did is what counts, what we can prove." Ashley started to respond but the first rumble of thunder cut him off, and had us on our feet. I told the president he shouldn't go. Before he could answer, the front door opened and Linda came in, and stared at the drawn pistols.

"She's my wife," I said. "I called her to say we were back."

"Obviously, something's up," she said. "I had customers or I'd have been here sooner. Nice greeting." She said hello to us, not a degree of warmth in her voice. The president apologized and introduced her to the agents she'd not yet met. "They were with you when you bought the bikes. I remember their faces. So, is anyone going to tell me?"

Jane said, "Koppler is back."

"And you're going after him?" The question was general, but aimed straight at me." I nodded. "Then I'm going with you."

The president shook his head. "No one is, Linda."

"Jane and I have a right to confront him. He may only be the mastermind, but he gave Joe free rein. This is personal."

"That's why I'm going alone."

Chapter 79

Jane

WHEN WE REACHED the school parking lot, Tony walked to the curb. Without planes, the generator wasn't needed. The president handed Fritz a photocopy of a section of Paris, which Fritz gave to Ashley.

"Why me?"

"It's Paris."

While Ashley set up the portal, I warned the president not to go alone.

"I'm meeting my informant," the president said. "Then we'll see. It's night there now."

The storm hadn't produced, so we waited in Ashley's classroom. The classroom acted as a catalyst for Fritz, and he walked to the front of the room and began a lecture, the story of his first day in the portal. Fritz said that since that day, our lives changed regularly. He didn't know the technical answers, but could provide live, vivid examples of how he had learned the intricacies of using the portal.

Tony laughed. "You know that none of this is possible. Even with all our technology and the greatest brains in the world, time travel has too many paradoxes to work. And the natural world will rebel against attempts to change physical laws." In spite of the seriousness, we had become a tiny extra-worldly family. We could smile at the unbelievers.

Ashley chuckled. "I read a lot of quantum physics when I was in the other universe to try to find a way home. Most of the pros think that. Some have hypothesized that bridges between worlds can exist, and that there are multiple dimensions, parallel universes. And none of that is possible, either."

Fritz continued, "Except that I've been in three universes, Ashley has crossed bridges into two, we've met Shakespeare, Robert E. Lee, Winston Churchill, the Wright Brothers, and we've seen Hitler and Lincoln." I glanced at Linda. Her eyes narrowed, but she bit her lip.

The storm outside began to rival the one in our conversation. Fritz said we should head to the hall. Tony asked if calling the new president might help.

"I've thought about it, but I don't want him to know more than he does. This is complicated."

"Who knew it could be so complicated?" I said. My sarcasm evaded Fritz and Ashley, but the others responded with smiles, smirks and a chuckle.

Fritz asked Ashley if he was ready, then tapped the doorknob. "Nothing."

We waited until the thunder began in earnest. Nine o'clock on a Saturday sounded more like the song lyric than the right time to go to Paris in the middle of the night. I had resigned myself that Koppler would slip away again. The story that I wanted to happen, Ash and I slipping away unbothered by the past, would wait until we could find an end to the current tale. Which one was the fairy tale, I didn't know.

We tingled with the lightning flashes and the booms of the late evening thunderstorm. The president said, "Bring the generator."

"We have planes?" Tony asked.

"Use the Oval Office picture. We have another guest. I asked him if he wanted to go to Paris. He doesn't know why yet."

Fritz said, "I don't want him to know. We've been in danger for too long. I promised when you left office, we were done with this. This is too much to ask."

"Fritz, he's never seen what the portal will do. So he hasn't internalized the danger. Maybe he'll get serious. The middle of the night in North Korea, and then the middle of the night in Paris, could also be the White House."

"That's a big 'if'," Linda said.

"It is. But going from his office to here, then somewhere else, alone, might shake him up. When you first portalled in, Fritz, I knew then the world had changed. I hope he can see that."

"He's done that already. Why would this time be different?"

"He's not part of a crowd. No accolades and pats on the back. Only a job to complete."

"You're still an optimist," Ashley said. "I'm not."

"Then let's find out."

The door opened and the new president stood a few steps away, talking to Bill Sharp. He walked through first, Sharp right after.

"Where am I now?"

"Same place as before."

"Where are the soldiers?"

"We don't need them," said the president.

"What about security? This is dangerous." He stared at the civilians surrounding him. "I've seen you before," he said to Fritz. "Where are you taking me?"

"Unfinished business. Are you ready?"

"I'm here, aren't I?" Listening to the tone, the belligerence covered his fear and uncertainty.

"We're going to Paris. It's four in the morning."

On a dimly lit, empty street, a solitary man viewed the new arrivals, his head cocked. Four secret service agents, two in front, two behind, escorted the two presidents. The stranger approached. I recognized him, and so did both presidents. Linda stared at the man, and ran into the portal. I followed.

I said, "Mr. President, this man is a Caballero. Isaac Martin. Please go back."

"I'm well aware of Mr. Martin. I'll tell you later."

"Mr. Martin, you may not remember me," Linda said.

"Of course I do, Linda. You're Tim Miller's daughter. You're married to the man who discovered the portal." She spluttered a confused response. I, on the other hand, touched the pistol holstered against my back, ready to act. Ashley and Fritz stood in the rear, not sure what would occur next.

"Okay, so you all know each other. Isn't that nice," said the new president. "Why am I here, Isaac? There better be a good reason."

Martin looked at the new president. "I've located Thomas Koppler. You've been told what he's done. Every accusation is true. He headed a conspiracy against the country."

"That's ridiculous. I've met him many times. You could say we're friends. He even contributed to my campaign."

"He tortured Linda and Jane, and almost killed me," Fritz said, pushing to the front of the pack. "He planned the attack on the White House during the Summit."

"That's enough, Fritz," said the president. "I'm here, you're here, Mr. President, to get a confession. And frankly, I want you to see how dangerous the portal can be. You think it's dangerous. You don't have any idea how right you are. Especially on your own."

"Why would it be dangerous for me? My agents will protect me, if they want to keep their jobs."

"If you get killed, they'll still have their jobs. You won't. Don't dismiss the enemies of our country, foreign or domestic. And don't take our allies for granted. We have more than you know, and they're not all leaders of countries."

"Stop arguing," Fritz said. "How are we going to get him?" Martin handed Fritz a floor plan of the apartment.

"I got this yesterday, but I wanted to be sure he settled in."

"So we need to go back. Are you coming, Mr. Martin?"

"Yes. No one is in there with him. He knows I'm nearby. I made a point of letting him see me. We talked for a few minutes. He has an unusual story that will interest you, Mr. Russell."

A minute later, we portalled to a room surrounded by windows. A balcony bordered our entire view. Sparse furnishing presented a different image from the man, Thomas Richter, who collected antiques and no-expense-spared decorations, but cared so little that he burned down his mansion. Yet they were one and the same man. A desk, two stuffed chairs and a coffee table sat on the bare parquet floor. Lights had turned on as we stepped through. Motion detectors covered all directions, so the muffled buzz behind the closed door ahead promised that we would be in the company of our prey shortly.

The door opened and a wide-awake Koppler sauntered in. "Nice of you to visit. I wish you had told me you were in the neighborhood. But never mind. Let's see, who do we have here?" He scanned the group. "Mr. President, highly unusual. Glad my help paid off. And your predecessor. You seem to call when I'm not at my best. Ah, Ms. Sanderson. Your blonde hair seems to have deserted you. I assume these are agents. I'm flattered that you think you need so much protection from me. And you two gentlemen, I believe we've met. I'm sorry I don't have my boots on to greet you again."

"He's with me," said Martin.

"Yes, Mr. Isaac Martin, my financial genius. I owe you for your training. But you seem out of place."

The president had run out of patience. "Sit down, Mr. Koppler. We're going to have a conversation that's been long coming."

Before the president could proceed, Fritz said, "Where did the portal take you?"

"Thank you, Mr. Russell. My curious location begged the question as to how that happened. I've been witness to the days leading to Napoleon's return from Elba. We aristocrats have become rather edgy of late. An interesting experience, but not enough modern conveniences for my taste. I'm quite happy to see Paris again, with running water. Is that glowing thing your transportation?"

Linda inched next to Fritz. "Why did you let Joe torture me?" Fritz took her hand, both in support and restraint.

"Because secret weapons belong in private hands. Your father can explain why. He so easily gave you up to Mr. Sapphire. Now if you're done with your questions, please leave and I'll return to a pleasant dream."

The new president said, "Thomas, I've heard some disturbing stories about the Caballeros. By the way, you never invited me. Are the stories true?"

"Of course not. If they were, I'd be in jail."

"You'd be in jail if you hadn't slipped the country," the president said.

While Koppler condescended, and the arrogance filled the room, I examined the apartment setup to see what tactical advantages Koppler had, even with us all around. His calmness as he baited the hook warned that he might have an exit or escape plan. I hated the man for his cruelty, but I grudgingly admired his attention to detail. I scanned the walls and ceiling, certain that cameras recorded each action, each word. Positioned where he sat, behind his desk, a weapon of some sort rested close by, I was sure. "Nice balcony," I said. "Does it go all around? It's like your ship. Except the water is a softer landing." I succeeded in distracting him. "Did you know that Joetta Dunsmore survived. She said you watched Joe toss her into the ocean."

"Who?"

"And we have recovered all the recordings from your peep-show cabin. Including the audio. Voice analysis reports that you gave the orders." I pressed my bluff. "We have an order to extradite, and Paris police are waiting for our signal."

I glanced at the others, engrossed in my speech, and not watching him. As if he had not a care in the world, he asked if we would like to experience the early morning beauty of the city coming awake. He walked to sliding doors which had camouflaged, almost invisible, handles. As though they had forgotten the mission, mesmerized by this modern-day Saruman, everyone followed him outside.

He said, "I like it out here. Two bakeries two blocks apart compete for business, but the aromas force me to dress and buy a fresh loaf." He pointed up and down the street. "There. Can you smell it?"

His manner disarmed and his voice hypnotized, as if he were guiding a tour. The new president wandered away, with two agents following. With fewer bodies, Koppler maneuvered closer, pointing out the tourist sites we could see.

The president said, "It's lovely. And distracting. Now, let's go back inside and finish this." Koppler grabbed Linda from behind, lifting a pistol from the pocket of his robe.

"Leave now. I'll keep her with me."

I slid my gun from behind, but another report beat me. A red mist puffed in the slight breeze. Koppler's left ear had flown off. When his instinct to grab the pain rose, his grip on Linda released, and she ducked, rose up, leaned back and pushed.

With so few people awake, the scream of his plunge dispersed and ended. Fritz said we needed to leave, but the president said he was going to the street to be certain. While the others took the elevator, Fritz poked through the portal, and said he would change the opening to street level, and meet us there.

Bill Sharp hustled the new president to the elevator and we all went to see what I hoped to be the end of that evil man, and the organizations he built. The elevator descended, almost as rapidly as Koppler. When we reached the lobby, a puddle of blood already covered the sidewalk. Fritz stood over the body, smiling. Though the broken body lay bleeding and immobile, Koppler's head overlooked the avenue a story above us, impaled on an iron fence spike.

"That's pretty messy," the new president said. His antiseptic and detached comment was almost funny. "Can we go home now?"

Before anyone moved, a shadow stepped into the light, a woman wearing a head scarf. Dark complexion, yet wearing make-up, clearly from the Middle East. She strode ahead despite the pointed pistols. "Mr. President, I would like to thank you."

"You're welcome."

"Not you. Mr. President, I am Safiya Massoud. My husband confided in me of his role with that man. I have waited many months to find him. His cousin's son, Mason Hamid, told me the full story. Ibrahim's ambitions overcame his caution, but I loved him. If you had not succeeded, I prepared to end the evil. You should go now. I will wait for the police."

"Mrs. Massoud, I regret your husband's death. I asked the Sheikh to fake the fall, and deliver him to us. He said your husband jumped. I am sorry."

Moments later, we had returned to the hallway. Ashley took my hand before I could cross. "Come with me. Fritz, keep the door open."

"Where are you going?" Fritz asked.

"To buy some fresh bread." In spite of the gore nearby, Ashley had dismissed Koppler's fall as easily as dismissing his first class of the day. Any regret he harbored hid behind the twinkle in his eye at the end of our long crisis. He didn't care.

Chapter 80

Fritz

LINDA SHOOK LIKE a sapling in a hurricane. I held her until we crossed into the school. She looked up at me asking question on question with her eyes. One emotion, fear, never materialized.

"You know how I feel, don't you?"

"Yes," I said. "Like I felt rescuing the president in Geneva. Like when I killed the Kopplers." The strangeness of saying that stuck in my head. "He had a lot of lives. Even in another universe."

"Will this feeling go away?"

"It will, when you accept that he might have killed you." Reassuring her, I refrained from saying she'd remember it. "But now, it's over. So let's get Jane and Ashley." Once they were back in Riverboro, with four loaves of fresh bread, returning the president to the Oval Office topped the list.

He said, "Before I go, who are you? Where are we? You just said you rescued the president, and killed Thomas Koppler. When? I just saw his body."

"Sir, my name won't mean anything, and it's safer that you don't know where you are. I killed Koppler in 2008 in another dimension. I've just returned after four years as an instructor at Robert E. Lee's college. The portal decides if I can be useful. Mr. President, you have just time traveled, watched a man die in the middle of the night in a city more than 4000 miles away. I set his location and we walked right into his house." The blank stare in my direction made me believe that he still didn't understand.

Ashley had set the brochure on his desk, and told me to open the door. "Wait. I want to do this again," said the new president.

"I'll be watching to see if you need me, sir. Good night." I gently turned him and Bill Sharp patted my shoulder as they left.

Isaac Martin chatted with the president, Jane and Linda, as Ashley and I moved up the hall. "Ike told me about the Caballeros after the cruise. With no chance to make contact then, he called me from the airport. He didn't know about you, Jane."

I asked him if the Wall Street genius story was true or a cover story. He told me that his background was real. When Koppler let slip that he had planned the White House attack, Martin determined how the story would have to end. "I bided my time, waiting for him to show up again. Although I avoid politics because people misinterpret, I have a personal stake with him. The president and I discussed the cruise and he asked me to keep an eye on Mr. Richemartel. Neither of us knew he was also Thomas Koppler, who most people believe to be a fictitious figure."

"What made it personal?" Jane asked.

"My sister. Her name was Lily Evans." In that moment, our shock and sadness matched his.

The president said, "I'd never made the connection before. I didn't know Isaac Martin. I'd met Ike Martin, Lily's brother. When Declercq told us the names of the people at that first meeting, we investigated, but Ike isn't a public figure. I didn't tie them together until he called."

Jane asked, "Mr. Martin, did you suspect Florian?"

"No. The group pushed him to take the lead. He had a prominent role in the Middle East development, had lost a major asset, and Richemartel played him, played each of us, looking for weaknesses to exploit. Declercq had daughters, young women. His attention to you, Ms. Sanderson, riled him. I have since learned the full story. I believe Richemartel threatened Declercq early on, and took advantage of him, knowing Florian wanted to protect you. In the end, he gave you up. What saved you on the cruise was the other woman, Joetta. Her late night walk changed their plan. You could be dealt with later. On land."

"Richemartel guessed right about each of his 'guests', except me. His one mistake. He and I talked about his investment plans. He openly analyzed each of our roles and who he thought would need more encouragement. As I listened, he became less cautious. He never said what he intended, but I didn't doubt his capacity for cruelty. When he repeated his expectation to influence government, with the election so near, I suggested that elections could be bought, results manipulated. He looked at me with those cold eyes and actually smiled. He said, 'We're going to have a change in policy, Mr. Martin.' I understood that the process had already begun."

"Where did you go when you left the ship?" Jane asked.

"Straight to the airport. I took the first plane that left. The cab drove by just as Ms. Ahn was hit. Joe drove the murder vehicle. He slowed enough to see and then drove off." Then Martin said that although he had enjoyed his evening, he wanted to go home.

Ashley said, "You must be familiar with guns. Or you were lucky. Your shot barely missed Linda."

"Astute observation, Mr. Gilbert. I am an expert marksman. With many weapons. Ms. Sanderson, sorry, Barclay, you distracted him when you reached for your pistol. He jerked just a tiny bit away from you. A split second sooner, my shot hits his forehead."

A crash of thunder above us prompted me to ask where he wanted to go. The president handed me a new floor plan. As Martin stepped into his Paris apartment, he said, "Linda, tell your father I said hello."

Our mission ended. First, the president and his agents left us. Last once again, Tony waved as he drove away.

As we all walked to the Mustang, Linda said, "It's finally over."

"Why don't you two come for breakfast," I said.

Linda squeezed my hand.

Chapter 81

Ashley

JANE REACHED INTO her physics background. "We're surrounded throughout the universe by what's called "dark energy. The force that enabled us to travel across universes shouldn't have been seen. It's just there."

"I didn't see anything, but I had to battle the force when I opened the door, the portal. And once I pushed the portal open, it sucked me into another universe. Where I wanted to go. That energy was the bridge, I think. Jane, you understand the physics and the hypotheses, but the electricity/water angle is so elemental, literally."

"Do you think you and Fritz have some kind of genetic structure or the ability to tap a new energy source that allows you to open the portal?"

"Honestly, I never thought of that. Are any tests capable of answering?"

"None that I know of, but I'll be checking the literature. Both professional and the science fiction. The novelists have come up with some fascinating ideas."

At last, we were alone. The last time Jane and I had been alone ... when was that? I'd always been accompanied by doubt, or some pending mission. The portal had loomed over us, ready to snatch those spare moments away. And she was always preoccupied. I'd become accustomed to early calls, late evenings and her focus on the events of the day. But now, as the adrenaline rush depleted, one hope, a single word shone ahead for us—normal. I hugged her, and our kiss could star in a movie. We sat on our new couch, well, mine anyway. And she started to laugh.

"What?"

"Everything is about to change. We've talked about how the portal changes us. How connected we all are. And right here, right now, it's all coming together."

I rubbed the couch cushion and glanced around my living room. The dining room table covered with small boxes had hosted the most powerful people in the world, and more parties would come. I put my arm around her and pulled her tight against my chest.

"Will you marry me?" I asked.

"Yes," she whispered, nuzzling her head into my shoulder.

"Shall we set a date?"

"I'll call my mother in the morning."

"Jane, I love you. I'm hungry."

Chapter 82

Jane

WITH ASH'S ARM around me, I looked out the dining room window, and a sunburst lit the sky, even though midnight closed in. I'd never been so comfortable. For the first time in my life, I sat still. The need to be doing something, anything, had evaporated. I studied his face, eyes closed, calm and content. I wanted to spend the rest of my life with this wonderful man.

"Do you want kids?" I asked. We'd never really talked about children. I had avoided this conversation.

"I think so. A couple maybe. I think I'd be a good father."

"You will be."

"Do you?"

"Yes. A boy and a girl. And a husband I love enormously."

He tugged me closer, kissed my forehead, then said, "I've waited for you forever. Thank you for waiting for me."

I kissed him again.

"We're alone," he said. "I suspected that would never happen."

"Fritz has been a good friend, and I'll share you with him. If he needs to come back, we'll adjust. I can't imagine our life without him. But I hope that he and Linda will find the road back together."

"They will. They're both too stubborn, too strong, to accept defeat. Now let's get something to eat."

Chapter 83

Linda

"WE'RE HOME, MOM."

Mom smiled at Fritz when she came into the kitchen. Without a word, she gave him a long, tight hug. When she let go, she motioned to the table, wiping tears from her cheeks.

"Don't cry, Emily. It's not that bad."

She brushed her eyes and blew her nose. "Maybe you're not stupid anymore."

"Mom!" Fritz just laughed.

"Private joke, dear. Remind me to tell you sometime. Do you want a drink?"

"I'll get it," he said, and went to the liquor cabinet, moved a few bottles, and pulled out a dusty bottle of whiskey. "A newly acquired taste. Irish." He poured three glasses.

"Welcome home," Mom said and clinked glasses.

I said, "I'm the happiest woman in the world, Fritz. And I'm so sorry. TJ will be glad you're home, too."

He raised his glass again. "We have a lot to catch up on." Fritz grabbed my hand. "Emily, you should have seen her. She was heroic."

I could feel the doubt exuding from my face. "I only ducked."

"He had a gun to your head, Lin." Emily gasped. "You didn't flinch. When you backed up, you knocked him off balance. When you stood up, you pushed him backward over the railing."

"I did?"

"When you're in the middle of a fight like that, a split second can seem like an hour. And you can't see yourself. You just react. That's what happened."

Mom said, "Drink up, you two. You've earned it. I hope this is over, once and for all. Fritz, pour me another."

"I invited Jane and Ashley for breakfast, Mom They'll probably be early. Oh, and do you remember Isaac Martin?"

Mom chuckled. "I've known Ike all my life."

"Really?" I said. "You never told me that. He was there tonight."

"Daughter, some things you will never know."

"Ripples," Fritz said.

Chapter 84

Fritz

I'D SAT AT the kitchen table more times than I wanted to count, but never with Emily and Linda alone. I sipped my whiskey, savoring the warm and unique flavor. Being home felt, well, it felt right. I had a new friend in my mother-in-law, and I told her I was grateful for her time and patience. She said I owed her 'a hundred bucks,' that I'd lost the bet.

"What bet?"

"I bet myself that you would come home and you and Linda would get your heads on straight. And I bet a hundred dollars that you'd pay me if I was right. So pay up."

"How is that a bet with me?" Linda giggled softly at Emily's audacity.

"Are you staying?" Emily asked.

"Yes."

"Then I won because I'm right."

Her logic defied argument, so I told her I'd pay her in the morning.

"Good. That'll pay for the gas and tolls. Now that you're here, I can finally go home. Tim will be here tomorrow." She glared, daring me to object. When I said nothing, she grinned. "Fritz, it's time to end the battle. I told him he'd always been wrong about you, and that if he wanted me home, he had to come here and apologize. Do you want to know what he said?"

"I don't know. Do I?"

"Stop it now. This minute. He said he was glad you were home safely. 'You're right,' he said. 'I underestimated him. I'll apologize and more. I've told Joe to come, that we are going to be a family again.' Fritz, I've never been so happy. But you need to pick Joe up at the airport."

I shook my head and chuckled. "I guess we're back to normal."

"So tell me where you've been."

"It's late, Emily."

"No time like the present. Besides, we won't have a chance to be alone or have this quiet again. I'll be gone."

Too much to tell in detail. No reason to save some for the morning because Ashley already knew most of it. I closed my eyes and called up an outline behind my eyelids for reference.

When I finished, I said, "It's hard to believe I've only been gone five months, or that I've only been home for four days. But you have the story now. You can ask questions tomorrow."

Sleep beckoned and pulled me up the stairs. Before I climbed in to a favorite memory, I kissed Linda for the first time in thirteen years.

Chapter 85

Ashley

NORMAL. MY FAVORITE word of the month continued to provide no surprises, no nuances, no disappointments. Life was returning to normal. I'd told George that I wouldn't be teaching again this year. Fritz and I would begin again after summer vacation, and I looked forward to catching up on the reading list I'd compiled. Science fiction led the way.

Although I hadn't been Linda's first customer, Jane and I bought bikes and rode all over Riverboro. She even biked to work. We met the president occasionally on his bike with his entourage of family and agents. Even Rachel and Nicole rode to work. I noticed that bikers rode everywhere we went. Linda's store attracted customers from all around the area. To get back in racing form, she planned to sponsor a two-day event in mid-September when holidays were memories and school had begun again.

When no one was paying attention, I rode. I rode with Jane to work daily and sprinted home. At the start, the workouts were painful. Muscles I hadn't used in a long time yelled for me to stop, but slowly they agreed we were doing the right thing. Fritz rode with me every few days, and we spent most of each day together. He said he wanted to adjust to being home, spending time bonding with TJ. He concentrated on writing a detailed memoir of all his experiences. When I told him

I wanted to read it, he said I could proofread the manuscript when he completed his first rewrite. I think his reluctance meant he hesitated to tell the whole story. Even Linda hadn't seen any of it.

The Sunday after we moved Jane's stuff, Emily invited us for breakfast, and an afternoon party. She said Tim and Joe would be there, and asked me to pick Joe up at the airport because Fritz was sleeping so deeply, she hated spoiling what he really needed.

Jane and Linda helped set up for the party. Emily had invited everyone who had been a part of the portal adventures. "Except Ben Franklin," she said, with a sad touch of nostalgia. Tim arrived while Fritz and I had gone to Hoffmann's for the party platters Emily had ordered. Enough for an army of party-goers. A real party needs a party atmosphere, and Emily made sure we were all in the mood. She had invited the president, and he said he wouldn't miss it. So a new level of noise greeted our delivery.

Fritz excused himself when Emily said that Tim wanted to talk to him. Linda and Joe were sitting with him in the sunroom. "Come on in, Fritz," Tim said. I hesitated at the entrance to gauge the battlefield, but both his kids were smiling. He asked Linda to get her mother.

"Sure, Dad."

"Did you have a good trip?" I asked.

"The best I've ever had. Sit down. I want to talk to you."

Emily must have already been near. Linda returned with her only a second later.

"Fritz, now that we're all together, I want to say I'm sorry. I've been awful to you for a long time. No more excuses. I was wrong about you. You've done things I would never have had the courage to even consider. I hope you can forgive me. I even apologized to the president."

"Understand this, Tim," I said with an edge. I watched smiles fade. "I left to save Linda from what we've endured. To stop it before it happened. I married your daughter knowing full-well what you thought of me. I've always done what I thought was right, even when I was wrong. And you did the same. I respect that. I hope that we'll find other common ground. My son will want to see his grandpa often.

And my wife will want her parents, and her brother," I glanced at Joe, "to visit regularly. I accept your apology." I stuck my hand out and he took it, and then gave me a genuine hug.

Jane and I eavesdropped from the doorway. We smiled for our friends' happiness, and then at each other.

With tears flowing, Emily said, "Lunch is served. I have to get the lasagna on the table, and I want a beer."

Two weeks later, we all went to the Riverboro commencement, where George announced his retirement and introduced his successor, Liz Chambers, Riverboro High's first woman principal. The audience abounded with former students, who all stopped to say hello. Rachel and Nicole had the final send-off speech, together, speaking about how important work can be done by individuals. Then, with a signal, students began to circulate with gallon jars. Nicole cheered them on, while those of us who appreciated her efforts just laughed. Ted O'Neil stopped in front of one parent who dropped a one dollar bill in the jar. Ted just stood there, not saying a thing, holding the jar out. A twenty finally landed on the pile, Ted said thanks and went to the next parent. Twenty dollar bills floated into the jar because no one wanted Ted to embarrass them as he had done to the superintendent.

One afternoon, as the Fourth of July rushed up, my phone rang while Fritz and I lazed in the yard, reading.

The first thing to hit my ear was, "Do you have a hundred dollars with you?"

"I do." I shook my shoulders to get loose. "I'll meet you at the high school in twenty minutes."

"Make it ten."

Fritz asked, "Game on?"

"About time. Let's go."

The basketball court behind the school should have been deserted. Instead, surrounding the perimeter, kids and teachers had gathered to watch. Rachel and Nicole had sent out a text alert, and the crowd surge was immediate. Nat commanded in the front, interviewing spectators, ready to report the game. Cheers rose when we arrived, but the decibel level skyrocketed when the president came around the corner, dribbling a basketball. Chief Dempsey and a couple of Riverboro's finest followed him.

"So, you ready to lose?" the president asked, and jabbed my chest.

"Trash talk. Already? Not ready. I've been working out."

"Me, too. On my bike. Let's warm up. How about a quick game to five?"

"You're on."

Spectators continued to arrive as the warm-up began. I watched each move he made. A left-handed shooter, quick moves to his left, a little slower to the right. My leg had healed, and all the riding gave me the confidence as well as stamina. We tied at four, and he said, "Win by two." I agreed. Elbows, hips, pushing and shoving, regular fouls. I wasn't losing this one. I stole the ball and shot a perfect jumper to take the lead. The president dribbled twice and I stuffed the jump shot, retrieved the ball and drove to the basket. I faked a lay-up, and smiled at the president flying by me. A little bank shot, and I'd won the warm-up.

Fritz announced, "Ladies and gentlemen, that concludes our first act. The real game will begin in a moment."

"First to ten, right?" I asked.

The president said, "Works for me."

I expected the game to be quick and that I would be an easy winner. I'd already worn him down and I had a fifteen year advantage in age. Our onlookers now surrounded the court, as many as five deep in places, cell phones extended to catch the action. They laughed and cheered at our non-stop trash chatter.

The end was memorable. And no doubt would become legendary. The last point, with a 9-8 lead, came when the president dunked over my straining, outstretched arm.

I said, "I can't believe you can still dunk."

"Neither can I. I may never do it again. I'll feel that tomorrow."

The long-awaited historical game ended with the crowd crushing in on us, with pens and pads being thrust in our direction while Jon

Charles and Mel Zack moved everyone back. Coinciding with the end of the game, a clap of thunder raced above our heads.

I'd forgotten the forecast, but Fritz dangled the keys, and the crowd exited to avoid the lightning. I suggested we get inside to cool off. We walked through the emptying parking lot to our usual entrance, as the rain began to fall.

I told the president that he could shower or just wash off in the boy's room, but Fritz had something else in mind.

"Boy's room is fine," said the president. We both cooled down with cold water. When we returned, Fritz had wedged his classroom door open. When we entered, he said that George replaced his desk with a used one from another room. He removed a book from his shelf, laid it on his desk, and put his key in the lock. "Mr. President, do you want to meet Albert Einstein?"

"Will it work," I asked. "I don't have my desk key."

Fritz shrugged. He said he didn't know, but we had the opportunity and would again, but he wanted to know if his time-travel days were in my hands.

"Let's do it, then," I said.

The first try was a nothing. Then a flash and a crash, and his hand twisted the doorknob.

"It seems we have company, Dr. Franklin," said the famous Austrian physicist, whose accented voice twinkled, as did his eyes.

"We don't mean to intrude, Dr. Einstein," Fritz said. Three men sat at the table.

"But of course you do, Mr. Russell," said Franklin. "That's what makes time travel fun. Ah, Mr. President, so good to see you again. I can tell you have questions. To explain, Dr. Einstein replicated your conditions, and here I am."

The third man stood, a wide grin on his face. All of us had met him. While all the other introductions were made, we couldn't keep our eyes off Eric Silver.

Epilogue

Fritz

Our story has ended. Richter, Richemartel and Koppler would never again shadow our lives. Linda and I have spent hours talking about what happened in the time I was gone. I haven't shown her my memoir yet, but I have told her most. Oral history.

The bike shop is booming, so Linda and I share the hours and I help her plan the September race. The president has referred business on a regular basis. He said he refused to allow his guests to sit idly and took them for short rides to have serious discussions in private.

Linda and I share TJ as well, and he's had a chance to know his dad.

The weekend before Labor Day, just as they had planned, Ashley and Jane were married, and left for Paris for their honeymoon. But Ashley said that when they returned, he still intended to take his bride to meet Ernest Hemingway. The wedding guests included the president and First Lady, General Beech and his wife, Colonel Mitchell, Eric Silver and Lenore, and in his last official appearance, George McAllister gave a toast. Rachel and Nicole entertained the guests as part of Jane's bridal party, and collected over $1000 for their current charity.

Linda acted as Jane's matron-of- honor. And as we'd always planned, I stood as best man at the side of my best friend.

When the ceremony ended, we co-conspirators joined together and vowed that if the world needed us again...

If you have reached this point, you have finished Quantum Touch, and I thank you. I hope that you have enjoyed reading the story, as much as I have enjoyed writing it. May I ask a favor? Strangely, reviews matter whether good or not so good. Your comments are important to me, but are important to those who have yet to read the series. So, if you would leave a review, I would be grateful.

If you wish to contact me, I welcome conversation with readers, some of whom have become friends over the past years.

sternmike52@gmail.com is my email address. Really, it is.

As I wrote the stories, I relied on other authors for information and inspiration. Please continue to the next page, where I have listed some of the books that helped me take you to historical places.

Again, many thanks.

Michael R. Stern

Dear reader,

We hope you enjoyed reading *The Portal at the End of the Storm*. Please take a moment to leave a review, even if it's a short one. Your opinion is important to us.

Discover more books by Michael R. Stern at https://www.nextchapter.pub/authors/michael-r-stern

Want to know when one of our books is free or discounted? Join the newsletter at http://eepurl.com/bqqB3H.

Best regards,
Michael R. Stern and the Next Chapter Team

Selected Bibliography for Quantum Touch

The Wright Brothers, David McCullough

Gettysburg: The Last Invasion, Allen C. Guelzo

Benjamin Franklin: An American Life, Walter Isaacson

From Manassas to Appomattox: Memoirs of the Civil War in America, James Longstreet

How to Teach Relativity to Your Dog, Chad Orzel

No Ordinary Time: Franklin and Eleanor Roosevelt: The Home Front in World War II, Doris Kearns Goodwin.

The Memoirs of Robert E. Lee, A. L. Long

Sylvia Beach and the Lost Generation: A History of Literary Paris in the Twenties and Thirties, Noel Riley Fitch.

Franklin and Winston: An Intimate Portrait of an Epic Friendship, Jon Meacham.

The Old Man and the Sea, Ernest Hemingway.

Revolutionary Summer, by Joseph J. Ellis.

The Portal at the End of the Storm
ISBN: 978-4-86750-282-2

Published by
Next Chapter
1-60-20 Minami-Otsuka
170-0005 Toshima-Ku, Tokyo
+818035793528
9th June 2021